Cold Blue

a novel

Cold Blue

Gary Neece

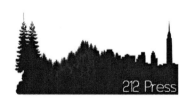

This book is a work of fiction, names, characters, places, and incidents are the product of the author's imagination or are used fictitiously. Any resemblance to actual events, locales, or persons, living or dead, is coincidental.

Copyright ©2011 by Gary Neece

All rights reserved. Except as permitted under the U.S. Copyright Act of 1976, no part of this publication may be reproduced, distributed, or transmitted in any form or by any means, or stored in a database or retrieval system, without the prior written permission of the publisher.

212 Press
212 Pope Rd
Windham, ME 04062

www.212press.net

212 Press is an imprint of Yellow Crane Press, LLC. The name and logo may not be used, except by prior written permission of the publisher.

Printed in the United States of America

First Edition: January 2011

Library of Congress Cataloging-in-Publication Data

Neece, Gary.
    Cold Blue / Gary Neece. — 1st ed
      p. cm.
    ISBN 978-0-9758825-3-5
    1. Cold Blue—Fiction. 2. Fiction—Crime
    3. Fiction—Mystery & Detective: Police Procedural

*For my parents,
whose only want was for their children*

"All the old knives that have rusted in my back,
I drive in yours."

—*The Phaedrus*
Plato

One

Monday
February 5th
Early Morning

Sergeant Jonathan Thorpe brought his eyes down from the desolate highway to the soft green glow of his dashboard lights. Five minutes till four. Up early, rather than out late, he enjoyed this time. The hours before dawn brought a spectral peacefulness to the city, a serenity disturbed only by fellow cops, hooligans, and the few unfortunate souls finding their ways to work. Most of the one million or so who made up Tulsa's metropolitan area still slept peaceably in their beds. Those not at rest resembled the Rapture's left behind, if Thorpe still believed in such things.

Shrewd criminals had long since retired from public view. They feared the slew of uniformed officers on duty, all of them bored and searching for someone, anyone, to pull over. "Big dope," as Thorpe referred to large quantities of narcotics, was mostly transported and sold during business hours when the cop-to-citizen ratio was much more favorable to the bad guys.

Driving, Thorpe's attention wandered. It's a trait those with driving experience share, though Thorpe's autopilot had adapted a few additional skill sets. While he efficiently operated his vehicle—feet working pedals and hands working steering wheel with little conscious effort—he also checked for tails in all three mirrors. He looked for suspicious activity in his peripheral vision. He stamped passing cars and faces into his short-term memory. With each landmark he passed, his random thoughts burst with a kaleidoscope of memories. Every street corner brought a memory of a shooting, car stop, fight, or foot pursuit.

While this activity fluttered in recesses of his mind, he considered the fellow "citizens" with whom he kept these late hours: The junkies and prostitutes and small-time drug pushers, all too damned ignorant or desperate to get off the streets. Dealers lurked in darkened doorways and urine-steeped alleyways. They slithered along side streets with no more than a fist-full of rocks destined for motel whores and twenty-dollar crack heads.

He'd encountered every kind. The cagey ones swallowed their dope as soon as you laid eyes on them. Later, they retrieved their cellophane-wrapped wares in the privacy of their own bathroom. The patient ones awaited nature's call. Those unwilling to postpone deliveries might introduce fingers to esophagus, subsequently plucking their illicit treasures from steaming gastric acid and last evening's meatloaf. Others were less cautious; they kept their products on them during the stop, concealed in the car or on their person. Often they kept the drugs under their tongue and only resorted to swallowing when their secret was discovered. Sometimes an officer would grab a suspect's throat to prevent the destruction of evidence. Meanwhile, citizens driving by witnessed a crooked cop choking the shit out of another *innocent* motorist. Then there were those who thought themselves particularly clever—believing they'd hidden the contraband where one would *never* look, let alone find it. As disgusting as it was, their fetid fingers usually gave them away. Maybe that's how crack *really* got its name.

This morning Thorpe was going after one of the smart ones, smart by crack dealer standards at least. As the supervisor of the Tulsa Police Department's Organized Gang Unit, Thorpe knew the difference. He pulled himself back to task as he made his way across the south end of the IDL. The Inner Dispersal Loop was a network of highways ensnaring downtown. Freeing himself from the commuters' version of an oval track, Thorpe took a series of side streets before turning north on Country Club Drive and cutting through the middle of a sprawling, government-assisted "community."

Thorpe thought about his tax dollars at work here. Yes, he was a cop but had to pay taxes like everyone else. Because of that, he often replied that he was self-employed when some dip-shit citizen told him they paid his salary. *Government-assisted housing*, Thorpe thought. *Free rent for freeloading assholes*. He knew he was being unfair; he'd met decent people who *had* to live in places like this. He felt sympathy for the innocents because animals of the two-legged variety mostly controlled the complexes.

Country Club Drive and its bifurcated housing complex were in close proximity to Tulsa's Country Club golf course. The course, surprisingly well maintained, was an occasional host to the LPGA. Thorpe doubted many lady pros would jump the fence and enter this complex to retrieve an errant ball—to do so would imply their balls were bigger than those used in golf—and therefore they wouldn't be needing the L preceding PGA. The entire complex was scheduled to be razed and rebuilt in a couple of years. For now, it was a good place to buy dope and get robbed—if that's your thing.

Thorpe exited the north end of the complex turning west. Several blocks later he approached Waco Avenue and looked north towards his target's home. In the distance, he could see Marcel's gold Cutlass parked on the west side of the street. Thorpe continued on before turning into the Greystone Condominiums. The condos were protected by a black iron fence and by an electronic gate to which Thorpe already had the code. He punched in the numbers from memory, pulled into the complex, and parked in a relatively low-lit area on the west side. The daunting security fence was the only security measure; there was no video surveillance, nor were there security companies that patrolled the grounds.

Garbed in dark blue coveralls, a hoodie, and full-face ski mask, Thorpe examined the area through deeply tinted windows before exiting his vehicle. The frigid conditions insured his clothing wouldn't garner unwanted attention, and it disguised the fact he was the only Caucasian within a square mile. Taking a sinuous route through the complex, Thorpe exited a pedestrian gate on the northeast side of the condos. Heading east, he resisted the urge to jog and remained alert for movement in the still morning. Except for his breath rising in the cold, nothing stirred. He passed Marcel's street once more and continued east another twenty-five yards before encountering a private drive that led north into a wooded tract of approximately five acres.

Despite the urban surroundings, there were occasional wooded areas on the north side of town. From previous surveillance, Thorpe knew the only structure on the property was a dilapidated barn, void of any human activity. An old, metal farm gate blocked the drive another ten yards north of the property line. Thorpe used a small pair of bolt cutters on a section of barbed-wire fence just west of the gate. He could have scaled the gate easily, but it was noisy and would slow him down if he needed to depart in a hurry. This was his primary escape route.

Faintly illuminated by moonlight, he strode up the old drive, wincing when the occasional patch of gravel crunched under foot. Though probably not audible more than ten yards away, in Thorpe's ears it sounded like thunder; his senses were in hyper drive, or as his father used to say, "maximum operational awareness."

Thorpe followed the drive deeper into the woods until reaching a stone marker that he lifted and tossed into the weeds. Turning and trekking west into the thicket, he stopped and uncovered a large, water-resistant canvas bag, which he'd concealed under dead vegetation and fallen branches during an earlier scouting mission. Collecting the bag, Thorpe began picking his way northeast through the trees. Branches and prickly vines grabbed at his clothing as he trudged toward the deserted barn. Winter-stripped of their canopy, the barren trees allowed just enough moon and starlight so he could navigate without use of artificial light.

Having reached a clearing, the barn loomed before him. Thorpe pulled open the rickety door and inspected the inky black with a flashlight. Drawing in a deep breath, Thorpe entered the darkness, removed equipment from the canvas bag, and began preparations.

Five minutes later, Thorpe emerged from the barn and made his way back southwest until he came to another barbed-wire fence. There, he secreted himself inside the tree line with Marcel's Cutlass twelve to thirteen yards directly in front of his place of concealment. The yellow glow from the distant street light didn't reach his position and neither would the illumination from Marcel's porch light when it was activated.

Marcel Newman was a member of the Fifty-Seventh Street Hoover Crips. One of the "smarter dealers," he was directly responsible for several murders that had occurred within the Tulsa area; he'd been charged with homicide twice. On one occasion the victim was an innocent six-year-old girl who just happened to be in the yard behind the target of Marcel's gunfire. Thorpe knew the charges were only dropped after chicken-shit witnesses refused to testify. Marcel Newman was a killer, and he associated with other known killers.

Thorpe's OGU investigators, along with the Vice Unit, had conducted a lengthy surveillance of Marcel's activities. The surveillance had ended approximately a week-and-a-half earlier because of a lack of results. During the surveillance, officers noted Marcel would leave his grandmother's house here and drive to a nearby convenience store where he would buy some breakfast sandwiches and drinks. From there, he would drive several miles to his girlfriend's apartment on the northeast side of town. Why Marcel arose so early and why he slept at his grandmother's house wasn't determined through surveillance.

As far as Thorpe was concerned, there was only one useful piece of information garnered from the investigation: Marcel left this residence every weekday at six in the morning. No exceptions. No one who led Marcel's lifestyle should keep such regular patterns; one day it would come back to bite his ass. This was the day.

MARCEL WOKE AT 5:45 A.M., groggily pulled the blankets aside, and slung his legs over the edge of the bed. He reached over and turned off an alarm radio blaring a nineties rap song, then slipped into his too-large black jeans, too-long white t-shirt, too-puffy black coat, and Timberland boots—his "Tims." Marcel liked to sleep here at his Nana's house because it was near the end of a dead-end street, which decreased the likelihood of his competition attempting a drive-by. Plus, he'd never conducted business at the residence so he wouldn't likely be bothered in the middle of the night by an annoying search-warrant service. In short, he felt safe at his grandmother's house.

Marcel shuffled into the kitchen, pulled the refrigerator out a couple of feet, and reached around until he felt the nylon holster duct-taped to the back. He slipped a Taurus 9mm Millennium Pro out of the holster and stood in the kitchen admiring the weight of the pistol. The weapon had a matte stainless-steel slide with a black-checked polymer grip. He'd had an acquaintance purchase the weapon for him at a gun show at the Tulsa County Fair Grounds; it was far superior to the Ravens and Jennings pistols most of his associates carried and was well worth the 400-plus dollars he'd paid. The magazine held ten rounds plus another in the chamber. At just over six inches in length, the weapon slipped easily into his coat pocket and could be withdrawn rapidly. Marcel pushed the heavy refrigerator back into place, walked to the front door, and flipped on the porch light. Pushing open the frost-covered storm door, he stood just inside the doorway for a moment, uncommitted.

He scanned the area, then offered himself to the dark, still morning.

WHEN MARCEL ACTIVATED THE PORCH LIGHT, Thorpe was ready. He'd already used the same pair of bolt cutters to cut three strands of barbed wire separating himself from the Cutlass. He watched as Marcel descended the front porch like an NFL running back alighting from the team bus. At an inch or two under six feet, Marcel was solid. Thorpe figured he'd been wise to bring along the weapon. Marcel probably fought like most any other gang-banger, his head down, swinging wildly with absolutely no technique. But just one lucky punch slipping through Thorpe's defenses could be devastating. It amazed him how some guys amassed so much muscle when all they did was sit around and smoke dope all day. During surveillance, his squad had never seen Marcel exercise once. Of course every time a guy went to prison, the state ensured they got their requisite time with the weights. They generally entered society with an extra twenty-five pounds of muscle along with a re-energized hatred for authority.

As Marcel rounded the front of the Cutlass and stood near the driver's side door, Thorpe watched through a red-dot scope as his target looked cautiously to the south. He kept the sight level as Marcel turned and looked directly into the woods where Thorpe was positioned. He held his breath fearing the rising condensation would be visible in the frigid morning. Marcel seemed to shrug off whatever had alarmed him and turned his attention back to the car. Thorpe thought, *Should have trusted your instincts, asshole*, as he sighted eight inches down and left from the edge of Marcel's right shoulder, taking into account approximately four inches of coat insulation.

AS MARCEL STEPPED AROUND THE FRONT of his Cutlass and reached in his right front pant's pocket for the vehicle's keys, he tried to shake the chill crawling its way up his spine. He turned back to his car, cupped his hands against the lightly frosted glass, and checked his backseat floorboard in one last salute to his paranoia. Seeing nothing, he took the key out of his pocket and inserted it into the lock.

Marcel heard it as much as he felt it—the thwack that drove his right shoulder forward. Instinctively, he reached across with his left hand to probe his shoulder for injury as the pain registered. He attempted to retrieve the weapon from his pocket but his right arm refused to respond. Trying his left arm, he was suddenly yanked back by the injured shoulder as if it were conspiring against him. Staring up into the night, Marcel attempted to push himself up with his good arm. But it was kicked out from under him. A boot crashed down on his injured arm. A knee pinned his other to the pavement. Above him loomed a masked man in coveralls. The dark figure pressed a large knife into the skin just below Marcel's left eye.

"If I wanted you dead, you would be. If you make one sound, I'll pop your fucking eye out and feed it to you." Burning green eyes, remarkably brilliant in the darkness, reinforced the stranger's threats.

NOT WANTING TO LINGER in the street, Thorpe quickly gagged Marcel with a rag and duct tape. He rolled him over and cranked his left arm behind his back. The wounded right shoulder offered little resistance as Thorpe brought the wrists together and bound them with tape. Thorpe removed Marcel's pistol, unzipped his own coveralls, and secured the weapon. Thorpe directed his captive to draw up to his knees. Marcel complied, and Thorpe assisted him to his feet. When Thorpe spun Marcel around and pushed him towards the woods, a muffled cry emanated from beneath the duct tape. Apparently Marcel had hoped they would be heading back towards the house, with the stranger unaware his grandmother would be inside. Marcel stumbled into the ditch and purposefully fell to the ground; Thorpe would have to drag him to the barn. Off the street and in the shadows, Thorpe could work more discreetly now. He switched on a hands-free LED headlamp mounted on his forehead and duct-taped Marcel's legs together above the boots.

Thorpe had shot Marcel with a crossbow. Attached to the arrow was high tensile, braided fishing line. He'd used the line to yank Marcel backwards as he reached for his weapon. The bolt with the barbed broad-head was still buried in Marcel's shoulder. Thorpe now cut the line so it wouldn't get caught on foliage when he dragged his cargo through the woods.

Thorpe was in excellent condition. At an even six feet with little body fat, his 190-pound frame was compacted muscle. He had a fighter's physique. Still, Marcel was a thrashing encumbrance. The fifty-yard haul through the woods and underbrush was grueling. Thorpe pulled Marcel through the open door and over to a support pole in the northeast corner of the pitch-black barn. He slammed Marcel's back against the pole and grabbed him by the throat. Holding the loose end of a roll of duct tape and Marcel's neck with his left hand, Thorpe used his right to wrap tape around the pole and his captive's throat several times. He wouldn't leave Marcel in this position for long as suffocation would soon follow. Having secured Marcel to the pole by his neck, Thorpe cut the tape on his captive's wrists, brought his arms behind the pole and secured them once again. Thorpe then cut the tape around Marcel's neck and placed a black hood over his head. Afterward, he used additional tape to cinch Marcel's lower back securely to the support pole.

Thorpe wore a police radio underneath his coveralls. A wire ran from the instrument, up his back, and into a bud inserted in his left ear. So far the radio had remained quiet. No one had phoned in any disturbance regarding Thorpe's activities, leaving him free to interrogate his captive.

First, Thorpe removed his own boots and exchanged them with another pair inside his canvas bag. He then left the barn to retrieve his crossbow and also Marcel's boots, which had fallen off as he was dragged through the woods. He needed to evaluate the crime scene he'd just created. The time Marcel spent alone, cloaked in silent darkness, would only help the interrogation process.

Contrary to what the movies would have you believe, Thorpe knew there was no magical truth serum. Several mind-altering chemicals had been used, including PCP and LSD, with varying degrees of success. Ultimately, drugs weren't reliable because the subject's reality became distorted. Plus, drugs took time—a commodity of which Thorpe was in short supply. Unfortunately, Thorpe didn't have access to a water-board, and he didn't have the time for implementing stress positions. He could use sensory deprivation to a degree, but he was mostly going to have to rely on pain, fear, pride, and humiliation.

Thorpe returned to the barn where his captive sat gagged, hooded, and bound to the pole. His headlamp cast an eerie glow on his prisoner as he circled Marcel several times in silence to build more tension. He knew Marcel could sense his presence; he turned his head to Thorpe's movements, desperately using his ears to gather information. Thorpe returned to the equipment bag, removed some items, switched on a battery-powered lamp, and again changed boots.

Thorpe returned to his captive, squatted, and spoke into Marcel's ear. "All I want from you are answers to my questions, nothing more. Do you understand?" Marcel nodded his head. Thorpe continued, "I'm going to remove the gag from your mouth; if you scream out, you're going to cause yourself a great deal of pain. Do you understand?"

Marcel nodded again as Thorpe raised the hood up enough to remove the tape and rag. He let the cloak fall back down into place. Thorpe spoke in an even tone, "Honest answers earn your freedom. Lies will cause you pain. What's your full name?"

"Marcel Newman."

"What's your girlfriend's name?"

"Which one?" Marcel asked.

"The one you take sandwiches and drinks to every fucking morning," Thorpe replied. He was asking baseline questions to gauge Marcel's responses. At the same time, he was letting his captive know his interrogator was an informed man.

"You tell me then, motherfucker," Marcel said.

Marcel's toenails appeared to be on a semi-annual clipping schedule. So it was no difficult task when Thorpe clamped a pair of needle-nose pliers on a yellowing nail and tore it from his captive's big toe. Marcel growled in pain but didn't scream out; he was still playing the tough guy. Thorpe stepped away from the ragged breathing of his captive. Marcel muttered an onslaught of profanity under his breath.

Thorpe gave him a few minutes to recover from the shock before continuing his interrogation. "Now what was your girlfriend's name?"

"Cynthia," Marcel relented.

"Cynthia what?"

"Cynthia Barnes."

"That's better."

Thorpe got to the reason for this meeting: "About a year ago, a woman and her child were shot to death in a South Tulsa home. They were the wife and daughter of a Tulsa Police Officer." Thorpe paused, letting the statement sink in before he asked his question, "Who murdered them?"

The question hung in the air. "I don't know nothin' bout that shit," he spit. The pause before his answer said more than his words.

Thorpe unsheathed his knife. He cut open Marcel's shirt from the waist to the neck. Marcel thrashed to the extent his restraints would allow, "Nigga! What the fuck!"

Thorpe stuck the knife through the hood into Marcel's left ear and slowly began to push. "Marcel, are you going to shut the fuck up, or am I going to have to kill you an inch at a time?"

Marcel shut his mouth as Thorpe used the knife up each pant leg until he was able to remove his captive's pants. He did the same with Marcel's underwear. His prisoner now sat naked, with a lot less pride, on the dirt floor. As Marcel sat contemplating his new predicament, Thorpe changed into yet another pair of shoes, using the lull to his advantage. Silence would accelerate fear. The freezing barn would increase discomfort and pain; everything hurts more when it's cold.

Thorpe directed his light onto Marcel, who was now shaking uncontrollably. Steam rose from his body. Thorpe knelt and spoke softly, "I know you know. Now this is where it's going to get real fucking ugly if you don't improve your attitude. I'm going to ask you the same question again, and if you don't tell the truth, you're going to cause yourself a shit-load of agony. It's up to you to help yourself." As Thorpe finished the sentence he clamped the pliers on Marcel's left areola, then asked, "Who killed the woman and her child?"

Marcel turned his hooded head toward Thorpe's voice and replied through clenched teeth, "Fuck you."

Tough guy. Thorpe used both hands and all his strength as he pulled and twisted at the same time. Marcel's left nipple was ripped away from his chest as a ragged piece of flesh. Thorpe tossed the skin to the side as Marcel shrieked and passed out, blood flowing down his bare chest.

Marcel was a soldier. Twice, he'd been "caught-up-short" on drug violations. On both occasions he could have avoided prison time had he cooperated with authorities. But to Marcel, his reputation and his name were more important than even his freedom. He went to prison, served his sentence, and came back to his neighborhood with a wealth of street cred. Thorpe was going to use that against him.

Short on time, Thorpe held smelling salts underneath Marcel's nose, bringing him back to consciousness. "Can you hear me, Marcel? You *are* going to answer my questions, or you're going to die here on this dirt floor."

Marcel stirred, and after a few seconds of coughing, sputtered, "Man, I'm fucking dead anyway. Just 'cause I'm black, don't mean I'm stupid. Don't take a fucking genius to figure out who you are. You the husband. You the cop." Marcel let out a long, wet cough then continued, "But I'll tell you anyway just so you fucking kill me quicker. It don't matter none anyway. Those two niggas killed your kin... they died same night as them. Now fucking end this shit!"

Thorpe considered Marcel's declaration. It was possible Marcel just wanted to give him the names of two dead men so he could protect the real killers and end his misery now rather than endure more pain. On the other hand, he doubted Marcel would remember the two murders occurred on the same night given it occurred a year ago—unless there was indeed a connection. Thorpe already knew the two men he was referring to but wanted to see if Marcel could also produce their names. "What were the names of the two who were killed?"

Marcel paused as if he were considering whether saying the names of two dead gang-bangers would be a violation of his personal code. He must have decided it wasn't. "Big D and Little D."

Thorpe knew Marcel was referring to the brothers Deandre and Damarius Davis, both of whom were killed in North Tulsa the same night Thorpe's wife and daughter were slain. Homicide had looked into whether the murders were related but had been unable to find a correlation. It didn't make sense. Out of all the people Thorpe had sent to prison, he'd had only limited contact with "the DD brothers." Having done little more than conduct a cursory pat-down of either man, he'd certainly done nothing to reap this harsh a retribution.

"Why would those two assholes kill a cop's family?" Thorpe demanded.

"How da fuck do I know?" Marcel replied, still able to muster up attitude. "Musta' been stealin' yo shit when it went bad."

Thorpe rose and walked away from Marcel, his mind scrambling to catch up. What were the chances two north-side bangers would end up in Thorpe's south-Tulsa neighborhood, attempt to burglarize his home, shoot and kill his family, and then be killed themselves a few hours later? *Not very damn likely!* If they were in fact the killers, then someone had sent them, and that same person or persons had bought their silence with a couple of bullets. Thorpe returned to Marcel, determined to get at the truth.

"Who sent the brothers to kill my family?!" Thorpe demanded.

"I don't know what you're fuckin' talking 'bout. Just kill me already."

Thorpe knelt and peeled off Marcel's hood. Then he switched off his headlamp and slowly pulled up his own ski mask, uncovered his eyes, and stared directly at his captive. "Marcel, you're right. I *am* going to kill you. No matter what you say, or what you do, you are going to die tonight. I know you're a soldier, and I doubt you're afraid of death. A part of me actually has some respect for you 'cause in your own fucked-up way you have some honor about you. But you're about to make the most important choice of your very short life."

Through the dim light, Marcel stared defiantly into Thorpe's eyes. *Good*. He had the man's full attention, and he needed it to drive home his next bluff. Death was nothing to Marcel; he'd accepted his ultimate fate years before. Most bangers have no respect for human life, sometimes not even their own. Marcel had no problem dying like a soldier. He would have the respect of his crew, and enjoy a legacy— much like a radical Islamic dreams of dying a martyr. Thorpe had to convince Marcel he would strip that respect away…even in death.

"Marcel, I'm about to ask you a series of questions. You can either answer these honestly, or you can lie…it's *your* choice. Either way, before I kill you I'll give you a moment to make peace with God. If I think you've told me the truth—and I'm pretty good at sifting through bullshit, Marcel—you'll die painlessly. But, and listen real carefully to this Marcel, I'm going to take a little insurance policy out on your ass."

Thorpe paused while staring into Marcel's eyes; he needed to insure he understood. "After you're dead, your body leaves here with me. It may be in one piece, or it may be in several; that's up to you. What happens to it afterward is also up to you. If I discover you've been truthful, your body will be found on a street somewhere. Your homies will automatically assume you've been killed by rival gang members. They'll come to your funeral and remember you as a soldier and pay you the respect you deserve. You still listening, Marcel?"

His captive nodded his head as he stared back with unblinking eyes.

"Good. Because if you lie to me, Marcel, they won't ever find your body. Instead I'll start writing search warrants on all your homies, and I'll name you in those warrants as my snitch."

Marcel's eyes widened and intensified with even more anger.

"That's right, Marcel. You will have disappeared and warrants will start popping up with your name all over them. All your friends will think you've turned informant. You'll be dead, but no one will ever come to your funeral to pay you respect. The only reason they'd show up would be to piss on your grave. Now look in my eyes and ask yourself—will he really do this?"

Thorpe really needed to sell this bluff to insure he got truthful answers. In effect, he was forcing Marcel to be a snitch in order to avoid being labeled one. He was about to find out what was more important to the man: real honor or the perception of honor.

Marcel stared into Thorpe's unwavering eyes for a full minute before he turned his head away, his body appearing to collapse in upon itself. All Marcel had in this world was his reputation, and this cracker motherfucker was prepared to take that away from him as well.

Thorpe watched as fear and doubt clawed its way into Marcel's being. He knew he'd won the battle. Marcel might still offer slivers of resistance, but he was now a broken man without pride.

"All I heard was—that it was something else got fucked up," Marcel finally admitted.

"Explain."

"'Bout a week after your daughter was killed, dude told me the two brothers were the hitters. He said it was some fucked-up shit. I asked him more about it, but he quit talking. He said he shouldn't have said anything. He tried to act like he was just being solid by keeping his mouth shut. But I could tell he was scared."

"Who told you this?"

"I don't know his name," Marcel lied.

Thorpe placed the blade of his knife at the base of Marcel's penis. He very slowly began drawing the serrated edge across when Marcel blurted out the name, "Kaleb."

"Kaleb...Kaleb Moment?" Thorpe asked.

"Yeah," Marcel said, defeated, "...Fuck!"

"What else did he tell you?"

"Just that it was no coincidence those brothers got killed the same night. That's it; he wouldn't say anymore. I think he knew he fucked up by talking about it. Every day after that he told me not to say a fucking word...and I never did."

Thorpe weighed the information. He believed Marcel was telling the truth. For one thing, he could *see* the devastation in Marcel's face and body posture. He had become almost demure and had substituted nearly Standard English in lieu of Ebonics. But most importantly, he'd just snitched on one of his best homeboys, Kaleb Moment. Marcel had to know he had just brought hell itself down on Kaleb; his friend would soon be in a similar predicament.

Thorpe leaned in, "Marcel, if you're withholding anything else from me, a lot of people are going to have warrants served on them...courtesy of you."

"Man that's it; I don't know nothin' else."

"One more thing, Marcel...I'm going to wipe away the word *cop* you wrote with your finger." Marcel's hands were taped behind his back, just inches off the dirt floor. Earlier he'd used his finger to spell cop behind the wooden pole. "That was very clever. After I wipe it away you're going to use the same finger to write the letters L.A." Thorpe smoothed the dirt with his gloved hands before telling Marcel to proceed.

"I'll make sure this barn gets searched after they find your body." Thorpe thought he caught the hint of a smile as Marcel etched the letters into the dirt floor.

"Marcel, you have two minutes to try and save your soul if you think you have one. Pray to whatever god you worship. I'll tell you when it's time."

Resigned to his fate, Marcel closed his eyes and appeared to be engaged in silent prayer. Thorpe used this time to gather equipment. A minute later, he returned to Marcel and informed him it was time. He checked to make sure the L.A. initials were still intact.

"Marcel, earlier tonight when you walked out of your house and approached your car, you paused and looked around. You even looked my direction. You see or hear anything?"

Marcel turned and looked at Thorpe. He seemed genuinely contemplative before responding, "No, I just *felt* something. Guess I fucked up."

Ain't no guessing 'bout it. Thorpe held up a rag in front of Marcel's face, "Open your mouth, I have to remove the arrow, and it's going to hurt. I don't want you screaming out."

It must not have crossed Marcel's mind Thorpe could have removed the arrow after he was dead. He did as he was told. But when Thorpe continued wrapping Marcel's mouth and nose completely shut with tape his eyes bulged with realization and fear.

"Marcel, when I told you I respected you, it was just one of several lies you bought tonight. You're a piece-of-shit child killer just like the ones I'm after. When you made peace with God, I hope you mentioned that little girl you killed."

With that Thorpe picked up a stray two-by-four from the barn's floor, went down on his right knee, and swung the board like a baseball bat at the front of Marcel's throat. Bone and meat were crushed between the board and the wooden pole. Marcel's bound body convulsed and lurched on the dirt floor as he suffocated in his own blood.

Even as Marcel sat dying, Thorpe went to work. He cut the back end of the arrow off with his bolt cutters and used the pliers to pull the arrow through the front of the shoulder. He put all of these items in a large, heavy-duty, plastic bag. Thorpe then removed a small Ziploc plastic baggy from his pocket, used a pair of tweezers to remove a hair from the baggy, and placed it on the sticky side of some loose duct tape attached to Marcel. Thorpe gathered his equipment and left Marcel's body bound to the pole. He stepped out of the barn at 0655 hours.

Though the sky was beginning to lighten, he still had twenty-seven minutes till sunrise. Thorpe walked around the outside of the barn, wearing the different boots and using different strides before heading south down the gravel road. Before he reached the gate, he walked a few yards to the east, removed the spool of fishing line from the crossbow, and concealed the weapon in some vegetation. He didn't want to be spotted with the crossbow out on the street. Thorpe didn't care if the weapon was found eventually—it couldn't be traced back to him. He put the spool in his pocket and monitored the police radio as he calmly walked back to his vehicle.

TWO

Monday
February 5th
Afternoon

TULSA, OKLAHOMA IS THE FORTY-FIFTH LARGEST CITY, by population, in the United States. Nearly four-hundred-thousand people live within its limits—almost a million in the metro area. Originally part of Indian Territory, the city really flourished when large pools of oil were discovered in the early 1900s. In 1927, a Tulsa businessman campaigned to create a highway system connecting Chicago to California. Because of his efforts, Tulsa earned its nickname of "the birthplace of Route 66."

Today, the swath old Route 66 cuts through Tulsa is the city's easiest place to locate "women of the night." An archaic name, for these days women of the night were just as likely to be peddling ass during the lunch hour as anytime. If the old highway were to be renamed today, Route

69 might be a more apt description—though that service would undoubtedly cost extra.

Tulsa sits in the northeast corner of Oklahoma in a region known as Green Country. Unlike the western section of Oklahoma, Tulsa is surrounded by lush woodlands, lakes, and rolling landscape. The climate can change forty degrees or more in a single day. In February a person can be braving freezing temperatures on Monday, and walking comfortably outside without a shirt by Tuesday. The fickle weather prompted the famous quote by native Oklahoman Will Rogers, "If you don't like the weather in Oklahoma, just wait a minute."

The city itself is generally divided into four major sections by locals. The North Side has a predominantly black populace and is comprised of older homes and very few businesses. It's the place most rookie police officers cut their teeth—at least those who join for the car-and-foot pursuits, fights, and action. The North Side is where Thorpe spent the majority of his career before supervising the Gangs Unit.

The West Side is mostly lower-income whites. The East Side is a kaleidoscope of whites, Hispanics, blacks, Asians, and is generally comprised of medium- to lower-priced homes and industrial complexes. The South Side is where the money lives.

These socio-economic dynamics were the basis for S.E. Hinton's *The Outsiders*, a 1960s book pitting Greasers against Socials or "Socs." Francis Ford Coppola would later take the high-school author's book and make it into a blockbuster movie. Today, with the proliferation of gangs and gun violence, South Side Socials generally keep their lily-white asses out of the North Side.

Though Tulsa wasn't a huge metropolis, it was still bigger and busier than Thorpe wanted in his off hours. He chose to live outside the city, near the small town of Mounds, Oklahoma. His neighborhood was a twenty-five minute drive, south of downtown. His community consisted of fifteen homes. Each home sat on ten to twenty acres and was heavily wooded. He'd moved into the place about seven months after his wife, Erica, and his daughter, Ella, had been murdered.

The previous home had been a constant reminder of better times. Every square inch pierced his heart with memories. Scents lingered on hairbrushes, pillows, clothing and toys. Sometimes Thorpe even thought he'd heard his daughter's giggles, finding himself rushing into an empty room only to find nothing but a new depth to his misery. Even the new carpet in his daughter's bedroom was a reminder; no doubt bloodstains were still visible on the plywood beneath.

He immediately listed the home with a Realtor. Not able to bear surrounding himself with his family's belongings, he also couldn't bear to discard them. He moved all their possessions into storage and rented an apartment. He'd located the new property shortly before the Realtor sold his house, taking a huge loss in the process. He wanted out and knew no one would pay top dollar for a place in which a double homicide had recently occurred. He needed the seclusion of his new home.

The house sat near the front of twenty wooded acres, with a creek running through the property forty yards behind it. An unattached wooden deck had been built above the creek; Thorpe spent many hours there. It was on this deck where Thorpe sat now with his two German shepherds, Al and Trixie.

Thinking of his family, Thorpe felt the familiar emotional undertow start to drag him under. He'd been there too many times, knowing it'd take him days to claw his way back to the surface if he allowed himself to dwell. Thorpe consciously pushed thoughts of his wife and daughter away, instead concentrating on his environment and current predicament.

The day was relatively warm for February, but Thorpe could still feel the chill though his sweats and

Under Armor. The steaming cup of coffee in his hand helped stave off the cold. He was enveloped by oaks, towering pecans, and the soft gurgle of the creek flowing beside him. The crisp, clean, air intermingled with the rich aroma of his morning brew as he ran through the events of last night, trying to uncover any mistakes he might have made.

Generally, there are four major pitfalls that resulted in a suspect's undoing—first and foremost was motive, followed closely by collaboration. There's an old saying, "Two people can keep a secret...if one of them is dead." Nothing is truer in the snake-eats-snake world of the criminal. Over the years, several high-profile thefts had been pulled-off to near perfection. The most notorious of these were generally burglaries or armed robberies of armored cars and other currency-transport systems, where the perpetrators made off with millions of dollars. Though these cases sometimes went unsolved for weeks or even years, invariably one of the suspects would do something stupid that brought the spotlight down on everyone else. The thieves might simply live above their means with no explanation for their newfound wealth, or might feel the need to brag about what they "got away with" to a buddy or girlfriend. Or, they might just get busted for something unrelated and turn witness to avoid prison time. Thorpe knew collaboration would be the downfall of his family's murderers. One or more of them had already spoken about it, the information filtering down to Marcel from Kaleb Moment and now to Thorpe.

The third pitfall was physical evidence, especially in the era of DNA. One hair follicle left at a crime scene was all it took. Blood, semen, saliva, fingerprints, bite marks, tool marks, ballistics—the list was nearly infinite.

The last of the major problems is potential witnesses. Witnesses are not reliable and in today's courtroom are the easiest to discredit. Thorpe had responded to many a crime scene to find witnesses giving completely different descriptions of the same suspect. Witnesses to stressful events were especially prone to making misidentifications. DNA testing had exonerated numerous suspects who had spent years in prison based on the testimony of "reliable" eye witnesses. Rape cases, where the victim is obviously under an extreme amount of stress, were some of the most common cases later overturned by DNA evidence. Even trained and experienced police officers were not immune to these errors.

When officers are involved in a stressful event such as a shooting or even a high-speed chase, huge amounts of adrenaline are dumped into the body. The mind is essentially under the influence of chemicals meant to help the individual survive, but they also alter perception. Studies have shown officers involved in high-speed chases experience similar physiological symptoms as a soldier in the midst of combat. At the conclusion of these chases, officers aren't able to just switch off these "fight or flight" chemicals; they are literally drugged. Some end up on the ten o'clock news *a la* Rodney King. Anyone who's been a police officer for more than a week knows if a suspect runs, the law and an ass-whipping are going after him. It has nothing to do with race. If Conan O'Brien decided to outrun the police, he would get his five-thousand-dollar suit beaten right off his back—and Conan's the whitest man ever to have walked the planet.

Thorpe figured eventually he himself would be discovered. He didn't have to worry about collaborators and was fairly certain there would be no witnesses who could provide anything valuable. But he certainly had motive. And one just never knew about physical evidence — despite how many precautions were taken.

He doubted his motive could be tied to Marcel, at least not at this point in his mission. Marcel had nothing to do with his family's murder except for hearing something he shouldn't have. Thorpe had gotten lucky. He hadn't known if Marcel was in the know. Thorpe had just chosen five killers in the Tulsa area—five gang-bangers who were in the information stream of the underworld of Tulsa, five men who deserved to die and who he would have little remorse killing even if it turned out they had no useful information. Thorpe had considered the possibility of killing all five of the thugs and still not acquiring useful information. Instead, he had found a starting place with his first target. Marcel had given him someone who knew something, his best friend Kaleb Moment. Now Thorpe had direction. But with each kill the connection would grow stronger between his family's killing and the ones Thorpe would be committing. He might eventually become a suspect, but hopefully not until all who were responsible for his family's death had been put in the dirt. Even then, being suspected and being convicted might be worlds apart.

Evidence was another matter. Thorpe had taken steps to avoid leaving incriminating DNA, while at the same time planting misdirecting physical evidence. He kept his brown hair short, had completely covered his body, and had shaved his goatee prior to the mission. Still, one dog hair transferred from his clothing to the crime scene would be enough to link him if he ever became a suspect. However he already had a reasonable excuse if that scenario ever arose. Because of his job, Thorpe had legitimate contact with most potential "victims" prior to engaging them. Tonight, he would dispose of many of the tainted items from last night's encounter with Marcel. He also had one more piece of misdirection to plant, contingent upon Marcel's body remaining undiscovered for just a bit longer.

Thorpe heard the crunching and popping of rubber on gravel as he turned his head to watch a gleaming silver Toyota 4-Runner dock in his driveway. It was Jeff, his good friend and old partner. Jeff Gobin was about the same height as Thorpe but a good forty pounds heavier. When Thorpe and Jeff had suffered through the academy together they had weighed nearly the same. Now they probably had the same amount of muscle on their frames, but Jeff had put on an insulating layer of fat. Jeff was still in excellent shape, he just really enjoyed his pizza, spaghetti, fettuccini, and anything else Italian. Jeff was black, but if someone had to guess his ethnicity from his stomach contents, he'd most likely surmise Jeff was fresh off the boat from Sicily. It'd been a few years since Thorpe and Jeff had been partners, but they remained close. Following the murders, Jeff had checked up on Thorpe almost daily. Lately, Jeff had been coming out to Thorpe's property to workout—religiously. Jeff probably thought he was being a Good Samaritan by coming out to Thorpe's *compound* as his friend liked to refer to it, but Thorpe figured he was probably coming out as much for his own mental stability as anything else. Jeff was stuck in a not-so-happy marriage though you would never hear him complain about it.

Thorpe rose from the deck and walked to a large, wooden barn that sat about fifty yards west of his home. The modern barn was 24 by 20. It had double doors, a loft, steel support, and stained concrete floors. Thorpe had outfitted it with weights, a heavy bag, wrestling mat, and various pieces of exercise equipment.

"What the fuck are you smiling at?" Jeff remarked, without a smile of his own.

"I'm thinking of the ass whipping you're about to get," Thorpe said as he opened a door beside the larger double doors.

"Why are you always talking about my ass? There something you want to tell me?"

"Huh, your ass ain't bad, but your boobs are a little big for my taste," Thorpe joked.

"Fuck you."

That's how their pleasantries usually went. A transcribed conversation between the two would look like two sworn enemies who were thrown in a very small room together. But that's the way they—and most cops—talked to each other. If another cop wasn't giving you shit, then he probably wasn't your friend.

Thorpe opened the door, and the two men walked inside. Having been trained, Al and Trixie remained outside and took their posts near the barn's door.

"Jeffro, it's chest day. Let's try to firm up those man boobs of yours. Otherwise I'm going to have to buy you a manssiere."

Jeff smiled and proudly displayed his middle finger.

Following strength conditioning, he and Jeff went through thirty minutes of cardio circuit training that involved jumping rope, working the heavy bag, and scrambling on the mat. Throughout the workout, last night's conversation with Marcel kept looping through Thorpe's mind. The trigger-pullers were already dead, but it was obvious there had been a more sinister undertaking than a burglary gone bad. Someone had *sent* the Davis brothers, someone who was going to pay dearly. Thorpe's workout intensity rose to meet that of his rage, until he collapsed on the mat, rolled over, and vomited on the smooth concrete.

Thorpe had always exercised regularly, but since his family's death he'd totally immersed himself in his workouts. The physical pain would, temporarily at least, help dull his emotional torment. Pain, adrenaline, and a mission—that was Thorpe's version of an alcoholic drinking himself numb.

"Damn, John, that's why I don't want to spar with you anymore. That shit ain't normal," Jeff said, scowling.

"People puke all the time when they workout," Thorpe sputtered—still hunched over the concrete.

"Yeah, when they got Bobby Knight all over their ass. Not when they're working out at their own home."

"I didn't throw-up from my workout," Thorpe smiled, "I got sick from watching your man boobs flop around inside that nasty shirt of yours."

"Have I told you to fuck off lately?" Jeff said sarcastically.

"Yeah, couple times."

"Good." Then Jeff added, "Man, you need to go see someone before this shit kills you."

"I'm working it out... It's getting better."

"You say so," Jeff said, knowing his friend was lying. Jeff had been there when Thorpe first met his wife, and he'd tried to be there as much as possible ever since her death. That is, when Thorpe didn't push him away.

The chance meeting had occurred seven years before. At the time Thorpe was 28 years old and enjoying the bachelor life. He'd been on the force for seven years, had not yet been promoted, and was working as a Strategic-Oriented Police Officer or SOPO. There were six SOPO officers assigned to Gilcrease Division. SOPO officers were selected primarily because they demonstrated a proficiency at tossing shit-heads in jail. Their assignment was basically to put out fires across the city. If a particular area was experiencing a high amount of violence or drug trafficking, it was the SOPO's job to come in and quell the criminal element. Tulsa police officers generally operate solo but because of the inherent danger of their assignment, SOPO officers worked with a partner. One Saturday night in August, Thorpe and his partner, Jeff, were patrolling outside a downtown Tulsa bar, the site of several recent shootings. They were conducting checks on a couple of pedestrians, who were dressed out in gang colors, when Jeff observed two ladies exit an adjacent bar and head toward a parking lot. Thorpe noticed Jeff's attention shift and followed his partner's gaze. Even at fifty yards, both officers could tell the women were extremely attractive, attractive enough that both Thorpe and Jeff forgot the term "officer safety," giving their full attention to the two women walking away from the bar. The two gang-bangers could have clubbed both officers over the head like baby seals had they wanted. But their attention had *also* been drawn to the women now walking down the street away from them. It must have been quite a sight: two uniformed officers standing next to two dressed-out "Red-Teamers," all four of them drooling on themselves like best friends and fellow deviants.

The two ladies walked west down First Street and rounded a corner heading north into a darkened parking lot and out of sight. Thorpe was returning his attention back to matters at hand when he observed two men across the street near where the women had passed. One of the men elbowed his buddy in the ribs and nodded in the direction the women had gone. The two men began to follow. Thorpe looked at Jeff and could tell by the look on his partner's face he shared the same concern. Jeff returned the I.D.s to the bangers, and both officers jogged toward the area where the two women and their stalkers had disappeared.

When Thorpe rounded the corner, he observed the two women near a red BMW. One of the men was just catching up with the women from behind. He estimated the guy to be about five-foot-ten, slightly over 200 pounds, and highly intoxicated. The man was doing his best impersonation of a drunken ninja as he unsteadily snuck up behind the nearest woman and lifted her black pleated skirt. The woman spun on the man and attempted a wide, right-handed slap, but Drunken Ninja was sober enough to catch her right wrist with his left hand and push her up against the car. The two drunks then began saying things only drunks think are clever. The second, smaller man began maneuvering toward the other, almost equally attractive woman.

Thorpe had come up behind Drunken Ninja, who now had a hold on both the woman's wrists. The woman caught the movement and glanced over her assailant's shoulder at Thorpe. Her assailant, probably a little sharper now because of an adrenaline rush, recognized someone must be standing behind him. Drunken Ninja stepped back with his left foot, spun, and took a right handed swing that seemed to start somewhere near the Canadian border. Instead of backing away from the telegraphed punch,

Thorpe stepped into and underneath it, driving Drunken Ninja's body over his right shoulder. Thorpe lifted Drunken Ninja off the ground and had him draped across his shoulders in a fireman's carry. Though the move isn't taught in any respectable martial arts dojo, it is a move handed down from every father to every son. It's a move you use on your buddies when you're horsing around, especially effective when they're drunk. It's not a practiced law-enforcement tactic, for good reason, but Thorpe was showing off a little now. He gave Drunken Ninja a "helicopter ride," spinning him rapidly through the air.

Thorpe released the man mid-flight. Drunken Ninja was unable to activate his landing gear and skidded painfully across the lot via his stomach and forearms. And, just like any self-respecting drunk, Ninja immediately jumped to his feet to address the threat. Unfortunately, his world was now spinning out of control, and he couldn't keep his feet. Drunken Ninja started staggering to his right and instead of just falling down (and saving himself further embarrassment), he picked up speed as he tried to stay upright. He took several sideways running steps before plowing head first into the tailgate of a blue, Ford F-150, knocking himself unconscious.

The woman in the skirt had just been in tears but was now quietly laughing as she looked down on Drunken Ninja, who was emptying his bladder through his jeans onto the gravel parking lot. All four began openly laughing. Thorpe thought he even heard a giggle come from Drunken Ninja's drunken sidekick. When the amusement eventually faded, his lady in distress, Erica, looked up at Thorpe and that was it. He could see it in her eyes; she was enamored.

One week later, he picked Erica up for their first date. For the occasion, she wore a white-lace halter cami with a plunging neckline and bare midriff. Again she wore a black skirt, but this time it was about three inches shy of being illegal. She looked, smelled, and oozed sex. The date began with dinner and drinks before Erica suggested going to a large country-and-western bar located near the center of Tulsa's city limits. He wasn't much on crowded bars but couldn't totally dismiss the idea of slow dancing with the beauty seated next to him. Her long, slender legs mostly made the argument for her. Shortly after, Thorpe found himself on a crowded dance floor with Erica pressed tightly against him. The couple lasted two songs before he invited her back to his apartment. Erica promptly accepted. By the time he turned the key to his apartment and pushed open the door, they were pulling at one another's clothes. The two fell into the apartment and a lovemaking session. They never made it past the front room.

After their first date, the two began seeing each other regularly, but not exclusively. Sex was the glue holding the relationship together. He didn't know if Erica was in love with him but knew she at least had a deep infatuation. Sometimes he wondered if she wasn't just attracted to the potential for violence she had witnessed when they first met. Some women crave that. Everyone's seen them—the woman with the fashion-model looks hanging on the arm of a Kid Rock look-alike. One thing Thorpe knew for certain; he wasn't in love with Erica. In fact, he'd never been in love with any woman and was beginning to doubt whether he had the capability. About two months after their first date, Thorpe decided he'd better call off the relationship. He was preparing to break the news to Erica when she informed him of her predicament. She was pregnant. The two had been careful, but these things have a way of happening. Erica seemed genuinely happy with the prospects of motherhood, and after the initial shock, Thorpe did his best to appear optimistic. Thorpe was raised to accept responsibility for his actions, and though today's experts would probably discourage marrying because of an unexpected pregnancy, Thorpe felt it was the only thing to do.

Erica came from money—old money. Her father, Phillip Hessler, made no attempt to hide the fact he was deeply disappointed in the man who had "knocked-up" his baby. He had higher aspirations for his daughter. Thorpe figured the man had hoped for an Ivy League investment banker as a future son-in-law, not some knuckle-dragging civil servant with a gun. The two were married in a large downtown Methodist church with Erica clearly showing in her white wedding dress. When the father gave his daughter away, he did so with a glare that should have burned a hole right through Thorpe's rented tuxedo. The relationship with his in-laws would never improve.

Thorpe was in the delivery room on the night Ella was born. He didn't experience any of those overwhelming emotions other fathers describe when excitedly recalling the births of their children. He made sure he said all the right things and smiled on cue. Two days later, mother and child came home to the apartment. Erica didn't feel well and Thorpe was burdened with the majority of childcare. One short week of caring for Ella—the diaper changing, the bottle feedings at 3 a.m., the standing over the crib to make sure the baby was still breathing, the worrying that comes with caring for something so small, fragile, and, yes, precious—had broken Thorpe down. He loved this baby more than anything he had loved in his entire life. Childcare wasn't a burden any longer; it was a privilege. This innocent baby, Ella, looked to Thorpe to take care of her, and that's just what he planned to do. Thorpe wasn't the only one changed by being a parent. Erica settled down and, to his surprise, turned out to be an excellent mother. As Ella grew so did the relationship between Erica and Thorpe. He may not have been in love, but at least he had a deep caring. Thorpe's love for Ella, however, was beyond even his own comprehension. He knew then if he lost her, he too would be lost forever.

FOLLOWING THEIR WORKOUT, JEFF LEFT Thorpe's property more concerned than when he'd arrived. When they'd partnered together, they'd spent upwards of eight hours a day with each other five days a week and had often hung out with each other on their off days. When you've spent that amount of time with someone, you damned well got to know him. Maybe not his history, if he were unwilling to share. But you definitely got to a point where you knew what another person was thinking, even if the words weren't spoken.

Jeff sensed a shift within Thorpe. He'd already been close to becoming unhinged, but now there was something... new. He couldn't quite pinpoint what it was but decided he'd be keeping a closer eye on his best friend.

Three

Monday
February 5th
Evening

POLICE LOVE THEIR ACRONYMS, and the Tulsa Police Department is no exception. Thorpe supervised the department's Organized Gang Unit, or OGU. The OGU operated out of the Special Investigation's Division or SID, which housed the department's undercover units. In addition to the OGU, the division was also home to the Vice Unit, two narcotics units, the Intelligence Unit, and the Organized Crime Drug Enforcement Task Force or OCDETF, a unit comprised of DEA agents and Tulsa Police Officers—both entities being cross-deputized. Tulsa Police officers, integrated with the FBI's counter terrorism unit, also worked out of the office. The personnel working at SID were a motley bunch. Some had the boy-or girl-next-door appearance while others looked as though they should be snorting crank in a darkened corner of some seedy bar.

The Special Investigations Division was more commonly referred to as the office by those who worked there. The office was relocated every few years in an attempt to keep the location secret, thereby deterring counter-surveillance. Currently the office was located on the southwest corner of a busy intersection in east Tulsa. The only way to enter the office was to drive up a concrete ramp on the south side of the building. When you reached the top of the ramp, you were faced with a large gate and an electronic card reader. The gate was posted "ITPS Inc., AUTHORIZED PERSONNEL ONLY!" ITPS stood for *It's The Police Stupid*—a testament that cops *do* have a sense of humor. Once you were granted access through the gate, you parked on a lot that—in reality—was the roof of the second floor of the building. The first and second floors were occupied by regular citizens who didn't have access to the third floor. The third floor was half parking lot and half office building.

The office was situated in a fairly nefarious neighborhood. Officers could literally sit in their own elevated parking lot, look to the south, and observe drug sales occurring on a daily basis. The Sheridan Commons, a low-rent, pay-by-the-night or by-the-week "whoretel," sat just to the south. It was operated by a Middle Eastern man who was shady to say the least and was a major prostitution and street-level narcotics hub.

Thorpe arrived at the office a few minutes before 6 p.m., darkness already descending. Thorpe had ten officers and one corporal under his command. The corporal and four officers normally worked dayshift hours from eleven in the morning to seven at night. Thorpe chose to work the late shift from 6 p.m. till 2 a.m. with the six night-shift officers. However, because of the nature of the work, schedules changed on a daily basis and overtime was abundant. Well, it was abundant until the new division commander arrived a few months ago. Now officers went home on time even in the midst of a developing investigation—all in order to make the new major, Richard Duncan, look like an overtime savior to his bosses. Thorpe parked his undercover truck beneath the amber lights of the parking area. He then walked across the lot, dimly illuminated by the yellow haze, and swiped his card a second time in order to gain entry to the building. As usual, the division's secretary, and all the brass had already left for the evening. Two of Thorpe's nightshift officers were already at their desks. Thorpe walked through the OGU bullpen passing one of his officers, Jennifer Williams.

"Hey, Carnac, can we serve a warrant tonight?" Jennifer asked. "Carnac" was a name Thorpe had picked up a couple of years earlier. For some reason, most criminals had cool nicknames like Deuce, Fast Eddie, Machine Gun Kelly, whatever. But a police officer would never give another cop a cool moniker. Some had tried to give themselves favorable names—always with disastrous consequences.

Thorpe's label was a reference to "Carnac the Magnificent," a character made famous by the late Johnny Carson. In the skit, Johnny would wear a ridiculously gigantic turban on his head. As always, Ed McMahon played the straight man. Carson as Carnac would produce an envelope, which McMahon would claim was "hermetically sealed." Carnac would then use his psychic powers to come up with a punch-line answer to an unknown question. After announcing the punch line, Carnac would open the sealed envelope and read the question. The bit would go something like this:

Carnac would hold an envelope to his enormous turban and state, "A triple and a double, catcher's and fielder's, and Dolly Parton."

McMahon: "A triple and a double, catcher's and fielder's, and Dolly Parton."

Carnac: "Name two big hits, two big mitts…and a famous country singer."

Thorpe had earned this nickname while serving a search warrant on a methamphetamine lab near Lewis and

Independence. One of his officers had obtained the warrant utilizing a trash-pull.

The courts have deemed once trash is abandoned at the curb it is no longer protected by search-and-seizure laws. Investigators generally "pull" the trash and replace it with another bag in the early-morning hours while everyone's asleep (though sometimes it's difficult to determine when a crankster sleeps, since they're often up for days on end). And it's always a bit awkward when you get caught stealing trash. Feigning being drunk off one's ass is usually the preferred tactic for avoiding lengthy explanations. No one likes talking to someone who's shit-faced, not even meth-heads.

You can learn a lot about a person from going through their trash, right down to their menstrual cycles. In this instance, officers found blister packs from numerous cold and allergy pills, which contained pseudoephedrine. They'd also located Heet bottles and items covered with iodine stains. All of these components are used in the "Red-P" method of methamphetamine production. A background check on the occupants revealed prior arrests for drug possession and related offenses. The contents of the trash, bolstered by the resident's criminal history, were more than enough to obtain a search warrant for the property.

Search-warrant services on methamphetamine labs are rarely fun. They're inherently dangerous because of a multitude of toxic chemicals used in the manufacturing process. In addition, the "cook" itself produces phosphorus gas, which is lethal. Added to the mix are human cooks who are at the extreme end of paranoia. Labs often explode, and the cooks sometimes implement booby traps to injure officers.

The house involved in this particular search warrant was the quintessential crank house. It was located in the midst of lower-class homes, had a large lot surrounded by an eight-foot privacy fence, had vehicles in various stages of repair carpeting the yard, had black-plastic sheeting on the windows to provide privacy, and upholstered furniture on the front porch. The only things missing were the requisite Chevy El Camino and Confederate flag.

In addition to their usual equipment, the first three officers staged at the front door were wearing self-contained breathing apparatuses and Nomex fatigues. The SCBA's protected against toxins in the air, while Nomex offered minimal protection against explosions and flash fires. The first officer wore an air monitor around his neck that checked for toxic and explosive chemicals. The monitor is designed to let out a piercing alarm if it detects specific elements above a certain threshold. If the alarm goes off, the search warrant is over, and everyone gets out. Immediately.

Thorpe was in charge of the search warrant and was the Emergency Radio Operator, responsible for all radio traffic if the search warrant went to shit. Strict radio discipline is paramount; the ERO is responsible for broadcasts which may include multiple tactical considerations, requesting medical personnel, calling additional officers and countless other contingencies—all of which are covered during the search warrant's brief.

Thorpe's squad used a ram to gain entry through the front door, before slowly and methodically searching the lower level of the two-story dwelling for suspects. The air quality was fine, and it didn't appear a lab was operational. Earlier, the surveillance unit reported observing the main target enter the house, yet Thorpe and his entry team still hadn't encountered the suspect. Two officers had "held" the staircase to the second floor as officers cleared the lower portion of the dwelling. Thorpe began to ascend the steps after notifying another officer to follow at a safe distance.

Hallways are one of the most dangerous portions of any search warrant. Officers call them fatal funnels because you progress down a corridor with no cover or concealment. If a suspect steps out and fires rounds down a hallway, he's most likely going to cut meat. Stairways are even worse. They're hallways with uneven footing where the bad guy has the high ground. Consequently, a bunch of officers on a stairway at the same time is a bad idea.

When Thorpe got to the top of the stairs, he found another hallway with three bedrooms and a bathroom. He motioned for additional officers and together they cleared the bathroom and two of the three bedrooms. The door to the final bedroom at the end of the hallway was closed. Thorpe took up a position in a bedroom on the left side of the hallway near the closed room. Another officer approached the door from a bedroom on the right side of the hallway. That officer approached from the right, hinged side, and reached across for the doorknob. As the officer was reaching across, Thorpe was overcome with a feeling of impending doom unlike any he'd ever felt. Thorpe hissed "stop" to the officer. Sensing the urgency in his sergeant's voice, the officer stepped back into the bedroom on the right, taking cover.

Thorpe remembered feeling flustered as he had not heard, seen, or even smelled anything indicating circumstances anymore dangerous than usual. The only thing substantiating his concern was that Intelligence was relatively sure the main target was inside the house; yet his squad had not encountered any suspects. Still, Intelligence had been wrong on numerous occasions. Thorpe called for an officer to retrieve a bullet-resistant shield and sent another officer to collect the ram, which had been discarded on the front porch. When both officers were in place, he directed the officer with the shield to approach the door and crack it open, just about an inch "to let the room cook." The room was dark inside, and there was still no movement. Yet Thorpe felt a *presence*. Thorpe was just inside the doorway on the left using the doorjamb for cover. Attached to his Glock was a high-intensity flashlight now illuminating the limited area inside the partially open door eight feet ahead.

Thorpe tapped all his senses in an effort to understand his foreboding of the room beyond. He was sure every officer now felt it, or maybe they just sensed Thorpe's unease. Regardless, he was so attuned he could literally hear the fabrics stretching and contracting as weary officers breathed heavily in and out under the mounting stress. Still, nothing tangible seeped from the room ahead, only darkened corners and silence. Despite the quiet, lack of odor, or any visual clues, the room may as well been aglow with brimstone based on the hairs standing on the back of Thorpe's neck.

Thorpe could smell Donnie Edward's cologne. In fact he could pinpoint the officer's exact location inside the room from his labored breaths. In addition to the stress everyone was feeling, Donnie had raced to fetch the ram and had lugged the heavy instrument back up the stairs. Donnie resembled in size a NCAA Division I defensive end, and with good reason; that's exactly what he was before joining the department. These days his appearance was closer to a "one percenter" motorcycle club member because his hair and beard came close to two feet in length. Because of his size, Donnie was often in charge of the ram—as he was on this warrant.

"Donnie, on my right," Thorpe ordered the officer to his side.

"What's up, Sarge?" Donnie asked.

"Donnie, I want you to launch that ram at the door and get your ass back in here before it hits. You think you can do that?" Thorpe whispered, never taking his eyes off the room ahead.

"Yeah, no problem," Donnie answered, "What's the deal?"

"Just a bad feeling." Thorpe directed his officer into the hall with a bit of pressure on the larger man's shoulder.

Donnie threw the ram but was back behind Thorpe when the eighty-pound ram slammed into the door, knocking it wide open. A shotgun blast came from the right side of the unsecured room, taking out a chunk of sheetrock just left of the battered door.

A shotgun blast in an enclosed space will definitely wake your ass up. Following the blast, a redheaded maniac with saucer-size eyes came running out of the room kamikaze-style, carrying a long-barrel gun in his hands. Thorpe fired one shot with his Glock .40-caliber handgun into the center of the suspect's face. The round caught the suspect in the bridge of the nose. Because of the suspect's forward motion, he began to fall face first into the middle of the hallway near Thorpe's feet. Not taking any chances, Thorpe fired two more rounds downward, directly into the back of the suspect's head before it even impacted with the floor. Then he immediately brought his weapon back up toward the open door, scanning for additional threats.

At the conclusion of the warrant service, one of the officers asked how he knew what was on the other side of that door. Thorpe had sarcastically responded, "Didn't you know I was psychic?"

The officer responded, "Yeah, right, Carnac the Magnificent." And the nickname stuck.

All shootings involving a police officer are investigated by both Homicide and investigators with the Office of Integrity and Compliance, formerly known as Internal Affairs. Thorpe didn't know the reason for the name change—maybe they thought the fancy name lent them more credibility or maybe they were just trying to soften their image. Police departments around the country were too busy trying to pacify leftwing liberals instead of doing their jobs, which was supposed to be fighting crime. Despite the official name change, officers still referred to them as Internal Affairs. Currently there were about a dozen ways to complain about a police officer in the city of Tulsa; anything from an on-line Internet complaint form to an anonymous phone call would do the trick.

Unlike their portrayal in the movies, IA investigators are actually pretty decent cops. Well, most of them anyway. Unlike fable, the busting of a fellow cop by an IA investigator was not a fast track to promotion—at least not in Tulsa. Recently, his buddy Jeff Gobin had become an IA investigator. As far as Homicide, Thorpe had the utmost respect for the sergeant in charge of that unit, Robert Hull, and most of the investigators under his command. In Thorpe's mind, and in many others on the department, Robert Hull was one of the finest cops on the department. During the subsequent investigation, most questions centered on how Thorpe knew a threat was in that room. Thorpe's disclosure that he "had a feeling" raised the eyebrows of several investigators though none officially called bullshit on the matter.

Another point of contention was the two slugs to the back of the head. The suspect was falling in such a way that he had a line of fire into the room where Thorpe's team was huddled, and Thorpe wasn't going to learn the suspect was still alive by a shotgun blast taking off one of his officer's heads. Homicide and IA had absolutely no problem with that explanation. However, the Tulsa district attorney's office almost didn't sign off on a justifiable shooting because of the last two rounds. Tulsa's district attorney loved to go after police officers. Thorpe was sure it was all politically motivated. That's the problem when you have private citizens reviewing deadly force situations. You have lawyers who would absolutely shit themselves if they were placed in situations officers face every day. Yet they believe they can sit back and Monday-morning quarterback events that at the time were tense and rapidly evolving. After five weeks of paid suspension, the DA blessed the shooting as justified, and Thorpe was reinstated to the Organized Gang Unit.

"Hey, Carnac, can we serve a warrant tonight or what?" Jennifer asked again. Officer Williams had a lot of good qualities; patience wasn't one of them.

"I don't think there are any in front of you. Let me see it," Thorpe said, carrying the warrant back to his office to review.

Every sergeant at SID had his own office. Most garnished theirs tastefully with lamps, pictures, and the requisite framings of all the accolades they'd received since kindergarten. Thorpe's was sparse. Besides his desk and computer station, he had a small television and a confiscated leather couch for late nights at work. Otherwise, everything that hung on his wall was functional. He had two cork boards filled with various documents and a large paper wall calendar serving as his décor.

Anyway, Thorpe spent as little time as possible inside his office. He answered emails, returned phone calls, and distributed case assignments within an hour of arriving. The rest of his time was spent doing what officers should be doing, throwing bad guys in jail. The new major, Richard Duncan, had arrived only a few months ago and was already making that job more difficult. He was trying to turn the whole division into a bunch of gun-toting secretaries. Officers now spent half their shift doing paperwork instead of crime fighting. They spent countless hours feeding a new case-management system that was more than cumbersome and less than beneficial. A simple drug arrest now turned into five hours of post-booking paperwork.

Major Duncan looked like a walrus—an ugly walrus. He was a good four hundred pounds, and no one could remember ever having seen the upper third of his pants because of copious amounts of fat spilling over his belt and submitting to the effects of gravity. Since transferring to the division, Duncan had taken advantage of the relaxed grooming standards and had grown a long mustache extending down his jowls. That, and his naturally bald head, only accentuated his walrusness.

The department had probably transferred Duncan to SID to get the man out of uniform and away from public view. Thorpe had heard when Duncan was a street officer he didn't do a damn thing and rarely saw the inside of a jail—*probably couldn't fit*. But here he was, commander of the Special Investigations Division, bogging a bunch of go-getters down with red tape. It was one of the many reasons Thorpe chose to work nights instead of days. He didn't have to see much of the fat-ass-brass.

Thorpe sat at his desk and reviewed the "controlled buy" search warrant Jennifer had prepared. "THE STATE OF OKLAHOMA, Plaintiff vs. CORRINDER RAY HIGHTOWER AKA: C-NOTE, Defendant." Tonight OGU would be searching for "COCAINE, COCAINE BASE, FRUITS, INSTRUMENTALITIES, MONIES, RECORDS, PROOF OF RESIDENCY, FIREARMS, AMMUNITION AND PROOF OF OWNERSHIP OF SUCH ITEMS. Simply stated, the warrant was for "crack" cocaine on a known 107 Hoover Crip's house and was written exactly like ninety-five percent of the other warrants he approved; the only differences were dates, location, and suspect information. All the rest was standard search-warrant fluff. He approved the warrant, called Jennifer's desk phone, told her it was a go, and set a time. He then went to work on Major Duncan's plethora of demands—for there were other matters needing his attention this night.

Four

Monday
February 5th
Late evening

THREE HOURS LATER, Thorpe and four of his investigators were in a 1997 puke-green Ford Aerostar van rumbling toward *The Kitchen*, a nickname given to one of the most violent and gang-infested sections of the city. The old family wagon was a certified piece of shit— the perfect undercover "jump-out" van. They were the lead vehicle of a five-car caravan. Two marked police units brought up the rear of the modern-day posse.

Because it was her warrant and she'd helped plan the approach route, Jennifer was behind the wheel. Jennifer was one of the more physically fit officers on the department when it came to strength conditioning. She spent several hours in the gym hitting the weights every day. Despite her efforts, she hadn't developed a mannish-looking body like some female body builders often obtain, but she could damn well kick some ass.

Thorpe looked over his shoulder at the three men squeezed into the rear bench seat as he made adjustments to his DEA-issued entry vest. The vest had built-in Kevlar throat- and pull-down-groin protectors. "POLICE" was emblazoned in white across the front and back. He also donned a Kevlar helmet, clear shooting glasses, and his nylon gear that sported a drop-down rig made to house his Glock .22C with flashlight attachment. Topped off with black Harley Davidson boots, dark jeans, and long sleeved black t-shirt, his appearance was intimidating. Wearing similar equipment, the entry team looked like a small band of black-clad warriors—or maybe a group of jack-booted thugs depending on your conservative or liberal leanings.

Thorpe was provided a good view of the three officers because the center seat had long since been removed to facilitate the rapid deployment of large men with bulky equipment and hostile intentions. At either end of the bench were men who only made the one in the middle seem even smaller. Donnie Edwards, the former college football star. And Jack Yelton. Jack was a couple inches shorter than Donnie, but was nearly the same weight. He sported a crop of red hair and a proud beer belly. The man/boy in the middle was Jake Holloway. At a hair over six-foot-one and a sandwich away from achieving a buck-sixty, he looked the part of a high-school senior. Which was one of the reasons he was such a great undercover. No one would ever believe he was a cop.

All of the men, and Jennifer, looked alert but relaxed. They'd been on too many search warrants to develop the nervous tics and wide eyes some of the less experienced officers show while en route to a search-warrant service. That's why Thorpe always put the new guys and the uniformed officers at the back of the line. Some of them were too keyed-up, and you just never knew what they might do. Thorpe had seen even veterans do some really stupid things on warrant services. A common occurrence was officers sprinting all alone into the fray, an action that put the whole team at risk.

As Jennifer turned north on Hartford Avenue, Thorpe conducted a radio check to make sure all the vehicles were still in line. When she turned west on 51st Place North, Thorpe advised the dispatcher monitoring the tactical channel they were "less than a minute out" and requested a time. Jennifer brought the van north on Frankfort Avenue, approaching the target from the south. The house was on the east side of the street and would be on the team's right as they dismounted their gas-powered steeds.

Because Thorpe was only able to assemble ten officers for the warrant, instructions were given that no officer would pursue runners who were standing outside the target house upon the team's arrival; they were already stretched thin enough without chasing rabbits in four different directions. As Jennifer neared the target location, she switched on the van's bright lights. The cars following extinguished theirs. The desired effect was to blind anyone in the yard so they couldn't see the caravan as easily, especially the marked police units.

Usually the team parked around a corner and approached the target house on foot, but the logistics of this particular warrant required a faster response. The neighborhood contained too many spotters to make an approach on foot feasible; any drugs would be well on their way to the Arkansas River via Tulsa's sewage system before officers made entry. The same concerns prevented Thorpe from having a surveillance team placed on the residence prior to their arrival. An unfamiliar vehicle or pedestrian wouldn't go unnoticed by lookouts. Spotters were generally young men patrolling the area on foot or bicycles. They were either paid cash or given a small amount of crack they could then sell on their own, keeping part or all of the profits. Sometimes the spotters were just crack-heads who got free product for their security services.

Jennifer pulled to the right of the street, one house short of the target. Thorpe advised over the radio that there were three black males in the driveway of the target house and reminded officers they were not to chase. Most cops seem to have extra nerve endings in their legs, which make them want to chase anything that runs from them. Sometimes they have to be reminded to switch the impulse off. Thorpe then advised "Police One," one of two helicopters owned and operated by TPD, to make their approach.

The team poured from the van with the distinctive sound of weapons being unloosed from molded-laminate holsters. One of the suspects immediately broke into a run for the back yard. Another ran directly into the open front door, slamming it shut behind him. The third froze—eventually dropping to the ground in compliance with officers' commands.

Two officers had the assignment of running directly to the back of the residence for rear containment. They had permission to pick one individual fleeing the house and pursue.

Thorpe went directly to the front door and, since the team had been compromised, was permitted to forgo the "reasonable amount of time" bullshit. He ordered Donnie to breech the front door while simultaneously shouting, "Tulsa police, search warrant."

Donnie swung the heavy ram. The front door exploded inward, catching a skinny female smoker directly in the face. The term "crack-head" took on new meaning as the woman, with a flap of skin hanging from her forehead, flailed backwards onto a glass coffee table. Jennifer and Jake tactically "split" the door. One was on the right side of the door opening with a view inside the left portion of the front room, and one was on the left side of the door opening with an opposing view. Thorpe performed a "step around," acquiring a sight picture of the center portion of the living room. After several announcements, Thorpe gave the order to enter the residence. The two officers did so simultaneously, Jennifer low with Jake coming over the top, both pistols scanning the deep corners as Thorpe followed on their heels.

Thorpe heard over the radio that his rear containment team had one target in custody in the back yard but another had dived out a window and was fleeing west towards a drainage culvert. Police One advised they were "10-97," or on scene, and were tracking the target running northbound in a storm-water drainage canal. The helicopters were equipped with "FLIR," a thermal-imaging camera that picks up differences in temperature. FLIR (Forward Looking Infrared) can track persons and vehicles by their heat signatures and is extremely effective in colder temperatures and at night. The projected image resembles a film negative. The best aspect of FLIR is that the helicopter can track someone without them knowing; there is no spotlight to indicate to the suspect they are being followed. In fact, the crew often directs the NightSun away from the "hidden" suspect to make them feel all warm and cozy, as if they'd successfully avoided detection. All the while, they're directing officers with boots on the ground right up their ass.

Back inside the residence, a black male stepped out of the kitchen, both hands in his coat pockets. Officers were ordering the suspect to get on the floor, but he just stood there expressionless, his hands stuffed in oversized pockets. The suspect very slowly and with exaggerated enunciation said, "Fuck you, cracker motherfuckers... Get out of my house." Thorpe inched his way across the room, his weapon out and pointed directly at the nose of the now smiling tough guy. Thorpe got to within three or four feet of the suspect. With his gun still trained on Smiley, he brought his right foot up and used all of his weight as he heel-kicked the man just below the tip of his sternum. Smiley went sailing, a countertop stopping his backward flight as he bounced off cheap Formica onto the rotting linoleum floor. Thorpe stepped into the kitchen and cleared it of additional threats before bending over the now frowning clump of meat on the kitchen floor. Smiley tried to talk some more shit, but the wind had been knocked out of him. Instead he just made squeaking noises as Thorpe secured him with handcuffs. "Who's smiling now, asshole?"

Cops love search warrants or "legalized home invasions," as they sometimes refer to them. Search warrants are no nonsense. Because of the inherent danger involved with warrants, failure to comply with commands are not tolerated. *Where else can a person get this kind of adrenaline pump and get paid for it?*

Thorpe and his team cleared the rest of the residence finding no one else inside except for the crack-head with the cracked head and Mr. Smiley. Police One advised they had observed the window-diver run north through a culvert underneath 56th Street North. The suspect had continued north from there to another street they couldn't identify from the air. When the suspect passed underneath, he never exited the other side.

Police One had also seen the runner "toss something hot" prior to hiding under the street. Depending on material and the outside air temperature, discarded items would retain a heat signature from the suspect's body for several minutes. Thorpe took Jake and another one of his investigators, Tyrone Benson, with him to the street that passed over the culvert. Police One directed Thorpe to where Frankfort Avenue and Elgin Avenue intersected. Technically the streets shouldn't be able to cross since they're both north-south streets. Yet they somehow managed to form a Y at this location. Police One had seen the suspect run underneath but not emerge from the other side. Here, the drainage canal leading to the culvert grew considerably smaller. It no longer consisted of walled concrete, but was instead wet mud and vegetation where it met the four-foot diameter tube.

Thorpe posted Jake and Tyrone on the south side of the culvert where the suspect had entered. Inside, the tube was ink-black, and Thorpe didn't particularly like the idea of silhouetting himself by sticking his pumpkin inside to have a look. He called for a K-9 officer, Justin Adams, who arrived about five minutes later with Thor, a very large German shepherd who took much enjoyment in biting human flesh. Thor didn't care if it was a bad guy, another cop, or sometimes even his own handler; if something got near his muzzle, he was going to eat it.

Generally, it's standard practice for K-9 officers to give the bad guy a chance to surrender before releasing their dog. Adams gave no such notice before releasing his partner into the lightless cavern. The clicking of nails and scent-gathering snorts eerily echoed out of the chamber as the dog worked his way down the tunnel. Thorpe thought if someone was still secreted inside, they were most definitely releasing another odor right about now which would only aid in their discovery.

Several seconds later, Thorpe heard a scream and the guttural sound of a large beast who'd found his prey. It didn't take long for the suspect to scream, "Get this fucking dog off me," and express his strong desire to submit. After a few more seconds, which probably felt like a week to the suspect, Adams called for Thor to "release" and return.

After Thor was tethered, Thorpe shouted instructions for the suspect to exit the south end of the tunnel with his hands clearly visible. Upon exiting the other end of the tunnel, the suspect was greeted by Officer Benson who promptly leg-swept the suspect to the ground. Tyrone then dropped his nearly 250-pound frame to one knee, landing squarely in the middle of the suspect's back. The suspect's arm was badly bitten, and he had a large gash on the back of his head. Thorpe requested an ambulance for the injured prisoner, then had Police One direct him to the area where the suspect had discarded the item. Whatever it was, it had cooled to air temperature and was no longer visible to thermal imaging.

Thorpe instructed Adams to bring Thor over for an article search, prompting the suspect to nearly jump out of his torn skin at the sight of the large German shepherd approaching. Thorpe decided to mess with the suspect a little: "Relax, he's just going to sniff you, maybe get in one last bite, and then he's going to find whatever it is you threw before entering the tunnel."

"Fuck that, I'll show you where I tossed the gun."...*Even better*. The ever-so-compliant suspect led officers to some vegetation near the base of a tree and nodded. With the aid of a flashlight, it only took a few seconds for Jake to locate a loaded Taurus 9mm lying on the ground.

"Hey, John! You know what the difference between you and Thor is?" Adams asked.

"He's better looking?"

"No, you have pee in your name."

"What...? Oh, Thorpe...Thor...Freaking hilarious, Adams." *Lame*. "Adams, you know the difference between you and your dog? He tells better jokes and licks his *own* balls."

Pleased by having won the verbal duel with Adams, Thorpe returned to the warrant location to check the team's progress. He found Jennifer walking into the living room from the rear of the house. She informed Thorpe they hadn't found any dope yet but had found about twenty-five-hundred in cash. Jennifer pointed back down the hallway and asked, "You see the little window that crazy fucker dove out of?"

Apparently, the guy they had just pulled from the culvert had fled the house by diving head first through a window. Jennifer led Thorpe to the back of the house and pointed to an incredibly small bathroom window. On part of the window was a tuft of black curly hair, flesh, and blood.

"He dove out of that? So that's where he got the gash on his noggin. I thought Thor had tried to tear his head off." Thorpe told Jennifer of the large gash on the back of the suspect's head.

"He was a determined little fucker. I'll give him that," smiled Jennifer.

Just then Tyrone called Thorpe on the tactical frequency. "I've got some good news, some bad news, and some more bad news. Which do you want first?"

"The bad news, and then the other bad news—of course." Thorpe was a get-the-bad-news-out-of-the-way-first kind of person.

"First, our little prisoner is going to need a lot of staples." That meant officers would to have to baby-sit him at the hospital for hours before booking him. Why they were called "emergency" rooms made no sense to Thorpe. It took forever for hospital personnel to get to you—this guy would probably lose another quart of blood before he was seen.

"The other bad news is our little dog treat here is only 17 years old." *Great,* even if they did find drugs that meant after babysitting him for hours at a hospital they were going to have to release him to a guardian. He'd be dealing dope well before Thorpe's squad finished the paperwork.

"What's the good news?"

"We did find a sack under his sack," Tyrone said, referring to a baggy of cocaine hidden under the suspect's scrotum.

"How much?"

"Haven't weighed it yet but looks like about ten grams, definitely trafficking weight."

"He got a record?"

"Couple of stolen cars. One previous marijuana arrest," Tyrone informed Thorpe.

"Maybe Juvie will take him then. Thanks." Since it was trafficking weight, and he had priors, it was possible JBDC would take him. The Juvenile Bureau of the District Court was overwhelmed and overcrowded, just like its adult counterpart. Thorpe knew even if the suspect *was* admitted, he wouldn't be kept long. Such was the job. Everyone screamed for the police to do more. The simple truth was the police did the job—very well indeed. It was the judicial system, no truth in sentencing, and the lack of prisoner space that was failing miserably. Every time Thorpe read about a murder in the newspaper, the article would invariably go something like, "The suspect was sentenced to twenty-five years in prison—five years ago." *Then what the hell is he doing out of prison killing people when he should be in prison another twenty years? It was damned ridiculous.*

The search wrapped up with trace amounts of cocaine being recovered from the toilet bowl. Before imitating Superman by flying out the bathroom window, Clark Kent had apparently flushed some of his stash down the toilet. Three suspects were booked on various charges. Two were transported to the hospital before being taken to the county jail.

While the rest of his squad guarded prisoners in hospitals and started in on the hours of paperwork requirements, Thorpe excused himself under the guise of having to do paperwork for The Walrus.

Five

Monday
February 5th
Late evening

IT WAS NEARING MIDNIGHT as Thorpe walked through SID's web of desks to a separate section that housed the equipment officer's space and most of the division's toys. There, he retrieved night-vision goggles and a handheld thermal imaging device much like the FLIR on the helicopter. Thorpe didn't bother signing out either piece of equipment; he planned on having both returned before the equipment officer arrived in the morning. Leaving the building and walking into the parking lot, he took a plastic bag from his assigned truck, then he borrowed one of the extra undercover vehicles. The vehicle was a red Chevy short-bed confiscated from a local drug dealer. Like all the other cars in SID's fleet, the license plate was not on file and was untraceable. The only drawback was that SID's undercover officers were routinely pulled over by patrol because their license plates were bogus. This could be a real problem when undercovers had a bad guy in the passenger seat and a patrol officer walked up and said something like, "Shit, Carnac, I didn't know it was you," marking the end of an operation. The Training Academy taught recruits not to show recognition when they crossed paths with an undercover—but people forgot.

His first objective was to scout out the residence of Dwayne Foster, aka "L.A," a drug dealer from New Orleans who had been displaced by Hurricane Katrina. How he got the nickname "L.A." was lost on Thorpe; as far as OGU could figure L.A. had never lived in California, let alone Los Angeles. *Whatever*, it didn't really matter. Despite the fact that both were Hoover Crips, L.A. and Marcel Newman were virulent enemies. They had purportedly fired shots at each other on several occasions without ever hitting their intended target. Thank God bangers held their weapons sideways in an attempt to look cool. They never acquired a site picture and rarely hit what they were aiming at.

When Thorpe instructed Marcel to write L.A.'s initials in the dirt of the barn, Marcel smiled. He knew what Thorpe was planning: L.A. was going to take the fall for Marcel's murder. Inside the plastic bag, sitting on the floorboard, was a pair of boots. The boot's distinctive soles would match imprints left in the dirt around Marcel's abandoned carcass. The dirt on the soles would match the barn's floor. The blood splatter on the boots would be linked through DNA to Marcel Newman. The hair Thorpe had placed on the duct tape binding Marcel Newman would be matched through DNA to L.A. Thorpe had retrieved the hair from a comb during an earlier search warrant they had served at L.A.'s residence. All this physical evidence would readily be found in search warrants that would be served after Marcel's body was found with L.A. written in the dirt by the victim's own finger.

The boots weren't absolutely necessary. If Marcel's body had been discovered by now, he wouldn't risk planting the boots. But if he could, the evidence would be insurmountable. It wouldn't matter how many witnesses L.A. could provide—placing him elsewhere at the time of the murders. Today, when juries think CSI Miami is the real deal, DNA and physical evidence is king.

L.A. lived in the area of 5th and Lewis Avenue. The place was a real shit-hole where the Vice Unit had an easy time snatching up whores and street-level drug dealers. The area was a combination of old, low-rent apartment buildings and decaying homes, inhabited by a combination of races and ethnic backgrounds—Hispanics, blacks, and white trash had an equal foothold in the neighborhood. Even some Middle Easterners resided there. Another peculiar aspect of the blighted neighborhood was that it butted right up against the grounds of the University of Tulsa, an expensive private university nationally recognized as one of the premiere universities in the nation. Yet a couple of blocks away you could get curb service for a blow job, crack cocaine, marijuana—whatever your particular vice might be.

Sometimes the police would be called in to bust heads in the neighborhood, but they would soon be redeployed somewhere else in the city. Geographically, Tulsa's land area was as large as San Francisco, Boston, Pittsburgh P.A., and Minneapolis—combined. If you placed all the city's arterial streets and highways together end to end, it would stretch all the way from New York City to Los Angeles, back to Tulsa again and beyond. The Tulsa Police Department had roughly 800 sworn police officers and was in desperate need of more. There was just no way to be proactive enough to make the city as safe as it needed to be with the limited amount of personnel.

The current mayor was the latest in a long line of trust babies. Every mayor Thorpe had worked for since he'd moved to Tulsa had been the son, daughter, wife, or husband of a multi-millionaire. Not one had earned that fortune on their own. Just once, he'd like to have a bona fide leader who hadn't bought his or her office. One who more reflected the common person. Empty promises, especially when it came to public-safety, were growing tiresome. In just a few short months the current administration had decimated the department, systematically reducing its ranks. Meanwhile calls for service continue unanswered for hours. Thorpe wasn't sure who he disliked more, politicians or criminals—or were the occupations synonymous?

Thorpe pulled into a parking lot and changed into a pair of woodland camouflage pants and an old Vietnam-era army field jacket he'd obtained from Goodwill. He put the boots into an old beat up backpack and slipped on a gray stocking cap and dark cotton gloves. Then he drove west on 11th Street—part of historic Route 66. The small motels left over from the famous highway's heyday were now homes to prostitutes, drug dealers, and meth-labs. Thorpe spotted a couple of the working girls along the way.

As a police officer, Thorpe had encountered hundreds of prostitutes in the city of Tulsa, but not one even approached Julia Roberts' character in *Pretty Woman*. Most were missing teeth, had open sores, and smelled like unrefrigerated, ten-day-old tuna. Why men stepped out on their wives for these walking petri dishes he would never understand.

Thorpe turned north on Atlanta Avenue and passed yet another dish at the corner of 7th Street. This girl was, in reality, a man. His name was Desmond Jones, and he was a fairly convincing transvestite. At least he was at night in poor lighting. Mr. Jones was giraffe like, with long skinny legs. The sad thing was, he looked better than most of the *actual* females walking the street. Jones had been in considerable fisticuffs over the years as many of his customers became rather disconcerted when they reached down and discovered an *outie* when they were expecting an *innie*. As a result, Jones had become quite the scrapper. Two Vice guys once picked up Jones and negotiated a threesome. When they identified themselves as police officers and tried to take Mister/Miss Jones into custody, well, the fight was on. Jones wore copious amounts of makeup to help disguise his true gender. He also sported two water-filled balloons to give him the appearance of having ample breasts. The fight with the officers started in a car and literally *spilled* out into the street as both water balloons burst. The water mixed with Jones' heavy makeup. When the two officers finally got Jones into custody, all three were covered, head to toe, in dripping makeup. They looked as though they'd been wrestling in a huge box of ink cartridges. The sight of the two officers booking Jones into the jail made a lot of police officers' and inmates' night. *Funny shit.*

Thorpe turned the truck west on 6th Street and drove past L.A.'s house. There were pedestrians on the street, as always in this area, but it appeared as if L.A.'s vehicle was not parked in front of his home. Thorpe continued to Lewis Avenue and pulled into a convenience store parking lot on the northeast corner. He parked on the side of the building, grabbed the backpack, and walked north towards an alley leading east. The alley was ominous; a portion consisted of wooden fences on either side and was completely covered by trees and flora climbing into a canopy high overhead. The alley was poorly lit, branching off into seedy apartment complexes, vacant plots, and parking lots. It usually had a few knaves lurking about—the last thing Thorpe needed now was for someone to try to rob him. He didn't want to be forced to shoot someone and have to explain why he was walking down the "alley of death," fearing no evil, with God and his Glock his only comforts. Carrying a backpack, he knew he'd be prime pickings for a robbery.

In the tunnel-like alley, Thorpe was dismayed to see a group of Tulsa's less-than-finest citizens about forty yards ahead. The group, four males wearing bloated coats, resembled malevolent arachnids awaiting their next meal. A distant street lamp cast an orange glow over the group as he neared. Thorpe walked confidently forward, placing his right hand in the zipper of his field jacket to imply he was armed, which he was. He hoped to intimidate the group enough so they would wait for a safer looking dolt to come along. As he passed, one of them said, "What you got in your pack man?"

Dammit. "Your death certificate. Ready to collect?" Thorpe said, trying to use intimidation to dissuade the pack.

Three in the group started laughing—much to the dismay of the one who had spoken. That man just stared straight at Thorpe, expressionless. Having passed the group, Thorpe turned—back-pedaling to face the threat—his hand still in his jacket. When Thorpe was about thirty yards east of the foursome, they turned away, scurrying. *Shit.* They were going to get a gun—probably stashed in a car.

He should have just kept his mouth shut; he had disrespected a gang member in front of his homeboys and was going to have to answer for it. He couldn't afford a scene, there was really only one option—disappear. Finding a gap in the chain link, Thorpe slipped out of the alley to the south and knelt down in an area where he could see through vegetation. He decided he would stay concealed until the potential threat passed. Twenty seconds later, Thorpe heard a car engine making a hard acceleration on the street to the north. Shortly after, he observed a dark SUV turn from southbound Atlanta into the alley and slowly drive towards his position. Because the alley was only partially lit, and because the SUV's windows were tinted, Thorpe couldn't see inside. Nevertheless, he was sure it was the foursome. He couldn't make out the tag but noted the SUV was a dark Chevy 4-door and was sitting on twenty-inch chrome rims.

Thorpe stayed put for another twenty minutes without seeing the SUV make another pass. Hopefully the group had concluded their prey had made it to its destination and they'd decided to move on to other troubles.

Thorpe reentered the alley and continued west to Atlanta Avenue. Before he stepped out, he scanned the streets for the SUV. Not seeing it, he walked south then turned back west on 6th Street. He walked along the north side of the street while eyeing L.A.'s house, which sat on the other side of the road. A few people milled about, but none in the immediate vicinity of L.A.'s house.

Thorpe sat down on the sidewalk across the street from his target house, removed the handheld thermal imaging device, and discreetly scanned the screened porch of L.A.'s home. No hot spots; the porch appeared to be clear of occupants. Putting the device back into his coat, he zipped his collar up to his chin before crossing the street. Thorpe entered the unlocked screened porch and swiftly shrugged off the backpack. Removing the boots from the plastic bag, he placed them in the corner of the porch and hurriedly left.

The boots were nice Timberland wheat nubuck leather, retailing for a around a buck-forty. They were L.A.'s size; this he'd also verified on the last warrant. L.A. would probably find them and wonder how the hell they got on his porch, but Thorpe figured he'd keep them; they were still in good shape. He had removed most of the blood splatters from the boots but made sure there were trace amounts to be discovered in lab tests.

Thorpe left the porch, walked back to the east and turned south, avoiding the alley. He sure as hell wasn't going through there again, just in case his buddies were back. Winding his way through the neighborhood, Thorpe neared the convenience store and observed a dark SUV approaching from the north. It pulled into the lot just as Thorpe was entering his truck. The dark Chevy SUV with chrome wheels backed into a parking space and sat. No one got out. *Damn*, either he had shitty luck or they had put spotters in the neighborhood to call if he was seen—probably the latter.

Thorpe sat there for a moment considering his options. It was obvious they didn't want to approach him in this parking lot. It was too well lit and too many police drove up and down Lewis. Thorpe didn't want to call the police; he didn't want to be placed this close to L.A.'s house. He could badge the SUV from a distance to scare it off—but what if one of the spotters had seen him enter L.A.'s house? *No*, he didn't want that coming up in an investigation—someone had seen a cop sneak into a murder suspect's home. He had to try and lose them. Thorpe decided to stay on main streets for a while so as not to get shot—always a good plan.

Thorpe pulled out onto Lewis Avenue, immediately getting a green light at the intersection. He continued south to 11th Street. The dark SUV followed. Catching a red light, Thorpe stopped in the inside lane with a compact car between his own truck and the SUV. The light turned green, but Thorpe didn't move, prompting the small car to blow its horn. The SUV did nothing. Thorpe ignored the impatient honking and waited for the light to turn red again. When it changed, Thorpe let cross traffic start moving before he accelerated hard. As Thorpe cut off traffic, the compact's horn was joined by the horns of other irate motorists. To Thorpe's surprise, the compact car also ran the red light, followed by the SUV. "Shit." Either the compact was really pissed or the group had split into two cars. Maybe they had called for assistance. There was one way to find out.

Thorpe made a hard left on 13th Place. A street sign indicated the road was a dead-end, but Thorpe knew that wasn't exactly true. The compact and the SUV followed. No doubt now; they were together. Thorpe knew 13th Place was only a block long here and was bordered by a steep, wooded embankment to the south and a closed charcoal-grill manufacturing plant to the north. The street came to an abrupt end at a wooded area, but you could make a sharp left turn and drive behind the plant on a gravel road that curved to the northwest and back to Lewis.

Thorpe pushed the truck as fast as it would go down the short street, pumped the brakes, and made a sharp left turn behind the plant. He briefly accelerated before slamming on the brakes again. The area was totally isolated, and the building was now between him and his assailants. He jammed the truck into park and jumped out the driver's door. He brought up a Beretta 9mm just as the nose of the compact car was making the corner of the building. Thorpe unloaded five rounds into the driver's side window and three more into the windshield of the car. He was already climbing back into his truck when he heard the SUV slam into the rear of the compact. Thorpe fed the accelerator and sped down the gravel road and back onto Lewis Avenue. He raced north checking his mirrors. Nothing was following. He had no idea if he had struck anyone in the vehicle, and he wasn't waiting around to find out. He turned up his police radio and concentrated on slowing his breathing. He disappeared into the neighborhood, avoiding major streets. If a shooting call did go out, officers would respond, lights and siren, driving as fast as they could on major streets.

Ten minutes after the shooting, Thorpe pulled into a parking lot near the office and changed back into his original clothes. *Shit, that had been too close.* He couldn't afford any more screw-ups. There was some radio traffic but nothing about his extracurricular activities.

He drove into the office lot and wiped down the truck. Gathering his belongings, he got back into his assigned truck. He spent the next twenty minutes traveling to the Arkansas River, where he threw the pistol in the water part by part. The Beretta had been a fine weapon he had acquired during an earlier search warrant. He had never handled the gun or its ammunition without first donning gloves. He would have to dispose of the clothing later, but now he removed his gloves. Then he made his way back east.

Forty minutes after the shooting Thorpe finally heard radio traffic that could be related: "Lincoln 101, Lincoln one-zero-one and a car to back. Shooting victim at St. John Hospital, 1923 South Utica Avenue, one-nine-two-three South Utica Avenue, break...See security in the E.R. Black male arrived with a gunshot wound to the face. Security reports the car he arrived in, a white Ford Focus, has multiple bullet holes." *That had to be the car.* Thorpe pulled out his cell phone and contacted one of his officers.

"What's up, Sarge?"

"Hey, Jack, I just heard a shooting call go out over the radio. Apparently someone got himself and his car all shot to hell. A couple of uniforms are en route to St. John Hospital to see the victim. Don't know where it happened. You mind running over there to see if he's one of ours?"

"Yeah, I'll start that way."

"Thanks, let me know what you find out."

Thorpe's Organized Gang Unit was responsible for investigating gang-related shootings. Sending Jack to the hospital wouldn't be seen as unusual. Jack would first check to see if the suspect was a certified gang member. If so, the OGU would handle the investigation. If not, Jack would check the suspect for gang tattoos, associates, and so on. If he discovered the victim should be certified, OGU would take the case. If Jack found no indications of gang involvement, it would be left to the uniformed officers.

Thorpe had planned to gather intel on Kaleb Moment tonight, but in light of recent events, he decided it would be best to stand down and assess the situation. He drove back to his office to tackle some of Major Duncan's deforestation experiments.

An hour later, Thorpe was sitting at his desk, working on his in-basket, when Jack used his phone's direct-connect feature to reach his boss, "Hey, Sarge, you over here?"

"Yeah, Jack, Whatta you got?"

"Kid's name is Christopher Ruble. He's not certified yet but probably should be. Got some tats indicate he's a Blood."

"What's the deal with the shooting?" Thorpe asked.

"Kid was hit in the face. Bullet went in his left cheek, fucked up his teeth, and exited his right cheek. He's going to live, but he'll be eatin' through a straw for a while."

"Who, where, and why?" Thorpe inquired.

"Don't know who the shooter is. Kid can't talk worth a shit, so he's literally lying out his ass. From what I can gather, he was just driving down the street minding his own damn business, when someone just lit up his car for no good reason. Typical deal. Didn't see anything, doesn't have any idea who would shoot at him."

"Got a crime scene?"

"Not that we know of yet. Kid said it happened on Apache somewhere. Uniforms are heading up there now to see if they can find anything. Going to have his car towed for evidence—let SIU process it. Guess the little fucker drove it here himself—no teeth and all."

"Okay, Jack, thanks. Let me know if you need any help." For once, an uncooperative victim was going to work in Thorpe's favor. It didn't look like the guy was going to provide any description of his assailant and was even lying about where the shooting occurred.

Before Thorpe left the office for the night, he removed a two-pound bag of sugar from the cafeteria, went out to the red Chevy he'd been driving earlier, and poured a good portion of the bag into the gas tank. That should cause enough engine damage to keep the car out of action for a while. In fact, since the vehicle was an older confiscation, the department would probably just scrap the truck instead of having it repaired. The last thing Thorpe wanted on his conscience was one of his fellow officers driving the Chevy truck and getting ambushed by some revenge-seeking gang-banger.

Six

Tuesday
February 6th
Early morning

THORPE DROVE THE GRAVEL ROAD alongside his property. It was just after two-thirty in the morning. Inside the fence, Al and Trixie paced the truck until both parties met at the gate. Ablaze in headlights, the dogs' wagging tails projected shadowy ribbons on the otherwise still barn. Removing the lock and chain, Thorpe reached through the metal gate and scratched both dogs under the chin before ordering them to back up. The dogs dutifully responded, allowing Thorpe to push open the gate, climb into his truck, and enter his property. Once through, Thorpe exited and gave his friends a proper greeting—a very thorough scratching behind each dog's ears. Thorpe replaced the gate and continued up the driveway, parking in front of the barn. After feeding the two shepherds, he removed equipment from his truck and walked to the front door of his home. Thorpe didn't have an alarm system; the house was so remote it wouldn't achieve much, besides that's what Al and Trixie were for. Thorpe unlocked the front door, stepped to the side, and ordered the dogs to search the interior. Thorpe hadn't found the inspiration to decorate yet. His living room consisted of a leather couch, a comfortable chair, an end table, a television, and not much else. Crossing the threshold, Thorpe removed a Glock 27 pistol from his ankle holster and a Glock 22C from his waistband. He placed both weapons on the end table. In the kitchen, he got a beer. He stood in hesitation for a moment, reopened the refrigerator, and removed the remainder of the six-pack; it had been that kind of night. Thorpe waited for the search's conclusion, then he walked out the back door—beer and dogs in tow.

Shortly after Thorpe moved into the home, he'd built a stone fire-pit next to the wooden deck. Now, he tossed some logs into the stone crater, lit a fire, and popped open a beer. Ice cold brew and a sizzling fire—the finer things. As he sat there, he considered the events that had brought him to this moment and had forged him into who he was—and who he was becoming.

Thorpe had been born and brought up in Kansas City, Missouri. During his childhood, his mother, Margaret, had worked as a school-bus driver for the North Kansas City School District. This allowed her to be home with little Johnny, and his sister, Marilyn, during the summer, weekends, and holidays. This was an important aspect of her job since she was, for all practical purposes, a single parent for interminable periods of time.

Thorpe's father, Benjamin, was a soldier. At least that was the profession as explained to little Johnny, Marilyn, and anyone else who inquired about Ben's line of work. This much Thorpe did know: Benjamin Thorpe was very poor as a child. His own father had disappeared when Ben was very young, leaving his mom to raise eight children. At one point the family's station was bad enough they split up for a time; Ben had lived with a neighbor. From what Thorpe had been able to learn, the neighbor turned out to be not much more than a local prostitute who was gracious enough to help feed and house Ben until the family got back on its feet. That never occurred. Ben dropped out of school in the eighth grade and lied about his age to take a job and help care for the family. Ben had been deprived of both a father and a childhood.

When Ben had turned eighteen, his fondness for fighting began to land him in jail and in trouble with the local authorities. This was back in the days when judges routinely gave young men the choice between the military and jail time. Ben had wisely enlisted and had discovered he was a natural-born soldier—except for one problem. He didn't like to take orders from idiots, of which the military was in no short supply. On more than one occasion he threatened bodily harm to those with higher rank, and, at least one time, he made good on that promise. Thorpe was reasonably sure that by the time he was ten or eleven-years-old his father was no longer in the regular army. Whether his father left voluntarily or was forced out, Thorpe didn't know. Ever since he could remember, his father had been gone for long stretches of time. "Overseas deployments" were what his father and mother called them. When Ben did return, sometimes with a new collection of scars, he spent every waking hour with his children and was a firm but good father—at least Johnny thought so. Some of the things Ben did back then would probably land a father in jail these days.

Ben began teaching little Johnny hand-to-hand combat skills shortly after he took his first steps. As Johnny grew, the lessons resulted in numerous scrapes and bruises. But Ben always let John know the sessions were conducted with the best of intentions. "It's a dangerous world with dangerous people, Johnny. This may save your life or the life of your family some day." To little Johnny, these activities seemed normal because it was all he ever knew. While other kids and their fathers were playing football and basketball, Johnny and Ben were going over the finer points of disarming an adversary and how to use household items as lethal weapons. Looking back, Thorpe figured his dad never had a father who taught him the proper way to throw a football or the other facets of team sports. Also, his father had dropped out of school and hadn't had the opportunity to learn sports there either. So Ben was teaching Johnny the only skills he had mastered. Before Ben would leave on a deployment, he would search for a boxing or martial arts facility to supplement Johnny's skills while he was away. Ben was maybe 5-foot-eight and weighed one-fifty or less: He was a small man. In those days, instructors would routinely accept challenges from other instructors or prospective students to prove they were worthy of teaching. Ben would take Johnny to a prospective school, meet with the instructor, and ask to spar before signing a contract. If the instructor refused, Ben would say that if he wasn't confident in his own abilities then Ben wasn't either and would stand up to leave. Sometimes the instructors would let Ben and Johnny leave. Other times, either because of financial reasons or pride, the instructor would accept the challenge and lay down ground rules like no biting or eye gouging. The sparring matches would generally last several minutes but always ended one of two ways—with John's father standing over a semi-conscious instructor or the instructor declaring the fight over before something precious was broken.

During those sparring matches, John saw that his father could have ended most fights much earlier but was merely auditioning the instructors to see if they had anything they could impart to his son. Thorpe remembered seeing his father equaled only one time in all those auditions: Ben had taken him to a boxing gym where the head coach had been a regional Golden Gloves champion and was now a retired professional boxer. The boxer outweighed his father by at least fifty pounds and bested his father during the match. However, Johnny was positive that if the fight had occurred in the street, his father would have picked the pugilist up by the hips and dropped him head first onto the concrete. A street fight might have lasted ten seconds.

Benjamin Thorpe would be "on deployment" from two weeks to six or seven months. He would usually return unannounced, although Johnny sometimes guessed when his father's return was imminent because it was foreshadowed by his mother receiving a mysterious phone call. Then Johnny would notice the house was getting a touch cleaner. But the big giveaway was when his mother began preparing an elaborate meal of Thanksgiving-sized proportions and spending an inordinate amount of time dolling herself up in the bathroom. These rituals generally concluded with Ben bursting through the front door, gifts in hand. His daughter, son, and wife would pounce on him. It was only during these moments John had ever seen his father cry; nothing vocal nor exorbitant, just a glistening of the eyes. Once, a teardrop had trailed down the cheek before quickly being wiped away.

The next day Johnny would usually be woken by a pair of boxing mitts landing on his chest as his father stood in his bedroom doorway silhouetted by the hallway light. "Let's see what you've learned, boy," was the standard line. With that, the two would go down into the basement and get on the mat. Father would spar with son for a few minutes before putting a solid whooping on the boy so as not to let his head get too big. "You're getting pretty good, son, but you'll never be able to whup your old man," his father would say with a big grin on his face.

When Johnny turned twelve, his father decided his son needed some real-world experience. "All the classrooms in the world can't prepare you for a single dark alley," his father would say. On their first such outing, his father loaded up some fishing gear and told his wife they were heading to the lake. In reality, they were headed to downtown Kansas City to pick a fight.

His father had driven around some of the seedier parts of town before coming across a closed skating rink where a group of kids was sitting outside doing a whole lot of nothing. "Johnny, just remember everything you've learned and concentrate on the kid you're fighting," Ben began. "I won't let anyone else jump on you, and you have nothing to worry about except maybe a black eye. But the most important thing is this—don't seriously hurt one of these kids. We're here for experience, not to put somebody in the hospital. They're going to say some nasty things to you, and rightfully so. We're coming into their place and picking a fight. Don't get angry about it; put yourself in their shoes. If you break someone's arm or go for an eye or anything else dangerous, you're going to have to answer to me. I'll take you down to the basement, and you'll get an ass whippin' like you've never had before." Ben held out his fist, and father and son did the over-under fist shake. Ben smiled, and they both walked over to the group of kids.

Thorpe could still picture the scene vividly after all these years. As Ben and John approached, one kid who had been sitting on a concrete wall slid off and walked right up to them.

"What you want, mister?" The question was meant for Ben, but the kid never took his eyes off John.

"I've got ten dollars in my pocket says not one of you can whip my boy in a fight. Any takers?"

The kid who'd approached didn't hesitate, "I'll take your money, mister."

"Good. Just a few rules. Only *you* fight my son. Anyone else jumps in, no money. Any weapons come out, no money. If you do pull out a weapon or jump in, I don't care if you're a kid or not, I'm going to kick your ass. And finally, if you lose, no money."

"I ain't gonna lose, mister."

The group formed a circle around John and the boy whose name turned out to be Levi, as in, "Whip his ass, Levi."

Ben shouted, "Lift up your shirts and turn out your pockets, both of you. Any weapons, no fight." John and Levi did as they were told. The one thing John noticed was how much more developed Levi seemed to be. John had the body of a child while Levi was beginning to look like a man. Despite his years of training, John was scared shitless. His father approached, put his hands on his son's shoulders, leaned down, and whispered, "Let him come to you, and don't forget to breathe." His father stepped away and simply announced, "Fight!"

Levi danced around on the balls of his feet in a boxer's stance: "I'm going to jack you up. Your daddy may as well give me that ten dollars now and save you a broken mouth." Levi then put his head down and came in with an overhand right. John had been through this drill so many times he didn't even think, his body just acted. John slapped the right hand to the inside with his left hand and slid in behind Levi's right shoulder. He slipped an arm under Levi's chin and locked him in a chokehold. Less than ten seconds later, Levi was unconscious. Feeling his opponent go limp, John released Levi and watched as he crumpled to the ground, silencing the circle of spectators. Knowing Levi would regain consciousness almost immediately, John locked his opponent's shoulder, elbow, and wrist, then waited for the inevitable. Levi woke in a compromising position with little recollection of what had just occurred. "What happened?"

"You lost," John answered.

"Bullshit, I..." Levi couldn't finish the sentence as John applied pressure to the back of his hand, causing pain in both his wrist and elbow joints. "Okay...Okay...You win."

Thorpe won the fight in a matter of seconds, never having to throw a punch. His father walked over, put twenty dollars in Levi's hand, told him he'd earned it, and left with his son. "Good fight, son. One thing: you didn't breathe until I paid Levi his money. If it'd been a prolonged fight, that would work against you. Your muscles need oxygen. Otherwise, good fight. How do you feel?"

"I feel okay. He didn't even hit me," John answered, looking up at his father from the passenger seat.

"I don't really mean physically, I mean *what* do you feel?'"

"A little bad I guess. I mean...he didn't really deserve that. He's probably embarrassed."

"Good, Johnny. I don't ever want you to start a fight—just end 'em. I started the fight not you, and that's the way it's going to stay. You're a good boy, Johnny, and you're going to stay that way...Understand?" It was a statement not a question.

Whatever it was he did for a living, Ben Thorpe didn't want his son to be involved in any way. The secret fights continued, and John's opponents got bigger and older until he was fighting grown men. Some fights were easy and some John lost. Some resulted in contusions and lacerations that had to be hidden from his mother.

In addition to fighting, Ben taught his son relaxation techniques, survival and navigational skills, and made him proficient with a variety of weapons and firearms. All the martial arts and boxing schools he had attended had been miles away from home and had been paid for in cash. Johnny had always been enrolled in these schools under a different last name. If John had ever bragged about his training or started fights at school, he would have been sharply disciplined. John's father was a living, breathing version of the book *The Art of War*. Many of the teachings imparted from father to son were principles of war craft. "You should never let your potential enemies know of your capabilities, son. The less they know about you the better." John had often wondered why his father was so intent on him learning these principles when his father's dream was for John to become a "nine-to-fiver." His father had many responses, most of which were along the lines, "Son, you never know what life is going to throw at you." Or when his father was in a particularly dark mood: "John, dynasties, empires, and civilizations have been collapsing since the dawn of time. Why should the U.S. of A be any different?"

But there were many lighter times as well; there were the family vacations and the weekend outings. His father and mother loved each other and rarely fought, though John knew his father's long absences were an emotional strain on his mom. There had been only one time when his mother threatened to leave Ben. It had been shortly after John's sixteenth birthday. John already outweighed his father by fifteen pounds but was still getting his ass handed to him during their sparring matches. Nowadays John was the one sparring with the instructors when trying out new schools. John could hold his own with the instructors for the simple reason the teacher had immersed himself in one discipline while John had been cross-trained in a variety of arts. John would simply find a weakness in the particular discipline and exploit it. It was during this time father and son had gone out for another "fishing trip."

During this particular trip, one of the fish had pulled out a concealed knife and had given John several slashing wounds across his arms and torso. Ben had been moving in to rescue his son, when John secured the wrist of his assailant with one hand and had driven the thumb of his other hand into the man's eye socket. John continued driving his thumb as deep into the socket as he could, as if he were trying to scoop out the inside of a pumpkin. Ben grabbed his son and fled, knowing he couldn't take his son to the hospital because he was fairly certain the knife-wielding man was dead. So his father drove him home, and the cat clawed its way out of the bag.

Ben and Margaret cleansed his wounds as best they could. Luckily, the blade hadn't penetrated deep enough to puncture anything vital, and Ben had a well-equipped combat medical kit that included local anesthetics as well as antibiotics. Though the injuries were not immediately life threatening, they were going to leave lifelong scars, especially since Ben himself had to crudely sew up his son. Ben had to explain to Margaret what had occurred and by the looks she gave her husband, John worried that after he received his makeshift medical treatment, his mother might shoot his father. After accepting a bottle of antibiotics and further instructions on how to care for her son, Margaret kicked Ben out of the house.

John's sister, Marilyn, had been sequestered to her room while his mother fretted over Johnny for three days and nights. The only thing that prevented her from taking him to the hospital was the fear her son would go to prison for the rest of his life. A week later Ben was allowed back in the house but slept in the basement. Things were never the same between his father and mother again. When his father was finally able to be alone with his son again, he asked, "How do you feel, son?"

"Dad, the thing I feel the worst about is I don't really feel much at all."

"It was my fault, son, and mine alone. You did what you had to do to survive. You're a good boy, Johnny, and you always will be."

The incident was never mentioned again. His mother and father were cordial, but Ben's sleeping quarters remained in the basement. His father was no longer allowed to leave the house alone with his son, and there were no more family outings. About four months later Ben left for a deployment and never returned. John had not seen or heard from his father since. As the months passed, John began to resent his mother. His father had taught him to respect his mother, so he didn't speak out. But secretly he blamed her for his father's leaving. One night he heard his mother's sobs from her bedroom and went to her side. She had lost a great deal of weight over the last month and her eyes had become dull and sunken. Thorpe put his hand on his mom's shoulder, which prompted her to speak, "I loved your father. You know that don't you?"

"Loved?" Johnny asked, fear creeping into his voice.

"I loved him, I still do."

"Then tell him to come back. Tell him you love him."

John's mother gave him a look that said, *You don't understand do you?* "Oh, baby, your father didn't leave us. He knew I was mad. Maybe I would always be mad. But he wouldn't leave us, baby! Your daddy may be a lot of things but he's no quitter. He wouldn't quit us, and he surely wouldn't quit you or your sister."

"Then why hasn't he come back, Mom?"

"Johnny, you knew he did dangerous work, you knew something might...happen."

"What happened, Mom?"

"I don't know. God's honest truth, baby! I swear I don't know what your father does. He wanted to protect us all from that. But he has never gone this long without contacting me in some way."

"Is he dead, Mom?"

"I don't know, but something's wrong. Your father...I'm worried. And he left with me being mad at him. That's never happened before and now...this. I could have taken it any other time...but...and now my son hates me too."

John broke down and cried. Soon his sister had heard the commotion and had joined them. The three stayed up and talked and cried until daylight. Thorpe no longer blamed his mother and realized she was in even greater torment than he was. Along with the agony of not knowing Ben's fate, John's mother was living with the guilt of sending her husband off with a cold shoulder. John, Margaret, and Marilyn bonded as they never had before. Despite their closeness, John's mother never recovered from her worry and guilt.

Margaret Thorpe died two years later after being diagnosed with bone cancer. She was given six months but only made it half that long. John believed she simply lost the will to live. It was during his mother's funeral when John realized how much his mother had truly sacrificed. There was scarcely a soul in attendance, a testament to the devotion his mother had bestowed upon her family. She had sacrificed her entire life solely for her husband and her children.

And then, just thirteen months ago, Thorpe's new family had been destroyed. Those images often intruded—Ella lying in his arms, her pale complexion, hair smoothed back on her head, cold to the touch. Thorpe pushed the memory of his dead daughter out of his mind. He couldn't go through that again, not right now. No wonder he was more than a little screwed-up. *Who wouldn't be?* Thorpe thought. But he *was* worried about who he was becoming. He was a Christian, but how could he justify what he was doing? The people he was hunting were killers and preyed on the weak. But did that give him the right to be judge, jury, and executioner? Thorpe hoped on Judgment Day he wouldn't be standing in line with the same people he had helped remove from this world. He hoped there were some exceptions to "Thou Shall not Kill." Deep down, he suspected he might be justifying his actions to himself. Thorpe took the last drink of his last beer, patted his dogs on the head, and walked back inside his home. After brushing his teeth, Thorpe took a long hard look in the mirror as he slowly traced one of the scars on his chest with an index finger. With moistened eyes, he spoke unconvincingly to his reflection, "You're a good boy, Johnny, and you always will be."

Seven

Tuesday
February 6th
Late morning

THE NEXT MORNING, Thorpe was gathering fallen tree limbs in the front of his property near the road when Al and Trixie tore off in a full sprint to the east, disappearing into the thick woods. The dogs didn't bark, and after a few minutes came trotting back to where Thorpe was working. Several seconds later the familiar form of Deborah Jennings came trotting down the road. Deborah was an avid fitness fanatic and also just a plain fanatic. The woman was trouble with a capital D—the "D" in reference to her surgically enhanced cup size, which was today also taking full advantage of the warm weather. Thorpe had chanced into a one-hour relationship with the woman just after he'd moved into the neighborhood. It was an encounter he had instantly regretted and was trying hard not to repeat. They had met on an occasion much like the one repeating itself today.

Then, he'd only been in his new house for a short time. He didn't know anything about his neighbors and the large acreage meant the situation wasn't likely to change. The day had been very hot, near or over a hundred degrees and Thorpe was clearing his newly purchased property. In a time when both fit and unfit men were wearing form-fitting T-shirts, he went to great lengths to conceal his muscular form. One reason he did so was because of the teachings of his father. "Don't ever show the enemy your hand, son. Make him think your strengths are your weaknesses and your weaknesses are your strengths." But mostly he covered his body to conceal the collection of scars he had managed to collect over the years. Some were acquired the night his opponent had produced a knife, but there had been other altercations as well. When people observed his scars, they always wanted to know the stories behind them. If the people were strangers, Thorpe could easily spew a line of crap they couldn't dispute. Cops, however, have the resources to call bullshit on a fabricated story, and Thorpe couldn't exactly be truthful with how he received his mementos. If only he'd heeded all his father's advice, such as, "Don't shit in your own sandbox," then he might not have found himself in his current predicament with this woman.

The day they had met, he had dispensed with his usual precautions and had discarded his shirt. He was working near the road in a pair of boots and khaki shorts, wet with sweat. Al and Trixie had not yet been trained, so the only warning Thorpe received was the sound of gravel crunching underfoot. Thorpe had looked up to spot Deborah running on the gravel road. She was wearing a black sports bra that barely contained her ample bosom and a pair of black Lycra running shorts. Her tanned, toned, and pierced midriff was on display, and Thorpe heard himself mumble, "Oh my God." As the woman approached, she caught sight of Thorpe and her pace slackened. Thorpe's body was nearly void of fat with muscle striations clearly visible in his chest, arms, back, and chest. His washboard stomach glistened. The woman slowed to a walk, altered her course, and sashayed right up to the fence. She said, "Hi neighbor...Deborah."

Thorpe walked over and took the hand extended over the fence. "John."

"John, I hate to be so forward, but you have the most amazing body I've ever seen on a man."

"I bet you say that to all the neighbors."

"Hardly. How'd you get the scars?"

"I'm a cop...TPD. Stuff happens." Not exactly an answer to her question, but not a lie either.

"Well, it makes me feel safe knowing I have one of Tulsa's finest as a next-door neighbor."

"Which house is yours?"

"The big obnoxious one on the hill."

"Nice to meet you, Deborah."

"Yes, it is." Deborah was in full flirt mode now. She was playing with her hair and repeatedly touching Thorpe's arm. "I'm sorry I've been such a poor neighbor. I haven't brought you and your wife a housewarming gift or anything."

"Not married."

"Divorced?"

"Not exactly," Thorpe replied.

Deborah didn't pursue the vague answer.

The double doors of the barn were open, and Thorpe's makeshift gym was visible from where the two stood.

"You have your own gym? Mind if I take a look?" Deborah didn't wait for a reply; in fact she was already headed for the gate while asking the question. She made sure she led the way to the barn, giving him a view from the backside. Her breasts were so large they overtook her small frame, and he could easily see their outline from behind. Deborah walked through the garage door and stopped at the punching bag. She threw a few punches. It was one of the most erotic sights he had ever witnessed, one that had immediately caused a southerly flow of blood.

"John, I think you would make an excellent personal trainer, *then* I wouldn't have to drive all the way into town every day."

"I'm expensive," Thorpe smiled.

Deborah laughed and tossed her hair back, "I'm rich."

She walked over to a squat rack, lowered herself under a bar with no weights, and began doing squats facing away from Thorpe. She arched her back and thrust her butt back and up during every repetition. "If you're that expensive you should at least give me a spot while I'm working-out."

Thorpe walked up behind Deborah and placed a hand on her bare sides just above her form-fitting shorts. Deborah stepped backwards, arched her back, and buried her firm buttocks into Thorpe as she dipped down with the bar. When she came back up, she again pressed herself into him. Thorpe promptly lifted the bar off her shoulders and tossed it behind them both. Deborah turned and ran her fingers down his chest and abdomen. She then grabbed him from the outside of his shorts. They both collapsed to the padded mat and made love with the double doors open — in full view of the road.

Thorpe had no idea whether anyone had passed by and had witnessed the show. Deborah had proven to be an insatiable and slightly violent lover. She had continuously traced his scars with her fingers and mouth as they made love, and he wasn't so sure he hadn't earned a few new ones, courtesy of her fingernails. Lying on the mat, Thorpe asked the question he'd probably consciously neglected to ask prior to their interlude, "Are *you* married?"

Deborah hesitated before responding, "Yes, but that doesn't mean we can't *see* each other from time to time."

"It does for me," Thorpe replied.

"Didn't seem too interested in whether I was married before we had sex."

"Like most people, I think a lot clearer after sex than before it."

"We'll see," Deborah said, smiling. With that, she dressed, bent over, flicked his nipple with her tongue, smiled, and began jogging toward the gate as if intercourse had just been a water station on her running route. Following the encounter, he'd avoided the fence line anytime he saw Deborah approaching. Eventually, his dogs were trained not to let anyone inside the gate with the exception of Jeff—unless Thorpe gave the proper command. This kept Deborah from coming onto his property uninvited. And she couldn't phone him because, like any decent cop, Thorpe had an unlisted phone number.

Recently Thorpe had encountered Deborah's husband, Mr. Jennings. Thorpe had been running on the road when he'd been approached by a Mercedes with tinted windows. At first Thorpe was afraid it was Deborah, but as it approached, the darkened driver's window slid down, revealing its sole occupant. Thorpe stopped running, but the man never left the vehicle, speaking to Thorpe through the open car window. Mr. Jennings appeared to be in his late sixties and had a red swollen nose indicative of a lifetime of alcohol abuse. He was also grossly overweight and generally appeared to be in poor health. He told Thorpe he was a corporate attorney in one of Tulsa's larger law firms. Mr. Jennings gave no indication he was aware Deborah and Thorpe had met. During their short conversation, Mr. Jennings had conveyed they had a live-in maid/chef and had bragged about several belongings, including Deborah. It was apparent she was the quintessential trophy wife and probably no more cherished than the man's other possessions, a thing to be worn on his arm and shown off at parties. Thorpe didn't have much sympathy for Deborah because she had probably married the money, not the man. Still, he thought maybe he'd been a little hard on the woman. But most of his avoidance was so he himself wouldn't fall again.

On this relatively warm winter's day, Deborah was wearing long tight pants and a pink Lycra shirt with a zipper in front. The zipper was pulled low, exposing her cleavage. As Deborah approached, Thorpe smiled and raised his hand. She slowed to a walk. Al and Trixie began to let out low guttural growls until Thorpe called them off.

"You're not going to turn your back and release your hounds on me today?"

"Sorry, Deborah. You were right. I was just as much to blame as you were. I didn't want to know the truth."

"I had it coming...Didn't give you much of a chance. Look, I know about your family now. You were in a bad place." Thorpe nodded his head; he was still in a bad place.

"My husband says you two met the other day?"

"Yeah. It wasn't as exciting as when we met though."

Deborah laughed. "I hope not. He told me we needed to move outta here. He said it was embarrassing to share the neighborhood with a civil servant."

Thorpe figured the guy would be really pissed to know what else they'd shared. "I take it he's not a big supporter of the police? Why do you guys live way out here anyway?"

"Thomas wanted a country retreat. You should see the entertainment area he had built behind our house and the view it has of the Tulsa skyline. It was great at first, but now he has trouble getting his colleagues out to visit because of the drive. He's all about entertaining and showing off. I have a feeling we'll be moving back towards town soon."

"Well, I'm sure it'll all work out."

"John, I just want you to know what happened between us...that's not something I normally do. I don't want you thinking I'm like that. I was just in a bad place too. I still am."

"Deborah, I don't want to sound callous, but it's really none of my business. I don't like hurting people, but I'm doing my damnedest not to break all Ten Commandments this month. You should be having this conversation with your husband." Thorpe backed away from the fence. "I wish you luck, Deborah. I really do." As he walked towards the house, he risked a glance over his shoulder, watching the overtaxed pink Lycra resume its burden on the road. *My God that woman looked good.* Thorpe looked down to Al and Trixie, who were following on his heels. "I should find a social life before you two start looking good to me."

Thorpe had been too consumed with finding his wife and daughter's killers to fall too deeply into loneliness. It was moments such as these—when he was confronted with an attractive woman — he was reminded of some basic needs missing from his life. He hadn't been celibate for the last thirteen months; he'd had several one-night stands—usually out of town. To engage in anything more substantial seemed to be an affront to his lost family. Not so much to his departed wife, as she would surely understand. But if he were to develop a relationship with a woman, it would suggest he was moving on and starting afresh. Thorpe knew he wasn't being logical, but he was afraid a meaningful relationship would lessen the bond between himself and his lost daughter.

Not long after Thorpe disappeared inside, Jeff Gobin rolled up the drive. In addition to being his best friend, Jeff was the only person to visit his home on a regular basis. Other than his sister, he was also the only person remotely aware of the combat skills Thorpe possessed. Still, even Jeff didn't know the extent of the training—only that Thorpe's father had imparted the skills to his son. He was also the only officer on the department Thorpe fully trusted. Not that he would tell Jeff what he was up to; he wouldn't want to put his friend in such a position.

"You look like shit," Jeff said as Thorpe pulled open his front door.

"Thanks...had a six-pack last night."

"You? A six-pack to *you* would be like a case to me. Thought you gave up drinking?"

"I figured, under the circumstances, I'd better keep away from it for a while," Thorpe said, pouring himself a cup of coffee.

"But you think you can handle it now?" Jeff inquired.

"No, but kicking your ass still gives me much more satisfaction and is a hell of a lot cheaper than alcohol."

"Uh-huh, you're in trouble today. I watched *The Last Dragon* last night. Learned some old-school moves."

"I remember that movie. Guess that makes you Sho'nuff, the Shogun of Harlem."

"I can't believe you actually know that movie," Jeff laughed.

"Hey, maybe after our workout we can rent *Breakin' 2: Electric Boogaloo*," Thorpe remarked.

"Very funny, you probably have a special edition of *Dirty Dancing*, don't you?" retorted Jeff.

"Another good movie. Nobody puts Baby in a corner."

"The sad thing is, you know the lines to all these fucking movies," Jeff remarked.

"It *is* sad isn't it? So what's new in the Rat Squad?" Jeff was an investigative sergeant with Internal Affairs. Some officers just referred to it as The Rat Squad.

"Same old shit...Officers beatin' the hell out of poor ol' innocent citizens," Jeff sarcastically declared as he waved off a cup of coffee.

"My name cross your desk lately?"

"Not this week, John. Maybe we should get you a pin...No complaints in a whole week."

"Yeah. The only people who don't get complaints are the ones who don't do real police work."

"You don't have to tell me, brother. You're acting like I wasn't your partner for four years."

"Just making sure you haven't gone totally over to the dark side," Thorpe jokingly said.

"Why does it have to be the dark side, asshole? Why can't it be the white side?"

Both men laughed, though it wasn't the first time Thorpe had heard his friend use the pun. Despite their lasting friendship, both men knew little of the other's past. Thorpe figured Jeff sensed his reluctance to talk of his childhood, or perhaps he didn't inquire because he didn't want to reciprocate. Either way, the arrangement was just fine with him.

Thorpe's pager started going off. He recognized the number of Robert Hull, the sergeant over Homicide. "Getting a call from Hull. A misdirected youth must have been on the wrong end of a bullet." Thorpe punched the numbers into his cell phone.

"Hull," the detective answered.

"Hey, Bob, what's up?"

"John, I think we found one of your boys. You know a Marcel Newman?"

Sure, Bob, I killed him just the other day. "Oh yeah, he's a regular." *They found the body.*

"This isn't your typical spray and pray. You'll probably want to see this for yourself."

"Whatta you got?" Thorpe asked.

"Son-of-a-bitch has been bound to a pole, looks like he's been tortured. Probably been dead for a couple of days."

Actually, Bob, it's only been about twenty-seven hours. "Where you at?" Thorpe asked, already knowing the answer.

"Go to Newton and Waco. A uniform will guide you in from there."

"Okay, Bob, I'm a ways off. You going to be there for a while?"

"Oh, yeah. This is a pretty fucked-up scene. We'll be here all afternoon and then some."

"Okay, I'll start some of my other guys. I should be there in about thirty minutes."

"Hey, John, one more thing..."

"Yeah?"

"You know anybody goes by the initials L.A.?"

"I know a couple guys. Why?"

"Looks like your boy wrote those initials in the dirt before he died."

"No shit?" Thorpe said, feigning surprise. "Marcel's been trading rounds with a guy named Dwayne Foster, goes by those initials."

"May be an easy case then," Hull remarked.

"Well, we definitely have a starting point. I'll see you in a few minutes, Bob."

Thorpe left Jeff to finish the workout on his own. A few minutes later, as he crossed from the house to his truck, Thorpe heard the song "*I touch myself*" coming from the barn's radio. Thorpe stuck his head through the door, yelling, "You better not be touching yourself in my barn." Jeff smiled and grabbed himself. Thorpe laughed and climbed into his truck. His smile instantly faded.

Eight

Tuesday
February 6th
Afternoon

THORPE TOOK THE SAME ROUTE to the scene as he had one day earlier. *Was it just yesterday?* It seemed to Thorpe like so much had happened since then. Traveling west on Newton, he noticed the towering boom cameras of the local television news vans. Thorpe passed the parasitic news reporters and drew near yellow "Police Line Do Not Cross" tape stretched across the road. Thorpe badged the uniformed officer manning the post, who swiftly lifted the tape, allowing Thorpe to drive underneath. He drove several more yards before parking behind an assortment of detective's vehicles. Climbing out of his truck, Thorpe noticed several cameramen had their lenses trained on him. He approached the cameramen, informed them he was an undercover officer and asked they not air his image or that of his vehicle out of officer-safety concerns. The cameramen assured Thorpe he would be edited out or given the standard pixelated treatment.

Thorpe returned his attention to the crime scene and noticed the gate to the gravel drive that led into the woods—and to the barn—stood open. A uniformed officer, whom Thorpe recognized, stood near the section of barbed wire Thorpe had cut just hours earlier. "Hey Todd, what's going on?"

"Don't really know, Sarge, haven't got to see the scene. I'm just guarding this fence and some boot prints. Heard Marcel Newman's body was found in a barn up there," Todd said as he threw a thumb over his shoulder in the direction of the barn, "and he was all fucked up."

"Couldn't happen to a nicer guy," Thorpe responded.

"Ain't that the truth," Todd agreed.

"Mind if I take a look?" Thorpe asked, pointing towards the boot prints.

"Go ahead; you can see it from the gravel here," the officer said while motioning Thorpe to an acceptable vantage point.

Thorpe could see a portion of a boot print in the dirt. A print he knew would never be traced back to him. "They think that belongs to the killer?"

"I don't know what they think. They don't let me in on their circle-jerks," Todd answered.

"I get to the scene this way?" Thorpe asked, pointing up the drive.

"Yeah, Sarge, but I gotta call you an escort. Hull says nobody comes up the drive without one."

"That's okay, I'll call Hull," Thorpe said, retrieving his cell phone from his belt.

About ten minutes later, Hull came walking down the drive and shook hands with Thorpe. Hull had been on the department for thirty-plus years but still had a fairly youthful appearance. He was a couple inches shorter than Thorpe with graying black hair. Today he wore a tan suit jacket and pants with a white dress shirt and no tie. He looked as though he hadn't shaved since yesterday, but

Hull always looked like that. He was a superlative detective and dedicated to his job—so much so it had cost him several marriages and any resemblance of a normal life.

"John, this is a good one, really gets my juices going."

"Bob, the last thing I want to hear about are your juices."

Both men laughed and Bob began leading Thorpe west down Newton. "It all started this morning," Hull said, talking with his hands as he made a large circular motion in the air. "Marcel's baby's momma, Lady Morgan—and, yes, Lady is her real first name—called Marcel's grandmother today and asked if she'd seen her grandson. Grandma tells Lady that Marcel stayed over the night before last, but must have caught a ride in the morning because his car was still parked outside of her house, and she hadn't seen Marcel since the night before. Lady tells grandma she and Marcel had plans together and he never showed up. Grandma doesn't get around too good, but now she's concerned. She walks out to Marcel's car and notices a blood smear on the driver's side window. She then notices what she thinks might be more blood on the street, goes back inside, and calls the police."

Thorpe and Hull were now standing at the corner of Newton and Waco Avenue. Hull pointed to the north. "That's Marcel's car parked up there with the police tape surrounding it. The blood was found just east of the car on the street. When the two uniforms show up, they also notice the blood and one starts looking to the east to see if Marcel had been dumped into the ditch or had crawled there. They notice the barbed wire had been cut at that location and began following a somewhat beaten-down path that led through the woods and to a barn. They open the barn door and about shit themselves when they find a bloody black male bound to a pole inside. They cleared the barn of suspects and, because it was obvious the person was dead, never directly approached the body. The officers backed out of the barn and called it in." Hull pointed back in the direction they had just come from. "Let's walk back to the gravel drive and we'll go in that way." The two sergeants walked back east towards the entrance of the gravel drive leading to the barn. Hull pointed to the cut barbed wire next to the gate. "We think the killers may have entered here, left here, or both."

"Killers, as in plural?" Thorpe asked.

"Yeah, there are multiple footprints left in the dirt floor of the barn that all seem to come and go from the pole where Marcel was bound. The prints are of different shoe patterns and sizes. We think we're looking at multiple suspects—at least three. We've got a partial print near this cut barbed wire that matches one of the prints left on the barn's dirt floor." Hull glanced at Thorpe with a question, "Any ideas why they cut the barbed wire instead of just climbing the gate or cutting off the lock?"

"You sure the killers cut the wire?"

"Pretty. It's definitely fresh," Hull answered.

Thorpe feigned contemplation before responding, "Maybe they'd been planning on dragging Marcel out through the opening and knew they wouldn't be able to lift his ass over the gate. I don't know."

Hull responded with a simple nod of the head as the two men continued north on the gravel driveway. As they approached the barn, Thorpe recognized several homicide detectives and crime-scene technicians.

"Marcel's still bound to the pole. No big hurry to move him—he ain't goin' nowhere," Bob said as he stopped outside the open barn door and pointed inside. We've marked off a path that's been processed already. We can access the body this way." The two men stepped inside and paused to allow their eyes to adjust. "We're in the process of getting some better lights set up in here," Hull offered.

Except for crusty, congealed blood and the ghastly swelling of flesh—puckered between bands of tape—the body appeared just how Thorpe had left it. Hull and

Thorpe walked over and stood beside the body. "From what we can gather so far, the killers took Marcel down at his car, dragged him through the woods and into this barn, and then bound him here. The victim has a wound in his right shoulder that appears to be through-and-through. One of his nipples has been torn off and tossed over there." Hull pointed to a patch of what now looked like dry leather lying in the dirt. "Don't know the cause of death yet. His mouth, nose, throat—all his airways—were taped up. If that occurred when he was still alive, it surely would have done the trick." Hull pointed down to the base of the pole behind Marcel's body. "There's the initials I was telling you about. So what do you think?"

Thorpe knelt and studied the setting for a couple of minutes. "It looks like he was still alive when they pulled the nipple off. Lot of blood. He's pretty fucked-up. I'd say his killers were trying to get some information from him or were really, *really* pissed off about something. My first impulse is to believe they were probably after something though—trying to find out where some dope or some money was hidden. Any signs of his car or his grandma's house being ransacked?"

Hull shook his head, "No. Why do you think they were looking for something instead of just out to kill him?"

Thorpe stood, "Because these guys just don't do this shit. Your Mexican and El Salvadorian gangs do this, sometimes motorcycle gangs, but generally not black gangs. These guys just get in a car with their buddies and a bunch of guns and go shoot the shit out their target's house, usually without checking if the target's even inside first. The dude's little sister is usually the one who ends up catching a bullet."

Thorpe looked at Hull who was slowly nodding his head. Hull knew all of this already but liked to hear what other people were thinking and see if it matched up to what was bouncing around in his own head. Hull always gave the appearance of studying you while you spoke, which he probably was. He was probably the best interrogator on the department and could smell bullshit like a fly in summertime. Thorpe didn't take alarm from Hull's behavior because it was usual. Thorpe could only remember one time when Hull didn't behave that way—the night Erica and Ella were killed. Hull went out of his way to make sure Thorpe knew he wasn't considered a suspect in the killings.

History suggests that when a wife and children are murdered, the husband is, more often than not, the culprit. Though Thorpe believed Hull didn't seriously consider him a suspect, it would be negligent of the department if they didn't cast part of their investigation his way. Hull's squad would have looked into Thorpe's life to some degree even if they only focused on folks who may have held a grudge against the supervisor of the OGU. There would be hundreds of arrest reports to sift through: What were the circumstances of the arrest? Were they sentenced to prison? If so, were they still in prison? If not, were they living in the Tulsa area? That line of investigation alone would be extremely time-consuming. Of course Thorpe's life away from the department would also be scrutinized. Just how much of his past and current life Hull had uncovered Thorpe wasn't sure. This he did know, Hull was a good cop but more importantly was a good man. If Hull had uncovered something not pertinent to the case, it would only be filed away in Hull's brain. And no one had a key to that labyrinth.

"What do you make of the 'L.A.' in the dirt?" Hull inquired.

Again Thorpe paused as if gathering his thoughts. In reality he had already anticipated this line of questioning and had prepared what he was going to say. The trick was for it not to sound rehearsed. "We've had several tips Dwayne Foster and the late Marcel here have been shooting at one another for some time now. They've never hit each other. But a couple of their homeboys have taken some superficial wounds. Foster's street name is L.A. The most logical conclusion would be L.A. and friends were kicking Marcel's ass when he realized he might not make it out of this barn alive. Marcel then wrote the initials in the dirt so the police or his crew would know who to look for." Thorpe paused before speaking again. "The other possibility is someone other than Foster killed Marcel, and set Foster up as the fall guy."

"Interesting. Anyone else out there want Marcel dead?"

"Shit, Bob, that list could be almost as long as the one for you."

"Not fucking likely," Hull laughed. "By the way, if I ever wind up dead, tethered to a pole, make sure my ex-wives are looked at extensively," he finished with a smile.

"You know this is weird, Bob, we just concluded surveilling Marcel a couple of weeks ago. Didn't get anything of use out of it." Thorpe spent a couple of minutes describing the investigation and what they'd learned.

"Too bad this didn't happen then, you guys would have been here when the shit went down," Hull commented.

"Yeah, the only bad thing is we might've stopped it," Thorpe said with a grin. "Bob, I've already got Tyrone dressed up like a hab and en route to L.A.'s house. L.A. lives near Sixth and Lewis so Tyrone should fit right in. Jennifer's at the office and ready—with help from your guys—to knock-out a search warrant. Given the documented background we have on these two and the physical evidence here at the scene, we should be able to get a search warrant pretty quick."

Hull spoke with artificial irritation, "John, I am the head Homicide dick around these parts, you know."

Thorpe smiled, "Too easy. What do you want from my end?"

"How 'bout you get eyes on L.A.'s house, and have one of your people start on a search warrant," Hull responded.

"Gee, that's a good idea. Where do you come up with these epiphanies?"

"Epiphanies... Big words don't compensate for your small penis," Hull shot back.

"Small penis. Your wife been talking in her sleep again?"

"No, but your sister has."

"Ouch. You cut me deep, Bob, *real* deep," Thorpe joked, "You or one of your boys can get together with Jennifer. With what we got on file, and with what you guys come up with here, we should be able to spit out a warrant in a matter of hours."

The two sergeants walked to Marcel's car where they met up with Hull's senior homicide detective, Chuck Lagrone. Lagrone was in his early sixties but looked eighty if he was a day. He was short and maybe weighed 130 pounds. Most officers get larger with tenure, usually with fat, but it seemed Lagrone weathered with each passing year and one day might disappear all together. Now he was just a thin layer of skin wrapped tightly around bone. Because of his appearance, he had earned the departmental nickname of "The Skull." The Skull was one hell of a detective and, despite his looks, a genuinely nice guy.

"How's it going, Carnac?"

"Good, Skull. How you doin'?"

"Ain't dead yet, but I got one foot in the grave and another on a banana peel."

"You're wearing that joke out."

"I'll try to come up with a new one *just* for you."

The three men discussed the case for several minutes before Thorpe excused himself. As Thorpe walked back to his truck, he reflected on his conversation with Hull. Thorpe had jokingly insinuated he was sleeping with Hull's wife, and Bob had instantly shot back about having relations with Thorpe's sister. No hesitation. The Skull had interviewed his sister following the murders. Standard stuff. But Hull had popped off with "sister" instantaneously. Thorpe wondered just how much Hull knew.

AS LAGRONE WATCHED THORPE WALK AWAY, he spoke to his boss out of the corner of his mouth: "Bob, I've been in the shit in Vietnam and been in three shootings on the force, so it means something when I say…I wouldn't ever want to get cross with that boy."

"Me either, Chuck, but that's because you and I know what he's capable of. Most people don't. And John's went through a lot of trouble to keep it that way—so we're going to honor that."

"How's he holdin' up?" Lagrone asked.

"This was the first time *in thirteen months* he didn't ask about his family's investigation."

"Huh. If John ever finds those cocksuckers before we do, they're in for one helluva bad day," Lagrone said.

"If we do find those cocksuckers first, I'll personally help John put those sons-of-bitches in the grave."

"Sounds like something worth going to prison for. Count me in boss."

"Shit, Skull, a life sentence for you is the equivalent of about three weeks. Whatta you got to worry about?"

"Fuck you. I'm going to outlive all you bastards."

"Probably, you're like a little cockroach," Hull said, heading back toward the barn, "Let's get back to work."

"Yeah. Dead body pick-up."

Nine

Tuesday
February 6th
Evening

I*T WAS 11:00 P.M. THORPE SAT IN A DARKENED CORNER of Monkeyshines Gentlemen's Club. The strip bar was in close walking distance to a cheap motel. If you wished, you could pick up a strung-out stripper-whore and retire to a flea-infested motel room. Liquor or beer could not be served inside Monkeyshines. Crack or crank, sure, but not alcohol. To compensate, the patrons took frequent bathroom breaks and trips to their vehicles to consume the mind-altering drug of their choice. To be fair, the bar's customers did include the "Average Joe" types who returned to their car every thirty minutes or so to slam a beer before returning to "the beautiful women of Monkeyshines."

Thorpe currently had one of those "beautiful" women sitting on his lap as he watched L.A. and two friends at a table across the dark, expansive room. The beautiful woman in question went by the stage name "Candy," and by Thorpe's reasoning, she must have had plenty of the sweets growing up because she had several missing teeth and the ones still in her mouth were in various stages of decay. Candy had the classic look of a crankster.

Heavy methamphetamine use caused calcium depletion in the bones, often resulting in a fine set of Billy Bob teeth. In addition to a winning smile, Candy was also emaciated and covered with crank sores. *Very sexy!* Most Tulsans didn't realize Monkeyshines was owned and operated by associates of an outlaw motorcycle club, who made a fair amount of their non-tax profits from the sale of methamphetamine and who were also, in all likelihood, Candy's supplier. One of the reasons methamphetamine had earned the name "crank" was because motorcycle gangs—in the early days of the drug—used to transport the illegal substance in the crank cases of their bikes.

Sometimes the employees of Monkeyshines were blatant enough to wear their patches inside the bar. Thorpe couldn't understand why black patrons like L.A. continued to drop huge amounts of money in a bar operated by a gang known to commit hate crimes against them. One thing was certain, they were happy to take L.A.'s money, and L.A. seemed to enjoy giving it away. *Everyone's a winner*.

As Thorpe sat in the bar conducting surveillance, he continuously received updates on his cell phone. Skull and Jennifer had obtained a night-service warrant for L.A.'s residence and vehicle. They had also obtained a warrant for L.A.'s person in order to collect DNA evidence.

Jennifer was the only officer from Thorpe's unit who would be participating in the warrant service on L.A.'s home, which would be executed any minute now. The rest of Thorpe's officers were concealed in the parking lot of Monkeyshines and were to execute the warrant on L.A.'s car after he drove it away from the bar. Thorpe had been sitting inside the club playing the part of a sexual deviant while he watched L.A. and his crew. Thorpe was wearing a wool skullcap pulled down to his eyebrows, blue jeans, and an insulated flannel shirt. He was thankful for the extra layers of clothing as Candy ground her wares into his thigh. Thorpe decided his first order of business upon returning home, would be to toss his jeans into the washer with an ample supply of detergent.

Candy had offered to take Thorpe to the "private" dance room, which was up a couple of stairs and separated from the rest of the bar. In the private room, hand-jobs could be had for a hundred dollars and blowjobs for two hundred. If you didn't bring enough money with you, an ATM machine was conveniently located next to the bathrooms. Thorpe politely declined the offer, claiming he wanted to watch the rest of the girls for a while. But he insisted she return later. Candy accepted a twenty from the city of Tulsa and promised she would be back. Investigators at SID were given "buy-money" to use for purchasing dope, beer, whatever. The Vice Unit dropped quite a bit of taxpayers' money on lap dances, massages, and beer—the poor bastards.

L.A. had removed his coat about thirty minutes ago, draping it across the backrest of his chair. Thorpe casually took a circular route behind L.A., noticing he wasn't wearing the boots that had been left on his porch. However, Thorpe did notice the right side of L.A.'s jacket stretched tight toward the floor, while the other side was slack. There was something heavy in the right side pocket, most likely a gun. Thorpe returned to his seat and spoke into his cell phone as a song blasted over the bar's speaker system. "Tyrone, I think L.A. has a handgun in his right coat pocket. Don't wait for him to get in his car. Take him down in the parking lot. Approach him from the east. If he runs he'll come right back towards me. Get some more uniforms set up around the neighborhood in case the other two guys run. Okay? Sound it back to me."

Several minutes later, L.A. took a call from his own cell phone, stood erect, and almost dumped the girl who'd been sitting on his lap to the floor. He said something to his buddies and began hurrying for the exit as he pulled on his coat. Thorpe slowly began to follow as he used the direct-connect to warn Tyrone. Candy—worried she was about to lose potential income—approached. Thorpe spoke into the cell phone, "Yeah, honey, I'm coming home now, RIGHT NOW!"

Tyrone received the words on the other end and decoded the message. "We're on boys." The six officers, dressed much like Thorpe, had parked a van next to L.A.'s car. They got out and stood behind it in a circle, pretending to be shooting the shit and drinking beer. L.A. tore out of the bar with his associates in tow. When L.A. drew to within ten yards, Tyrone pulled out his neck badge and yelled, "Police!" The six officers simultaneously drew their weapons. L.A. friend number one was farthest away from the officers. He broke and ran towards where Thorpe was staggering across the parking lot.

Being an ex-con, L.A. would be sent back to prison if caught in possession of a firearm. He took off and followed on the heels of his friend. Tyrone and Jake pursued him. Associate number two stood where he was and was immediately given an up-close introduction to the gravel lot.

L.A. would try to run far enough to get rid of his weapon without being seen, but this was not going to happen. L.A. was headed right towards Thorpe, who was still impersonating a staggering inebriate. L.A. risked a glance over his left shoulder at his pursuers, giving Thorpe the opportunity to move in and put a shoulder into L.A.'s ribs. The blow knocked L.A. completely off both feet, sending him crashing to the lot. He landed awkwardly on his right side. Thorpe was already on L.A. as Jake and Tyrone drew near, "I'm okay. Get his buddy."

Associate number one was fast. Jake was faster. And Tyrone wasn't fast at all. Jake caught associate number one in the parking lot of a different bar. Though fast, Jake wasn't much in a fight. He grabbed the larger suspect from behind by the collar of his shirt. The suspect spun and caught Jake with a left hook just under his right armpit. To Jake's credit, he held on to the suspect's collar as he fell to the ground so that the bad guy was still on his feet and bent over at the waist.

What Tyrone lacked in speed, he made up for in mass. Just as the suspect was about to deliver another blow to Jake, Tyrone drove his 250-pound frame into the backside of the jackknifed suspect. With Tyrone on top, the suspect was driven forward and landed face first onto the asphalt. The landing peeled off a good portion of flesh from the suspect's forehead and nose. Tyrone almost ripped the suspect's arm off as he brought it behind his back and placed him in handcuffs. It turned out suspect number one was also an ex-con in possession of a firearm, not to mention seven grams of crack cocaine in his briefs.

A lot of people who shouldn't see the undercover officers' faces were now coming out of the two bars and watching the show. Thorpe and his team quickly turned the suspects over to uniforms and got out of sight. Thorpe called Hull. "What's up, John?"

Thorpe filled him in, then asked, "What's happening with the warrant?"

"Just got the house cleared a little bit ago. No one at home. Haven't really started searching yet. I'll let you know if we come up with something," Hull answered.

"Be careful out there. L.A. got a phone call right before he leapt out of his chair to leave this place. Someone's watching you guys and gave him a call...You going to try and interview L.A. tonight?"

"Think he'll talk?" Hull asked.

"Doubt it. This ain't his first rodeo. Don't know about his buddies yet."

"Ok, John. By the way Jennifer's been a huge help."

"Yeah, she knows her shit. Best warrant writer I got...Bob, if you don't need me for anything else, I'll probably be taking off after I fill out my supplemental report. Go home and get some sleep."

"Squeeze in a couple of hours for me...No. Go home. I appreciate your help, John."

"You bet. I'll talk to you tomorrow."

"Don't call me, I'll call you. Gonna get some sleep of my own. Maybe."

Thorpe doubted Hull would get much sleep if any. Robert Hull put in more hours than anyone else on the department. He made good money from overtime, but it had cost him much more. What guys like Hull did for entertainment after leaving the department Thorpe had no idea, probably had a heart attack and died six months into retirement.

Thorpe wouldn't be getting much sleep tonight either, though it had nothing to do with job devotion.

Ten

Wednesday
February 7th
Early morning

ACCORDING TO MARCEL NEWMAN, Kaleb Moment held secrets about the murder of Thorpe's family. What Marcel hadn't known was that his good friend was a police informant. Kaleb had been caught trafficking crack cocaine and was looking at prison time. Instead of spending his early twenties in the custody of the Department of Corrections, Kaleb had signed a contract with the Tulsa County District Attorney's office and was now "working off" his charges by setting up his friends and associates. SID maintained a CI file. CIs, or confidential informants, were the backbone of undercover dope investigations. Without them, ninety percent of the top cases would cease to exist.

SID supervisors were the only people who had access to CI files at the office. Each CI was assigned a number, and those numbers were the only identification on any document. The CI file was kept in the administrative sergeant's office in a locked file cabinet. Via several simple Rolodexes, you could look up sequential numbers to obtain a CI's identity. Once you had the CI's name, you could retrieve his information and case history from a set of alphabetically marked file cabinets secured with a combination lock.

Earlier, Thorpe had gone to the file cabinet marked "M," entered the proper combination, and pulled Kaleb Moment's file. In addition to the cases resulting from Kaleb's cooperation, it listed personal information including contact numbers and addresses. Thorpe recorded this information and noted Kaleb's handler was Brian Hickey, an evening-shift narcotics investigator.

The files had led Thorpe to the Bainbridge Apartment complex. Bainbridge, by any name, was one of the most malignant complexes in the city. It was federally funded and constantly changed names. As an officer, Thorpe had once been assigned to the Foot-beat unit. Foot-beat officers had patrolled these housing complexes nightly, but the program had faded away with grant losses and manpower shortages. Now it seemed like the only crime-fighting program the apartments applied were name changes. When a particular housing complex was aired one-too-many times on the evening news, preceded by the words "another shooting at," the complex would simply change its name.

About a month ago, uniformed officers had cornered a homicide suspect in one of the units inside this complex. A mob formed and started throwing rocks at the police. During the subsequent melee, a reporter became part of the story when she was grabbed by the hair and thrown into her own news van. A couple of shots were fired at officers. As with most incidents like this, the complex was one of the safer places in the city for the next week as officers made examples of anyone who poked a head out a door. The community had complained because there hadn't been enough police enforcement in the complex; then they complained because there was too much. *Damned if you do...* Police personnel had since been shuffled to other hotspots, and the complex had resumed its status as federally funded gang housing.

A few minutes ago, Thorpe had driven through the complex with the hope of spotting Kaleb's car parked outside his girlfriend's apartment. The car wasn't there, and Thorpe couldn't park inside without drawing attention to himself. He had to find Kaleb soon; these guys had a way of leading short lives, and if Kaleb went and got himself killed before Thorpe had a chance to interrogate him, the secret would die with the little shit.

Thorpe drove to a nearby convenience store, which was yet another prime location for selling crack and a place where Thorpe had initiated many foot pursuits. The location provided a payphone, which the drug dealers appreciated, and it had no outside surveillance cameras, which the drug dealers loved. Thorpe climbed from the vehicle and used the payphone to dial Kaleb's cell phone number.

"Who this?" A male answered.

"This is Sergeant Thomas Brightling. I'm a detective for the Tulsa Police Department's Office of Integrity and Compliance." Thorpe pulled the name out of his ass.

"Office of what?"

"I'm an Internal Affairs investigator," Thorpe explained.

"So?" Kaleb said with feigned disinterest.

"So...I know you're working for the Tulsa Police Department as an informant. Your case officer is Brian Hickey."

Several seconds of silence preceded Kaleb's response, "What do you want?"

I want to kick your ass. "I need to see you right now. What you need to know is this: Your case officer is suspected of providing information to people he shouldn't. He will be relieved of duty before this night is over. I need to speak with you in reference to the Chamberlain case you just handed Hickey. If you cooperate, you're done, your contract is fulfilled; you won't have to do anymore work for the department. If you don't, or if you call Hickey when I hang up, I will personally negate any progress you've made on your contract and send your ass straight to prison. Where you at?"

"Shit! I'm at my place."

"Where's that?" Thorpe asked.

"Bainbridge."

"I just drove through Bainbridge and didn't see your car."

"My car ain't there 'cause the fucking thing got stolen," Kaleb said with overt hostility.

"Anyone inside with you?"

"My woman."

"Make up an excuse, and walk to the park just north of the complex. I'll be in a dark gray Chevy Tahoe. Don't tell her what you're doing."

About five minutes after Thorpe pulled into the park, he observed a figure crossing the darkened grounds. Kaleb approached the passenger side door, opened it, and climbed inside. A blast of cold air and the smell of marijuana entered the car along with its new occupant.

"You don't look like a cop," Kaleb remarked.

"I thought you might appreciate that since I came to pick you up in your 'hood. You want to see my I.D.?"

"No. What's this about?"

"We think Hickey's been giving information to bad guys, including the names and addresses of his informants." Thorpe intended to scare the shit out of his guest. It worked.

Kaleb sat in stunned silence before his lips started working, "FUCK! FUCK ME! THIS IS FUCKING BULLSHIT! FUCK, I'M A FUCKING DEAD MAN!" Spit was flying out of Kaleb's mouth onto the dash. That was going to cause Thorpe additional cleaning later.

"Kaleb, I need you to calm down. We're going to take care of this, and you."

"Take care of ME! You fucks can't even find my fucking car! Fuck!"

"Kaleb, we can't let this get out. What did you tell your girlfriend when you left?" Kaleb didn't respond. He wasn't even listening. Probably all he was thinking about was his homeboys finding out he was a snitch. In Kaleb's mind, he was already dead. Thorpe needed to refocus Kaleb's attention, "Kaleb, listen to me! What did you tell your girlfriend when you left?"

"I didn't tell the bitch shit! She don't need to know what I do."

"Bullshit, Kaleb, you told her something."

"I told her I'd be right back, that's it."

"Well it's going to be a few minutes. I need to get a recorded statement. I'm taking you to a motel room. My captain and I are going to get a statement from you there."

"A motel room? Why are we going to a motel room?" Kaleb asked, sounding worried.

"Do you want a cop seeing you and me walk into Internal Affairs together? This can't get back to Hickey." Thorpe was playing on Kaleb's fear.

"Motherfucker! I don't want to testify against no cop. I'll have fucking everyone huntin' my ass then!"

Thorpe was already driving. "You won't have to testify. He won't know you talked. He's done a lot more than this. You're just another nail in the coffin."

"Fuck! I always knew that motherfucker was dirty." For some reason all drug dealers think all cops are dirty. Maybe it makes them feel better about themselves.

Thorpe had the keys of several motel rooms. Scattered around the city, the rooms were in repellent motels. The managers let police use them under the guise that they were cooperative with law enforcement. Everyone knew different. These particular managers relied on drug dealing and prostitution; otherwise their establishments wouldn't have any customers. The Vice Unit used them for John stings and other vice operations. The motel's rooms were never filled to capacity, so it didn't cost anything to let officers have keys to some of the 'suites.' Management didn't bother to clean the rooms but once a week or so, but Thorpe figured other rooms didn't receive much more cleaning than theirs.

As Thorpe drove to the motel, he gave Kaleb instructions: "We've rented this room for at least a week, until we figure out what all information Hickey has leaked. You're welcome to stay here, call your girlfriend, whatever, until we get this cinched up." Kaleb nodded his head dazedly. "I'm going to let you out around the corner. Here's the key to room 142. It's located on the south side of the building. You don't want everyone to know you're here with the cops. I'll wait a couple of minutes before I follow you in." Thorpe parked in a secluded lot just east of a Whataburger fast food restaurant and let Kaleb out. "You take off, it's your ass! I'll have a warrant out for your arrest in an hour. You give a statement, you'll never see us again. You have my word." Kaleb ambled off toward the motel, his head down as he mumbled profanities.

Even though the Tahoe's tags weren't on file, Thorpe walked to the back of the SUV and removed the license plate. He then climbed in the back and spread heavy plastic over the cargo area. Having completed those tasks, Thorpe drove to the motel and backed the Tahoe up to room 142.

Pulling a baseball cap low on his head and rolling up his collar, Thorpe grabbed the roll of plastic and a backpack. He walked to the motel's door with his chin tucked to his chest. Arriving, he knocked lightly. Kaleb opened up. Thorpe stepped inside the musty room, closed the door, and tossed the equipment on the bed. As Kaleb's eyes followed the equipment through the air, Thorpe stepped toward Kaleb with his right foot and cracked him on the jaw with a sharp elbow. The informant reeled backwards onto the floor. In a matter of seconds, Thorpe had Kaleb's mouth, hands, and feet secured with tape.

The blow didn't knock Kaleb unconscious. Instead, he lay on the floor and stared at Thorpe with wide, terrified eyes. Thorpe searched Kaleb's person and found a voice-activated tape recorder in a pocket of his jacket. Thorpe hit rewind on the small machine and then pressed play. Some of the conversation he and Kaleb had on the trip over played on the machine. *Fucking snitches*, Thorpe thought as he rewound the tape to the beginning and hit play again. The recording began in the middle of his earlier phone conversation with Kaleb. After the phone conversation terminated, a woman's voice was heard: "Who's that?"

"Fucking pigs again. They won't leave my ass alone. I ain't done shit," Kaleb replied over the tape.

"What they want?"

"They keep trying to blackmail me into giving up my homies. I ain't told them nothin'. Just keep feedin' 'em fulla shit."

"Just tell them to fuck off," replied the woman's voice.

"Baby, who's going to take care of you if they send me to prison on some bullshit case?"

"Always fuckin' with the black man," the female agreed.

"Ain't that the truth. Don't tell anybody what I'm doin', baby. Nobody will understand I'm just playin' em.' I'll shovel some shit into this cracker and be right back."

Thorpe hit stop on the tape recorder. "Kaleb, Kaleb, Kaleb… I wish you hadn't told your girlfriend." This was a problem but there was nothing Thorpe could do about it. Thorpe pulled out his knife—the act instantly bringing about muffled cries and a thrashing on the floor. He carried the knife to the bed where he cut off a section of plastic and spread it out on the floor at Kaleb's feet. He then propped a wooden chair in the middle of the plastic before lifting Kaleb off the dirty brown carpet and seating him in the middle. It was all very theatrical.

Thorpe used duct tape to secure the prisoner to the chair by wrapping it around his chest. Then, he stepped toward the door, engaging the deadbolt and chain. Thorpe approached the bed and opened his backpack. For added effect, he removed several crude instruments, including a pair of small pruning shears and a rusty hacksaw. After, Thorpe approached his captive and stood to the side where he couldn't be kicked. "Kaleb, I need you to listen very carefully. Are you listening to me?"

Kaleb nodded his head briskly, causing several beads of sweat to drip onto his lap.

"Good. First of all I apologize for lying to you. It was the only way I could get you here without causing a scene. I don't like scenes." Thorpe was doing his best impression of a man deranged; then again maybe an act wasn't required. "Second, as you may have figured out, I'm not a detective with Internal Affairs, but I assure you I am a cop. My real name is Jonathan Thorpe, Sergeant Jonathan Thorpe. You may have heard my name mentioned about thirteen months ago."

It took a few seconds to register, but Kaleb's eyes morphed from confused fear to terror.

"I see you recognize the name. Good, then you know why you're here." Thorpe was almost whispering now. "Kaleb, I want to know who killed my family, and you're going to tell me. If you give me this 'I-don't-know bullshit,' you're going to instantly regret it." Thorpe nodded his head toward the instruments on the bed. "If you don't cooperate, you're leaving this room chunk by chunk in bloody sheets of plastic. I know that's pretty fucked up, but, given the circumstances, you can understand I'm pretty pissed off. Can't you, Kaleb?"

Kaleb didn't respond—possibly couldn't—and Thorpe decided to ease up on the scare tactics before his captive went into shock. Kaleb wasn't like Marcel Newman; he was broken already. Thorpe snapped his fingers in front of Kaleb's face. "But none of that has to happen, Kaleb. Just answer my questions truthfully. Some things I already know, so it had better match up. I'm going to remove the tape now and you're not going to scream are you?" Kaleb shook his head and Thorpe removed the tape. "Who killed my family?" Thorpe began.

"Deandre and Damarius Davis," Kaleb stated. His body and voice were trembling so violently he was difficult to understand.

"*How* do you know?"

"They called me the night they did it. Wanted to meet. They said they were doing something for somebody and they..." Thorpe held up a finger then walked over to the bed while repeating Kaleb's words "something for somebody?" as he reached for the pruning shears.

"Okay! Okay! Deandre called and said he had to see me right now. Me, Deandre and Damarius was real tight, friends since back in the day. I talk to the police, but I would never rat them two. We was like brothers. Anyways, he calls, and I can tell he's spooked. Wants to meet me at my apartment. Tells me to kick whoever I got inside the fuck out. So I tell my girl to get lost—that some serious shit is going down and she don't need to be a part of it."

Kaleb was talking fast, not the kind of speech pattern someone has when they're fabricating details. He was rattling information off rapid fire, his adrenaline causing him to speak in streams. "Anyways, Deandre and Damarius show up about twenty minutes later, and they're scared crazy. Deandre says he met Stephen Price earlier and Price gave him a half key of cocaine. Says he wanted them to plant the coke at some cracker's house to set him up...."

Stephen Price? Thorpe's head felt as though it were going to explode. He momentarily lost all his auditory sense and had to steady himself against the wall. His heart rattled like a drum, and it felt as though his throat had swollen shut. He started employing relaxation techniques and hoped the shock hadn't registered on his face too badly. When Thorpe finally regained control of himself, he noticed Kaleb was still rapidly imparting information. As shocked as Thorpe had been, it wasn't even close to what his captive was experiencing. He didn't want to interrupt Kaleb's recounting of events, but Thorpe had missed a good portion of what the man had just said.

"Just a second Kaleb, I lost you back there. I want you to start again at the point where Stephen Price gave Deandre a half-kilo of cocaine. You do mean Stephen Price, the TULSA POLICE OFFICER, don't you?" Thorpe asked, hoping against all logic that Kaleb was referring to a different Stephen Price.

"Yeah, Stephen Price, the cop. So Deandre says Price gives him a half-kilo of soft and wants him to hide it in this dude's house on the south side of town. We're all tight: the brothers, Price, and me and we've all done work before. But this shit was a little different so Deandre asks Price what's up. Price won't tell him shit, just says the less he knew the better—won't tell him who the dude is or anything. He just says if they do this they'll be taken care of... *forever*. He tells them the job's a piece of cake; that he's got someone watching the house and no one is home. He even gives them a key to the fucking house."

Kaleb suddenly stopped talking. He looked hesitant to continue.

"Go on, asshole, I already know how this story ends," Thorpe demanded.

"Anyway, Price gives them instructions on how to get there and describes what the place looks like. Well, Deandre and Demarius go over there and check it out. They notice lights on, but they don't see anybody moving. Shit, everybody leaves their lights on when they're away anymore, so they figure Price knows what he's talking about. They find a place to park and decide to go in the back. They get to the backdoor, and there's two locks. Well the key fits one of the locks but not the other. Now they're like…What the fuck do we do now? So they end up kicking in the back door. What dumb fucks. I mean they're there to plant drugs in a fucking house, and they end up kicking in the back door. Kinda fucks-up the purpose, doesn't it?"

Thorpe just nodded. "Yeah, real dumbasses."

"Sorry man, I…"

"Just go on," Thorpe said, not wanting concocted sympathy from a man he was going to kill.

"Anyways, they kick in the back door and get in the house when a woman comes down the hall with a fucking gun in her hand. They told me they had no choice but to…shoot her. Then they hear a scream and see this little girl standing at the bottom of the stairs. I guess the girl…your girl…well those dudes didn't have any masks on or anything…so they decide they had to…"

"Kill her?" Thorpe finished the sentence with the faint taste of his own bile.

"Yeah, man. They killed her. Killed 'em both, I guess."

"No guessing about it, asshole. Why would Stephen Price, *the cop*, want to plant dope in my house?"

"I don't know. I sure as hell wasn't going to ask. If Price knew I know what I know, I'd be dead too."

"Tell me the rest. Tell me everything."

"After they…did your family, they panicked. They forgot all about the dope they was supposed to plant in your house and just took off. That's when they called me and headed over to my place. They was *jacked*, started telling me what I just told you and were talking bout bouncin'. They were sayin' how Price was going to kill them for fucking up. They were talkin' about flippin' the half-kilo to make some money while they got the fuck outta Tulsa. But while we was talkin', Price calls them on their cell phone and asks what went wrong. They start to tell him the story over the phone, but he tells them they gotta meet in person. Tells them they can still fix this shit—make it look like the husband killed the family. Those two dumb fucks actually bought that line of shit and left to go meet Price. That's the last I ever saw of 'em. They were killed the same night. That motherfucker Price killed 'em—I know it."

"Where were they supposed to meet Price?'

"They didn't say. I didn't ask."

"Did they know they'd killed the wife and child of a police officer?"

"I don't think so. They never said...I think if they'd known they would have said."

"How did Price get a key to my house?"

"Man, I don't know...honest!"

"Kaleb, you said Damarius, Deandre, and you all 'done work' with Price before. What'd you mean?"

"Shit. Price was movin' dope since we was kids. He was always the smartest of us...never got caught — well at least nothing his uncle never got him out of." Stephen's uncle was also a Tulsa Police Officer. "We couldn't believe it when he became a cop."

Neither could anyone else. "He keep moving dope when he became a police officer?"

"He'd front us every once in a while—we'd pay him part of the bank. Some brothers were bitchin' he was takin' dope off 'em and never puttin' their asses in jail. Makes you wonder where that dope was goin'. We been tight for years, but lately he's been hangin' with a bunch of Nabahoods. Wouldn't be surprised if he didn't have something goin' with them. Still, he didn't move near as much shit after he went five-o. Didn't wanna touch it anyway, maybe had other niggas movin' it for him. I'm not sure, man...just rumors of rumors. If he was in the game, he was keepin' that shit sealed."

"Besides the Fifty-Seven's and the Nabahoods. Who else was Price friendly with?"

"Shit, everybody. He even postin' with Slobs."

"What other cops do you consider friendly?"

"Shit, you know already."

"Pretend I don't," Thorpe growled.

"Besides Price? Phipps hangs with us Fifty-Seven Streeters. Pretty sure he might sell some stuff on the side or got some homeboys do it for him. I know he used to hang out with the Double D brothers, but not much when I was around. Shit, I wonder if he knows I been talkin'?"

"Officer Andrew Phipps? Who else?"

"Man, a few of the black officers. I mean, shit most of 'em grew up here—they ain't just gonna forget where they come from. But as far as livin' the life? Corn Johnson hangs with some ballas. Don't know shit bout 'em though. He used to jack up some of ours for dope but didn't arrest 'em. Man, but lots of those guys don't mess with you for nuttin'. Know they'll be an Uncle Tom in the 'hood."

"What about Stephen's uncle, Marcus, he dirty?"

"Nah. He's old school. He don't fuck with us much either. Damn sure kick a nigga's ass though. Good thing is, he don't take you to jail—just kicks your ass and leaves you bleedin' in the street."

"Officer Charlie Peterson?" Thorpe asked.

"Same thing, his boys sling, but he don't."

"What are you forgetting to tell me, Kaleb?"

"Man, I told you everything I know. Fo' real."

Thorpe was pacing the room like a caged animal. "I want you to sit there and think awhile. I have to do some thinking of my own. Don't start running your fucking mouth until I tell you to. When I do, you better have thought of something else to give me."

Thorpe sat on the bed's cheap comforter and tried to gather himself. Why would Stephen Price, fellow Tulsa Police Officer, want to plant dope in Thorpe's house?

Thorpe decided this wasn't the time or place to dwell on Price. He cleared his head to deal with more immediate problems, namely Kaleb Moment. He had spent enough time in this motel room with his cooperative guest. Sooner or later his cooperation would end and he'd have a problem on his hands. Thorpe had come to this room with the intent of killing Kaleb and discretely disposing of his body. He had become infuriated during Kaleb's revelations, but the anger had been redirected. This kid had only come by some information he wished he'd never heard. On the other hand, he had known the circumstances behind his family's killings for thirteen months and had offered nothing, not even an anonymous phone call.

Thorpe tried to place himself in Kaleb's shoes. Had he been raised by the same people, in the same neighborhood, he may have reacted the same way. Thorpe realized he was facing a similar crossroads now: What would the average parent of a slain child do with the information Thorpe now possessed? He figured most would probably take what information they had to the authorities and hope for justice. But Thorpe knew justice wouldn't be served in this case—unless he dealt it. All the information Kaleb possessed would be considered hearsay in court and wouldn't be admitted as evidence. And that would be *if* you could get Kaleb to testify in the first place. Then there was the fact that Kaleb was a known drug dealer whose testimony couldn't be relied upon anyway. The only two people who could directly testify against those responsible were killed the same night as his family.

Thorpe had a decision to make here and now: If he let Kaleb go, Thorpe would surely be headed straight for prison. However, if he killed Kaleb just to avoid being incarcerated, then he wasn't any better than the shit bags he was hunting down.

Thorpe knew he'd been speeding down the proverbial slippery slope head first, but this was too much. He had to maintain some degree of self-respect even if it meant a lifetime behind bars. Thorpe could deal with prison, as long as he got justice for his slain family. Thorpe stood, walked back over to the wooden chair beside his captive, and sat. "Mr. Moment, what have you thought of to tell me?"

"Man, I swear I've been thinking—that's everything man. I don't know no more!"

"Kaleb, what do you think I should do with you?"

Kaleb had begun to relax ever so slightly, but after this question, all the previous tension could be seen returning to his body and facial muscles. A vein appeared on his forehead. His heartbeat became visible as it pulsated above his sweaty brow. It was almost as if Kaleb hadn't even considered he might be killed despite his cooperation.

"Relax, Kaleb. I'm not going to kill you."

"Bullshit, man! You're going to kill me."

"I'm not going to lie to you, Kaleb. I was going to gut you right here in this room on the sheet of plastic. But not now. I tried to look at this deal from your point of view, and I probably would have done the same thing you did—nothing. If you would've talked, you'd have been a dead man. Besides the two true killers were already dead, right?"

"Yeah, man, that's fo' real man. I—"

"Kaleb! Shut up and let me finish. I'm going to let you go because I think you got put in a fucked-up spot. However, someone like you is liable to see my generosity as a weakness." Kaleb was shaking his head and started to open his mouth to speak. "Kaleb, I said to keep your mouth shut until I tell you to speak. As I was saying, a guy like you might see this as a weakness. To tell you the truth, the *smart* thing to do would be to kill you. But the *right* thing to do is give you a chance. Kaleb, you may've had a shitty life and been put in a shitty spot but what you chose to do with your life was your decision. You chose to be a dope dealer, and you chose to be a snitch. Since you snitched on your homeboys, I know you'd have no trouble snitching on me. Over the next few weeks, there's going to be a lot of fucked-up shit happening, and you're a smart enough guy to put two and two together."

Thorpe glanced at the crude cutting instruments still lying on the bed, "If I hear you've breathed a word of this to anyone, you will die a slow and painful death. If you don't believe me, watch the news the next few days. In fact, first thing in the morning you're going to see on T.V. how your good friend Marcel Newman died a horrific death in a lonely barn next to his house. In case you haven't figured it out yet, Marcel is the one who gave me your name. I decided I didn't like—or trust Marcel—and he got fucked-up royal for it. I may be letting you go now, but I barely came to this decision. I figure it this way—I let *you* decide if you live or die. If you talk, then you've decided your fate for me. My conscience won't be bothered because it was your decision. Do you think I'm capable of killing you, Kaleb?"

Kaleb nodded his head but didn't say a word.

"Someday, Kaleb, you're going to get caught pushing dope again and you're going to think, "If I give up a cop, I'm home free," and then you'll consider protective custody—DON'T. I can, and I will, find you *anywhere*."

Thorpe hoped he was driving the point home. He needed to at least put enough fear into Kaleb so he would keep his mouth shut for the immediate future. "Kaleb, I'm a different kind of cop. That's something you're going to realize in the next few weeks." Thorpe pulled out a serrated knife and held it up to Kaleb's face. He then leaned down and cut the bindings on his captive's legs. He tore the bindings from Kaleb's chest and instructed his captive to remove the excess tape. Thorpe gathered up his belongings and told Kaleb to walk out the door and get in the truck—holding his jacket so as to conceal his still-bound hands. Thorpe drove around the building and across the street to the dark parking lot of a nearby biker bar. Thorpe parked the SUV and turned towards Kaleb. "Kaleb, are we friends?"

"Uh...sure..."

"Bullshit. We're never going to be friends, asshole. You so much as mention my name and your family won't be able to recognize your remains. Thorpe grabbed Kaleb by the chin, and watched his eyes flash with fear. With one swift motion, Thorpe slashed Kaleb with a knife diagonally across the face. "Now every time you look in the mirror, you'll be reminded what I'm capable of." Thorpe cut the tape on Kaleb's wrists and removed his bindings. The blood from Kaleb's head wound was now running down his face and onto his shirt. "Get the fuck out of here, and be glad you're still alive. Your first test will be explaining that head wound to the hospital staff."

Kaleb staggered out of the SUV on weak legs. As Thorpe drove away, he noticed Kaleb making his way toward Memorial Drive. Wherever Kaleb's first stop would be, it sure as hell wouldn't be the biker bar. Thorpe turned north on Memorial and couldn't help but think he was on borrowed time.

Eleven

Wednesday
February 7th
Afternoon

THORPE HAD A LONG BUT RESTLESS SLEEP during which he had recurring dreams. In them, he was hunting large game with an assortment of weapons. The terrain in his dreams oscillated from city, jungle, forest, and desert. But one thing remained constant, every time he had his quarry in his sights, he was overcome with a sense of being hunted himself. Feeling a presence looming over him, he'd turn to find nothing. When he would return his attention to his prey, he'd discover the animal had disappeared.

The meaning of the dreams wasn't lost on Thorpe. Just because the Rat Squad hadn't rousted him out of bed in the middle of the night didn't mean an investigation hadn't been launched or that Kaleb hadn't notified the FBI. The smart thing would have been to put a bullet in the kid's head. Because he'd left Kaleb alive, Thorpe was feeling the pressure to act immediately. But mistakes were generally the fruit of haste. Thorpe decided he would take no action until tomorrow. He needed time to formulate a plan. Thorpe picked up his cell phone and called Gail, a civilian employee who served as the office's secretary. All the investigators referred to her as "Ms. Moneypenny," in reference to Ian Fleming's fictional character in James Bond novels and films.

"Special Investigations Division."

"Hello, Miss Moneypenny," Thorpe said, attempting a British accent.

"Hello, James."

"Actually it's John."

"Hello, John."

"Do you ever get tired of this routine?" Thorpe asked.

"Never," Gail lied.

"I'm sure. Could you put me down for a vacation day?" he asked. "I've decided to give aspiring world dictators a holiday."

"Everyone needs a holiday."

"How's M?" Thorpe jokingly asked. 'M' is James Bond's and Miss Moneypenny's fictional boss in the British Secret Intelligence Service. In this case, he was referring to their actual boss, *Major* Richard Duncan.

"She's an idiot and a bitch," Gail replied. Duncan was actually a man, but the gender-swap allowed Gail to insult the Major even if he were standing right next to her. It also added an extra bit of amusement for parties on both ends of the line. "I think she needs to find a man," Gail giggled.

Having called in a vacation day, Thorpe had the entire afternoon and night to himself. He entered his barn for a workout. As he lifted weights and worked on the heavy bag, he obsessed about the connection between Stephen Price and his family's murder. *Why would that asshole want to set him up to take the fall on a drug charge?* Thorpe could only remember one incident with the man.

Thorpe had been in his current position as supervisor of the Organized Gang Unit when one of his officers arrested a suspect with trafficking weight in crack cocaine. The suspect was a first timer and didn't want to waste his get-out-of-jail-free card from the District Attorney's Office. He agreed to do five deals to keep the incident off his record.

The first credit on the confidential informant's payment plan would be a man he knew only as "Rocc." According to the CI, Rocc was always good for at least an 8-ball on short notice. The CI refused to do a buy-bust; he was too scared to purchase dope as officers swooped in and arrested the dealer. Instead, the CI called Rocc and ordered an 8-ball of crack. He agreed to meet Rocc at a convenience store at a busy intersection. The only information Thorpe's unit had on the suspect was he usually drove a newer, white Dodge Stratus.

The plan, if possible, was to get the Stratus stopped for traffic violations *before* it reached the convenience store—a common tactic used to keep from burning informants. The CI wouldn't be waiting there; he'd be sequestered away. As with all dope deals, the plan changed and changed again. After a long game of musical "meets," the Stratus finally showed. Of course by this time the marked patrol units were spread all over the city and weren't in position to make a stop. Thorpe and his team donned raid jackets and took the Stratus down in a parking lot.

Two sons of a Tulsa police officer were inside the vehicle. Lyndale Peterson was behind the wheel. His younger brother, Leon, occupied a back seat. Interestingly, a Hispanic gang member—a Latin King out of Chicago—was riding shotgun. Eventually, officers found an 8-ball in Lyndale's sock and two loaded handguns under the driver's seat. More cocaine was found hidden in the engine compartment, and Leon had a small amount of marijuana in his pants' pocket. All three suspects were arrested. Surprisingly, Lyndale manned-up and took responsibility for both weapons and all the cocaine. Unfortunately, that led to the release of the Chicago gang member, who never said shit. Leon received a stint in the county jail because the marijuana charge was a second offense, but Lyndale got hammered. He was a three-time loser and was sent to prison for a serious stretch.

After the incident, Officer Charlie Peterson filed a complaint with Internal Affairs stating Thorpe planted dope on his sons: Because the CI was confidential, Thorpe couldn't tell Peterson that his boys had been set-up in a sting or share any of the details of the investigation. Doing so could get the informant killed. However, the information was provided to Internal Affairs investigators, and Thorpe was exonerated.

Afterward, Thorpe heard rumors that the Peterson sons were close friends of Price. If Price thought Thorpe had framed his friends, it could explain why he'd be interested in returning the favor.

If Thorpe were caught with an unexplained half-kilo of cocaine in his house, he would—at the very least—be fired and almost assuredly sent to prison. Price would have his revenge.

If this theory were accurate, was the elder Peterson involved? Were any others? Thorpe wouldn't be satisfied unless he was sure all responsible had paid with their lives. He needed a way to reveal all the players and establish their guilt.

Thorpe was pulled away from his thoughts and workout by an irksome beeping. He recognized the number displayed on his pager's screen. Thorpe punched in the numbers on his cell phone.

"Hull."

"Hey, Bob, it's John. You paged?"

"Yeah. Just wanted to give you a quick update on the search warrant. We found a pair of boots in L.A.'s closet and guess what?"

"They matched the tread patterns left in the barn?"

"Correct, Carnac. He tried to clean them up, but it appears there may be some blood stains remaining on the boots."

"What's L.A.'s story?"

"He says he's happy as a dog with two dicks that Marcel's dead, but he didn't have anything to do with it."

"Go figure. You hit him with the boots yet?"

"Yeah, we told him we have the boots he wore at the scene. Told him he didn't clean them good enough. Blood stains were still on them. Told him if the lab proved the blood was Marcel's, he was fucked. He asks, 'What boots?' So we show him. You know what he says then?"

"I have no idea."

"He says, 'Those aren't my boots.'"

"Ah, the old 'those aren't my pants' ploy." It wasn't uncommon to arrest someone, find dope in his pocket — only to have the suspect claim, "These aren't my pants." Apparently dope dealers would like cops to think they share pants with one another, which *would* explain why they were always ill fitting and falling halfway down their asses.

"Yeah. So we say, 'How come you have someone else's boots in your closet?' and you know what he says to that?"

"He claimed you planted them there," Thorpe answered.

"Close. He said someone left them on his front porch. He thought they were mint, and they fit, so he decided to keep them."

"Yeah, people leave anonymous boots on my porch all the time. How did he explain the 'L.A.' Marcel wrote at the scene?"

"He didn't. He said 'Fuck you, I want my lawyer now.'"

"Probably the smartest thing he's ever said. You guys find anything else?"

"We're still sifting through a lot of stuff at the scene and the warrant. Plus we're still waiting for the autopsy. That's the biggest news so far. What time are you coming in?"

"Sorry, Bob, I know it's bad timing, but I took the night off. Needed a break. Something you should consider doing every once in a while."

"I'll rest when I'm dead."

"That won't be long if you never take off. In the meantime, can I take out…what is it now…wife number twelve…for you tonight? I'll show her a real good time."

"Fuck you, Thorpe. She'd rather get twelve inches from me once a month then three inches from you every night."

Thorpe laughed, "Sounds like you've used that line before, Bob."

"Maybe once or twice. We can make do without you, John. Take a break. You've earned it."

"Your wife's earned it."

"You're relentless."

"Bob, that's why your wife puts up with my three inches."

"Have I told you to fuck off yet?"

Hull was a good cop and one hell of an interrogator. Thorpe had noticed Hull kept prompting him to hypothesize what L.A.'s responses were to questions. *Was he being interrogated himself?* It was hard to determine—Bob was a tough guy to read. Thorpe hoped he was as equally tough to read; he had tried to respond as though he hadn't known the truth. Thorpe also noticed Bob hadn't mentioned L.A.'s hair fiber on the duct tape. But, there was a lot of evidence to sift through and the results of the autopsy were still out. Thorpe doubted L.A. could come up with an alibi strong enough to contradict the physical evidence mounting against him. These guys were notorious for producing not-so-credible witnesses who would swear the offender was in their presence at a far-away location at the time whatever heinous crime was committed. Unless L.A. was sitting in a casino with two hundred cameras trained on him during the time period Marcel was killed, he was going to be convicted. Thorpe had no remorse about L.A. serving a life sentence or possibly being condemned for a killing Thorpe had committed. L.A. was a murderer and everyone knew it, even the judge who was forced to release him because of uncooperative witnesses—witnesses who were probably threatened into silence.

Thorpe looked at his watch and realized he'd been working-out for nearly two hours. He'd been in such a state of concentration he wasn't even sure what exercises he'd completed. Earlier, he'd convinced himself not to act until tomorrow. But now he realized that wasn't going to be possible; he needed to act quickly and decisively. He hadn't thought it was possible for this to get more personal, but it had. His family may have been murdered by fellow police officers—by his *brothers in blue*. It might not have been their intention to kill his wife and daughter, but that consideration wouldn't be enough to spare those responsible. They had intended to falsely accuse Thorpe of a crime that would cost him his job and his freedom. Instead they had taken so much more. Thorpe had waited thirteen months for Hull and his crew to find the killers. Had Hull found them, they would never have lived long enough to see prison. But Thorpe had found the bastards on his own and was prepared to secure reparations.

Twelve

Wednesday
February 7th
Evening

THORPE SAT OUTSIDE THE RIVER FALLS APARTMENTS near 81st and Memorial Drive in the privacy of a blacked-out Chevy Impala. The complex had neither a river nor falls but was a nice, fairly expensive apartment complex situated behind a QuikTrip convenience store and a Wendy's fast food restaurant. Thorpe had entered the complex riding the rear bumper of a car that had remotely activated the apartment's iron gates.

Earlier, Thorpe had stopped by Riverside Division or RID, the department's uniformed subdivision that covered the south and west sections of the city. Because of current manpower shortages, the front desks of the uniformed divisions were only manned during business hours. Thorpe found it ridiculous the substations were closed at any time, day or night—people should be able to find and talk to a cop at a police station. However, on this evening, the lack of basic services had been to his advantage: He had needed information contained behind the front desk of the substation, and no one was around to watch him snoop. Thorpe had used a four-digit code to enter RID, walk behind the desk, and locate a Rolodex filled with Riverside officers' names, addresses, and phone numbers. Once he recorded the necessary information, he checked third-shift's line-up and was pleased to see Stephen Price was on duty.

His next stop had been at SID to procure equipment for the night's activities. He'd hoped to get in and out of his office without much fanfare but had engaged in a brief conversation with the sergeant over Vice, Gary Treece. Thorpe had explained that despite taking the night off, he'd needed to come in for a few minutes to "get some shit done for Major Duncan." Treece, who also worked for Duncan, needed no further explanation. Following the encounter, Thorpe had made it out of the building with a "Birddog" tracking device, directional microphone, voice changer, and keys to a gray Chevy Impala—none of which he signed out.

The Birddog device consisted of a magnetic transmitter easily placed on a vehicle's undercarriage. It emitted an RF signal detected by a directional receiver with a range of two to four miles. Thorpe could have selected a GPS tracking device, which was much more accurate and functional, but the Birddog did have an advantage crucial for this mission; it left no electronic signature that could later be traced back to the device or to Thorpe. GPS utilized satellites and could be traced back to the particular unit if anyone bothered to check. Plus, SID's GPS tracking devices had external antennas, which were more easily noticed by someone you were following.

The disadvantage of the Birddog was its short range. If you got out of range, the only way of reacquiring your target was to drive around until you came within the spectrum of the transmitter. Then it became a game of Marco Polo. But in this case, Thorpe had no choice. He couldn't use a unit that could be traced back to SID equipment. The directional microphone he had borrowed was fairly good at picking up conversations in open areas but could not penetrate enclosed spaces. The federal government and military had laser microphones that could pick up conversations from outside a building by converting vibrations off window glass into spoken words. Unfortunately for Thorpe, SID had yet to acquire this expensive technology.

Outside Stephen Price's apartment, Thorpe lurked behind the Impala's deeply tinted windows as a patrol car turned the corner and found a parking space. He watched Price, who was built like an NBA forward, uncoil his long, lean body from the cruiser and lumber off toward his apartment. It was some thirty minutes before his shift was scheduled to end. If Thorpe had to guess, Price had snuck home early without putting in for leave. He was probably still checked out on a call somewhere on the other side of town. Thorpe had hoped Price would give an indication which personal car was his—but no such luck. Waiting a few seconds, Thorpe exited his car and located Price's apartment on the second floor of the three-story apartment building. The balcony of Price's apartment overlooked the parking lot where his patrol unit sat.

Thorpe returned to the parking lot and scanned the vehicles around the patrol car looking for any clues that might indicate which one was Price's Privately-Owned-Vehicle. Thorpe ruled out several just because they didn't fit what he thought a single male would drive. He was still trying to formulate a plan when he noticed Price descending the stairs wearing slacks, a leather jacket, and size fourteenish dress shoes. Price got into a vehicle befitting his size, a silver Hummer III, *nice ride*. Thorpe waited until the Hummer backed out of its space and rounded the corner before he followed.

Despite how it's portrayed in the movies, it's almost impossible to follow a car using one surveillance vehicle—unless the person you're following is totally clueless or you're utilizing a tracking device. Thorpe barely caught a glimpse of the Hummer turning west on 81st Street before he himself pulled up to the complex's exit. He let several cars get between himself and Price, then fell in line. The traffic lights at 81st and Memorial turned green allowing Price to turn left on Memorial Drive. Thorpe watched as the Hummer traveled south a quarter of a mile before pulling into the parking lot of The Ocean Floor, a night club that attracted a younger, sexually driven clientele.

Continuing south on Memorial Drive, Thorpe watched the Hummer search for a parking space outside the busy bar. He continued on, glancing over his shoulder every few seconds to make sure the Hummer didn't leave the parking lot. Another quarter mile south of the bar, he found a safe place to conduct a U-turn. Back at the Ocean Floor's parking lot, he found a space several rows behind the Hummer, waited about ten minutes, retrieved the transmitter, and exited his Impala.

Thorpe was wearing a heavy jacket over a hooded sweatshirt, which he pulled over his head as he passed in front of the unoccupied SUV. He scanned the cars near the Hummer and, not seeing anyone inside, walked up to the passenger side, bent down, and attached the transmitter near the rear of the vehicle. Thorpe then reentered his own car and drove to an Irish bar on the northeast corner of 81st and Memorial, directly across the street from QuikTrip. There, he activated the Birddog's receiver, which was, so far, receiving a strong, accurate signal.

Thorpe grabbed the voice changer and walked across Memorial to the QuikTrip. He didn't want to drive his car onto the lot because he was unsure about the presence of surveillance cameras. From experience, he knew the cameras didn't provide quality pictures, but they could often pick up the make and model of a car. In addition to his heavy jacket, Thorpe was wearing gloves and baggy pants. He still had the hood pulled over his head. As he approached the convenience store, he changed his gait and the manner in which he carried himself. He would have liked to make this phone call farther away but was afraid Price would drive out of range of the receiver before he returned. In the age of cell phones, it was becoming more difficult to find pay phones, but QuikTrip kept the antiquated devices outside their stores.

The handheld voice changer he'd acquired from SID was a cheap model, and he wasn't certain why they even had one. Whatever the reason, it was good enough for his purpose. Thorpe stood with his back to the cameras and punched in the cell phone number listed on Price's Rolodex card. He hoped Price would answer. After five rings he heard a male voice answer the phone. Loud techno music thumped in the background.

"Hello?" boomed Price's unmistakable baritone voice.

Thorpe spoke into the cheap electronic instrument, producing an unnatural metallic voice.

STEPHEN PRICE WAS INSIDE THE OCEAN FLOOR NIGHT CLUB enjoying views of short skirts and plunging necklines when his cell phone vibrated on his hip. Price retrieved the phone from his belt but didn't recognize the number on its screen. "Hello?"

"Get somewhere you can hear me."

Price thought one of his friends was fucking around with him again. He was obviously using some kind of contraption to alter his voice. "I can hear you...Who's this? This some kind of joke?"

"I know you killed Demarius Davis. I know you killed Deandre Davis." Price felt an acute pressure in his chest as though his heart was being inflated with an air compressor. *No fucking way he just heard that.* He must have misunderstood. "What? Who the fuck is this?"

"You killed them both and I can prove it."

Motherfucker! Motherfucker! Price's mind was racing. Feigning ignorance was all he could come up with as a defense, "What the fuck you talkin' about?"

"I want twenty-thousand dollars, or I'm going to the police. I'll call you in exactly one hour at this number with instructions. Understand?"

Price's brain was waging an internal battle with itself. *This can't be fucking happening! I knew this shit was going to happen!* "I don't understand shit, Motherfucker! Who is this?"

"One hour, at this number, with instructions." The stranger cut the call. Price slammed his cell phone closed. He pushed against people as he hurried towards the exit. Once outside, he flipped open his cell phone, retrieved the last number received, and hit send. The phone rang with no answer. Price paced up and down outside the bar, sweating in spite of the cold weather. Price brought up the number and again hit send. This time a male answered — but without the ominous metallic voice that had shattered his night's festivities. "Hello?"

"Who are you?" Price asked.

"Who are you?" the voice replied.

"Who the fuck is this?" Price demanded.

"I'm answering a damn pay phone, asshole!"

Price couldn't get his mind to settle down. "Damn it! Shit! Did you see who was on the phone before you?" Price asked.

"Look buddy, there wasn't anybody on the phone. I was walking into the store, the phone was ringing, I thought 'what the hell' and answered it."

"What pay phone is it? Where you at?"

"The Q.T. at 81st and Memorial."

Suddenly Price felt very exposed. His head was on a swivel as he closed his phone. He ran to his Hummer, peeled out of the lot, and dialed a familiar phone number.

THORPE WAS STILL PARKED on the southwest corner of 81st and Memorial. He was about to get "eyes on" his target when his tracking receiver notified him of Price's approach. Thorpe watched as the silver Hummer pulled up to the intersection and turned east. He listened to the audible alert on the Birddog receiver and realized Price had driven past his apartment. *He's on the move.* Thorpe followed, trying to stay well behind his quarry.

Halfway between Memorial and Mingo, Thorpe noticed the signal slow, stop, and reverse directions. Price was headed straight back at Thorpe, prompting him to hastily pull off into a neighborhood and kill the lights. He watched out his rear window. After a few seconds, he observed the Hummer traveling back to the east. Thorpe turned around in a driveway and was pulling back up to 81st Street to follow when he noticed the signal was coming towards him again. Price was performing a classic tail shaker, making U-turns in an effort to identify follow cars. Good. If he was trying to shake a tail, it meant he was going somewhere he didn't want to be followed. Thorpe backed into a driveway on the darkened street, watching as the Hummer passed on 81st Street. Thorpe waited for the signal to weaken before leaving the driveway and following. The receiver indicated an easterly route for nearly a minute, then it turned north and the signal began to weaken rapidly. Price was northbound on Highway 169. On the highway, Thorpe pushed the Impala as fast as it would go.

The Hummer was about a half mile ahead with several cars separating the two vehicles. At this distance, the Impala would only be a pair of obscure headlights in Price's rearview mirror. As Price topped a small incline, Thorpe noticed the signal on his Birddog begin to quicken. Price had come to a stop on the other side of the hill. If a car had been conducting a visual follow, it would crest the hill and pass Price before the driver realized what had happened.

Thorpe was impressed. Price was pretty good at shaking a tail for someone who had never done UC work.

Of course Price *had* been a dope dealer, and a lot of those guys learned the same skills on the streets. Thorpe pulled to the shoulder and waited for the signal to indicate movement.

For the next twenty minutes, Price continued to use similar tactics in an attempt to identify a tail. But Thorpe successfully stayed within range of the Birddog's transmitter and eventually tracked Price to an area in north Tulsa. Thorpe drove the neighborhood several times in a circular pattern, spiraling closer with each cycle, finally isolating the parked Hummer. Thorpe halted his car to the southwest, retrieved a gear bag, and set out on foot.

This particular neighborhood had been going through redevelopment and consisted mostly of black middle-income families. Thorpe was glad for the colder temperatures, the late hour, and the amiable neighborhood. All three elements helped Thorpe walk through the area without encountering fellow pedestrians.

The Hummer was parked on the south side of the street in front of two-story house with a brick face. There were two vehicles in the driveway and another car on the street in front of Price's Hummer. Thorpe memorized the license plate of the car in front of the Hummer and continued walking east. When he reached the end of the cul-de-sac, he turned and walked back along the north side of the road. He scanned for a hiding place. There wasn't any foliage sufficient to conceal an adult on the north side of the street, and the backyards of the homes were surrounded by wooden privacy fences. Thorpe risked a glance over one of the fences and noticed the yard was fairly deep. As quietly as possible, Thorpe called to see if any dogs were inside the yard. No growls or barks sounded in reply, so he scaled the fence.

This particular yard gave him the best view of the house across the street. Thorpe hit the ground with a large fixed-blade knife at the ready. Even though he'd heard no barks, he half expected to be fighting or fleeing a large dog any minute. Had this been a neighborhood anywhere north of here, he most likely would be leaping back over the fence with a disagreeable pit bull at his boots.

He ventured deeper in the yard and again called quietly for a dog—better to encounter one now than to feel Brutus breathing on the back of his neck later. Both the house and backyard remained quiet and dark. Feeling more relaxed, Thorpe returned to where he had leapt the fence. Using his knife partly as a cutting instrument and partly as a prying tool, he removed a section of fence at eye level. Now he could watch without sticking his head above the fence and silhouetting himself. Thorpe took a pad of paper from his jacket and recorded the license-plate number he had memorized. Next he retrieved binoculars from his equipment bag and recorded the make, model, and plates of the two cars in the driveway.

After about ten minutes, another vehicle turned onto the street and into the driveway. It activated motion lights on either side of the garage door. Thorpe trained his binoculars on the exiting driver. His theory was falling apart: the distinctive form of Brandon Baker walked toward the front door. Brandon was a white police officer who worked out of Gilcrease Division's Street Crimes Unit. He resembled Big Foot, not because of his size but because every square inch of his person was covered with coarse black hair. What the hell? He had a passenger with him who accompanied him to the front door. The second man was dressed a lot like Thorpe—in heavy garb; Thorpe couldn't even determine his race from this distance.

Five minutes later, an old beater pulled onto the street and illegally parked on the north curb line, directly in front of where Thorpe was concealed. Thorpe's original theory seemed to be reviving itself: Leon Peterson stepped out of the car. Leon was the youngest son of TPD officer Charlie Peterson. When Thorpe's unit had executed the "buy-bust," arresting a Latin King and both of Charlie's sons for trafficking in cocaine, Leon had received a thirteen-month sentence, though he was released much earlier. His brother, Lyndale, had received a twenty-year prison sentence and was still locked up. The diminutive Leon, who stood all of five-foot-four, appeared nervous as he left his car. He looked in every direction. Once he arrived at the doorstep, he searched his surroundings again before ringing the doorbell. As he waited for the door to be answered, he faced away from the house and shifted his weight from one foot to another. *He's scared shitless.* After a few seconds, the door opened.

Leon stuck his head in the door and looked around before committing his body to the interior. Thorpe figured Leon had ample reason to be nervous. Unlike his associates, who probably felt beyond reproach, Leon had once been held accountable for his actions. He had done time. Thorpe checked his watch; it was five minutes until he was due to make his phone call demanding a ransom. Of course Thorpe wasn't going to make that phone call—his goal had already been achieved: He had discovered at least some of those involved in his family's murder. With a few simple interrogation techniques, he would soon have his answers. Still, Thorpe desperately wished he could hear the conversation inside the home. The directional microphone he'd brought with him would be totally useless. He'd been hoping for an outdoor meeting.

Thorpe imagined there were heated discussions occurring inside the house: *Who all knew about the murders? Which one of the group had been talking? How should they handle the ransom call*—the one that wasn't coming? Thorpe wondered if they were bright enough to figure out this had all been a ruse to get them in one place and identify them. Thorpe considered what his plan of action would be if he were in their place: He'd make a phone call or send someone out the backdoor to conduct counter surveillance. Suddenly, Thorpe's back felt very exposed. There wasn't a whole lot he could do about it except try to stay attuned to his surroundings. It was a quiet night, and hopefully if someone started slinking around he would hear him coming. The yard Thorpe occupied was scattered with dry leaves. If the other yards were similar, Thorpe should be able to hear someone in time to take evasive action.

Despite the dropping temperature, Thorpe removed his hood, favoring hearing capabilities over shelter. It had been some time since the last arrival. Periodically, Thorpe would do squats in an effort to warm himself. Thankfully, he'd dressed for the occasion. The nip, however, was beginning to chew at his ears and through his boots.

Climate aside, if the group didn't disperse before daybreak, he'd need to find an alternate location or risk discovery by a homeowner or a dog let out for its morning bladder movement. But he needed to maintain surveillance as long as possible; undoubtedly there were others who had arrived before him, and they needed to be identified.

Thirty minutes passed before Thorpe caught a flash of movement to his left. A figure was walking in the front yards on the north side of the street. Based on height, it was probably Leon. Walking from east to west, the man's path would carry him in front of where Thorpe was concealed, separated only by the wooden fence. Thorpe noticed the figure disappear around the far side of the house to Thorpe's east. *Was the man going to jump the fence and search the backyards?* Thorpe quieted his breathing and focused his auditory sense. The sound of rustling leaves announced the appearance of the man in front of the house to his east. He was probably peering over the top of the fences. The man walked to a car that was parked on the north curb line, cupped his hands against the glass, and looked inside. *He's definitely looking for surveillance.* The gloom made it difficult to see, but Thorpe was almost certain it was Leon.

The one non-police officer was the only person who had considered the phone call might have been a set-up. As smart as Leon may have been though, he wasn't smart enough to arm himself; his hands were empty. If he did possess a weapon, he didn't have it at the ready. Leon was probably concerned about a police sting rather than being followed by a grieving, revenge-seeking killing machine. Leon abandoned the car and headed towards Thorpe's position.

Thorpe had a decision to make. He needed to act quickly. He could disappear around the house and hope that if Leon noticed the recently cut hole, he wouldn't determine that it was fresh. Or he could take Leon down now. Both options had negative and positive aspects; ultimately, Thorpe couldn't take the chance Leon would see the hole in the fence for what it was. Thorpe gathered his equipment and, in a crouched position, moved towards the back of the house. When he reached the rear of the home, he dumped his equipment and ran around to the west where he found a gate. Thorpe quietly unlatched the gate and walked to the southwest corner of the home. Peering around the corner of the residence, Thorpe just caught a glimpse of Leon disappearing around the east side of the house. Thorpe took one quick look around before sprinting across the concrete driveway and down a walkway in front of the residence. When he reached the corner of the house, he didn't even slow down to locate his target. Instead, he rounded the corner at full speed, spotting Leon in the process. Leon was positioned with his back to Thorpe, looking through the hole Thorpe had just abandoned. Leon heard the footsteps crashing behind him and turned to find Thorpe closing in on him at full speed. Thorpe held a knife concealed in his right hand. The knife, including the blade, was black as night, and Thorpe held the weapon so it wouldn't be noticed until it was too late. As Thorpe neared, Leon raised both hands, palms forward, above his head, in the classic "I surrender" stance.

Leon obviously thought he'd just been caught in a police operation. Thorpe hit the brakes and decided to play along with Leon's misguided thought process. "FBI, turn around." Leon complied immediately. *This was going to be too easy.* "Get down on your knees...Cross your ankles...Put your hands on the back of your head." Leon executed every command, allowing Thorpe to approach from behind and place him in Flexcuffs. Leon began spouting his defense, "Man I didn't have anything to do with this shit, they..."

"Shut the fuck up, you're going to blow our surveillance," Thorpe interrupted.

"Alright, alright, man, it's cool."

Thorpe pulled up his hoodie and kept Leon facing away from him. He couldn't afford to let Leon recognize him, not yet anyway. "You're going to fuck up this whole investigation, asshole. I'm the only one who has surveillance on this side. You're coming with me."

"That's cool man. I was just getting ready to call you guys."

Thorpe held Leon's cuffs and grabbed the back of his neck. Directing Leon from behind, Thorpe retraced his route, picked up his equipment, and took Leon back behind the hole in the fence. He put Leon on his belly with his head facing away from him. "Do they know you're out here?" Thorpe asked.

"Yeah, I told them I was coming out here to look around, but I was really coming out here to call you guys."

Yeah, right. Thorpe hadn't even discovered a cell phone during his pat-down. "How long do they expect you to be gone?"

"Man, I don't know. I said I was going outside to check things out. They just nodded their heads."

"Remember we've been watching this place. Who all's inside?"

"There's Price and..."

"I want first and last names," Thorpe demanded.

"...There's Stephen Price, somebody Baker—I don't know his first name, Thadius Shaw, Andrew Phipps, Corn Johnson, and another white dude I don't know."

Thorpe unwittingly shook his head. Not counting the unidentified "white dude," five of the men were, or had been, Tulsa police officers. All five had a reputation for being dope chasers. "White Dude" and Brandon "Big Foot" Baker were white guys. The other three men were black.

Andrew Phipps was about the same size as Thorpe, except thicker. His short hair exposed a skull shaped like a battering ram. His eyes set deep under a pronounced forehead. Phipps served on the department's Special Operations Team as a sniper. The Special Operations Team, SOT, was Tulsa's version of most departments' Special Weapons and Tactics Teams, SWAT. Unlike some other departments that had fulltime SWAT teams, Tulsa's SOT was a part-time assignment. The team practiced twice a month but otherwise held regular positions on the department.

Corn, short for Cornelius, was Phipps' best friend. Whoever said you can't judge a book by its cover had never met Corn. He walked around with a look of perpetual confusion. His mouth was always half open just begging for some drool to spill out. He didn't look very bright, and he wasn't. He'd been a member of Gilcrease Division's Street Crimes Unit. He resigned when he was caught providing drug dealers with sensitive information about investigations against them.

Phipps had worked in SID's day-shift narcotics unit but had been booted out after a year. The whole affair had been hush-hush, and Thorpe still didn't know the circumstances behind the removal.

"Who else is inside?" Thorpe continued.

"No one, man. That's it."

Thorpe wanted to ask whose house it was, but didn't want to sound uninformed. He still wanted Leon to think he was a federal agent here on official business. If that were actually the case, he'd damn well know whose house he'd been conducting surveillance on.

"Who else is involved that didn't show up?"

"Hey, man, I'm willing to cooperate but I want a lawyer. I want a deal on paper."

Leon was thinking about his future—he didn't have one. "At least tell me this...is there anyone else involved who didn't make it here tonight?"

"Yes," Leon answered.

"What have you been talking about tonight?" Thorpe asked.

"They're all fucked-up. They think one of us has been talking because someone has found out about this shit and's trying to blackmail Price. They're trying to figure out how to handle a phone call from some ransom motherfucker."

"Do they know we're on to them?" Thorpe continued with the FBI ruse.

"Those hole-diggers didn't even consider that until I brought it up. Now they don't know what to think."

Thorpe decided he didn't need to conduct surveillance any longer. Leon would provide any necessary information. But Thorpe needed to get him somewhere he could question him properly. Thorpe pretended to have a two-way conversation on his police radio: "Copy...You want me to remove the prisoner? Ten-four...I have to walk him to my car...No, I don't think he'll be a problem...We need to get his car outta here, or they'll know something's up. Okay, we'll just take his car then."

"Okay, Leon, I've got a replacement coming, so I'm walking you to your car. Understand?"

"Yeah, man, that's cool."

Leon was working so hard at appearing cooperative that it blinded him to the snake pit he was willingly walking toward. "We're both going to stroll out of here like best friends. You try to shout a warning or try to take off, and you can kiss any deals goodbye. Got it?"

"Yeah, man, I never wanted anything to do with this shit. I wanna help."

Thorpe retrieved Leon's car keys from his coat pocket. "If you do yell out or try to run, I'm going to knock the piss out of you. With your hands cuffed behind your back, you won't be able to break your fall with anything but your face. Okay, you're going to walk in front of me and listen to my directions. Let's go."

Thorpe easily lifted Leon by the shoulders, pointed him west, and told him to move. The two men walked to the passenger-side door of Leon's aging Cutlass. Thorpe kept an eye on the target house. After stuffing his captive in the car, he leaned against Leon's throat with his left forearm as he buckled him in with his right hand. Thorpe walked around the back of the car, making sure his hoodie covered his face, and let himself into the driver's seat as he tossed his bag in the back. Thorpe turned the car around in the cul-de-sac, then made his way out of the neighborhood.

Leon was in a talkative mood. "Where we goin'?"

"We have a mobile unit a couple miles away from here where we're monitoring this operation," Thorpe lied.

"Man, I can't have any TPD see me with you. There's too many of those bitches involved in this thing. They'll kill me."

I'll kill you. "Don't worry. We have a command post set up in a secluded area. No one is going to see you with us. When we get there, we'll let you use a phone to contact your lawyer. If we get pulled over by TPD in this piece of shit, just let me get out and handle it—you stay in the car."

"Cool."

Yeah, cool. Thorpe let Leon nervously ramble on about irrelevant topics as he drove past the North Side's only significant grocery store. Well, it used to be. Now it was an abandoned building. The area's city councilmen always accused city leaders of neglecting development in their part of town. The truth was, it wasn't economically viable to locate here. Let's face it—if people were able to make money at something, they were going to do it. Problem was, any retail store would lose more money to theft and robbery than they would make in sales. Pizza-delivery outfits wouldn't even come here because their drivers were always having their pizza paid for with threats and the occasional bullet. Thorpe continued north on one of the nicer streets in Tulsa—even though it ran through some of the harsher neighborhoods. The street had recently been expanded and was constructed of concrete rather than cheaper asphalt. The four-lane road was divided by a "green" median with decorative trees and flowers. Thorpe had cut his police teeth on this side of town and was very familiar with the area. He turned the Cutlass east on 36th Street North and passed a Tulsa Housing Authority complex on his left. Thorpe had worked shootings, murders, stabbings, rapes, and engaged in numerous foot pursuits in and around this complex. Just east of the complex, on the north side of 36th Street North, was a dirt road leading back into a large wooded area that still had working oil wells. Sometimes car thieves would drive their newly procured "hot boxes" to this secluded area, where they could strip the vehicles in privacy. Thorpe pulled left onto a dirt road he knew branched off into more tracks.

"You guys are back here?" Leon asked—finally getting a whiff something might not be kosher.

"You don't want to be seen do you?" Thorpe reassured him.

"No...Look, man, I don't know....this is...Can you show me some I.D.?"

It was dark in the car. Thorpe pulled out his neck badge and pointed it in Leon's direction.

"Look, man, this is kinda fucked up. Why don't you just take me to the FBI office?" Leon's survival instinct was finally throwing the red bullshit flag.

"The command post is just around this corner, Leon. Relax."

Thorpe could tell Leon was considering bailing out of the car. He could sense Leon eyeing the door release. *Too late now, asshole.*

Thorpe passed a black pump jack on his right. Also known as a nodding donkey because of its appearance, the pump jack was an over-ground drive for a piston pump on an oil well. Oklahoma's landscape was punctuated with the contraptions as Tulsa was once considered the oil capital of the world.

Thorpe heard the seat belt release and the distinctive sound of the belt retracting back into its housing unit. Leon had finally realized he was in some deep shit and was making an ill-conceived escape attempt. Thorpe didn't even try to stop Leon. Instead he rolled down both front windows, removed the key from the ignition, grabbed his gear bag from the rear seat, and stepped out of the Cutlass. He rounded the back of the car just in time to watch Leon slide through the window, land on his head, and somersault onto his back. He rolled to his feet—an acrobatic move and probably a painful one considering Leon was still cuffed behind his back. The man was definitely motivated.

Just as his prisoner gained his feet, Thorpe used a front-heel kick near Leon's kidney. The force sent the small man crashing to the ground on his left shoulder. Not being able to use his arms to control his balance, Leon landed awkwardly. When he attempted to stand again, his left shoulder drooped at an unnatural angle; the fall had apparently dislocated his left shoulder. Enough adrenaline coursed through his system to block the pain. Only determination registered on his face. There were no cries of agony.

"Take these cuffs off, motherfucker, and let me go to work on you...Fucking bitch," Leon screamed.

Thorpe slung the gear bag over his shoulder, sidestepped a kick, and grabbed Leon by his coat collar. He dragged him over to a pair of large oil storage tanks. A metal staircase led to a small catwalk spanning the tops of the tanks. Thorpe propped Leon against the metal railing, unzipped Leon's coat, and pulled the coat's shoulders down to his elbows, using the coat as a makeshift straightjacket. He then looped another cuff around the plastic still attached to Leon's wrists and wrapped it around the railing. Thorpe cinched the cuffs so they dug deeply into

Leon's skin. He didn't want to leave any space — motivated prisoners have been known to tear off their own skin in an attempt to free themselves. Thorpe stepped back from his prisoner, knelt down, and pulled back his hood. The two men stared at each other until recognition finally flooded into Leon's eyes.

"Aw fuck, man! That shit wasn't supposed to happen."

"But it did."

It was bitterly cold, but Leon sat drowning in sweat, fear and pain. Thorpe attached Flexcuffs to Leon's ankles, cinching them. Then he retrieved a rag and told Leon to open his mouth.

"Fuck you," Leon spit.

Thorpe walked behind his captive, isolated Leon's index finger from the rest and cranked it sideways until it snapped. Leon let out an agonizing moan but didn't scream. "Open your mouth," Thorpe repeated.

Leon opened his mouth, and Thorpe stuffed a rag inside, careful not to get his fingers bitten off. Thorpe secured the rag with duct tape, walked to the Cutlass, and backed the car up to where Leon was sitting. Thorpe retrieved a section of rope from the bag and secured one end around the Flexcuffs on Leon's legs. He then took the other end toward the rear of the car as he listened to Leon's muffled cries; he realized what was about to happen. Thorpe attached the rope to the underside of the Cutlass and returned to his thrashing prisoner.

"Leon, shut up and listen." His prisoner continued to thrash and squeal like a bound hog. Thorpe grabbed Leon by both ears and looked directly into his face. "Listen, Leon, you want to get out of this shit?" Leon looked pleadingly at Thorpe and nodded his head. "Good, it's important you listen carefully. Do you understand?" Leon nodded his head. He was openly crying now. "I'm going to ask you a series of questions. I know the answers to most—others I don't; you don't know which ones. All I want is honest answers—no matter how bad it may make you look. If you answer all the questions truthfully, you won't have to endure this." Thorpe motioned to the rope and the car as he spoke. "If you tell one lie…Just one…I'm going to fuck you up. And, Leon, I won't pull away fast; I'll tear you in half slowly like a sheet of paper. The first that'll go are your shoulders because of the way they're positioned. It's going to hurt like a bitch. And when you pass out—and I promise you Leon, you will pass out—I have some smelling salts to bring you back. And then we'll start all over again. Understand?"

Leon nodded vigorously.

"I'm going to remove your gag. If you scream, I'll smash your teeth in and force this rag back into your mouth, and then I'll start stretching you out…Understand?" Leon again nodded. Thorpe pulled off the duct tape and removed the rag from Leon's mouth. "Leon, tell me what's going to happen if you lie to me."

"You're going to fuck me up…But you're going to kill me no matter what I say."

"That's true. But it's your choice, Leon. Tell the truth, and you can die quick with a clear conscience. Lie and you can be slowly ripped apart and go straight to your maker with a lie on your lips. They killed my family, Leon, and those child-killers aren't worth protecting. They're not worth the pain I'm willing to dish out."

"Shit…man, I didn't…"

"Shut up with the whining, Leon, or so help me…"

"Fuck," Leon said, crying. "What do you want to know?"

"I want to know everything."

"Fuck, man, this whole thing started out so small and just blew up. My pops was so fucking pissed off at me and Lyndale when you popped us with that dope. He was mad at Lyndale, but he was crazy fucking mad at me. Lyndale had already had some trouble with the law, but I had done a pretty good job staying away from that shit. I even had some college. Fuck! It all started when Pops bailed me out of jail. He was talking about kicking me out of the house, disowning me, just flushing me down the fucking toilet. Man, I panicked…and I felt bad about letting down my old man. He's a good guy, a Christian, always tried to do right…"

"Get to the fucking point, Leon," Thorpe interrupted.

"Anyway, I start trying to convince him that you guys planted the dope on us. I wasn't lookin' to get anyone in trouble man; I was just tryin' to get out of it. So I keep on him about this shit, tell him this sergeant pulled some dope out and planted it on Lyndale. Told him you said they weren't going to let a bunch of niggas run around like we own the place. Man, I see this shit starting to take a hold on him, so I just keep workin' it. Pops starts making some phone calls, tells me to stay put, and leaves. A couple hours later he shows back up, tells me some others had been set up by you too. He wants me to come with him—tell my story to some other officers.

"So Pops puts me in his car and drives me over to Shaw's house. I walk in and about shit myself. Those two white dudes weren't there but all them other niggas was. Plus another that wasn't there tonight…Cole Daniels. Now I know this thing was snowballin' now, but by this time…You know, it's too late now. Pops tells me to tell them what happened, so I start telling them the same shit I told my pops. I could see these guys just getting more and more pissed. Especially Price and Phipps, they was workin' those other motherfuckers up. They start tellin' 'em 'bout other blacks they heard you set up. Man, it starts getting real bad then. They was wantin' your head. Everybody started arguin' about what to do. Some people wanted to report you, but most said that wouldn't do any good. Said all you white boys stuck together, that nuttin' would be done. Finally Price just told everyone to settle down. He'd handle it. Told everyone to stay quiet about this, that they couldn't trust the white man to do shit. Later, Price pulled me aside and got my cell phone number. Told me he would call later. Then Pops drove me away and told me not to talk about this anymore that it'd be handled…"

Thorpe could just picture the scene. Leon had fed their paranoia perfectly. They didn't even bother to question the validity of Leon's or Price's outrageous statements. They only heard what they wanted to believe, they were being targeted by a racist white cop. Thorpe decided not to interrupt Leon's recollection. He would pose questions when Leon had finished talking.

"…So I thought my part in all this shit was done. They wasn't going to report it. Nothing official would be said. I went about my merry fuckin' way. A few days later, Price calls and asks me if I remembered how to get to Shaw's house. He gave me a time to come over that night and told me not to tell anyone, not even my pops. So now I'm nervous, I don't know what the fuck he wants. So I shows up at his house, and there's about half the people there than was there was the first night. There was Baker, McDonald, Price, Phipps, Corn Johnson, Thadius Shaw, Daniels, and that same white boy that's there tonight."

"Is that Shaw's house you were at tonight?" Thorpe asked.

"Yeah."

"You said you don't know who the white guy is?"

"No, man. I just seen him that night and tonight. That's it."

"What does he look like?"

"Man, I don't know. He fo' real don't want to be seen. Both times he sits off in a corner with one of those fucking black ski-masks on. Hardly says a word and when he does he whispers like in that fucking Bat Man movie. Don't want to be known."

"You think he's a cop?"

"Fuck I know. Even though he don't say nuttin' the others kinda look at him like he's running the shit. Know what I mean? Fuckin' wait for him to nod and shit."

Thorpe was frustrated, "You gotta know his height, weight, something?"

"I don't fucking know, man. He's always sitting and wearing a big coat and shit. Might be about your size, might be fatter."

Thorpe wasn't getting anywhere in regards to the mysterious white man. "Go ahead with your story, Leon."

"So Price asks me how I'd like to get back the guy who was gonna send my brother to prison. And I ask how I was gonna be able to do that. Price pulls out a fat bag, points at me, and says, 'You gonna plant this in his house.' I said no fuckin' way I was gonna do that, but they kept pressing me, and I kept sayin' no. Finally Price says he'll take care of it, but they won't let me off the hook. They say I gotta be a part of it 'cause of what I know. They gave me your address and told me the times you worked and the days you was off. They told me you was married and had kids. Wanted me to watch the house and call when it was empty. The next night, I find your house. There was a car parked in the driveway, and the lights were on. I didn't want to sit in your neighborhood...You know a black dude sitting in your neighborhood is going to attract attention, so I just drove down the street every once in a while. That car was parked there the whole night. The next night I drive by your house, and there's no car, no lights, nuttin'. It looked empty, so I call Price and tell him. He tells me to keep watchin' the house and let him know if anyone comes home. I thought to myself *fuck that!*

"About an hour later, Price calls and asks me if the house is still empty. I told him yeah, but really I wasn't even watchin' the place anymore. Price didn't know that. He told me to keep watchin' the house until I was told I could leave; told me to call him if anyone went to the house. Shit, I was already halfway across town, but I wasn't going to tell Price that. Later that night, Price calls me, and he's mad as a motherfucker...Tells me the house wasn't empty. He wants to see me, but I made up some excuse...I wasn't about to go meet him. He tells me to keep my mouth shut until we could talk.

"The next day the shit about what happened at your place was all over the fuckin' news. Then I saw those two brothers were lit up the same night. I put two and two together, man...Fuckin' Price used, then killed those niggas...I know it. Figured he was going to kill me too. I was the only non-cop left in the know—my dad being one was probably only thing kept me alive. I put all this shit I'm tellin' you to paper and gave it to someone to keep safe. I told Price he'd better make sure I stayed healthy or that letter would be sent to the Feds with a copy to my dad. I bet they would've killed my ass if it hadn't been for that little insurance policy I wrote for myself. That's it, man! That's the whole story. I didn't want anyone to get hurt. I didn't even want to watch your house, but they made me. Please don't kill me, man...I feel real bad about what happened to your wife and kid. That shit wasn't right. Please man! I promise I won't tell nobody. Just kill those motherfuckers...I'll fucking help you do it."

Leon put all this on paper? "Where's that letter you wrote?"

"My law...Hey...that's...uhh...If I die the cops are going to know all this shit. They'll know the whole story. You *can't* kill me! You'll be suspect number one if you start doing these other motherfuckers. You gotta let me live. Killing me will get you in the joint."

Leon made a good point—smart little bastard. "Where's the letter you wrote?" Thorpe repeated.

"Fuck you, nigga, that letter gonna keep me alive. Got your ass now—cracker motherfucker." Leon began to show his ass now that he thought it was saved.

Thorpe grabbed Leon's ankles, lifted both legs off the ground, stepped back, and yanked on the small man with all his strength. Tendons and bones gave way as Leon's arms, which were still restrained to the railing behind his back, now extended straight above his head. Thorpe dropped his captive to the ground. Leon looked like a disfigured referee signaling a touchdown while lying on his back thrashing and screaming. Thorpe pressed a towel across Leon's mouth to stifle the sounds of his suffering.

"Leon, we were doing so well, but then you had to go and get disrespectful. You *are* going to tell me where that letter is. It's just a matter of how much pain you're willing to endure first." Leon began vomiting, prompting Thorpe to remove the towel from his face. Thorpe cut the Flexcuffs off and rolled Leon over on his side to prevent him from asphyxiating on his own puke.

"Leon, where's the letter?" Thorpe persisted.

Leon sputtered, his breath smelling of bile as he attempted to speak. "…It's at home, under my mattress."

"Bullshit, Leon, that's going to cost you." Thorpe grabbed Leon's wrist, locked his elbow, and slowly began to twist, rotating Leon's already mangled shoulder.

"Wait!…My lawyer has it…Jessie Leatherman."

"Leon, are you lying to me again? If you are, I promise I'll work on you all night."

"Man, he's got it. If I die, he walks it to the Feds. You can't stop it."

Thorpe considered what Leon had told him—it made sense. Jessie Leatherman was a private criminal attorney who often served the North Side drug dealers. The police loved him because he was a horrible lawyer. They often joked Jessie put more people in prison than any police officer ever dreamed. The only time he got people *out* of prison was when they went to appeals court and it was determined Jessie had provided ineffective counsel. Earlier Leon had started to say his lawyer had the document before he attempted to use the letter against Thorpe. If Jessie did have the letter, it was a significant obstacle. Thorpe wasn't prepared to start hurting innocent people, which made retrieving the document a tricky proposal.

"What about your brother? He know about any of this shit?" Lyndale was still in prison.

"No."

"I find that hard to believe."

"He's in fuckin' prison. They monitor his phone calls and his mail. I'm not going to talk about this shit with him."

"What else you have to tell me, Leon?"

"I'll be waiting for you in hell," Leon growled between clenched teeth.

Thorpe stood, "You have two minutes to make peace with God. Then I'm sending you to one place or the other."

Thorpe gathered up equipment as he heard Leon praying under his breath. *There truly are no atheists in foxholes.* In spite of the damage Thorpe had inflicted on Leon, there was very little blood to show for it. Thorpe wanted to keep it that way. After a couple of minutes, he walked back over to his captive and pulled up on Leon's collar until he was sitting upright with his arms hanging unnaturally at his sides. Thorpe stood behind Leon and dug a knee into his ribs. "It's time."

Leon began to protest, "Please don't..." But he never finished the sentence. Thorpe grabbed his chin with his right hand and palmed the top of Leon's head with his left. In one violent motion, Thorpe pulled up and back with his right as he pushed down and away with his left, snapping Leon's thin neck and fatally damaging the spinal cord.

Thorpe dropped the limp vessel of what was once Leon to the ground. He needed to find a place to conceal the body in an attempt to prolong its discovery and buy enough time to complete his mission. If there truly was a letter, and if Leon's body were discovered, it wouldn't take long for investigators to focus on Thorpe, especially after TPD officers started dropping dead.

Thorpe considered burning the body to destroy physical evidence. But a fire would likely lead to an immediate discovery of Leon's remains. He also considered severing Leon's hands and feet above where the Flexcuffs had been attached. Those marks would be distinctive: Police officers would immediately be considered as potential suspects even though the cuffs were readily available to civilians. But he dismissed the idea as too Jeffery Dahmerish. Thorpe figured on paying fully for his sins and crimes. He had little doubt he would be captured, charged, and convicted of several counts of premeditated murder, kidnapping, and a myriad of other felonies—but not until it was *over*.

Thorpe used a flashlight and searched the surrounding woods for a place to secrete the body. When he located a suitable spot, he returned to Leon's remains, hoisted it onto his shoulders, and shuffled into the woods toward a dense thicket of brush surrounded by a thorn forest. Thorpe felt the long prickly vines pulling at his clothing as he trudged through the thicket. He was wearing enough layers so as not to be concerned about his skin being ripped open and leaving DNA evidence, but he'd definitely have to ditch his clothing. The annoying, flesh-tearing thorns would keep the casual teenager out of the area.

Not having brought a shovel, Thorpe concealed the body by tossing it in the thicket and covering it with fallen limbs and other vegetation. He had no doubt it would eventually be found, but he hoped it wouldn't be for a few days. By then the crime scene would have deteriorated because of the elements. Thorpe trekked back through the barbed scrub and scanned around the oil tanks for signs he'd been there. The only evidence were footprints, tire tracks, and the contents of Leon's stomach.

Thorpe entered Leon's Cutlass and drove down the dirt road with his lights off, navigating by starlight. Having seen no headlights approaching from either direction, Thorpe pulled out onto 36th Street North hoping a patrol unit wouldn't see him emerging from the woods. Thorpe guided the Cutlass west on 36th Street North and south on Peoria Avenue.

The chances of Thorpe being pulled over driving this piece of shit at this time of night were fairly high. He hoped his luck would hold out just a little bit longer. He worked his way southwest until reaching a convenience store near Shaw's house. Thorpe selected an area on the east side of the store that didn't appear to have video surveillance. He left the car running, grabbed his bag, and stepped out of the vehicle. With any luck, the car would be stolen in a matter of minutes. Thorpe began the hike back to Shaw's neighborhood where his Impala was still parked. The temperature had dropped into the teens, and he was thankful to be on the move. He was equally thankful to hear a wobble tone on his police radio. A shooting had just occurred in deep north Tulsa, ensuring all the graveyard officers would be headed that direction.

Thorpe disappeared into the neighborhood and broke into a jog back to his car. He wondered what the crew back at Shaw's house was making of the disappearance of Leon. Given the information Leon had just imparted, coupled with his obvious paranoia and the disappearance of his Cutlass, Thorpe figured their first conclusion would be that Leon got scared and fled the city. Their biggest fear would be whether Leon was talking to the authorities. That and the fact they'd never received a second phone call from the anonymous blackmailer were probably making for some very nervous people right about now.

Thorpe would have liked to walk by Shaw's house to see if any activity was afoot but decided it wise to quit pushing his luck and bug-out. He approached his car and passed it, wanting to make sure no one was watching his vehicle. Not spotting any surveillance, he got in his car and drove through the neighborhood. As he passed the convenience store, he noticed Leon's Cutlass was already gone. The car had been stolen within ten minutes. And its owner wouldn't be filing a stolen vehicle report anytime soon. The Cutlass would probably pass hands several times before it was recovered or stripped. Any physical evidence Thorpe had left in the car would be greatly degraded. Thorpe made his way back to the office to trade out cars.

WHILE THORPE MADE HIS WAY BACK TO THE OFFICE, three men stood in the front yard of Shaw's home speaking in hushed tones. Leon's disappearance was almost as disconcerting as the ransom call they were still waiting to receive. Phipps had been inside listening to the heated discussion. Growing impatient, he'd looked out the window and discovered Leon's car missing. He summoned Price and the other man outside to discuss what needed done. With limited information the three could only agree on two things. One, Leon Peterson and Jonathan Thorpe were threats to their freedom. Two, both men needed to die.

Thirteen

Thursday
February 8th
Near midnight

Foot on the gas, revenge on the mind, Thorpe was in route to South Tulsa. His unit had wrapped up a search warrant an hour ago. During the service no one ran, no one fought, and everyone complied. In other words, the warrant wasn't much fun, but two people did go to jail for cocaine possession. Thorpe had excused himself explaining he had a pile of paperwork that needed attention in order to keep Major Duncan off his ass. He returned to SID and switched cars. Now he was driving a plain Ford Taurus. His gear and a change of clothes were in the back seat. A Tulsa Police beat map was spread out beside him.

Looking at Price's beat, Thorpe chose an isolated neighborhood just west of Yale between 81st and 91st Streets South. The neighborhood was secluded with large houses and heavily wooded back yards. Thorpe drove south on Yale before turning west into the rolling neighborhood. He drove around until he found what he was looking for—a large, dark home on a wooded lot. The house displayed a Smart Dog alarm sign in the front yard and a newspaper wrapped in yellow plastic lying at the end of the driveway. Thorpe decided the house, which sat near the end of a dead-end street, had an empty feel. The road was an east-west street but at this location curved back to the north before it ended in a cul-de-sac. Thorpe memorized the features of the house and tried to picture what the rear of the home would look like. He exited the neighborhood, pulling the Ford into a shopping center on the northwest corner of 81st and Yale. He found a dark parking spot and climbed into the rear seat of the Taurus. Shielded by dark tinted windows, Thorpe changed clothes, exited the vehicle, and removed the license plate. Climbing back into the driver's seat, he laid the license plate facedown on the passenger floorboard and drove to a neighborhood west of his target location. He parked just north of the Thousand Oaks housing addition, which, unlike most neighborhood names, actually made sense.

A vacant lot sat east of where Thorpe was parked. Isolated homes were situated on either side of the empty property. A street light was about thirty yards north of where the Taurus now sat. If someone did notice his abandoned car, they would likely only recall it was a white Ford Taurus with tinted windows. That would narrow the search down to a couple of hundred-thousand cars. Because Thorpe was wearing heavy garb, anyone who might see him wouldn't be able to provide much of a description.

There was no point hanging around any longer than needed. Thorpe was still monitoring Riverside's frequency and had heard Price go "10-46" on a dinner break about ten minutes ago. Thorpe took a cursory look around, grabbed his equipment, and walked briskly east across the street and through the vacant lot. As he crossed, he noticed a greenbelt ran north and south directly behind the allotment. The air was glacial; Thorpe left puffs of condensation like a train as he chugged up a steep incline across the greenbelt toward a heavily wooded area. Enough moonlight was shining that Thorpe, laden with equipment, could possibly be spotted by a neighbor as he traversed the greenbelt. Because of this, he walked steadily; he didn't run as running always drew attention. If he heard a call on the radio in reference to his suspicious activity, he would simply return to his car and choose another location—after switching out vehicles once again.

Thorpe entered the dark sanctuary of the trees, squatted, and peered down at the area he'd just crossed, scanning to see if any eyes had followed him into the woods. It was cold, nearing midnight, and a weekday, so Thorpe hoped his entry into the woods had gone unnoticed. The radio was dead silent; apparently it was a slow night as far as police work went. Turning toward the blindingly dark woods, Thorpe retrieved the night vision goggles he had obtained from the office. The goggles were not military grade and were a bit disorienting, but he didn't want to use a flashlight and risk being spotted by a neighbor. Thorpe continued his climb up the hill, navigating through trees displayed through the goggles in hues of green and black.

Approximately ten minutes later, Thorpe was fairly confident he'd rediscovered his target house – from behind. He removed his night vision goggles, noting the house and trim were painted in the same colors, and the house appeared to be the same style. The back of the home was surrounded by a six-foot wooden privacy fence, the planks attached so the support beams were on the exterior. Avoiding the clamor that kicking pickets would generate, he used a large knife as a prying instrument, loosening and removing several planks. After making an opening through which he could easily escape, Thorpe stepped into the yard.

A wooden storage shed and clumps of trees rose out of an angry sea of copper and brown. Waves of raspy leaves, feet thick in places, covered every inch of yard. A raised wooden deck, three feet off the ground, was attached to the back of the house, and you had to walk up steps to reach the back door. An outside porch light was illuminated seven feet off the deck to the right of the rear entrance. Thorpe waded through the yard, stepped up onto the deck, and let loose three booming knocks on the back door. Then he retreated back into the deep yard. He looked for a light or any sign someone might be home as he continued to monitor the police radio. He listened for anyone to call in his car or other suspicious activity—nothing.

He did hear Price go "10-8" on the radio, indicating the officer was now available to take calls. Thorpe noted the gate leading to the front yard was on the southeast side of the home—to Thorpe's right. The storage shed was located on the other side of the yard and was about thirty yards from the deck. Because of the deck's handrail and elevation, a firing position from the shed was not optimal. Thorpe needed to be about ten yards closer to the home. But the shed would have to do because the tree trunks were not large enough in diameter to conceal his form if a flashlight were cast his direction.

Thorpe removed a small pair of bolt cutters from his pack and cut the lock on the shed. Inside the shed, Thorpe felt comfortable using a flashlight. It didn't take him long to find what he was looking for—a leaf rake. Thorpe used the rake to clear an area behind and to the left of the shed. He then cleared a ten-yard path leading up to the house. Thorpe tossed the rake aside, walked up to the house, and kicked in the back door. Then he pulled the door shut and hurried down to the shed. Thirty seconds later, the still night was shattered by the piercing alarm system.

Nearly ten minutes passed before dispatch assigned the call, which Thorpe intercepted through his ear piece, "Ida 304, Ida 304 and a car to back. Smart Dog intrusion alarm, 4530 E. 86th Street, four-five-three-zero east eight-six Street, break."

Price answered the call. "Ida 304, I'll advise."

"Ten-four, Ida 304. Trip is rear entry. Copy you'll advise. Time zero-zero-three-six hours," Dispatch acknowledged.

Price had done exactly what Thorpe knew he would do, what almost every police officer does; he advised on an alarm call. Advising meant no backing officer would accompany him on the call. It was a bad habit of even seasoned officers. TPD responds to so many false alarms they're rarely taken seriously—especially in south Tulsa. An officer generally advises and checks the perimeter of the home solo; only if a break is located will he call for additional officers or a K-9 unit to clear the house. Thorpe stood behind the shed monitoring the surrounding houses for lights or movement in reaction to the shrill alarm.

After a few minutes the audible alarm went silent. Thorpe ceased to watch the gate and retreated fully behind the shed. Anyone walking into the yard now would be announced by footsteps thrashing through leaves. For the next nine minutes, Thorpe stood at the ready beside the shed, bow in hand, arrow loaded, concentrating on his breathing. Finally Thorpe heard Price go "10-97" on the radio. The announcement spiked his heart rate ever so slightly. Price had arrived on scene.

STEPHEN PRICE HAD BEEN ON AUTO-PILOT ALL EVENING, not having the proper state of mind to be on patrol. In the academy, rookies learned about three different mindsets, which were based on the traffic light system. "Condition Green" was the mindset you have when you're sitting in the sanctuary of your own home watching reruns of Seinfeld on television. "Condition Yellow" was cautionary, a condition you needed to shift into anytime you donned a police uniform—danger could be around any corner. From the minute you leave the house, you should be scanning your surroundings for threats. "Condition Red" was when you were "in the shit," or likely to be soon. Price had been operating exclusively in the green after the ransom call. He wasn't focused on his surroundings.

Price pulled up in front of the address with the sprung alarm. *Another rich asshole who wouldn't shell out his inherited money for a decent alarm system.* Price was tired of responding to false alarms. After having performed a cursory check of the front, Price found a gate on the left side of the house and stepped into the backyard. Price walked around the corner of the house, feet shuffling through accumulated leaves, towards the lighted back porch. Price directed his flashlight to the wooded back yard but quickly turned his attention to the back door. *Who the fuck called me last night?* Price stomped up the wooden stairs. As Price crossed the wooden deck, his mind focused enough to realize the rear door frame had been splintered. His mind was just registering the good break when he felt the thud in the small of his back.

What the hell? Price felt no pain at first, only a rapidly spreading warm sensation. Then came the pain and the realization he was "in the shit." As Price's mind was trying to bridge the gap between green and red, he finally realized he should be drawing his pistol. His right hand on his weapon, Price heard something on the deck behind him. He had both snaps undone on his retention holster, was lifting the weapon and turned—only to get knocked off his feet and through the back door. The pain in Price's back, which was excruciating, intensified even more when he landed on the kitchen floor. His tormented mind registered a piercing noise, a brightening of the room, then pressure on his arms and torso. His eyes focused. Looming above him was Sergeant Jonathan Thorpe.

Fuck.

THORPE'S HOPE of interrogating Price was dashed. The man reacted faster than Thorpe had hoped. Price had been close to clearing his holster by the time Thorpe reached him. His safest option had been to knock him off his feet. Unfortunately the blow had knocked Price straight through the back door, reactivating the alarm.

The recognition of imminent death in Price's eyes gave Thorpe a measure of satisfaction. He buried a large hunting knife in the right side of Price's neck, severing both the internal and external carotid arteries as well as the internal jugular vein. He must have also penetrated Price's spinal cord: Death was instant. Thorpe left the knife inside his victim so he wouldn't be sprayed with blood while removing the blade. He then took Price's radio and a cell phone off his police belt and backed out the door.

Thorpe recovered his bow and left the way he'd come. As he made his way through the woods and down the steep hill he tossed the bow to the side and continued towards his car. When he reached the end of the woods near the greenbelt he knelt down and pulled out a black Hefty bag. Thorpe pulled off his gloves and jacket and put them in the bag, then he pulled on another pair of gloves and began walking to the car.

Thorpe drove south through the neighborhood until he found a secluded place to reattach the license plate. He also activated the emergency button on Price's radio; Thorpe saw no sense in having a family traumatized by returning home and finding a slain police officer in their home. The activation of the emergency button would have officers respond immediately to Price's last known location. His lifeless body would be discovered within minutes.

Fourteen

Friday
February 9th
Early Morning

As SUPERVISOR OF THE DEPARTMENT'S HOMICIDE UNIT, Sergeant Robert Hull didn't respond to every murder scene. He did respond to most—and absolutely responded to any killing where a police officer was involved, especially when a police officer was the victim. When Hull had answered his page at 1:30 this morning, all he'd been told by dispatch was a police officer had been killed on an alarm call and no suspects were in custody. He hadn't asked for a name; he wasn't eager to know.

As Hull approached the entrance to the neighborhood on Yale, he noticed a patrol unit restricting access to the area. The officer manning the post recognized Hull and waved him through. Hull wove his way through the neighborhood. As he grew closer, he noticed the towers of several news vans. The carrion-enticed media were circling

Urbana just north of 86th Street. There would be no shortage of discussion for the talking heads this Friday morning. Hull passed the hungry-eyed reporters and continued to another checkpoint manned by three officers and police tape. There, he parked his car behind similar plain, American-made sedans lining the street. As he stepped from his car, a blast of artic air reminded him to reach back in for his gloves before walking towards a large home that appeared to be the center of activity. He stepped under more police tape as an officer in uniform marked his arrival with some notations on a clipboard.

"They're all around back, Sarge. Take the gate on your left." Hull walked across the yard's dormant grass, through the gate, and around the corner of the home, where he was met by his gaunt detective. Chuck Lagrone was standing shin deep in an ocean of leaves.

"Skull, whatta we got?"

"I've never seen a killing like this before, boss, let alone a cop. You know who it is right?"

Hull had been afraid to ask. "No."

"Stephen Price."

Hull felt a bit relieved—then a bit guilty for that. "His uncle been notified yet?"

"Got police chaplains en route over to his house. Should be arriving any minute now," answered Lagrone.

"Better get some more officers on the perimeter. We don't need him showing up, knocking down our crime scene."

"I'll get some guys on it. Come on, Bob, you better see this for yourself instead of me trying to describe it for you." The two men ascended the wooden stairs taking care not to step on potential evidence. The rear door stood open. Price lay on his back just inside the kitchen door, his dark form in sharp contrast to the stark white tile. The first thing Hull noticed was the large knife protruding from the right side of Price's neck. When he got closer he noticed a metal arrow shaft underneath Price's body. There was a significant amount of blood pooling around Price's neck on the white tile floor. Hull was taken aback. "Son of a bitch!"

"Fucked up, ain't it!" Lagrone agreed.

"That's an understatement," Hull breathed, then, "How pure is this scene?"

Lagrone began narrating: "Three officers stepped over the body and cleared the rest of the house for suspects. Two firemen entered and pronounced him dead. After that, everyone exited the house and locked it down. The list of people who have been crawling around the backyard is more extensive. SIU did video already." SIU was the department's Special Investigation Unit. Its detectives were responsible for collecting evidence at major crime scenes.

"Son of a bitch! This isn't your typical cop killing; he's been assassinated," remarked Hull.

"Fucking looks that way."

"He wearing a vest?" Hull asked.

"Yeah. Looks like the arrow penetrated. Don't know how deep yet. Need to process the scene more before we start poking around the body."

"Fuck! Tell me everything you know so far," Hull requested.

Lagrone began reading his notes to Hull. "According to dispatch, Price went 10-46 in his car at 2345 hours and 10-8 at 0015 hours. At 0035 hours dispatch received a rear-entry alarm at this residence—we'll check with Smart Dog to get an exact time the alarm was tripped. At 0036 hours, dispatch assigned the call to Price who stated he would advise. At 0050 hours, Price went 10-97. At 0101 hours, Price's emergency button was activated on his handheld radio. At 0108 hours, the first officer responding to the emergency activation arrived. At 0110, the responding officer reports an officer down; he requests EMSA, a supervisor, and additional units. Fire shows up and pronounces Price DOA, while three officers are clearing the rest of the house. The officers determine the residence is secure, tell the firemen to get out, then the officers go out the front door so they don't have to step over the body again. Other officers clear the backyard and notice the lock to the shed has been cut off. They clear the shed. They also discover several boards have been removed along the back fence." Lagrone motioned back towards the fence where the boards were missing. "The fence is in pretty good shape, and it looks like the boards were just recently removed. That's about all I got right now, boss."

"Shit! This is going to be big, Chuck. A fucking bow and hunting knife! Son of a bitch." Both men were unconsciously looking down with unfocused eyes at Price's body while shaking their heads. "What about the homeowners?"

"Not home and haven't been able to contact them yet. There's a newspaper sitting at the end of their driveway, which may indicate they haven't been home today. Neighbors don't know where they're at; says they were here yesterday." Lagrone looked at his watch, "I guess it would be the day before yesterday now. Neighbors said they saw them Wednesday."

"What do we got going?" Hull asked.

"We have a full call out. All the homicide detectives are either here, en route, or being sought. Uniforms are still conducting a canvass in the neighborhood asking if they've seen any cars or people that don't belong in the area, asking about the family who lives here and if they've heard or seen anything suspicious. Got some lights en route so we can light up the backyard."

"These damn leaves are so thick the suspect could still be in this yard and we wouldn't know it," Hull said, only half kidding.

"Don't I know it; it'll take us two weeks to sift through this shit."

"Chuck, I know it's early, but you got any theories yet?"

"Yeah, but I don't know if I want to say them out loud."

"Price had a lot of people who didn't like him and a lot of them are on the department," Hull answered for him.

"Yeah; remember 1982?" Lagrone was referring to a case in which a former Tulsa Police Officer, Jimmy Dean Stohler, shot the former girlfriend of another ex-TPD officer in the chest, killing her. The weapon was a crossbow.

"Fuck...That's all we need! With this being Price — Tulsa will have another race riot."

Price was a notorious black activist on the department. His name had been attached to many a lawsuit. None of his allegations had ever proven to be factual, but sometimes fiction becomes the truth—particularly when the media gets hold of it. Price was always good for a quote in the local liberal rag. The allegations had earned him plenty of enemies on the department. No one likes to be constantly accused of being a racist.

"Oh, I almost forgot. Look at Price's gun belt. Notice anything?" Lagrone asked.

Hull studied the body for a minute, "His police radio's gone."

"Yup."

"Huh. Do me a favor, Chuck. The chief and every other high-ranking fucknut are going to want in this backyard. Pass it on to the uniforms: No one goes in the house or backyard without my permission—that includes our illustrious chief; he can get his face time with the media some other place."

Hull descended the deck and shuffled through leaves where he found a mature tree with rough bark to lean against. He stuffed his gloved hands into his coat pockets and watched as SIU and his men went about their work. Hull blocked out the activity swirling around him and tried to picture the scene without emergency personnel.

The wash of crime-scene lights snapped Hull to attention, causing him to look down at his watch. He'd been leaning against this tree for nearly a half-hour though it only felt like minutes. His toes were well aware how long he'd remained stationary—they were numb. Hull stepped away from the tree and began trudging around the yard. After a thorough inspection, Hull walked back up on the deck and again spoke to his senior detective.

"Got it figured out, boss?" Lagrone asked.

"Got some theories bouncing around inside my skull. Anything new?"

"Just a few things. Both the porch light and the kitchen light were on when the first officer arrived. The first responding officer reported climbing the deck and seeing Price lying on his back. He retreated and waited for his backers to arrive before clearing the house. One of the three checked Price for a pulse when they made entry, couldn't find one, and continued searching the residence. Looks like the arrow penetrated the back of Price's vest but doesn't appear to have penetrated the front. May have hit bone, or just didn't have the oomph to get through two panels of Kevlar and muscle. We were able to get hold of the family who lives here. They were in Texas because the husband's father had suffered a heart attack. One or both will be back en route and should be here in five to seven hours. The house doesn't look like it's been rummaged through, but we'll have to wait till they arrive to know if anything's missing. Marcus has been notified, as well as Price's mother. I heard Marcus was somewhat unemotional about the whole thing, but who knows what's going on in his head. Everybody grieves in different ways."

"Where's Marcus at?" Hull asked.

"I think he's still at home. He told the chaplains they could leave. We got someone sitting outside his house—just in case."

"What are we doing with Price's car?"

"It's already been towed. We'll process it in the barn."

"Chuck, I'm going to talk to the PIO." The Public Information Office was responsible for disseminating information to the press. "Then I'll talk to the brass. After that, I'm going to head back to the office and start jotting some things down. If you come up with anything significant call my cell. Also make sure the woods behind the house get a thorough search. We'll be looking for clothing, Price's radio, a bow, whatever."

"Okay, boss."

"One more thing, Skull. You notice the path that's been cleared in the leaves?"

"Yeah, I saw that. Whattaya make of it?"

"Wouldn't make any noise if you approached the deck from that path would you?"

"No, no, you wouldn't."

Fifteen

*Friday
February 9,
Early morning*

JONATHAN THORPE SAT IN HIS LIVING ROOM sipping a cold beer. After activating Price's emergency button, he'd driven a good distance from the scene and gone through Price's cell phone. Most of it was useless. Price seemed to have the entire TPD roster saved in his contacts. But there was one number that stood out. Thorpe had gone through Price's call history, where he found an incoming call. The actual phone number meant nothing to him and no name was attached with it. But it was the exact time Thorpe had phoned Price with the phony ransom threat. A couple of minutes after receiving that call, Price had made an outgoing call. That number had the name "Carl" attached with it.

Thorpe had wanted to spend more time with Price's cell phone but couldn't with today's technology. Many an armed robber had been caught because they took their victim's cell phones. Detectives would work with phone companies to triangulate the phone's location. Usually the dumb-assed robbers still had the phone in their pockets.

Thorpe had removed the battery from Price's radio. He did the same with the cell phone and had tossed all the items in the river. Maintaining appearances, he'd returned to SID where he pretended not to have heard the frantic radio traffic. Several of Thorpe's investigators had responded to the scene to help canvass the neighborhood, but otherwise the scene and investigation were being handled by homicide detectives and uniformed officers.

It wouldn't take long for detectives to figure out the killing was premeditated. Whether they determined Price was specifically targeted remained to be seen. Thorpe also realized two murders involving a bow within a week wouldn't go unnoticed. Thorpe couldn't remember ever being involved in a homicide investigation where a bow was involved. The only one he had ever heard of were the Tulsa crossbow murders that had occurred before he joined the force. An ex-Tulsa Police Officer was convicted of being the shooter.

On the way home, Thorpe had driven to another pay phone and tried the two numbers he'd retrieved from Price's cell. It took several tries but someone finally picked up the first number and confirmed that it was the same payphone he'd used to call Price with the ransom threat. The second number went straight to voice mail — the voice mail of one Carl McDonald. McDonald was a TPD sergeant who happened to be the previous supervisor of the OGU before Thorpe had replaced him.

The fact that Price had called McDonald didn't condemn him. But it sure as hell was incriminating. Price receives a phone call accusing him of murder. The very next call Price makes is to McDonald? Thorpe wondered if McDonald was the mysterious "white boy" who liked to don ski masks in clandestine meetings.

As Thorpe sat in his living room, he thought about some consequences of his actions he hadn't fully explored.

He might not yet be a suspect with *investigators*, but if his targets were anything short of unmitigated idiots, they'd soon reach the conclusion Thorpe was likely responsible. Leon's disappearance could be attributed to him getting cold feet and skipping town, but Price's killing would be sure to flip on a few light bulbs: First, Price receives an ominous phone call from someone who claims to know what he's done. Then the supposed extortionist never calls back to make his demands. Then Price gets an arrow in the back and a hunting knife lodged in his throat. If someone was blackmailing the group they wouldn't kill a potential cash cow. They'd have to start theorizing about who'd be pissed off enough to start killing them — and it wouldn't take long to reach the conclusion Thorpe was their surest bet.

Thorpe mulled what their course of action would be then. They couldn't go to the authorities. *"Hey, we killed Thorpe's wife and kid, and we think he's really pissed about it, and now he's killing us. You guys need to do something about it."* No, they didn't have a lot of options except to kill Thorpe first—if they had the balls. *Would they find someone else to do their dirty work, or would they do it themselves?* They tried getting outside help last time with the DD brothers and that didn't work out so well. Thorpe's greatest threat was probably Andrew Phipps. Phipps was an ex-military and current Tulsa SOT sniper. Thorpe was nearly certain the Surgeon General considered having a trained sniper as your enemy detrimental to your health.

Would they try to kill me at work or at home? Thorpe didn't list his address with the department and only a couple of people with TPD knew where he lived. Still, it wouldn't take much detective work to come up with his address. Thorpe tried to put himself in his enemies' shoes and decided he lived in the perfect place to be ambushed; it was remote and secluded. If he were hunting himself, he would find a place to hide across the road from his house and take a shot when his target was working in the front yard or getting out to open and close the gate.

Thorpe decided he would try and use his home to his advantage. First thing in the morning, he would make sure he changed his contact information at the division so his correct address could easily be located. He'd also take protective measures while at work. But he was confident if they came for him, it'd be at his home—and he'd be ready.

Beyond his personal safety, there were other consequences to consider. Price's killing alone would be bad. If Thorpe killed a second black officer the town would become a political nightmare. It'd be better if Thorpe could go after McDonald and Baker first—because they were white. Thorpe wasn't a hundred percent positive McDonald was involved, and he wasn't about to go killing police officers on hunches and circumstantial evidence. Baker would have to be his next target; otherwise the city would become a circus. It would surely get national attention. The media would be quick to point out the city's history of disastrous race relations.

Most people weren't aware that Tulsa, Oklahoma was the site of the United States's largest and deadliest race riot. In 1921, the city erupted into two days of rioting. More than thirty city blocks were destroyed. By the time it was over, at least eight hundred people were admitted to hospitals. Most of those admitted were whites because the two black hospitals were burned to the ground. Blacks' injuries were likely vastly underreported. The official death count was thirteen whites and twenty-six blacks killed, though it was generally believed the black death-toll was much higher. Some estimates put the number of blacks killed as high as three hundred. Most of the rioting occurred in the Greenwood section of Tulsa, a prosperous commercial district owned by black businessmen. At the time the area was known as "the Negro Wall Street."

The spark occurred on Memorial Day 1921 when a 19-year-old black shoe shiner was en route to a "colored" wash room on the top floor of a downtown building. Some accounts suggested the shoe shiner tripped when he entered the elevator — and grabbed a white, 17-year-old female elevator operator in an attempt to break his fall. Others suggested the two were lovers and had a loud quarrel. There is little doubt the two were at least acquaintances because the shoe shiner would have had to use the elevator every time he needed to use the restroom. Regardless of the circumstances, what happened next was less ambiguous. A clerk from a clothing store on the first floor of the building heard the scream, saw the black male hurriedly leave, and found the elevator operator in distress. The employee concluded the operator had been sexually assaulted and called the police.

The next morning, a detective and a black patrolman located the shoe shiner, Dick Rowland, on Greenwood Avenue and brought the man in for questioning. Later that day the Tulsa Tribune printed a story titled "Nab Negro for Attacking Girl in Elevator." By evening several hundred whites had assembled outside the courthouse and demanded Rowland be handed over. The sheriff reportedly fortified the courthouse by disabling the elevator and having his deputies barricade the stairs with orders to shoot anyone attempting to breech their defensive perimeter. The sheriff unsuccessfully attempted to disperse the increasingly agitated crowd. Fearing Rowland would be lynched, a group of armed black men assembled on Greenwood Avenue then marched to the courthouse. Having seen the measures the sheriff had taken to assure Rowland's safety, the group reportedly returned back to the Greenwood district. Whites, having heard of the actions taken by the blacks, armed themselves and the crowd outside the courthouse grew to 2,000 or more.

Details are sketchy but it is widely believed the armed black men kept returning to the courthouse to ensure Rowland's safety. During one of those occasions an altercation ensued and a white man was shot dead by one of the armed blacks. Whites then began firing on the group of blacks and both sides exchanged gunfire killing one another. The group of black men fled to Greenwood Avenue with the large group of whites in pursuit. Throughout the night whites and blacks engaged in firefights and many black owned businesses were set afire. By morning, an estimated 5,000 whites had assembled and attacked Greenwood in a coordinated effort. Black residents began fleeing the area to the north where they were reportedly gunned down by white rioters. By any account the riot was a horrific event.

Thorpe hoped history would not compare what happened in 1921 to the events he was about to set in motion. In Thorpe's mind, his wife and daughter had been unjustly lynched. But he wouldn't fire indiscriminately like the rioters of 1921; he'd be a precise instrument of death with no collateral damage.

For the first time in a long time, Thorpe retrieved a family photo album and began turning the pages. As he wept, he asked for forgiveness for what he had done, what he had neglected to do, and what he was prepared to do; he asked forgiveness not from God, but from his daughter.

Sixteen

Friday
February 9th
Morning

THE DETECTIVE DIVISION was located inside the Civic Center building near 6th and Denver in downtown Tulsa. It was sandwiched between the Public Safety Communications Center and Municipal Courts. Officers referred to the building as "the Main Station." In addition to the Detective Division, the Main Station housed the Chiefs Section, the Office of Integrity and Compliance, the main property room, and various other support divisions of the Tulsa Police Department. The Detective Division sat on the second floor of the three story building. Sergeant Robert Hull, supervisor of the Tulsa Police Department's Homicide Unit, sat in his office adjacent the homicide bullpen. He had just got off the phone and was staring blankly at the wall when Chuck Lagrone, a.k.a. "The Skull" walked in and plopped down in a chair.

"Boss, you daydreaming again?"

"Just thinking, Chuck. Got anything new?"

"Neighbors didn't see dick. One of them heard the house alarm but weren't about to get out of their warm cozy bed to see if anything was happening. As for Price, we're pretty sure the arrow went through the lower back panel of his vest and traveled upwards, but doesn't look like it penetrated the front panel. It's possible the arrow hit the inside of his trauma plate," Lagrone said, while tapping his chest. Most officers wore the plates in front of their vest. The plates are nothing more than a piece of steel wrapped in additional Kevlar. Bullet resistant vests typically only stop projectiles fired from handguns. Rifle rounds will go through a vest like butter unless it directly strikes the trauma plate. Kevlar only provides minimal protection against sharp objects like ice picks, thin sharp knives, and arrows.

"Your theory about the path through the leaves would fit the trajectory the arrow took through his body," Lagrone continued.

"Tell me how you think this thing went down."

Chuck gathered his thoughts before speaking, "I think someone knew there was no family in that house and knew it had an alarm system. I think that someone then cleared a path in the leaves so he could close ground on the officer in silence. I think that *same* someone then kicked in the back door and waited for Price behind the shed. When he saw Price, he waited for him to walk up the stairs and then moved in on him from behind, fired the arrow, ran up the stairs and knocked him into the kitchen. Then he stuck a knife in his neck."

Hull sat silently for a few moments. "That would take a pretty cool customer."

"Ice cold," Lagrone agreed. "What's your theory?"

"I was thinking the same damn thing…but I was hoping I was wrong. The last thing we need is a professional killer running around knocking off cops. How long of a shot would that have been with the bow?"

"I don't have the measurements on me but I'd say between twenty and thirty yards."

"So besides picking the perfect locale and all that bullshit, our shooter has the foresight to clear a path in the leaves so he can stalk his prey silently, waits in the freezing cold, takes a shot at a uniformed police officer with a fucking bow and arrow at around twenty-five yards, and then has the balls to charge up there on an armed officer and plunge a knife in his neck. Is that what we're saying?"

"Sounds about right."

"Jesus Christ, Chuck! I got buck fever the first time I shot a bow at a deer—shook like a little girl. I can't imagine shooting a bow at an armed cop at that distance and having the nuts to follow the arrow up there. Whoever our *someone* is—he's killed before."

"I'd bet on current or ex-military. Maybe special forces," Lagrone agreed.

"Or SWAT. Something to check into," Hull noted.

"There's something else we should consider. What if Price didn't activate his emergency button? What if our shooter did? We never did find his radio."

"Why the hell would our killer hit the emergency button?" Hull asked.

"The only thing I can think of is he wanted us to find him sooner rather than later. Either that or he was sending some kind of message."

"That damned knife in his throat was message enough! Maybe the killer was only hitting buttons—didn't know what he was doing?" Hull pondered out loud.

"If what we've been guessing about this guy is true that doesn't sound too likely."

"I agree. We pretty sure our killer hit the button?"

"No. Just something to consider. But his emergency button was activated eleven minutes after he went 10-97. If I were a betting man, I'd guess Price was killed within a couple of minutes of arriving on scene."

"You're probably right." Hull agreed.

"One other thing; everyone says Price carries a cell phone—always. We couldn't find one on his person or in his car."

"No shit? We need to start pinging that phone, Skull."

"One step ahead of you. It's off the grid."

"Interesting. Why would someone take the time to take a phone off Price's body when that house alarm was waking up half the neighborhood?"

"Only one reason boss. Whoever killed him really wanted that cell phone. The question is, why? To get information or to destroy it?" Lagrone pondered.

"We need to get his phone records ASAP, Skull…I know, I know, you're one step ahead of me."

"Always am. Don't have 'em yet but we're working on it."

The two men sat in the office staring at the desk between them before Hull broke the silence again, "You said something interesting when you were giving me your theory. You said our someone waited for *Price* behind the shed. Not waited for an officer, but waited for Price."

"I didn't mean to imply the suspect knew the specific officer he was going to kill, though that is obviously something we'll have to look at," Lagrone said as he studied his boss's sour expression. "There's something more, Bob. Let's hear it."

Hull paused for a few moments before he responded, "Close the door, Chuck."

Lagrone closed the office door, and returned to the chair.

"From the scene it's fairly obvious this was a premeditated murder on a police officer. Let's have a discussion presuming Price specifically was the target. Of course we have no evidence of this, but let's travel down the road a ways and see where we end up."

"Okay, Bob, somehow I get the feeling you've already traveled down this road."

"A little; just wild speculation on my part. My speculation was facilitated in part because it was Price who was killed. He just happens to be one of the most loathed officers on the department and in my opinion, dirty as hell. In fact, if he were killed in a drive-by I'd just chalk it up to one of his associates popping him. But this bow-and-arrow shit doesn't fit that profile. I think we're looking at someone with a tactical background."

"I know what you're saying. Bit of a coincidence one of the most despised officers on the department gets taken out with a professional looking hit."

"If Price was targeted specifically, I'd have to say the hitter was a cop. What do you think?" Hull asked.

Lagrone sat still and thought for a full minute before responding, "I'd have to agree with you. First, the killer would have to know what days and what hours Price worked. He'd also have to know what beat Price worked to insure he was the officer who responded. He'd almost have to be in possession of a police radio to know if Price was available to take the call. He'd more than likely be knowledgeable about how we responded to alarms. So yes, if we are *assuming* Price was specifically targeted, I'd say the killer is probably a cop and probably TPD."

"Big assumption—yes. We're just tossing around ideas. I don't want to think one of our own did this either. In addition, the killer probably would have known officers have a tendency to advise on alarm calls. I also agree he'd have to be in possession of a police radio, not just a scanner that would be skipping around all the different frequencies; otherwise he'd never be sure he was going to end up with Price in the backyard. It would also explain how the killer would know how to activate an emergency button—if in fact the killer was the one who hit the button. Okay, with all these assumptions taken into consideration, who on this department would have the motivation, the skill, and the cold bloodedness to pull this thing off?"

"Again, I think you'd be looking at someone ex or current military. Someone who has killed before. Maybe someone fresh from sand-land who doesn't get the shakes about taking someone's life anymore."

"I agree the suspect has killed before. You don't carry out your first killing with a fucking bow and Buck knife. I could see someone using a rifle or something but I can't see a first-timer taking a guy out the way Price was dispatched."

"We'd have to consider some SOT guys also; a couple on the team have multiple kills," Lagrone added.

"So assuming Price *was* targeted, we're looking for a Tulsa Police officer with an array of tactical skills who has killed before and has a beef with Price."

"I can start compiling a list," Lagrone offered.

"Do it on the down-low. If the brass comes up with the same theory and asks you about it, just tell them we've already considered the possibility and we're investigating it. If they want more, refer them to me."

The two men sat on opposite sides of Hull's desk both staring at the cluttered workspace with unfocused eyes. Chuck brought his eyes up to his boss, "There's something more you're not telling me."

"Skull, are you having those psychic fantasies again?"

"Kiss my ass. I've worked with you long enough to read you like a cheap comic book."

Hull looked up at the ceiling and let out a long breath, "Chuck, we've been making a ton of assumptions, and I'm about to throw out a name with absolutely no just cause. I'm way off the fucking reservation with this one and I don't want my mentioning his name to turn him into a suspect on this deal. Okay?"

Chuck slowly nodded his head; he rarely saw his boss this concerned. "Understood."

"Let's talk about Jonathan Thorpe."

Hull didn't follow the announcement of Thorpe's name with any more words. He let it hang in air and watched Lagrone's reaction. Having worked with his lead investigator for decades now, Hull watched the older man's face parade an assortment of responses—surprise, contemplation, and possible acceptance.

"But before we talk about John, let me ask you a question. If someone killed your wife and children, and you found out who they were, but the police didn't know, what would you do?"

"You know what I'd do. I'd kill 'em deader 'n' shit. So would you," Lagrone emphatically stated.

"It's hard to even imagine something like that. But, yes, I'm pretty sure I'd kill them. If I didn't have any proof which could be used in court, I know I would."

"You think *Price* killed Thorpe's wife and daughter?"

"I don't know shit. I'm fucking thinking out loud and pretty pissed at myself for doing it."

Chuck had worked with Hull long enough to know not to interrupt with his process. Hull would keep questioning Lagrone to see if his line of thinking lined up with his own. He wouldn't lay out his theory until the questioning was over, if he revealed it at all. Generally he let Lagrone reach his own conclusions through the questions he had been posed.

"Okay, Chuck. We both agree if our family had been murdered and we knew the shit-head who did it, we would most likely kill the bastard...Especially if we didn't think the police would have enough to get a conviction. First, do you think John would react the same way?"

"Without a doubt."

"I agree. Secondly, for months John has been pestering me for information in reference to his family's murders, every time I've seen him and understandably so. Then, when Marcel Newman was killed, I spend an hour with the kid and he never brings it up. Chuck, tell me the reason why someone who has asked me about their family's murders every time I've seen them for thirteen months, suddenly stops asking?"

Chuck thought for several minutes before responding to his boss. "Either they've stopped grieving and decided to move on, or they've given up hope."

"Can you think of any other reasons?"

"Or they've discovered the answers."

"Which one do you think most likely applies to our boy?"

"He doesn't strike me as a quitter, Bob."

"Me either."

"Chuck, this morning I called the ME's office. You know the shoulder wound Marcel Newman had? ME said the injury was likely caused by an arrow."

"That's definitely strange, but doesn't implicate Thorpe; just a possibility these two murders are related," Lagrone responded.

"We haven't had a murder with a bow and arrow in twenty-five years and then we have two within a week of each other! Not to mention the one twenty-five years ago involved a Tulsa police officer as a suspect." Hull paused for a few seconds before continuing. "Assuming our killer targeted Price we agreed our killer most likely would be TPD, has killed before, has tactical skills, is one cool customer, and has a beef with Price. Now the motivation is unknown, but John certainly possesses all the other attributes... Again, this is just pure speculation, I can think of other officers who possess these skills as well."

"I know we're just talking here, Boss. I like the kid and I know you do too."

"Hell, yeah, I like him. This discussion doesn't go past the two of us. Let's discuss what we know about John, starting with the murder of his family."

THIRTEEN MONTHS AGO Thorpe had come home from work pulling his undercover truck into the driveway of his south Tulsa home. It was the early morning hours and Thorpe had noticed a couple of interior lights on. The lights were normally off but his wife, on occasion, forgot to extinguish them before turning in. According to subsequent interviews with Thorpe, he reported sensing something was wrong as soon as he inserted his key into the front door. He opened the door, scanned the interior of the house, and registered the shattered rear door standing open and then the body of his wife lying in the hallway surrounded by a pool of blood. He reported running to his wife's side to check her condition and instantly recognized she was dead. He then reported running up the stairs to his daughter's room where he found her lying on her bedroom floor, bloodied, dead.

Thorpe reported he was overcome with emotion and did not immediately phone police or check the house for possible remaining assailants. Instead, he sat on the bedroom floor and held his fallen daughter. After some time had passed, Thorpe hadn't been sure how long, he used his cell phone to call 911 and report the murders. Uniformed officers responded to the scene immediately, but because homicide detectives were already working another double homicide, it took them an hour before they responded.

Hull had been at the scene of the double homicide in north Tulsa where two brothers, Deandre and Damarius Davis, had been murdered and their bodies set on fire. While working the scene, he was informed by dispatch officers had another double homicide in south Tulsa. He'd told dispatch to inform the Southside officers to hold what they had, that it would be a while before they could respond. About a half hour later an officer called his cell phone and notified him the other crime scene involved an officer's family. Hull was enraged he hadn't been notified of that fact earlier and immediately responded to Thorpe's home.

Usually Hull assigned one of his investigators to a particular homicide—with his oversight—but decided to take the lead on this investigation himself. He found

Thorpe in a semi-state of shock sitting in a patrol car outside his home. Hull felt a great deal of empathy for Thorpe; he had children of his own and couldn't fathom having to go through a similar experience. He also knew, regardless of the circumstances, Thorpe would have to be investigated for any possible involvement in his family's murder. It's just a matter of statistics the husband/father is generally the offender in situations such as these. It's tragic enough to lose one's family in such a manner, but to have your peers suspect you of being involved would devastate most men.

During the course of the investigation, Thorpe's whereabouts during the times of the murders were verified; he had been with several of his officers during the time frame. Speculation arose the murder of the DD brothers the same night in North Tulsa may have been related. Damarius and Deandre Davis were shot to death on a dead end street before their bodies and vehicle were doused with gasoline and set afire. The heat from the fire was so intense the bodies were barely discernable inside the car. The seats had completely melted down to the coils. The vehicle in which they were burned, did fit the general description of a car that'd been seen parked in Thorpe's neighborhood the night his family was murdered. The Davis brothers were documented gang members and Thorpe was the supervisor of the Organized Gang Unit. The possibility of a revenge killing was investigated but the two brothers and Thorpe had only limited contact with each other. Associates of the Davis brothers were interviewed, but as usual didn't know anything about anything.

The angle also had to be investigated that Thorpe had hired the brothers to kill his family, and then later killed the brothers to cover his tracks. Luckily, Thorpe's whereabouts could also be confirmed during the murders of the Davis brothers. The only thing looking bad for Thorpe was the fact he'd taken out a life insurance policy on his wife shortly before her murder. Thorpe's explanation was he and his wife's family didn't exactly care for one another. He didn't want to have to ask his father-in-law for help raising his daughter in the unlikely event his wife died. Hull, as well as most of the department, was certain Thorpe had no involvement in the death of his family. However, the media loved these types of stories, and this one had made the national network. Despite Hull's assurances, he was ordered by his superiors to find out everything he could about Thorpe's past so there would be no surprises from the media. Hull led this discreet investigation himself with Chuck's help. During the investigation they learned more than they'd anticipated. Some of this information was passed along to their superiors; some they thought best kept to themselves.

Investigating Thorpe's history, the first thing Hull had done was pull his pre-employment background investigation. Every officer who is considered for the Tulsa Police Department undergoes a background check by an investigator assigned to the Tulsa Police Department's Training Academy. Some of the backgrounds are more involved than others depending on how many flags are raised during criminal checks, initial interviews, and so forth. Hull learned, because Thorpe possessed only one documented traffic citation, zero arrests, and a superior scholastic record, he'd earned only a cursory background check.

Hull immediately found one glaring flag somehow overlooked by his background investigator. The city physician documented a myriad of scarred lacerations on Thorpe's torso, head, and limbs during his mandatory physical. The physician questioned Thorpe about the scars and was told he had received them when he was assaulted by an assailant with a knife as a teenager living in Kansas City, Missouri. The background investigator had never followed up on Thorpe's claims. Hull and Lagrone were unsuccessful in their attempt to locate any paperwork substantiating the assault. Had this actually occurred, surely the boy's parents would have insisted upon a police report.

Thorpe's only documented contact with the police was the aforementioned traffic citation.

Thorpe stated in his background his father, Benjamin Thorpe, was in the United States Army and had been MIA since he was around 17-years-old. Hull learned Benjamin Thorpe was a sergeant in a supply company for the army but had been honorably discharged when Thorpe was eleven. From tax records, Hull was able to determine Benjamin Thorpe had been employed by USA International, a private security corporation which hired mostly ex-military personnel especially ex-commandos. Hull and Lagrone repeatedly got the run-around and could barely get the corporation to admit it once employed Benjamin Thorpe. Cooperation from the US Army was lacking as well. Both men were preparing to pay a personal visit to USA International when Hull was instructed by his major further investigation into Benjamin Thorpe wasn't warranted. Hull had asked if that meant he were to cease his investigation of Jonathan Thorpe. His boss informed him the investigation would continue but anything relating to Thorpe's father was irrelevant and off limits. Clearly, Hull had been poking his nose somewhere sensitive. He didn't know what Benjamin Thorpe had done in the Army or what he did for USA International, but he was certain it didn't have a damn thing to do with ordering supplies.

Also during the investigation, Hull had learned Thorpe had acquired an Oklahoma Driver's license under the name 'John Sullivan.' Many undercover SID investigators get the driver's license to use during undercover operations. Sometimes during undercover work, criminals insist on seeing an individual's identification. The last thing the investigator wants to do is hand over a driver's license which has all his personal information on it including a home address. The driver's licenses are actual valid licenses which can pass checks by law enforcement agencies. Hull decided to run an NCIC, records, and license check under the name and date of birth on Thorpe's undercover license. Nothing came up; he hadn't even used it to dodge a speeding ticket.

Not expecting to find any results, Hull Googled the name on the internet and found several hits under Thorpe's alias. Most of the results were in reference to John Sullivan the American general of the Revolutionary War and also the Oklahoma representative of the same name. After wading through numerous returns he noticed the name also kept popping up on several mixed martial arts sites. There were no pictures of John "the Scar" Sullivan but his physical description was similar to Thorpe's. At six feet in height and 195 pounds "the Scar" fought in the light-heavyweight division. Hull also discovered the name on an upcoming fight-card in Dallas, Texas. Hull noticed none of the previous fights had occurred in Oklahoma but all were within easy driving distance of Tulsa. Figuring it was a long shot, he talked Lagrone into the five hour trip, telling his senior detective they were going to Dallas, book a hotel, watch some fights, and check out Dallas' West-End nightlife, all on Hull's dime. Lagrone knew there was something fishy going on but wasn't about to pass up a free weekend of drinking in Dallas.

When the two detectives arrived at the arena for the night's fights, Chuck noticed his boss had purchased seats on the row furthest from the ring. As the night progressed, the two men continued ordering beers and thoroughly enjoyed the exciting bouts. With just two fights left on the card, the arena's speaker system began cranking out some tune by Lynyrd Skynyrd. Lagrone was in mid-swig from his plastic beer bottle when he observed Thorpe's head bobbing up and down in the arena's aisle. After doing a double take, Lagrone turned to Hull who was staring up at the ring, "That's our boy." Even from the furthest row they could tell the man was in phenomenal condition, prompting a response from Lagrone, "I had no idea that boy was in that kind of shape."

"I think there's a lot about the kid we don't know."

The ring announcer called out the vital statistics of "John Sullivan" over the speaker system. "Standing at six feet zero inches, one hundred and ninety five pounds, with a perfect professional record of seven wins zero losses, from Kansas City, Missouri, John 'the Scar' Sullivan". The scar was a fitting name for the man who stood in the ring with an assortment of healed lacerations. As the announcement of Thorpe's 205 pound opponent was echoing through the arena, Thorpe quietly paced in his corner and seemed to be scanning the crowd. His eyes appeared to lock momentarily on the two detectives near the back row before moving on. Lagrone spoke as both detectives kept their eyes ahead, "I think he just spotted us."

"It sure looked that way," Hull agreed.

Whether they'd been seen or not was still unknown to the two detectives; they'd never brought it up to Thorpe, and Thorpe had never mentioned the incident. The Scar dominated the fight standing *and* on the ground, ending by referee stoppage in the third round—but it seemed to the detectives Thorpe could have ended the fight anytime he wanted. Later, when the two detectives had left the arena and were drinking beers at a downtown Dallas bar, they'd discussed the bout. As usual Lagrone was the first to breech the subject, "John was just practicing on that poor bastard wasn't he?"

"Jesus, he could have ended the fight anytime he wanted; he had him in a deep choke hold in the first round. I think he released him just so he could get some more rounds in."

"What the hell is he doing fighting in Texas under an assumed name anyway?" Lagrone asked.

"He either doesn't want the attention or doesn't want anyone to know he has those abilities. Fucking bad ass. Bet he learned that shit from his old man."

"You mean his old man who never existed. That's some cloak-and-dagger shit if I ever seen it. Makes sense though; might also explain how he got some of those scars."

"Yeah, all those undocumented scars."

"You know what the most amazing thing was. The kid—before a fight in front of a huge crowd—is calm enough he spotted our sorry asses sitting in the back row."

"I think he did too. Most guys wouldn't be able to focus one row outside the ring under that kind of pressure."

"Yeah...most guys."

AS HULL AND LAGRONE SAT IN THE OFFICE discussing their knowledge of Thorpe, Hull paused, pulled a pad of paper from his desk and grabbed a pen. "Let's summarize what we have so far before we continue." Hull began writing on the pad of paper as he spoke. "First, we agree Thorpe has the mind set capable of killing those responsible for his family's murders. Second, the day Marcel Newman was found tortured and killed was the first time I've had contact with Thorpe when he didn't ask about his family's investigation. Third, Price was shot with an arrow and it's very possible Newman was also incapacitated with an arrow. Fourth, it's highly likely our killer has some type of military background. Fifth, Thorpe's father most likely was special-forces in the army and probably continued in that capacity with USA International. Sixth, Thorpe has some nasty fighting skills he works hard at keeping secret. Seventh, he also has an assortment of jagged scars with no record of medical treatment. Now this is pure speculation so I'll put this off to the side...I think his father passed on some of his military skills to his son and I think the lessons may have been severe. Okay, what else we got?"

Lagrone began speaking, "The problem with the murders of John's family has always been the sheer number of possible suspects. You talk about people with motive. John and his unit have tossed a ton of assholes in prison. We've always wondered if the murder of the Double D brothers were related—though John didn't have much known contact with the two. But anyone of those people he threw in prison could have enlisted those two to do their dirty work for them."

"What about the department? Who on the department doesn't like Thorpe?" Hull asked.

There was no hesitation from Lagrone; he had already begun speculating: "Charlie Peterson made an Internal Affairs complaint claiming Thorpe had planted drugs on his son. And it's no secret Price was good friends with those two shitheads."

"And we've always known Price plays on both sides of the fence," Hull added.

"So Price might have killed Thorpe's family as some sort of pay back?" Lagrone asked. "That's a bit of a stretch."

"May be more than payback. Like I said, Price was dirty. Plus we're just thinking out loud here—remember?"

Lagrone began to vocalize what he thought his boss was theorizing, "Okay, so Price thinks Thorpe is some crazy racist who is planting dope on his buddies. So he talks Deandre and Damarius into killing Thorpe, but things get fucked-up and they kill his family instead. Price then decides to tie up loose ends and kills the DD brothers before they start running their mouths like they all eventually do. But somehow, Newman is involved in this, or at least knows more than he should. Somehow, Thorpe finds out Newman has this knowledge, takes him captive, and gets the information out of him through torture. Then Thorpe grabs his trusty bow and takes out Price."

"It all fits. Except the part about Price wanting to kill Thorpe over some bullshit drug-planting conspiracy. Price had to know those two assholes were dirty. The only reason he'd pretend to buy into that shit would be in order to protect them." Hull thought out loud.

"Maybe he was trying to protect them because he was in business with them. The older son was looking at some serious time. Maybe Price was afraid Leon and Lyndale would snitch on him to avoid prison," Lagrone offered.

"Fuck, this is making my head hurt. Does this shit really fit or are we forcing it?" Hull asked.

"We're definitely forcing it, but don't stop me now I'm on a roll," Lagrone continued. "We said Price's killer would have to be ice-cold. Remember the shooting John was involved in during that meth warrant? Put a fucking bullet right between a man's eyes who had just fired on him then put two more into his head before it hit the floor. When we interviewed his squad later, they reported after John fired the shots, he was ordering the unit to maintain focus on the uncleared room. He's definitely cool under fire."

"Chuck, you know what we know so far? Shit. That's what we know. But some of it fits and I just got this…*feeling*. But really, I don't know how my mind got here with the miniscule amount of information we have. The question is…what are we going to *do* about my feeling?"

"My vote, Bob? Not a damn thing. If it did go down like that then Price got exactly what was coming to him. Plus, like you said, we don't have shit. Even if Thorpe wasn't a cop we wouldn't take this to the District Attorney's Office. This is one thin-assed theory."

"Yeah, Chuck, but under normal circumstances we'd at least look into it."

"Boss, I say we just keep our mouths shut about the whole damn thing. Like you said, we're just making wild guesses anyway. We don't know shit."

"Right now, I'm in agreement. I just have two *huge* concerns. First, in your theory you assumed Price was the only one—other than the brothers—involved in the murder of Thorpe's family. What if he wasn't? What if there *were* others involved? What if there were other police officers involved?"

"If that's the case, it's going to get real fucking ugly 'round here."

"If that's the case…damn right it is. I have a feeling if there were others besides Price involved, we're going to find out soon enough."

"What's your other worry?" Lagrone asked.

"This is going to be a big fucking deal, Chuck. The brass and politicians are going to want progress and we've got nothing. The only trail I can even start to sniff is a path I don't want to go down."

"Boss, we really don't have shit. Marcel Newman's case leads directly back to L.A., I mean the case couldn't be any tighter."

"That's another thing bothering me. I mean a lot of cases are easy, but that damn thing was served-up on a silver platter. Our victim writes our killer's name in the dirt? Our killer stomps all over the crime scene in a pair of boots...Those boots are recovered from his closet?"

"We don't catch the smart ones," Lagrone pointed out.

"Sometimes we do. Did you know Thorpe's unit served a search warrant on L.A.'s house a month or so before Marcel was killed?" Hull added.

"Doesn't mean shit. He's served warrants on three-quarters of the gang bangers out there—that's his job."

"I know, Chuck. I don't know if the kid's done a damn thing. Honestly, I hope if he did, he gets away with it."

"I know what you mean. The kid is different though. He always seems to be...evaluating. It's real subtle but he's just always scanning his surroundings. I think he tries to throw people off with his humor. Guy rarely seems to be troubled but you know he's gotta be fucked-up with his family and all."

"Yeah, interesting kid. Let's leave it be for now. Don't discuss this with anyone—not even your blow-up doll."

"As a matter of fact, boss, the kid kind of reminds me of you. Except he can see his own dick when he pisses."

"Skull, you're a real funny sumbitch. We've went way down Fantasy Avenue. Hopefully, this was nothing more than some bow hunter with a grudge against the police, who'll turn himself in this afternoon," Hull said.

"You don't believe that, do you?"

"I don't know what to believe. Right now, we work the case business as usual. Compile a list of potential TPD suspects but keep it under wraps. We'll see what physical evidence pops up and if the ME is able to give us anything useful."

Skull rose to get back to work. Hull asked him to close the door on his way out. Alone in his office, Hull flipped over a sheet of paper that had been lying face down. It was a Field Interview Report (FIR.) The report had been completed by an officer conducting a canvass of the area near Marcel Newman's murder. The officer had been approached by a citizen who lived inside the Greystone Condominiums. The citizen wanted to report a suspicious vehicle that had parked inside the gated condos the day before Marcel's body was found. The vehicle was a Ford pickup, and the citizen had recorded the license plate number. The officer making the report noted that the plates weren't on file and surmised that the citizen likely recorded the tag incorrectly.

Always thorough, Hull had called the equipment manager for SID and requested the tag numbers for all the undercover vehicles assigned to the division. The tag on the FIR matched the tag of Thorpe's SID-assigned Ford. Hull remembered Thorpe telling him at the scene that the Gangs Unit had been conducting surveillance on Marcel. But he'd also said they'd wrapped that surveillance up over a week ago. Hull's leap to Thorpe as a potential suspect wasn't as great as he'd led Skull to believe. If Hull decided to *misplace* a piece of evidence, he didn't want Skull to have to compromise himself as well. Hull picked up the Field Interview Report and stared at it for a full minute before tearing it into very small pieces.

Seventeen

Friday
February 9th
Afternoon

BECAUSE OF HIS ASSIGNMENT, Thorpe was required to keep a pager and cell phone on his person at all times. Because of Price's untimely death, he knew his phone would be lit-up with gossip seekers, so he'd turned off both devices before bed. He'd never missed a page before so he wouldn't be in much trouble even if he missed a call-out. After rising from bed in the early afternoon, Thorpe checked his messages and, as expected, most were inquiries about Price's murder. No pages had been sent directing him to come into work—good, he wouldn't have to explain why he hadn't responded. Out of all the missed calls, he returned only one—to his best friend in Internal Affairs.

Jeff answered: "What's up, Carnac?"

"You rang?"

"Just letting you know I won't be working-out today. We're all too busy with Price's murder—no long lunch breaks today. Crazy shit. I assume you've heard?"

"Oh, yeah. That's why I turned off all my stuff. Didn't want to be woken up by the grinding of the gossip mill. You guys have any leads?"

"Not according to homicide. Looks like it was premeditated though. Fucking bow and arrow! That's some crazy shit."

"Yeah. How's Marcus handling it?"

"I heard he took it pretty well. Who knows what's going on inside though. Gotta be rough losing your…uhh, sorry, man."

"Jeff, don't you start that crap, too. I'm tired of everyone walking on egg shells around me."

"Well, just wanted to let you know I wouldn't be working-out. We might be on a tight leash for a few days."

"That's okay. When we're fighting, I hardly notice you're there anyway."

"Bite me. I'm going to whip your ass someday soon."

"You're gettin' there."

"You want to go out this weekend? I may be able to get a pass from the wife."

"How 'bout you go out, and I'll make a pass *at* your wife."

"She don't like white meat. We on or what?"

"We're on. How 'bout Saturday night?"

"Sounds good. See you then."

While Thorpe was speaking on the phone, he'd been looking out his front window and was happy to see Al and Trixie chasing one another around the yard. He was going to have to do something about the two dogs. He'd selected the German shepherds primarily for security reasons; companionship being secondary. Over the last few months Thorpe had realized his need for the dogs had flip-flopped to where companionship was foremost. They, like most people's dogs, had become part of the family—in Thorpe's case his most immediate family. He loved his sister, but she lived several hundred miles away with her own family. The two rarely visited one another. Thorpe decided he needed to take measures to protect his dogs—even if it meant lessening his own security. If someone came after him here, the perpetrators would most likely want to remove Al and Trixie from the equation. Thorpe would lock them both up in the barn at night when he was away from home. Hopefully, they wouldn't shit all over his gym equipment.

Thorpe dressed and grabbed some cash. Since the dogs weren't showing any concern, he felt safe walking out the front door without fear of a bullet to the head. He entered the barn and rolled up his wrestling mat before calling the dogs and locking them inside. Then he left his property to do some shopping at Bass Pro Shops in nearby Broken Arrow. The business had some equipment he was interested in—plus he needed to replenish his outdoor clothing. He'd been getting into the unfortunate but necessary habit of destroying his garments.

THERE WERE SIX OFFICERS PRESENT in Cornelius Johnson's north Tulsa home. All of them were having heated discussions about the killing of Stephen Price. Sergeant Carl McDonald sat back and carefully regarded his fellow officers, wondering who'd crack first.

Technically Corn Johnson wasn't a police officer any longer, having resigned after a nasty little affair in which he was suspected of providing sensitive information to some of his old neighborhood friends. The department gave him an option—resign or face criminal charges. Corn wisely resigned. Though he was no longer a police officer, he remained in the group; he needed his lucrative friends now more than ever. Knowing the man's financial desperation, McDonald had asked Corn to host this meeting. McDonald sure as hell wasn't going to have The Band assemble at his own home.

McDonald had started referring to himself and his associates as The Band a couple of years ago. Not because it was cool, but because it simplified things in conversation. Price had accused him of naming the group after the mini series *Band of Brothers*, said he'd been trying to pull an inside joke because four of the six men were black—brothers. In reality, a different movie, *Band of the Hand*, was the source of the name.

Whatever. The Band they were. How they'd come into being was one of those things McDonald had never foreseen. It was almost as if it had just happened.

Though perhaps not the most moral of men, McDonald had joined the department with good-enough intentions. His first years on the department were spent in the Gilcrease Division, or as it was called then, Uniformed Division North. Between marriages, he earnestly went about putting criminals behind bars. He was promoted early in his career, and his work ethic earned him the supervisory position of the department's Organized Gang Unit. That's where he first dipped his toe in murky waters.

An extensive background check is performed on all applicants for the Tulsa Police Department. Officers who later transfer to the Special Investigations Division go through additional checks, mostly financial. SID guys are perpetually around large sums of money and drugs, an environment not lending itself to officers with debts.

McDonald had been in the unit for several months and was succumbing to a feeling most officers experience during their career—the feeling that he was nothing but a hamster on a wheel. No matter how many people he and his unit tossed into jail, no matter how many drugs and how much dirty money they took off the street, it seemed their efforts were useless. The drug dealers were often back out on the streets only days after being arrested.

The DA's office, wanting a high conviction rate, offered plea deals to everyone. Those given prison time normally had their already-short sentences cut by half. The whole thing was just a big game, and everyone was making money but the good guys. *Why shouldn't he profit as well? Is stealing from criminals really stealing at all?*

After a while, a twenty started disappearing here and there, enough to buy his lunch for the next week. Then one day, he pulled his toe out of that murky water and dove right in. It happened on a search warrant where he found himself alone in a bedroom staring at sixty-thousand dollars in cash. *If he took just a little, who would notice? If he turned it in, who would get it? A bunch of fucking politicians who hadn't done a damn thing except make his job harder anyway.* Fifty-five thousand dollars were turned in as evidence. No one ever missed the five K. No one even asked about it.

He'd filled his pockets that night but in the process had emptied his soul. After that, it just was. Having taken the first step, walking was easy.

People of like mind always have a way of finding each other. Before he knew it, he'd formed a loose group of officers who began planning search warrants and other stings with the purpose of financial gain. The Band was born. Before long, they'd started stealing dope as well. They'd either give the drugs to informants to sell, or they'd give people they busted an option: Lose your dope and go to prison, or retain it and give the proceeds to The Band. It was an easy choice for most.

McDonald knew better than to deal with any of these people directly. The best way for a criminal to avoid prison was to give up a dirty cop, and McDonald sure as hell wasn't going to go down that way. On those rare occasions where a personal visit was warranted, he'd always disguised himself.

As for The Band, he made it perfectly clear that if any one in the group talked to avoid prison, he and their family were fair game—a promise he intended to keep. If any one of these assholes even *thought* about turning on him, he'd kill them and their families. They knew the score. Just as he knew if he talked, Phipps would kill his family. The cost of talking had to be more expensive than the threat of prison. It was the only way he could survive; a simple but effective technique he'd learned from Mexican gangs: Talk and your whole family pays.

Everything had been going fairly smooth until that fucking Jonathan Thorpe replaced him as supervisor of the OGU. The man had been doing serious damage to his enterprise and was arresting far too many people who were "associates" of The Band. Sooner or later, one of those associates would decide to talk. They wouldn't be able to give up McDonald, but they'd damn sure be able to name other members. Then someone in The Band would consider federal protection despite the threats to their family's lives.

Then it had all escalated when Thorpe had arrested Charlie Peterson's sons. The two sold dope for The Band and were extremely close to Price. Lyndale was sentenced to prison for one hell of a stint. McDonald and Phipps in particular feared that Lyndale would tire of sitting in prison while the rest of The Band continued in prosperity. That's when McDonald hatched the idea of planting dope in Thorpe's home. If Thorpe was found to be a dirty cop, all the cases he'd been involved with would be closely scrutinized. That, paired with the original complaint that Thorpe had planted drugs on the men, would almost guarantee Lyndale's release. As a bonus, Thorpe would be fired and perhaps sent to prison. The man wouldn't be around fucking up McDonald's business anymore.

Within The Band, Daniels was his biggest worry. The man simply didn't have the stomach for what needed to be done. He'd been a concern of Phipps' even before this mess. Folks with a conscience as developed as Daniels' had no business swimming with sharks. He'd have Phipps keep a close eye on him— maybe give him a reminder of what awaited him if he talked.

Phipps was by far the most dependable in the group. His conscience had left him years ago, if he'd ever had one. The man was formidable, ex-military. He was the only one here with the guts to do what needed to be done.

Unfortunately, he'd just announced his opinion to the rest of The Band.

"We need to do *what*?" Daniels asked.

"You heard me the first fucking time, Daniels. You wearing a fucking wire or something?" Phipps accused.

Daniels started taking his clothes off.

McDonald had remained silent till now. Things were getting out of control, and he needed to instill some calm. McDonald, shaved white head gleaming, pulled his thick six-foot frame out of his chair.

"Keep your shirt on, Daniels," McDonald said. "We know you're not wearing a wire."

"Damn right, I'm not. I'm also not going to be part of no killin'."

"If we don't act first, he's damn sure going to kill us," Phipps argued.

"We don't even know if Thorpe killed Price," Shaw added.

"Let's go over this one more time, moron," Phipps said. "On Wednesday night, Price received an anonymous phone call from someone saying he knew the facts of the incident last year."

"*Incident*? We killed an innocent woman and child," Daniels interrupted.

Phipps gave Daniels a look warning him off. "Let me finish. The anonymous caller told Price he was going to the police with this information unless he was paid twenty-thousand-dollars. After receiving this call, Price called McDonald, and we all met at Shaw's house. Daniels, we couldn't reach you that night, so you weren't there. Price, Leon, and the rest of us met, and we discussed who might have this knowledge. We figured someone in this group had been talking. Leon argues and says the call might be a police sting. He went out the back door. He says it was to see if anyone was watching us. After a few minutes, we look for him and find his car missing. We all figure he got scared. Either afraid of us or the police; anyway we all figure he skipped town..."

"I guarantee he got as far away as he could. That boy was scared to death," Corn interrupted.

"Corn, you mind?" Phipps rhetorically asked. "Now, as we all know, Price was killed last night. I heard Homicide believes the murder was more of an assassination. Now this could all be a coincidence, but I don't think so. I don't think Price was blackmailed about the *incident* one night and killed the next without it being connected."

Phipps took a deep breath and looked around the room at the nodding heads before continuing. "If that's not enough, this morning Shaw's neighbor calls him over to look at some damage to his fence. Shaw said there was a hole cut in the fence. The hole faced Shaw's house. That's why we're not meeting there today. I think whoever called Price that night followed him to Shaw's. I think when Leon went outside to look for surveillance, he was killed. No one has seen or heard from him since."

Phipps looked around the room making eye contact. "I believe Leon is dead—murdered. I believe Thorpe killed Leon, then turned around and killed Price." Phipps raised his voice to drive home his next point, "I believe every one of us who were at that last meeting is in danger of being killed next!" Phipps paused to let his last statement sink in. "Baker, you've been awfully quiet. What do you think?"

Baker cleared his throat, "I'd have to agree. This is no coincidence. The phone call, Leon disappears, Price is killed. We all know Thorpe is behind it. Who else would start killing people over this shit? Anyone else would just turn us in. The only question is, what are we prepared to do about it?"

"We all fucking know what we need to do about it. We just gotta nut-up and do it," Phipps screamed. "This is war!"

"We're the ones that started the war when we killed his wife and kid," Daniels shouted back.

"That was an accident; that was never supposed to happen," Baker chimed in.

"That's all bullshit, Baker. You start fucking around like that and people get hurt. We never should've done what we done."

"Doesn't matter. It's done now, and you're a part of it, Daniels. Right now we need to concentrate on the threat to our lives. We have to deal with Thorpe before he kills each and every one of us!"

"Phipps, the way I see it, I'm safe," Daniels said as he headed for the door. "I didn't show up to your little meeting the other night, and Thorpe doesn't know I'm involved in this shit. I can't believe you fucks are actually discussing murdering a man...I won't be a part of it!"

As Daniels stormed out the front door, Shaw also stood up to leave. "Daniels is right, I ain't gonna be part of no murder."

"Sit down, Thadius. We're not getting anything accomplished by fighting with each other," McDonald said.

"Fuck that. I'm gone."

"Please, Thadius. Have a seat. No one is killing anyone. I think I have an idea where no one will get hurt," McDonald implored.

The five remaining men sat down in their seats, shiny with sweat despite the relatively cool temperature of the room. McDonald began laying out his plan to the rest of the group. Every time he looked Phipps' direction he was rewarded with a shaking head and a piercing glare.

McDonald finished laying out his plans. He stood, telling the other four men he needed some time to work on the details. When he walked out the front door, he sent Phipps a text that simply read, "Lacy Park. Now."

Five minutes later, Phipps pulled up next to McDonald with murder in his eyes, "You sit in there the whole fucking meeting not saying a word and when you finally do…"

McDonald held up a hand, cutting Phipps off. "Everything I said in there was bullshit. You're right. But we have to be careful about what we say and who we say it around. The others don't have the balls to do what needs to be done…understand?"

"I know, man. So what are we going to do?"

"I don't think Daniels can be trusted any longer."

"I've never trusted him," Phipps agreed.

"He and Shaw are tight, right?" McDonald asked.

"Real tight. They're like brothers."

"Phipps, I think I have an idea that will eliminate one problem and get the rest of the group on board."

RETURNING FROM HIS SHOPPING SPREE IN BROKEN ARROW, Thorpe called dispatch and obtained the phone number for his neighbor, Deborah Jennings.

"Well this is an unexpected surprise," she told him. " What can I do for you?"

"I hate to impose, but I was wondering if I could park my truck on your property for a little while."

"Park your truck on my property? Is that what you men call it these days?"

Thorpe laughed, "Not that I know of…No, I've got some bad guys who've learned where I live and what I drive, so I'd rather not announce when I'm home."

"Will you be putting me in danger?"

"Not if you have some place I can hide it."

"You sure you're not talking about sex?"

"Deborah, you have a one-track mind."

"My gate code is 5432. I'm sure I have a place it'll fit."

Thorpe instantly regretted having made the phone call. Later, when he pulled onto the Jennings' estate, he was surprised when Deborah appeared in slacks and a conservative blouse and coat. He'd expected something form-fitting but easily removable. She directed him to the west side of the property where a large barn stood out of sight from the road. Deborah was friendly but not overtly sexual. She said she would explain things to Thomas, her husband, so he didn't think they were having an affair. She said he probably wouldn't be too happy about it, but, he could kiss her ass—she was doing it anyway.

Having pulled his truck inside the barn, Thorpe transferred his purchases to a new duffel bag, slung it across his shoulders, and thanked Deborah. He passed through the gate onto the gravel road then into the woods. The first part of the trek would be tough going with the duffel; there was a lot of underbrush to wade through. But within a couple of minutes he was on a trail that would lead to his house. Thorpe had carved out this trail through the woods as a running route. It passed through his and several of his neighbor's properties, with one loop being nearly two miles. Thorpe enjoyed trail running, feeling it used more muscles and was more of a total-body workout than road running. After a few minutes, he came up on the back of his house and could see the deck overlooking the creek. Thorpe descended into the brook, waded through a foot of water, and climbed the opposite embankment. Before he reached the crest, he sat down his bag and pulled out a pair of binoculars.

If a competent sniper had been secreted in the undergrowth facing his home, the human chameleon would be nearly impossible to spot, a scenario Thorpe considered unlikely. His assassins would come at night; and though that was an assumption that could get him killed, he couldn't spend every waking hour peering into the deep dark across the road, flinching at every windblown limb.

Thorpe rose swiftly, sprinting to the back of the barn so as not to make an easy target for any lurking marksman. If someone were to shoot him, they'd have to earn it. His footfalls elicited a volley of barks from a startled Al and Trixie, who had not yet gathered his scent. When Thorpe reached the rear of the barn, he threw open the door and greeted his dogs. Then, he ordered the animals outside with the command, "Search." A cacophony of scratches echoed off the metal walls as the dogs' toenails searched for traction on the concrete floor. Gaining momentum, Al and Trixie tore off toward the front of the property, finely tuned muzzles in exploration.

As the dogs went about their work, Thorpe turned his attention to the interior of the barn, conducting his own search—for evidence of outdoor dogs having been confined indoors. Pleasantly surprised to find a sanitary gym, Thorpe waited for the dogs to finish their search and empty their bladders before retrieving his duffel bag near the creek bed.

Thorpe summoned the dogs, opened the front door of his house, and ordered a search—aware muddy paw prints would most likely be their greatest accomplishment. Al and Trixie scattered to opposite ends of the home, returning a minute later wagging their tails. Thorpe walked inside and dumped the contents of the duffel bag on the living room floor. He had a lot to do before reporting to work.

Eighteen

*Friday
February 9th
Evening*

OFFICER COLE DANIELS sat in the living room of his modest home wringing his hands in contemplation. *Were those crazy shits really going to kill Thorpe?* He knew Phipps wouldn't hesitate. War had fucked that man up. He'd known him for years, but ever since his last deployment, Phipps had been so detached he was robotic.

It was bad enough the group had decided to frame Thorpe. And Cole hadn't even known about that until the act had been set in motion. *He sure didn't do anything to stop it though, did he? Tried to justify it by acting like it was out of his hands. Then those two dumb fucks kill Thorpe's wife and daughter. Oh God, how had he got to this point in his life?*

Even after the killings he'd sat back and said nothing. He was afraid. Afraid of prison. Afraid of losing his wife and son. He'd been weak. Well, not anymore. First thing in the morning, he was going to get his wife and son out of town. Then he'd march down to the local FBI office and tell them everything. Maybe he could work out a deal and stay out of prison.

COLE'S WIFE, SAMANTHA, was in the kitchen preparing dinner – she loved to cook. Samantha knew something was bothering her husband but had been asked to be patient while he worked matters out on his own. Having put the finishing touches on her trademark lasagna, Samantha called for her husband, announcing dinner was ready. While she was transferring the steaming dish from stove to table, she heard the faint but distinct sound of breaking glass followed by a thud in the living room. Samantha hurried around the corner to find her husband face down on the floor, the right side of his head missing. Her living room wall was stippled with blood, bone fragments, and brain tissue.

THORPE WAS WRAPPING UP A SEARCH WARRANT in east Tulsa when the emergency tone broadcasted over the radio. "Adam 303, Adam 303 and a car to back. Off-duty officer shot at 1450 E. 56th Street North, one-four-five-zero east five-six Street North, break. Wife reports her husband is DOA from a gunshot wound. Wife was hysterical and provided no other information. EMSA and Fire are staging…"

Tyrone recognized the address, "Shit! That's Cole Daniels' house. What the fuck is going on?"

Thorpe was thinking the same thing, *What the fuck was going on?* According to Leon, Cole was one of those involved in the attempted dope planting at his home. Why would he be killed? It was too early to start speculating now. He instructed Jennifer and Donnie to transport the lone prisoner and complete all necessary paperwork. Thorpe and the rest of the unit would respond to the shooting scene to see if they could lend assistance. It would give Thorpe a chance to gather information.

En route, Thorpe tried to piece together what must be happening. Thorpe's presumption was that Daniels had become a liability to the rest of the collaborators. The group was desperate now, and they'd be coming for him sooner rather than later. They'd also inadvertently given Thorpe an airtight alibi; he had been surrounded by fellow officers as another suspect in his family's murder was killed. This was all speculation. For all he knew Cole's wife may have killed him—but that would be a nearly unfathomable coincidence.

Thorpe listened to the radio as the first responding officers arrived on scene. Their first responsibility would be to protect human life. That meant they would check to see if the downed individual was confirmed DOA or in need of medical treatment. They would then clear the house of potential threats and establish a safe perimeter. After safety was ensured, scene security and the preservation of witnesses would come next. An inner and outer crime scene would be set up, and a crime scene recorder would document the arrival time of every person who entered the outer ambit, including officers, detectives, medical examiners, police chaplains, funeral personnel—everyone. Every officer noted by the crime scene recorder would be responsible for completing a supplemental to the original homicide report, documenting actions he or she took while on scene.

Thorpe arrived about fifteen minutes after the alert tone was dispatched, finding nearly twenty police units parked in the drive and on the street. Daniels' house was on the northern edge of Tulsa's city limits on the south side of the street. The houses had large properties which sat back from the road a good forty yards.

Thorpe walked up to a patrol sergeant who had over twenty years on the department but had only recently been promoted, "What you got, Mike?"

"It's bad," Mike said as he glanced back at the house. "He's lying there in the living room with half his head missing."

"Cole Daniels? Gunshot, I guess?"

"Yeah...Cole. Wife says she was in the kitchen, heard a thud, ran in the living room and found her husband lying there with his brains all over the wall. There's a hole in the glass in the living room window. Looks like someone fired a high-caliber gun through the glass and killed him with one shot."

Sniper, Thorpe thought. But asked, "We're sure the wife didn't do it?"

"We're not sure of a damn thing right now; this thing's only fifteen minutes old."

"Okay, Mike. Some of my guys are heading this way. You need any help from us?"

"We've got too many people here already, tripping over each other. Right now we're mainly working at keeping people out of the crime scene. We already have a canvass going, but there's not a whole lot of houses within view 'round here. I guess the most I can ask of your guys is to start driving the neighborhood and cracking some heads, see what you can come up with."

Thorpe already noticed one thing about the crime scene that needed to be corrected. They'd cordoned off the property at 56th Street North to prevent sightseers and the media from getting too close, but the inner perimeter only extended about twenty yards from the front of the house. Thorpe decided not to raise the issue of extending the inner perimeter, which was based on his concern that a sniper might have fired the round from a considerable distance; this was not his crime scene. Thorpe was still speaking with the sergeant as he observed Detective Hull walking up the driveway.

Hull stepped up and spoke quietly, "Hey, John. Hey, Mike, fucking some week we're having, huh?" Hull nodded towards the house, "What we got?"

Mike reiterated all he had just told Thorpe—just as he would have to do twenty more times in the next thirty minutes. Hull took it all in, then asked, "So what do you think?"

"Two black officers killed two nights in a row. I don't know what to make of it," Mike said with a shrug of the shoulders.

"How bout you, John? What do you think?"

Thorpe looked directly at Hull: "You've got two black police officers killed one after another in what looks like professional work. Not only that, but both officers constantly complained about racism on the department. I think you've got a possible cop as a killer, and absolutely have a political nightmare on your hands."

Hull returned Thorpe's gaze. "Have you been reading my mind?"

"I only subscribe to the Sunday edition," Thorpe unsmilingly joked.

"Good, the rest is just filled with funnies...But I think you're right. I also think it's not going to take long for the media to reach the same conclusion. These are going to be some rough times ahead. Some have accused TPD of being racists forever, and now they finally have something resembling evidence."

"Bob, I've got some of my guys here; can you think of any way you can use them right now?" Thorpe offered.

"You can start by asking them where they've been for the last couple hours. We're going to have to start compiling information on where every police officer was during these two murders. The whole department will have to do it so we can start eliminating potential suspects. We may as well start while it's fresh in their minds."

Thorpe gave Hull a hard look, "Well, you can scratch my entire evening-shift unit off your suspect list. We've all been together the last two hours serving a search warrant. I'll have everyone in my unit send you an interoffice giving their whereabouts for the last two nights."

Thorpe turned and walked away just as Chuck Lagrone walked up next to his boss. When Thorpe was about ten feet away, he turned back with feigned anger, "And the next time the fucking Hull-and-Skull show comes to watch me fight, sit on the front row and buy me a beer afterwards."

MIKE ARCHED HIS EYEBROWS, "What the fuck was that about?"

"Nothing, Mike. Let me talk to Chuck alone for a minute," Hull said as he grabbed Lagrone and pulled him to the side.

"What the hell, Boss! Did you accuse him of being the shooter or something?"

"No. I just suggested he poll his squad about their whereabouts during these shootings. I told him everyone was going to be a suspect."

Lagrone pointed his finger at his boss, "Yeah, but he was the first person you told to do it. No wonder he took it personal."

"I wanted to give him a little shock, see how he responded. The good news is he said his whole unit was in the middle of a search warrant when this went down. If that pans out, it puts him in the clear."

"No shit...well...good!"

"He'll get over it—he's got a thick skin. Besides, we're going to piss off a lot of people before this thing is over," Hull assured his lead detective.

THORPE'S PLAN HAD BEEN TO DRIVE BACK TO THE OFFICE, but he decided this was the perfect time to tie up a loose end. As he drove, he considered the feigned anger he had directed at Hull. Thorpe wasn't actually mad at the man; the department was going to have to consider its own force as primary suspects—especially after tomorrow's headlines. Thorpe could just imagine what those would be. Besides, even if Hull *was* making insinuations, he was absolutely correct—at least about one of the killings.

With every north-side officer tied up on the homicide of Cole Daniels, Thorpe decided to make a brief stop at the law offices of Jessie Leatherman. The office was just a few miles south, sitting across the street from a convenience store where crack cocaine was the commodity most often sought and sold. Next to the convenience store was a restaurant which served excellent barbecue. The rest of the neighborhood, however, was one "shotgun" crack house after another. Thorpe wasn't sure why the small homes were referred to as shotgun houses, but thought it might have to do with the fact that if you fired in the front door, you'd probably stand a fair chance of striking everyone inside.

Thorpe didn't like using his assigned truck for the task but decided to take advantage of all the police officers being in one place at the same time. Earlier, Thorpe had made an excuse to enter the law office during daylight hours — to get a layout of the place. Though there were signs advertising an alarm system, none was active. Thorpe's truck contained the primitive equipment he knew he needed to gain entry. Apparently Jessie wasn't too worried about burglars—and after Thorpe had a look around the office he understood why—there wasn't anything inside worth stealing, not even a computer. As usual, Thorpe wore an earpiece connected to a police radio and oversized clothing.

Thorpe parked his truck in the barbecue parking lot, removed a pellet gun from the glove-box, and retrieved a wire clothes hanger from the back seat. Thorpe carried the pellet gun in his truck for a variety of reasons, primarily for search warrants when porch lights needed to be extinguished from a distance. When Thorpe stepped out of his vehicle, he was enveloped with the woody aroma of slowly smoked meat. Ignoring his mouth's salivations, he walked behind the barbeque joint towards the convenience store. He was grateful not to encounter friendly citizens behind the store who might think he looked like a good robbery target again.

Thorpe crossed the four-lane street a block to the east and began making his way towards the back of the law office. The windows were the type with an inside lever you turned clockwise then up to unlock. Once unlocked, the window was opened by pushing out from the inside. Thorpe approached the glass and noticed the lever was in the locked position. Retrieving the pellet gun, Thorpe shot a small hole just above and to the left of the lever. He then fashioned a hook on the wire hanger and fed it through the hole and down towards the handle. It took a couple of tries, but Thorpe was able to hook the lever and pull it up into the unlocked position. He then used his knife to break the seal on the window and pull it open.

Thorpe casually took in his surroundings before peeling off clothing so he could fit into the opening. Once inside, Thorpe rummaged through a cheap, laminate-covered metal desk before moving on to a pair of unlocked metal file cabinets. He located a drawer labeled "K—R" and inside found a file with the name Leon Peterson. Along with other legal papers, Thorpe located two unopened envelopes one of which was addressed to Leon's father, Charlie Peterson. *Could it really be this easy?* Thorpe opened the envelopes and found what he'd come for—handwritten statements detailing the events of Thorpe's wife's and daughter's murders. It included the names of all those involved. Thorpe looked around the office a few more minutes, checking for additional documentation. Finding none, he attempted to replace everything as he'd found it, and shimmied out the window.

Hopefully, no one would ever know there had been a break-in. The only evidence was a tiny hole in the window that would most likely be attributed to vandals. If they did suspect a burglary, they wouldn't find anything missing. If Leon's body was discovered and Jessie went to retrieve the letters but couldn't find them, maybe he would chalk up the missing documents to old age and forgetfulness; he wasn't the sharpest tool in the shed.

Returning to his truck with the smell of mesquite still ensnared in his nose, Thorpe decided to head to the office, tackle some paperwork, then head home for some rest. Tomorrow would be a long day of the brass trying to prove to the public and politicians they had everything under control.

As Thorpe made his way under a pregnant, starless sky, he wondered if he might have a surprise or two waiting for him at home.

Nineteen

Saturday
February 10th
Early morning

THE TEMPERATURE HAD PLUMMETED and a light sleet had begun to fall by the time Thorpe arrived at Deborah's property. He'd taken an unusual route to enter the neighborhood, being careful not to pass in front of his own residence; the last thing he wanted to do was endanger Deborah or her husband.

Thorpe stabbed at the numbered buttons on the keypad and was granted entry through the estate's imposing gate. He drove his undercover truck to the large barn on the south side of the property and pulled inside behind his personal truck. He cut his lights.

Thorpe shut the barn doors, turned on the interior lights, and began preparing his equipment, part of which included an AR-15 equipped with a flash hider, collapsible stock, and Aimpoint red-dot scope.

As Thorpe organized his equipment on the tailgate, he heard someone working the door latch of the barn. Thorpe released the bolt on the AR, feeding a .223 round into the chamber. He shouldered the weapon as he turned. Deborah let out a sharp cry as she looked down the muzzle of Thorpe's rifle.

"Deborah, you should damn well know better!" Thorpe lowered the weapon. "Close the door; people will be able to see the light."

Deborah held both hands over her heart as though she were trying to keep the organ from escaping her chest. "Sorry, I didn't know you were so jumpy."

"Did I not tell you why I was parking here? Knock next time...I could've taken your head off."

"You're right. You have to be careful."

"What are you doing down here? Your husband's going to come inside and shoot us both."

Deborah remained near the barn doors—as if she were afraid to approach. "He's not here; we've separated."

Trouble. "Oh...When did this happen?"

"It's been a few days...I wasn't going to tell you...but I've been thinking..."

Oh, shit. Stay strong, Thorpe. "Deborah, I'm not ready for a relationship right now, and technically you're still married."

"I've been doing a lot of thinking lately. Thomas has been treating me like trash for years. He hasn't been faithful since the day we married. I should've left him a long time ago, but I didn't want to lose all this..." Deborah gestured with her hands, referring to her possessions. "I just put up with it. And when you and I slept together I didn't feel bad about it because he had been doing the same thing to me for years. I finally had enough and confronted him about it; told him I knew about his affairs; told him I had one of my own. He was livid; tried to kick me out of the house. I told the old drunk bastard to get the hell out. It's over. Even if I wanted to make things work he wouldn't have me back. I've insulted him."

"Good for you, I guess...If that's what you really want."

"I don't want a relationship, John. I just want to be with you...from time to time." Deborah was wearing an ankle length fur coat. She undid the belt and slowly opened it wide. She stood there in black, knee-high leather boots, a fur hat, and nothing else. Her pale body stood in sharp contrast to the theatrical black scrim behind her. Her flesh was covered in goose bumps; her nipples stood in mock salute of the frigid air. Deborah took three catlike steps toward Thorpe who promptly lifted her off her feet and sat her on the tailgate, her fur coat spilling beneath her. Deborah spread her legs and undid Thorpe's belt. She pulled Thorpe closer as he entered her. She leaned back on Thorpe's canvas bag and pulled her feet up onto the tailgate so the heels of her boots dug into the liner of her fur coat. Deborah's bosom was pointed skyward, and as Thorpe's thrusts became stronger her large firm breasts rolled to the rhythm of their love making. Deborah pushed Thorpe away and forced him down where she had been lying. She straddled him, arching her back as she rose and fell. Her breath was visible in the cold air, and her entire body was covered with gooseflesh.

When they'd finished, Deborah spoke breathlessly, "Don't worry yourself about this. I'm not looking for a relationship either. And I know as well as you, it wouldn't work between us. But that was good." Deborah wrapped herself in her coat and walked to the barn door where she paused and looked back at his semi-naked form. "That's a big gun you got there," Deborah said with a smile. She nodded at the assault rifle lying next to Thorpe.

Damn it! Thorpe was mad at himself, and not for the first time with this woman. *How can a man be so disciplined in some areas of his life and have absolutely no willpower in others?* From Thorpe's personal and professional experience, he knew good sex was an excellent indicator of a woman's mental fitness. It seemed the better they were in bed—the crazier they were. With that reasoning, Deborah must be loonier than hell. Hopefully she'd keep her promise and not expect any commitment from Thorpe; at this point in his life he wouldn't be able to give it, and Deborah wouldn't be at the top of his list as a deserving recipient. He had needed that though; he'd had enough tension building up inside of him the last few days to power a small town.

Thorpe slipped out of his remaining clothes and into Under Armour Cold Gear. He covered that with several layers of additional clothing, topping it off with a three-dimensional RealLeaf suit, a commercial hunting accessory that breaks up the human silhouette with realistic man-made leaves. It's a watered down version of the ghillie suits used by military snipers. Underneath the camouflage, Thorpe wore a layer of Gortex and a black balaclava to protect against the falling sleet. He stashed his equipment in his camouflage CamelBak HAWG. The backpack was fairly low profile but capable of carrying 1280 cubic inches of gear. The pack was also fitted with a water bladder system capable of carrying a hundred ounces of water. Thorpe checked his watch—it was nearing two in the morning. He grabbed his weapons, slung the pack over his shoulders, and pushed open the barn's doors as he simultaneously pushed thoughts of Deborah out of his mind.

BEFORE ANDREW PHIPPS BECAME A SNIPER with the Tulsa Police Department's Special Operations Team, he had been a "Dark Green" United States Marine. More specifically, he was Force Reconnaissance or "Force Recon," a special operations force within the Corps, like the SEALs in the Navy, and the Green Berets and Delta in the Army.

Tonight he found himself in a situation he'd been in countless times before, except this time he wasn't miles behind enemy lines in some godforsaken third-world country. Instead, he was just outside Hicksville, USA, on a direct-action mission. He sat beside a gravel road with a 30.06 rifle and no scope. The weapon was nothing compared to the equipment he carried in Recon or even on the police department, but it was more than adequate for tonight's black-op.

This mission's HVI—High Value Individual—should appear in his sights at a mere forty yards. Phipps' position was far from optimal but was necessitated by the terrain and made acceptable by the fact that he didn't have to worry about an enemy force returning fire or overrunning his position. He'd never take such an up-close shot during a military action. He'd arrived with a cheap Bushnell scope but quickly found the woods were so thick, the only way he'd be able to acquire his target was to get close and personal.

No worries. He'd drop Thorpe with one well placed, high powered round, then Phipps would casually stroll out of the woods. The poor, clueless bastard would probably illuminate himself with his own truck's headlights. *This would be a piece of cake.* The only thing that made Phipps unhappy was the man lying on the ground beside him; Thadius Shaw was acting as his "spotter," though Phipps didn't plan on using him for anything other than an accessory—*that* would keep his mouth shut.

A few hours ago, Shaw would never have agreed to come along on this mission. But that changed when Sergeant McDonald convinced him that Thorpe had murdered his best friend, Daniels—and wouldn't stop until they were all dead. Shaw wasn't aware that the man who had actually killed his friend was lying next to him. Phipps hadn't exactly enjoyed killing Daniels...or maybe he did—he didn't know anymore. He had always gotten satisfaction from killing the enemy in combat but now wondered if he just didn't enjoy killing—period. He knew one thing: He'd relish putting a bullet in Thorpe's head, and his only regret would be that Thorpe wouldn't see it coming. In the sniper's world, death is like a light switch; you're dead even before the sound waves of the blast reach your corpse.

Both men were dressed in cheap camouflage. Phipps didn't want to wear his ghillie suit and risk tearing a piece of it off on a branch. He'd handled the material enough that his DNA was probably all over the suit.

Instead, he lay concealed in the bush, wearing cheap discount store camouflage, and using a cheap rifle. He was here to kill a man who'd become a threat to his freedom, and Marines had always been in the freedom-protection business. He didn't know much about the man he was here to kill. Thorpe had always seemed cordial, but that didn't mean anything; McDonald appeared to be a nice guy too. One would never guess the shit he was into.

Phipps looked over at Shaw—who was visibly shivering—and thought to himself, worthless. He'd told the dumb-ass to dress warm. There's nothing colder than sitting completely motionless on the frozen ground for hours waiting to kill someone. He didn't know if Shaw was shaking from the cold and sleet, or from nerves; probably a combination of both. Phipps was glad this would be a simple kill because Shaw wasn't inspiring a lot of confidence. Plus, Shaw wore eyeglasses which Phipps had forced him to remove. He didn't want light reflecting off the lenses and giving away their position. So, besides being an untrained, non-combat pogue and out-of-his-element, shivering little bitch, he was also half-blind. Phipps wouldn't be surprised to hear the man's teeth begin to chatter.

If Phipps were to be perfectly honest, his own toes were starting to feel a bit numb. He wished Thorpe would hurry up and get his sorry white ass home so he could put a bullet in it and go home to a heated den and ESPN. While these thoughts were swirling around his head, he noticed movement in the darkness of Thorpe's property. Two shapes were running towards the front gate—dogs. Where the fuck did they come from?

"What the...?" Shaw said loudly.

Phipps whispered, "Shut your fucking mouth." *What the hell was this?* They'd been here for two-and-a-half hours and hadn't seen a thing—and now two dogs were roaming the fence line? One of the dogs paused and looked across the road and just to the left of where he and Shaw were lying. It began to growl.

"That fucking dog sees us," Shaw said with obvious fear in his voice.

"He doesn't see us; he smells us…And now he probably hears us. If I have to tell you to shut your mouth again I'm going to slit your throat right here in these woods."

As soon as his words came out, the woods in front, above, and behind them burst with light. Shaw immediately jumped to his feet and turned to run deeper into the woods. The distinctive crack of supersonic rounds sliced air above Phipps head. The rounds were followed by a short yelp from Shaw as he continued his flight into the woods. *Fucking automatic gunfire*—sounded like a three-round burst from an M-4. The lights prevented Phipps from clearly identifying a muzzle flash.

Too fucking dark, Phipps thought as he fired off a round.

Another burst came in from another location. *Goddammit! The son-of-a-bitch was shooting and moving!* Phipps hugged the earth and began to crawl away from the gunfire—some of which came too close to finding its mark. When he had some cover between him and his attacker, he stood and began making his way deeper into the woods. He had to find that fucking Shaw. Or, maybe he didn't.

THORPE LAY PRONE IN THE CREEK BED with the bank as cover. Near him lay two connected extension cords. The hot end came from his house and the other led into the woods across the street. Thorpe had picked a trough through the gravel road and buried the cord. On the other side of the road, he'd connected a three-way splitter. Those cords fed several different lights which were concealed in the woods. Thorpe had even used clear Christmas lights in the branches high above the ground. Unlit, the lights were hard to spot in the limbs of the trees.

As soon as Thorpe had connected the two extension cords, the tree line had come alive with a curtain of light, and he had caught movement several yards to the right of where he had his weapon trained—something moving fast. Thorpe had let out a burst from his AR-15 towards the moving figure, then tucked his head and rolled several feet to his right. As he did so he'd heard the distinctive sound of a bullet tumbling through the air to his left—*ricochet*. The bullet must have struck a limb in the woods before reaching his location. *There were at least two of them*—one was fleeing through the woods and the other fired at Thorpe's last position. *Phipps must have a spotter with him.*

Thorpe popped up and let off a short burst near where he'd seen the first person rise and run. He fired these rounds lower anticipating Phipps was lying on the ground. Thorpe tucked his head and moved again, noticing there was no return fire this time. He figured one of three things was occurring: He'd either hit Phipps with the last burst; Phipps was retreating; or Phipps was relocating—waiting for Thorpe to let off another burst, a burst that'd be met with a rifle round between Thorpe's eyes. Deciding he'd pushed his luck enough, Thorpe slid down into the creek bed and began running to the east. When he reached a wooded area east of his house, he left the creek bed and began making his way back to the gravel road. He wasn't sure if he'd struck either man with gunfire.

PHIPPS MADE HIS WAY NORTH THROUGH THE WOODS, then stopped and considered his options. He could call out to Shaw and the two of them could wade out of this debacle together. Or he could lie still in the woods and hope Thorpe would come in after them. With all the dead foliage, maybe he'd hear the man coming—then again the sound of the sleet might cover his footfalls. Or he could quietly locate Shaw and use him as bait.

Phipps lay down on the floor of the woods to think. Thorpe didn't have any military background, but it sure as hell seemed like he had some training somewhere—*and where the fuck did he get an automatic rifle?* The more Phipps considered it, the more concerned he became. Not only did Thorpe anticipate an ambush, but he correctly anticipated from where it most likely would occur. Then he laid down some damn accurate fire on Shaw who was a moving target at considerable yardage. Plus, Thorpe shot and moved. He didn't get tunnel vision, even anticipated there could be more than one threat in the woods. Phipps had definitely underestimated the man.

Phipps figured Thorpe was smart enough to know it would be suicide to follow multiple adversaries into the woods alone at night. The man most likely would wait alongside the road, concealed, and hope to ambush them as they made their way back out of the woods. That's what Phipps would do. But Thorpe might make his way north through the woods to Phipps' east or west—in an effort to cut off a retreat.

Phipps' extraction element—Brandon Baker—was a few miles east in his personal car. The plan had been to kill Thorpe, hike east, call Baker, and get picked up. *Well that plan had gone to shit.* Phipps decided his best bet at surviving was to get up and haul ass north fast enough to ensure Thorpe couldn't get in front of him. He might have to spend the entire night in the woods, but it wouldn't be the first time he'd done it. As he began picking his way through the underbrush, he heard Shaw screaming his name—*Fuck 'im; that Gomer was on his own.*

SHAW DIDN'T KNOW WHAT DIRECTION HE WAS HEADING. *Goddamn Phipps!* His left arm was killing him. It hung like a piece of meat from the elbow down. A round had caught him near the left elbow and had completely disintegrated the joint. Shaw needed medical treatment but instead was out in the middle of who-knows-where in freezing temperatures with stinging sleet in his face. His glasses had been in his chest pocket when he began running but broke after he bounced off a couple of trees. Now he had one cracked lens and was afraid to use his flashlight for fear it would give him away. Because of the weather, he couldn't even use stars to navigate—not that he knew how to anyway. And Phipps...that motherfucker, wouldn't answer. Who knew where he was or even if he was alive. Fuck it was cold. Shaw, convinced he was going to die if he didn't get medical help, pulled out his phone and called Baker.

"Yeah?" Baker said, answering his phone.

"It's me."

"Is it done?"

"Yeah...Change of plans though. You need to come in the neighborhood and pick us up. We're lost in the woods, but we're close to the road."

"You're fucking kidding me, right?"

"Just get your ass in here and pick us up. You need to honk your horn when you get close to Thorpe's house so we can follow the sound."

"Bullshit. You trying to get us all arrested?"

"Look, ain't nobody the fuck out here! It's colder than shit so people's windows are closed; they're not going to hear you."

"Fuck that!"

"If you don't come get us, and the police pick us up in these woods, the first person I'm going to throw down is you. Now get your white ass in here and pick us up." Shaw hung up the cell phone. Hopefully Baker wouldn't call Phipps. There's no way Baker would come in here if he knew Thorpe was alive and running around with an automatic weapon.

THORPE HEARD THE SCREAMING before he even reached the road. Someone was yelling Phipps' name, "Phipps...I'm hit...Where are you? Phipps!" Thorpe was tempted to follow but was concerned it was a trap. *Go ahead—follow the voice and get a bullet in the back of your head for your troubles, dumbshit.* Instead, Thorpe crossed the road but stayed about a hundred yards south of the commotion. He hid behind a fallen tree and waited in the black. Thorpe removed the SID-supplied night vision goggles from his pack and secured them to his head. He knew he should use his dogs, but he'd become too attached to his furry family members. *Better he die in these woods than Al and Trixie.* The thrashing and yelling to the north ceased, allowing Thorpe to tune-in to the sounds of his environment; it was difficult with the falling sleet. Several minutes later he observed a wash of headlights on the trees above his position. A vehicle was approaching from the east on the road behind him. A minute after the car passed, Thorpe observed a faint glow of light through the trees ahead.

SHAW CAUGHT A FLASH OF HEADLIGHTS and began picking his way towards the road. He decided he needed to call Baker again.

"Where you at?" Baker answered.

"Did you just drive down the road?" Shaw asked.

"Yeah, I'm passing Thorpe's house now."

"Turn around and come back the way you came. You don't need to honk your horn; I could see your lights. Stay on the phone, I'll tell you when to stop." Shaw was having a hell of a time navigating through the trees. It was impossible to see, particularly with only one sleet-covered lens. After a minute, Shaw picked out Baker's headlights approaching from the west. "Stop. Stay right where you are and cut your lights. I'll be in front of you in a minute." Shaw couldn't wait to get out of the woods. He still didn't want to use his flashlight but decided to use the light from his cell phone's LCD screen to see at least a couple of feet in front of him. He picked up the pace towards the waiting vehicle.

THORPE SAW THE VEHICLE APPROACH from the west and stop on the road twenty yards behind and to his left. Then he picked out a glow cutting through the woods toward the waiting automobile. *What the hell?* Thorpe slid the goggles up on his forehead. It was a blue light. *This is too easy...It's got to be a trap.* On the other hand, the car in the road was a sitting duck if he wanted to step out and light up the windshield. The more Thorpe thought about it the more he didn't think it was a trap after all. *They're actually that stupid.*

Thorpe pulled down the goggles and began angling towards the approaching light. He should be able to intercept his target before it reached the roadway. Whoever was utilizing the blue light was carelessly crashing through the woods; Thorpe could even hear the footfalls above the cascading sleet. Thorpe timed his own steps to those of his prey.

The glow was closer now. Whoever he was stalking was using a damn cell phone to light his way through the woods. The light would provide a couple of feet of visibility at the most and would totally wreck the person's night vision beyond that distance. Thorpe propped his AR against a tree and retrieved his personal Sig Sauer .357 caliber pistol from his side holster. He didn't really want to use the weapon because he'd purchased it himself, and it was registered in his name. If he was forced to use the weapon he would be disappointed in having to destroy it—he was already going to have to dispose of parts of his personal AR.

Thorpe held the pistol in his left hand, in his right was a black tanto knife with a seven-inch blade. The knife was the weapon he preferred to use. He stood behind a large tree as his target passed about eight feet in front of him, moving right to left. His target held the cell phone in front of him with his right hand—his left arm dangled at his side, hand empty. *Was this guy really walking through these woods without a weapon at the ready?* Thorpe checked again to see if his target was being followed. He doubted someone would willingly sacrifice themselves as bait but Thorpe was genuinely perplexed at how easy this man was making matters. Just in case, Thorpe decided to take the man to the ground; at least he'd be a harder target lying prone.

Thorpe holstered his Sig. He charged his phone-wielding adversary. His prey heard death descending upon him and turned—too late. Thorpe tackled him with a well placed elbow to the side of the face, both men crashing to the ground with Thorpe on top. Thorpe secured the man's right wrist with his left hand and ignored the noodle-like left arm that slithered about the leaf-strewn forest floor. Thorpe held his knife across the man's trachea and looked down into a pair of wild eyes, *Thadius Shaw*. Thorpe lowered himself to within inches of Shaw's face, partly to instill fear, but mostly to get his head closer to the ground if Phipps was following. "How many of you are there?" Thorpe hissed.

"Just me and Phipps...And Baker's in the car," Shaw declared without hesitation. "Please don't..."

"Is Phipps still alive?"

"I don't know, I..."

Thorpe ended Shaw's sentence, cutting deep into muscle and cartilage with the razor-sharp knife. He was up and moving well before Shaw's heart stopped pumping steaming blood onto the frozen ground. *Thadius Shaw...That meant Phipps was dead, injured, fleeing, or stalking.* Thorpe reattached his night vision goggles and found Shaw's cell phone lying on the ground a few feet south of his gurgling body. Retrieving the phone and his AR, Thorpe found some cover and listened. He heard nothing except for the sound of sleet striking the trees and the idling engine of the vehicle on the road.

Good fight, son. One thing: you didn't breathe until I paid Levi his money. Thorpe often heard his father's words. He immediately concentrated on his breathing and simultaneously considered his options.

He could approach the vehicle from behind and take out Baker up close. Or he could just step out in the road and permeate the vehicle with .223 rounds. *What* would he do if he were in Phipps' position? He decided if he were Phipps, he'd sit in a locale where he could see the vehicle and take out his opposition if it moved in. He decided taking down the vehicle at this location was too much of a risk. Thorpe quickly came up with a plan he figured had an above average chance of success but was low risk for himself.

Thorpe moved into a position where he was concealed but had a limited view of the vehicle; it appeared to be a dark SUV. He pulled out Shaw's cell phone, covered the light, and found the last dialed call—Brandon Baker. Thorpe tracked east, being careful to stay low, stop, and listen. When he was out of view of the vehicle, he popped out on the road and sprinted east before finding another place to take cover. If Phipps was in fact watching the car, Thorpe would be out of range at this location. He retrieved Shaw's cell phone, brought up Baker's number, and punched the send button.

"Where *in the fuck* are you?" Baker answered—obviously thinking he was speaking to Shaw.

"Looking at you," Thorpe answered.

"Who's this?"

"That's a nice SUV you got there, Baker. Too bad I'm about to decorate the interior with your brains."

Thorpe could hear the roar of the engine and the spray of gravel. Baker would probably drive with his head down for a stretch then rise up when he thought he'd reached a safe distance. Thorpe could see the dark form of the vehicle approaching on the road. Then the lights flashed on—that meant his head was up. Thorpe was at a bend in the road, so he was firing at a ninety-degree angle at the front windshield. His main concern was that a .223 isn't much of a penetrating round; most of the bullets would be deflected, particularly the first few. Thorpe set his AR to semi-auto and placed the Aimpoint's red dot just above where the steering wheel should be located. He systematically began pumping rounds into the windshield.

BRANDON BAKER HAD BEEN SITTING ON THE ROAD with his lights off for what seemed an eternity. His nerves had caused him to break into a sweat, and, even though he wasn't driving, his knuckles were white on the steering wheel. Then he heard Thorpe's voice on the phone.

Fucking Thorpe was still alive and getting ready to put a bullet in his head. Baker ducked down in his seat, pulled the gearshift into drive, and stomped the gas pedal. He drove for a short distance before he realized he would probably leave the road, strike a tree, and die at the hands of that crazy fuck.

Baker peered over the dash and turned on his headlights to make his way through the darkness. *Shit; he still couldn't see.* He activated the windshield wipers to clear the accumulated sleet and noticed he had an approaching right turn. Baker rose fully in his seat to better handle the high-speed turn when his windshield started to spider web. Glass tore into his eyes. Baker reflexively ducked and as a result wasn't able to navigate the turn properly. He yanked his wheel to the right, anticipating where the turn should be. He felt his left wheel dip down into the ditch and lost complete control as his Durango violently left the road. The SUV came to an abrupt stop as Baker lay across the front seats bleeding from the eyes—awaiting death.

PHIPPS HAD WORKED HIS WAY NORTHWARD, unsure of his precise location or where he was headed. All he knew for certain was he'd survive the night. Occasionally, he'd stop and listen for unfriendlies over the deluge of sleet. It was during one of these pauses he heard the distinctive report of a high-powered rifle fired at a steady, semi-auto pace. The shooter had to be Thorpe, who was apparently still at work behind him—a good distance behind him based on the sound of things. Phipps' good news likely indicated the demise of Shaw, however. *Probably for the best. That nigger was a walking Charlie Foxtrot.*

With the gunfire safely in the distance, Phipps figured it would be safe to use his cell phone and make Baker aware of recent developments. Baker could look for a road that might intersect his path to the north. Phipps retrieved his cell phone—which had been silenced—and noticed he'd missed two phone calls from Baker within the last few minutes. Phipps returned the calls.

AS THORPE PLACED ROUNDS IN THE WINDSHIELD, the SUV entered the turn at too high a speed, then jerked to the right—too late. It left the roadway and struck a stand of scrub oak. Thorpe slapped in a fresh magazine then fired into the driver's side as he approached the vehicle. Reaching the SUV, Thorpe knelt behind the driver's side door before yanking it open with his left hand. Stepping around, he illuminated the interior of the cab with a flashlight attached to his rifle. Brandon Baker lay in a heap across the center console.

Thorpe fired two additional "insurance" rounds into Baker's upper back, slung the rifle over his shoulder, and ran to the passenger side. He pulled open the door and hoisted Baker's body onto the ground. A check of the pulse confirmed Baker was dead. Thorpe needed to do something with the truck—at least it was still running. Hopefully he'd be able to dislodge it from the trees.

Thorpe opened the rear passenger door and, with considerable effort, lifted Baker's limp body off the ground. He stuffed him in the back seat. Thorpe hurried to the driver's seat, put the vehicle into four-wheel drive, and was pleased when he was able to reverse the Durango several feet. He shoved it into drive and got back onto the gravel road. Thorpe drove the Durango south, away from his home. Then, he heard a cell phone ringing on the floorboard near his feet. He retrieved the phone and saw the name displayed on the lit LCD screen, Phipps. Thorpe flipped open the phone and let out an indiscernible grunt.

"Baker?" Phipps asked.

"Baker is feeling a bit under the weather at the moment; can I take a message?"

"Thorpe?" Phipps correctly guessed.

"And I believe they call you Mr. Phipps."

There was a long silence on the other end of the phone. Phipps was probably deciding whether or not he was going to play this little game.

"You're a funny motherfucker—even when you're about to die," Phipps finally said.

"I am a funny motherfucker. But you're a little confused on the 'who's going to die' part."

"You know who you're fucking with, motherfucker?!" Phipps shouted.

"I do, but you obviously don't. Otherwise I wouldn't be talking to you on your dead buddy's cell phone. Would I, Recon?"

"I'm still standing, motherfucker!" Phipps screamed defiantly.

"You're probably running scared, or as you Recon guys like to call it 'tactically retreating.' Aren't you, pussy? In fact, I bet you take some R & R for a few weeks like a good little bitch," Thorpe said, purposely pushing the man's buttons.

"I ain't goin' nowhere."

"Well then, why not come back and we'll finish this like warriors?"

"I'll finish this on *my* terms, motherfucker; but I'll stay in town—you can count on it."

"If you do leave, we'll both know you're the biggest gaping pussy this side of the Grand Canyon…By the way, is 'motherfucker' the only four syllable word you know?"

"Fuck you," Phipps growled.

"Way to improvise, marine."

Thorpe figured that should send Phipps into a mild rage. Hopefully he'd be pissed off enough to hang around and try to finish the job. The worst thing for Thorpe would be for Phipps to take three weeks vacation. Then, for a month, he'd have to worry if the guy was really out of town or actually the new bush in Thorpe's back yard.

For now, Thorpe turned his attention to the huge problem currently on his hands: He was driving around in a Dodge Durango with about seventeen bullet holes and front-end damage. Oh yeah, and there was also a dead guy in the back seat. He needed to get the car well out of his neighborhood—and do it without getting pulled over. Afterwards, he'd have to find a ride back home that wasn't traceable. Thorpe had one thing working in his favor: Cops hate to stop cars in poor weather, and it didn't get much nastier than it was tonight. Thorpe sometimes jokingly commented if he sold drugs for a living, he'd only move his product when it was raining outside.

Thorpe found a secluded area alongside the country road where he could stop to survey the Durango's damage. A headlight was busted. The windows on both front doors were nearly gone. The windshield was shattered. And there were bullet holes in the driver's side door. Thorpe located the vehicle's lug wrench and used it to rake the remaining glass from the two front windows. He then entered the cabin and kicked out the windshield. *Yet another pair of boots I have to replace.*

It was going to be hell driving sixty miles an hour in the sleet without a windshield, but visibility through the shattered glass was already difficult. Wiper blades would only shred trying to remove accumulated sleet. Thorpe grabbed a pair of sunglasses from his pack and put them on. The tinted lenses weren't optimal but would be an improvement over speed-driven sleet ripping at his eyes.

Thorpe dropped the SUV into drive and sped toward Tulsa in an open cockpit. When the city limits neared, he retrieved Shaw's cell phone from his pocket and began thumbing through its phonebook. Thorpe recognized several Tulsa police officers names on the menu. He began dialing. He didn't have any luck with the first two numbers, but got an answer with the third.

"Thadius? What are you doing calling…" Samantha Daniels—Cole Daniels' recent widow—answered the phone, clearly irritated.

Hoping to keep his voice indiscernible, Thorpe interrupted her using a raspy, whispering voice, "Samantha? Samantha I need help. They've got me…the same people who got your husband got me…" Thorpe didn't like using Samantha, considering the woman had just lost her husband, but now was not the time for niceties.

"Thadius, what's going on I…?"

"Listen! I'm in the trunk of a white Lincoln Town car. They're going to kill me, Samantha. My phone couldn't get through to 911. You gotta call the police."

"Where are you?"

"I don't know. We're parked somewhere in North Tulsa. I think we're close to Reservoir Hill. White Lincoln Town car. Three white males. You gotta call. They're going to hear me…I gotta go."

Thorpe hung up the cell phone. Hopefully Samantha would phone the police and make for a credible caller. Even if she thought it was a prank, she'd most likely report the phone call. Every available unit would respond to north Tulsa looking for three white males in a white Lincoln Town car. Taking into consideration the caller and recent events, even the State Troopers and Tulsa County Sheriff's Department would be notified. Thorpe should have a "police free" zone where he was headed.

Even if units did remain in the area, they'd be looking for three white males in a white Lincoln Town car—a far cry from a black Dodge Durango with one headlight. Thorpe turned east onto the Creek Turnpike making his way around the south side of the city before connecting with Highway 169 and continuing north. There weren't many cars on the highway, but the roads weren't too slick. Sleet was nothing compared to the freezing rain Tulsa often experienced during this time of the year.

Thorpe merged with I-244 before exiting onto Memorial Drive, thankful he hadn't yet spotted a marked police unit and angry with himself for not having brought along a police radio. Thorpe turned west into a neighborhood just north of McClure Park, where he removed his equipment from the Durango and set out on foot.

The Special Investigations offices were just over a mile away, but since he'd be traveling peripheral streets, his urban hike would be closer to two miles. He was looking forward to the exercise; sixty-mile-an-hour subfreezing winds had taken its toll despite the layers of protective clothing he wore. Thorpe hid his rifle and equipment in the shrubbery of a nearby house. Not many people were up at this hour, but a man ensconced in camouflage toting an assault rifle would definitely raise an eyebrow or two. Thorpe had some distance to travel but in an effort to keep all eyebrows at an acceptable elevation, he resisted the urge to run.

Twenty-two minutes later Thorpe approached the offices from the southwest. He had only one set of keys for an extra car at the office. If that car was gone, he'd have to enter the building via his key-card, which would electronically record his presence. His preference was to avoid leaving any indication he'd been in the area tonight.

Thorpe ascended the parking ramp and avoided using his key-card by scaling the chain link gate. He felt relief at the sight of the green Jeep Wrangler he needed. Thorpe got into the vehicle and pulled up to the gate, where a weight-sensitive pad released him and the Jeep without any electronic documentation. Outside the gates, Thorpe wished he could buy a gas can and petrol, but he knew every convenience store in the Tulsa area would receive follow-up investigations after tonight. And most stations had video—at least on the inside of the stores. Instead of using a gas can, Thorpe had another idea.

Thorpe drove the Jeep to a dark, isolated place inside McClure Park where prostitutes often serviced their johns. He doubted any police officers would check the area because they were busy searching for a kidnapped police officer and because hookers rarely walked the streets in such poor weather. Having parked, Thorpe walked back north to the area where he'd stashed his equipment. There, he retrieved the items and made his way back to the Durango.

Thorpe had considered his options on how to collect an accelerant. There were really only two. One, he could slide under the Durango and go to work on the plastic gas tank with his knife. It probably wouldn't take long to puncture the tank, and the drainage would be fast—there was just one problem; he'd end up with gasoline—a.k.a. evidence—all over his person and clothing. Plus he'd transfer that evidence to the Jeep when he drove away. He decided on his second option, which was much cleaner but unfortunately more time consuming.

Thorpe climbed into the driver's seat, inserted the key and turned it to the forward position activating the fuel pump. He then popped the hood, removed the bladder from his Camelbak, stepped outside and dumped the water on the street. Lifting the hood and using his knife as a screwdriver, Thorpe released the fuel rail and slowly began filling the bladder. When it was full, Thorpe dumped the gasoline in the cab of the vehicle and on the body of Brandon Baker. He was careful not to get it on his own clothing.

Taking one last look around, Thorpe used a lighter he'd found in the console. Flames leapt into the air. This time, Thorpe did run. As he approached the Jeep, he removed his gloves hoping to avoid leaving traces of the accelerant on the steering wheel. Thorpe started the Jeep and headed for home. He still had work to do there.

Twenty

*Saturday
February 10th
Morning*

It was 9 a.m. when Thorpe's pager started going off. He'd been asleep for exactly one hour and still had a dead man lying in the woods across the road from his house. Thorpe returned the page and reached his captain, Don Cory.

Cory filled him in: "Brandon Baker was killed last night, and Thadius Shaw is missing. I'd give you more details, but I have about a hundred calls I need to make. There's going to be a full briefing at SID at 1300 hours. Everybody's coming in, regular days off or not. Vacation and comp days are cancelled."

"I'll be there." The phone clicked dead.

Thorpe was going to be paid overtime to help search for the killers. He conceded to the irony, looked at his watch, and decided to get a few more hours of sack time. His father's words floated alongside him into unconsciousness: *Sleep is like water son—if you don't know when you'll find it again, get as much of it as you can.*

Three hours later, Thorpe was packing up his gear while watching the Fox News Channel in his living room. Tulsa had become the lead story on the national networks: Two black Tulsa police officers had been killed within the last two days and a third had gone missing. The story went on to describe the methods used to kill the officers and brief biographies of their lives. The requisite "experts" were on hand to lend their opinions, and, as usual, the experts were full of shit. However, they did suggest fellow police officers were potential suspects. This was based on the fact that the slain black officers were very outspoken about alleged racial inequalities on the department and had been parties to several lawsuits. The only hitch in their theory was the murder of Baker, a white officer. Several of these same "experts" spun several possible explanations. One suggested that Baker might have been a suspect in the black officer's deaths and had been silenced. As always these days, reporters were generating news rather than reporting it.

There were sound bites by TPD's inept interim police chief, Jason Kampmann. The man was a certified imbecile.

TPD, as a general rule, had usually promoted its chief from within. Being one of the first departments in the country requiring newly hired police officers to hold the equivalent of a bachelor's degree, the department was stocked full of competent, educated personnel. Unfortunately, Tulsa's mayor didn't like the fact the chief had civil service protection and couldn't be completely dominated. He declared that although several TPD candidates were certified as being qualified, he was going to seek a chief from an outside department and make him an "at will" employee. He essentially made the position a political one in which the chief would have to ask 'how high' when ordered to jump. These arrangements were currently being contested in the state supreme court.

In the meantime, the department was stuck with this bozo who had no idea of TPD's history. Among many embarrassing episodes, he was known to fall asleep during meetings and was incapable of simple tasks such as figuring out how to turn on a police radio. One of his first declarations was that he'd make the department college educated. He was promptly notified he was approximately twenty years late with the idea but was congratulated on such an enterprising concept.

Now Kampmann, wearing a TPD uniform he hadn't earned the right to wear, was on the national stage doing a damned good impersonation of Captain Kangaroo. Thorpe couldn't help but wonder how such idiots rose to positions of power in this country. The most important information Thorpe took from the news report was that the Federal Bureau of Investigation was now taking the lead on the homicides. *Great, now there'd be a pile of armed accountants in the mix.* Thorpe flipped off the television and stepped outside. He'd left the dogs out last night and noticed they didn't seem too concerned with their surroundings. He doubted Phipps would take another shot at him here; his next attempt would most likely be when Thorpe was at work. He was happy to see coyotes hadn't dragged Shaw's body out to the middle of the road, yet. He'd have to deal with that problem tonight after dark. At least it was cold enough the body shouldn't get too ripe.

The first thing Thorpe noticed when he pulled into SID's parking lot was the deluge of plain sedans and black Chevy Suburbans. Inside the office, he was greeted by Gail. "Hello, James," she said, looking up from her desk.

"Miss Moneypenny...You are bewitching."

"Oh, James, you're such the flirt."

"Only with you, Miss Moneypenny. Are we being absorbed by the Famous But Incompetent?"

"Uhhh? Oh, I get it. The FBI. Seems like it; they're everywhere."

"That's what people with tinfoil on their heads have been saying for years," Thorpe joked. "I guess I have a meeting to make. Arrivederci, Miss Moneypenny."

"Arrivederci, James."

Thorpe walked to his office, threw his gear onto his couch, and meandered through the building to the conference room. When he entered the rectangular chamber, he was reminded of a junior high school dance: SID supervisors occupied one side of the room opposite a bunch of uptight looking men in suits—neither group acknowledging the presence of the other. In this case the dance floor was a long, oval-shaped conference table which might as well have been the English Channel. Thorpe took a seat near the exit and glanced at the VICE sergeant, Gary Treece, who promptly rolled his eyes, leaned to one side, and farted. The SID guys burst out laughing, but the suits didn't seem to get the joke—very unprofessional.

A couple of guys were near tears, either from the laughter or the stench, when Deputy Chief Brad Elias strode into the room. His appearance reversed the direction of gaseous output as assholes collectively sucked up oxygen, tempting Thorpe to check the barometer on his watch to gauge the loss of atmospheric air pressure. Deputy Chief Elias was the head of a foursome. He was followed by Major Duncan and Captain Cory. Bringing up the rear was an attractive woman wearing a conservative pin-striped skirt-suit. With a furtive glance Thorpe ascertained the woman was long, slender, and walked with an athletic grace. Her thick black hair was pulled back and bundled tightly on the back of her head.

As the foursome made their way to a podium, Thorpe noticed every SID supervisor was locked on the raven-haired beauty...*Cops*. There's an old saying with police officers, "You can trust a cop with your money and life, but don't leave him alone with your wife." The woman had a dark complexion suggesting Mediterranean, Brazilian, or some other exotic descent. Thorpe noticed not one of the suits gave the woman more than a fleeting look. Maybe they knew something the SID guys didn't. Thorpe decided to give the woman a break and consciously chose not to drool on himself as she pulled up a seat next to the podium. The other TPD personnel in the room had no such concern. They looked like a pack of schoolboys who'd been given a Playboy bunny as a substitute teacher. Chief Elias took a position behind the podium and introduced the three figures who sat to his right, including Special Agent Ambretta Collins.

Chief Elias spoke for several minutes. He touched lightly on the direction the case was taking. It was obvious he was being careful not to disclose the entire scope of the investigation or the FBI's role in the matter. Towards the end of his comments, he was more candid, "To be perfectly honest, as of this moment, a member or members of this police department are possible perpetrators of these murders. Therefore, I can't fully disclose the details of this investigation to potential suspects. I'm not accusing anyone in this room. But you understand our predicament. Regardless, SID personnel will not be involved in the investigation of these murders. Your assignment will be—with the assistance of the FBI and U.S. Marshals Service—to help provide security for specific officers on the department. Particularly individuals who have initiated litigation against the department. Again, because we can't inadvertently assign the killer to guard his next victim, you and your units will be working in conjunction with the FBI and Marshals and more than likely will have an agent or marshal monitoring your activities. We'll be addressing the entire division at 1400 hours but wanted to have the supervisors on board first. Ms. Collins..."

Special Agent Ambretta Collins rose effortlessly out of her chair and took to the podium. Despite dressing conservatively, she hadn't been completely successful in smoothing out her curves with layers of wool. One of her most striking features was her hair, which was black as night. Thorpe managed to focus on her words as she introduced herself as a special agent out of Dallas and made the obligatory I'm-honored-to-be-working-with-you bullshit speech. When the hand-job was over, she asked the rest of the group sitting at the table to introduce themselves and state their current assignment.

Thorpe was worried he would be assigned a "Feebie" for a partner. *How the hell would he end this thing if he had a Fed riding beside him all night long?* Maybe he'd be spared because he had an alibi for the Cole Daniels murder. That alone might not be enough to save him; as far as the detectives and the FBI knew, it could be a *group* of officers involved with the murders. The man to his left quit speaking and everyone around the table directed their gazes at Thorpe.

"Sergeant John Thorpe...Supervisor of the Organized Gang Unit."

When introductions were over, Special Agent Collins outlined SID's role in the protection assignment, thanked those around the table for their cooperation, and returned to her seat.

Major Duncan won a hard-fought battle against the effects of gravity as he un-wedged himself from his seat and waddled behind his pulpit. "Right now we plan to work officers in twelve-hour shifts. Twelve hours on, twelve hours off. We have a preliminary schedule outlined, and we realize it will have to be tweaked as we move along. Right now we're not going to be accommodating. Everyone who signed up to work in this division did so knowing work hours, schedules, days off, were all subject to change. Anyone who doesn't like it can put on a uniform at shift change." Threatening to send his investigators back to patrol, was Duncan's favorite pastime—as if patrol were a bad thing.

Major Duncan plopped a stack of paper in front of the supervisor to his left, and with his regular diplomacy, told him to hand out the schedules. "For the TPD personnel in the room, understand this—Special Agent Collins is in charge of the protection detail. What she says goes. I know you don't take orders from federal agents, but I'm ordering you to follow her directions. Therefore, you can consider her commands to be my commands..." Thorpe privately wished one of her commands would be to kick Major Duncan right square in the balls—if he could find them. "That's all for now. We'll be meeting with the whole division in the bullpen in...twenty minutes. Any questions?"

Treece piped up, "Why are we only guarding black officers? Forgive me if I'm wrong but Brandon Baker was white the last time I checked."

Duncan replied, "Two black officers are dead. One black officer is missing. The only common thread is that all three initiated racial lawsuits against the city. It is the only connection we have. Baker seems to be the anomaly. If another black officer gets killed while we sit on our hands we'll be crucified in the media."

Treece continued, "Are supervisors going to be assigned a federal babysitter too?"

Duncan took a deep breath, clearly irritated with Treece's questions, "I think that was answered already..." *Not exactly.* "...There obviously aren't enough federal agents to assign to every officer on a continual basis, but they will be monitoring your activities continuously." *What the hell does that mean?* "That's it for now, you're dismissed," Duncan finished.

As everyone gathered paperwork and prepared to leave, Special Agent Collins spoke across the room, "Sergeant Thorpe, would you please remain behind for a few minutes?"

Thorpe halted his retreat for the door. *Shit! This can't be good.* "Yes, ma'am." Thorpe stepped deeper into the room and approached the special agent who briskly rose and offered her hand.

"Sergeant Thorpe, it's good to meet you," Agent Collins said.

"Nice to meet you," Thorpe lied.

"Sergeant, you and I will be working together."

"Ma'am, I don't think..." Thorpe noticed Deputy Chief Elias giving Thorpe a shut-your-pie-hole look. "I'm looking forward to working with you, Agent Collins."

The agent gave Thorpe a knowing smile that said "bullshit," but her mouth said, "Good. Please come find me when I'm finished addressing the rest of the division."

Thorpe walked away thinking he should have leered at her like the rest of the group; maybe she wouldn't have singled him out. When he left the conference room he found Treece waiting for him in the bullpen.

"What was that about?" Treece asked.

"Apparently Miss Collins was offended by the putrid smell in the room. She wanted to launch an investigation into the matter, and she put me in charge. I immediately gave you up and...case closed."

"Eat me," Treece laughed. "What'd she want?"

"I guess she's going to be my federal babysitter," Thorpe answered.

"Oh, you son of a bitch! I'd give my left nut to ride around with that woman."

"You'd give your left nut to ride around with a monkey for an hour if you thought you'd get some."

"Not true. I have a rule not to date women who are hairier than me...Well it's more of a guideline."

"Collins seems pretty icy to me," Thorpe offered.

"All women Feds are like that. They gotta act tough so they're taken seriously. Put her in a car with me for twelve hours and I'd melt her."

"The only thing you'd have is a bad case of blue balls," Thorpe laughed.

"I already have those."

"Don't worry, I bet you'll get a nice looking man in his early thirties to ride around with. Maybe he'll take care of your problem."

"I wouldn't doubt he'd try. Hope I at least get a marshal and not some Sudoku-playing FBI agent, fresh from advanced accounting."

Thorpe shook his head, walked to his office, sat behind his desk, and studied his new schedule. He noticed he was working from 8:00 a.m. to 8:00 p.m., but the rest of his squad was working evening shift hours. He had obviously been chosen to partner with Agent Collins even before the supervisor's meeting; he wondered why. One positive facet was his nights would be free to operate—and he needed the darkness. As Thorpe sat at his desk in contemplation, he caught movement at his office doorway. Special Agent Collins was standing at the threshold.

"May I?" Collins asked politely.

Thorpe motioned for her to enter, and from parent-ingrained conduct on being a gentleman, rose out of his seat.

"Please, don't get up."

Thorpe motioned to the couch across from his desk. Collins settled on the edge of a seat cushion.

"Sergeant, I could tell by your reaction in the conference room you're not thrilled about working with me. The fact is, most everyone is going to be paired with someone until they are cleared as potential suspects. Those who don't have agents with them will be getting unannounced visits periodically. If not me, you'll be with someone. A possible benefit for you will be that I'm working in conjunction with the investigative unit. I'll be splitting my time between that aspect and protection. As a result, you'll find yourself with ample time away from me. If you think I chose you because you were the only one in the room not making an ass out of yourself, you're mistaken. I just need to know if we will be able to have a positive working relationship, or if I need to have you…reassigned?"

Collins dark brown eyes were locked on Thorpe's. The gaze wasn't exactly challenging, but it was close. Thorpe heard some things he liked and some he didn't. If he was going to be forced to have federal oversight, it may as well be with a person who was going to keep his evenings free and who would be tied up on other assignments for half the regular shift. Collins was direct and to the point which was good, but she was also a little too sharp. The last thing he needed was a Lieutenant Columbo riding around in the car next to him—*just one more question.*

"Ma'am, you don't need to have me reassigned. I have nothing against you personally…I'm just not used to having a partner. I've been working on my own for several years now and have gotten used to it. Also, though you graciously keep referring to us as *working together*, I know, in reality, I'll be working *for* you. But you'll have no problems from me, and I'll do my best to make this collaboration work."

"Thank you. I appreciate your professionalism."

"May I ask why we were paired together?"

Collins paused for a few minutes before responding, "Detective Hull has a very good reputation in the investigative community. He has one of the highest clearance rates in the nation and has been involved in some very high profile cases. Detective Hull, as well as others, has a very high opinion of your capabilities. Plus, as I mentioned earlier, you will be working without an…*escort*…for extended periods of time. Taking that into consideration, you were one of the few SID supervisors with an airtight alibi—at least for one of the murders."

"I see."

Agent Collins rose off the couch. "I need to prepare to address the division. I just wanted to ensure we were okay. Thank you for your time, sergeant."

Thorpe added, "Please call me Thorpe or John. Whichever you feel more comfortable with."

"Okay. Since we're on the subject I'd prefer to be called Agent Collins…not Ma'am."

"Habit. See you after your speech, Agent Collins. Oh…and if you thought the supervisors were bad, you're in for a real treat with the investigators."

"I'm sure."

Collins walked out of the office and Thorpe couldn't help but watch her leave—only to have her figure replaced by another. It was Treece. The Vice sergeant stood gazing after Collins. He winked at Thorpe, "Asshole. Ready for meeting number two?"

The second meeting was more of the same just on a larger scale. There was grumbling from investigators who were going to have to can their work, let search warrants expire, and drift away from informants. Sometimes when investigators took long breaks from undercover work it took some time to get reestablished. However, most investigators realized the situation and accepted the setbacks. The most grousing occurred when officers realized they were considered potential suspects and were going to have federal oversight—that and the drastic change in schedules which were going to disrupt daycare schedules, side jobs, and extracurricular activities.

When Agent Collins spoke there was a lot of elbowing and whispering taking place in the room. Deputy Chief Elias looked like he was about to explode. He rose out of his chair. A hush fell over the bullpen. Deputy Chief Elias was in his mid forties—young for his rank, about six-two, and a bear of a man. Though he had a hefty mid-section, most of his bulk was muscle. In addition, he was well spoken and could expertly "dress one down." He absolutely enjoyed the art of intimidation.

Following the briefing, most personnel were sent home and given times to report back. Thorpe met with Agent Collins who was off to yet another meeting downtown. The two exchanged phone numbers and agreed to meet around 7 p.m. Until then, Thorpe would be without a chaperone. He decided to go to his office and shuffle through his email, phone messages, and case assignments—most of which would be put on hold until the current situation passed. Thorpe would have liked to deal with the mess in his woods, but he didn't have time, and it wasn't yet dark.

Twenty-One

Saturday
February 10th
Evening

BY 6:30 P.M., THORPE HAD NEARLY FINISHED getting the scutwork off his desk. Everything was being put on hold. Suspending his work was great for now, but once this thing was over his case assignments would look like a mountain range erupting from the gentle plains of his desk. But by then Thorpe figured he'd be dead or in prison—so why worry about it? While he continued to wrap up his affairs, Thorpe grabbed the remote and tuned his wall-mounted television to a national news program. It didn't take long for the news to loop back around to the recent events in Tulsa.

A prominent black leader was giving his opinions on the matter and advising he'd be making a personal visit to Tulsa to insure the "black voice" was heard. He cited recent events to "validate" black Tulsa police officers have been working in an "extremely prejudicial environment." He went on to express his sorrow to the families of the fallen officers but declared they did not die in vain. "Their deaths have irrevocably unmasked the tyranny that is the Tulsa Police Department." Normally this would piss Thorpe off, but he knew it was coming and had no one to blame but himself. Thorpe's phone rang and Agent Collin's cell phone number was displayed on the screen.

"Hello, Agent Collins," Thorpe answered; he reminded himself of the *Get Smart* character Maxwell Smart.

"Have you had dinner yet?" she asked.

"No."

"I haven't had anything all day. If you don't mind I'll drop my car off at SID and we can go grab something to eat. Are you close?"

"Never left the office.."

Fifteen minutes later, Thorpe slipped a tattered black leather coat over his hooded gray sweatshirt and went outside to meet Collins. When he stepped into the parking lot, he pulled the hood over his head. There was only one location from where a sniper would have a clear shot at Thorpe on the elevated parking area, and that was the motel across the street. Even from there, the shooter would only have a clear view if Thorpe walked near the south end of the parking lot. Regardless, Thorpe kept his hood up.

"Could you drive since you know your way around town?" Collins asked.

"Sure. This way."

"I was hoping we could take my car since I have a lot of stuff inside."

"Okay," Thorpe conceded. He would have preferred to drive an SID car.

Collins tossed Thorpe the keys to the gray Ford Crown Victoria and walked around to the passenger side of the vehicle. Another investigator was climbing out of a nearby Suburban with his federal escort.

"Hey, Carnac, I'll trade you babysitters," the investigator yelled across the lot.

"No, thanks. Yours looks constipated," Thorpe remarked as he entered the Ford. Thorpe thought he caught a glimpse of a grin on Collin's face. *A crack in the armor; at least she has a sense of humor.* "Where to?" Thorpe asked.

"You pick. It's your town. Let's just skip the chains."

"You like sushi?" Thorpe asked, as he adjusted the seat and rearview mirrors.

"I like sushi."

"We'll go to Fuji's. On Saturday nights it's hard to get a seat at most places, but I know the people there. We'll get right in," Thorpe explained.

Fuji's, located on the southeast corner of 71st and Memorial Drive, was Thorpe's favorite sushi joint. More importantly, there were no views inside the restaurant from the street. Thorpe turned south on Sheridan Road and drove in silence.

"Thorpe, this is going to be a long assignment if you never speak."

"I'm letting you set the pace, Agent Collins."

"Okay...Why did that man call you Carnac?"

"You read my file yet?"

Collins paused briefly before answering, "Yes."

She's being honest so far. "You read about my shooting?"

"Yes."

Thorpe let go of the wheel and made quotation marks in the air. "*Psychic Powers*, warned me of an armed suspect behind the door."

"How *did* you know?" Collins asked with genuine curiosity.

"I didn't. You know the feeling you get when you think you're being watched, or you think you're not alone?"

"Yeah," Collins answered, turning her head to study Thorpe.

"I had that feeling—a strong one—and trusted it."

"Huh...interesting."

"I figure my subconscious heard, smelled, or saw something that just didn't register consciously. But who knows," Thorpe offered.

Thorpe was now traveling down Memorial. Memorial Drive on a Saturday night is not a place one wants to travel unless they are between the ages of thirteen and eighteen and looking for a race, a fight, or members of the opposite sex. Thorpe hoped if he were being followed, his tail would be lost in the sea of adolescent drivers. Arriving at Fuji's, Thorpe pulled into a strip-center parking lot and found a place near the restaurant's front door. He pulled the keys from the ignition and held them out to Collins, who spoke as she received the keys, "Thorpe, what's going on?"

"What do you mean?"

"I mean you drove all the way over here with a hood pulled over your head, and you spent more time staring in the rearview mirror than you did on the road in front of you."

This woman is going to be a pain in the ass. "I'm an undercover Organized Gangs Unit investigator driving a plain Ford Crown Victoria with government plates. This car screams "police officer." Since you're so observant you probably noticed passing several cars with occupants dressed suspiciously like gang members. If one day I'm standing in an alley making a dope deal, I sure would hate to get a bullet in the back of my head because they remember studying my face behind the wheel of a cop car." That was all bullshit of course, but hopefully Collins would buy it. In reality he was hoping to avoid being on the wrong end of a .308 sniper round.

"Are you always this paranoid?" Collins asked.

"Agent Collins, I believe we've established my paranoia has already saved my ass at least once."

Collins smiled, *"Touché."*

This woman was definitely observant. *Not good,* Thorpe thought. The two walked into the restaurant and waded through the waiting customers. Thorpe noticed other couples showing an inordinate amount of interest in them: Collins was dressed in a smart business outfit while Thorpe had a couple days of beard growth and was dressed in a ragged leather jacket, worn hoodie, blue jeans and Harley Davidson motorcycle boots. Thorpe spoke to Collins loud enough to be overheard by the waiting patrons, "I guess everyone's thinking I could do better." A couple of women in the group let out some giggles as the men redirected their attention to the floor.

"Hey, John, we have a corner booth." It was Sue, the hostess. As with most employees at the restaurant Sue was Japanese.

"First-name basis. Are you Norm to their Cheers?" Collins asked with friendly sarcasm.

Sue led Collins to a booth against the back wall. Thorpe had been to the restaurant enough times the staff knew he'd only sit with his back to the wall in a position where he could observe the front door and fellow customers. He'd been coming here for years, even when he was in uniform; the entire staff knew he was a cop. It was one of the few routines Thorpe allowed himself.

When they reached the table Agent Collins sat on the side of the booth Thorpe had wished to occupy. This left him a bit unsure how to proceed, but eventually he sat down right next to his new partner.

"Excuse me?" Agent Collins said with surprise.

"Relax. You don't have anything I want—except a seat facing the room," Thorpe smiled. "If you want to get away from me, you'll have to sit on the other side." Agent Collins sat and stared at Thorpe for what seemed like a full minute before she relinquished and slid over. Collins redirected her gaze to a menu while a waitress brought two waters and placed a large Sapporo in front of Thorpe. Collins returned her gaze to Thorpe, accompanied by a pair of arched eyebrows. "Sushi just doesn't taste right without Sapporo. You going to report me?" he asked.

"Actually, a beer sounds good. Waitress, please bring me one of those."

Thorpe smiled, "Step one...establish trust. Check."

"Are you going to be a smart ass this entire assignment?" Collins asked with a hint of hostility.

"I've been a smart ass my whole life; I don't see any reason to change now."

"So this is normal behavior?"

"Unfortunately...yes."

Agent Collins put down her menu and faced Thorpe. "You know...every TPD officer and official I've come into contact with has been incessant with their questions regarding this case. You, on the other hand, despite knowing I'm also part of the investigative detail, haven't asked one question?"

"Would you tell me anything I haven't seen on the news already?"

Collins kept her eyes locked on Thorpe but paused before answering, "No."

"There's your how come," Thorpe remarked. "Thanks for being honest."

"I believe in diplomacy—when I'm dealing with people who may be thin-skinned. But I didn't think I needed to be anything but blunt with you."

"Where did you get your psychology degree?" Thorpe asked, taking a shot in the dark.

"Is that another joke or a legitimate question?"

"Legitimate question."

There was another long pause before Collins responded, "Florida State University."

"Is that where you got your undergraduate degree or your doctorate?"

"Undergraduate."

"Where did you get your doctorate?"

"Boston University," Collins answered—reluctance in her voice.

"People who earn their doctorates usually insist on being referred to as 'doctor,' it generally supersedes 'agent,' and absolutely overrides 'miss.' Why don't you want people to know you're a doctor?" he questioned.

"Sometimes it puts people on the defensive. And considering the circumstances, I thought the title might make people... *paranoid*." Collins finished the sentence with a wry smile. "How did you know I had a doctorate?"

"I didn't."

"Had one of those *Carnac* feelings again?"

"Just fishing."

"You're very deductive."

Thorpe smiled, "Please, let's keep this professional."

"But you're not funny."

Thorpe laughed, "So you think a person like—oh let's say *me*—might be paranoid if the FBI blew into town to investigate a series of murders where the most likely suspect is a cop. The '*me*' finds out his FBI partner—who claims to be in charge of protection—is most likely a criminal profiler. Now why would *anyone* find that worrisome?"

Collins took a long pull from her Sapporo before turning and facing Thorpe, "Frankly I didn't expect to be having this conversation within the first hour of riding with you. For someone who doesn't ask a lot of questions, you somehow deftly reversed this conversation so I'm on the defensive. I bet you're one hell of an interrogator." Collins paused and now seemed to be very carefully choosing her words. "How bout we jump to the end of the path you've been leading me down. Yes, I am part of the investigative detail. Yes, part of my assignment was to garner your trust and get you to open up about potential suspects in your unit, division, or department. That's all I can reveal at this time, and, believe me, I wouldn't be telling you this if I didn't think you already had that much figured out. I hope you appreciate my honesty and will choose to be an asset to this investigation."

"That wasn't so hard was it?"

Collins smiled, "By the way I *really* am in charge of protection, so let's focus on shoring that up first. Deal?"

"Deal."

Collins and Thorpe ordered sushi rolls and stuck to their one beer. They were both on duty and still had work to do. During the meal the conversation mostly centered on TPD operations, chain of command, and various specialty units. Before the two left, Collins excused herself to the ladies room, and Thorpe removed a notebook and pen from the interior of his jacket. He wrote, *Feb 10. The man who killed me tonight is Officer Andrew Phipps. He, Cornelius Johnson, and Sergeant Carl McDonald are the only three left responsible for the death of my family.* Thorpe replaced the notepad and pen inside his leather jacket.

ANDREW PHIPPS WENT THROUGH A LOT OF EFFORT to get a room in the Sheridan Commons. The three-story motel sat across from the secret offices of the Special Investigations Division where Thorpe worked. First, though he had declined protection, Phipps had to slip out the back door of his own home to avoid a two-man unit guarding his home. Then, because his car was parked in his driveway, he had to borrow a car from a friend with the excuse he was afraid to drive his own because he might be recognized and killed. The friend had promised not to let anyone know he was borrowing his car for the evening. Finally, he'd given a prostitute a hundred bucks to rent this thirty-dollar, third-story room, then give him the keys and disappear.

The room faced north towards the Special Investigations Division. Because of SID's elevated parking area, Phipps couldn't see the entire lot but he could see as cars stopped at the gate while entering and exiting the property. His shooting nest left much to be desired; on the outside of his room, he had a five-foot balcony that extended the length of the building. Because all the rooms opened up to the same balcony, he couldn't use the structure as a shooting platform. He considered concealing himself inside the room and shooting through an open door but soon found having an open door in this motel was an invitation for prostitutes and drug dealers to stop in and have a look-see. He'd even had a 60-year-old man stumble in his room asking to buy crack; it had taken Phipps about five minutes to shoo the pest outside. Even then the bastard kept walking up and down the balcony, mumbling to himself.

Phipps was not going to be able to take a shot from this position. If he tried a shot from inside the room he'd have to fire through the motel window, between the balconies' iron rails, and through the window of his target's vehicle. Dismissing the idea of firing from the room, Phipps had left his rifle in the trunk of his borrowed vehicle and was armed only with a pistol, binoculars, and police radio. He'd been monitoring the special sub-fleet that had been assigned to the protection detail but had yet to hear Thorpe's voice over the radio. He'd hoped to see Thorpe's truck pull up to the gate—either entering or exiting the offices—and wait for it to leave. Phipps' plan was to exit his room via the motel room's southern door, which opened to an interior hallway, go down to his car, and follow Thorpe until he found an opportunity to take the man out.

From what Phipps understood, every TPD officer and supervisor would be partnered with a federal agent or at least have one checking in on him. Which meant Phipps wouldn't have to worry about being the hunted instead of the hunter. Of course Phipps would be in a lot better position, and would have much more information if McDonald hadn't fled town—*fucking pussy*. McDonald had called him earlier to say he'd taken three weeks of vacation while things settled down. He wouldn't even tell Phipps where he was cooling his heels.

Phipps should never have revealed to McDonald what happened in those woods. He could see fear grip the man as he learned how the ambush had been turned inside out. He advised McDonald that *despite* what his file said, Thorpe must have had military training—more specifically commando training. Now instead of helping to finish this thing, McDonald had packed up and fled town. So Phipps was waging war for the both of them. This was just like the military. *The REMs—rear-echelon motherfuckers—relaxed in comfort while grunts swam in the shit.* If Phipps weren't successful tonight, he was going to *force* the enlistment of Corn Johnson; he too had been less than willing to volunteer his help.

Several years ago Corn and Phipps had been best friends. They worked and played together. Phipps got a position in SID's day-shift narcotics unit, and Corn worked in Gilcrease Division's Street Crimes Unit. Both units performed basically the same job except SID investigators had access to more toys and money. Corn got caught providing sensitive information to nefarious citizens on the North Side. Some of that information had been filtered down through Phipps at SID. In fact, Phipps had disseminated just as much, if not more, sensitive information as Corn—he just didn't get caught. Corn wouldn't voice it, but Phipps knew he was bitter that he'd had to resign while his friend skated on the whole affair. *What did Corn expect, for him to confess and resign out of friendship?*

So far, Corn had remained on the sidelines during this fight. But it was time for the man to come off the bench. Phipps checked his watch for the third time in the last fifteen minutes and decided Thorpe must've left in a different vehicle. His only option now was to monitor the radio and hope to get a location on his quarry. If that didn't work, he'd make sure Corn entered the game.

THORPE LEFT THE RESTAURANT half expecting a bullet to punch through his cranium. His only consolation: He'd never see or hear it coming, and he had a note in his pocket that would make life hell on Phipps, Corn, and McDonald. Thorpe was relieved when he reentered the Ford and drove away with his brain stem still attached. If he had been followed, he would have already been killed in the parking lot. Thorpe reached up and pulled his hood down.

"You're not afraid of blowing your cover anymore?" Collins remarked.

"I just felt it unfair..." Thorpe remarked, jokingly pursing his lips—giving his best runway look. "...denying you the privilege of my profile."

Collins rolled her eyes, "Oh, brother."

Thorpe and Collins discussed the night's agenda. There were nine officers under the umbrella of their protection detail. Officer Andrew Phipps declined protection but remained in town. Against Phipps' wishes, a team had been ordered to watch his house anyway, and follow at a distance when he traveled.

That meant there were nine two-man surveillance teams and four two-man relief teams. Two shifts, meant there were fifty-two men and women assigned to the protective detail, the bulk of which were TPD officers. The remainder was filled with United States Deputy Marshals, FBI agents, and a couple of OSBI investigators—OSBI being the Oklahoma State Bureau of Investigation—a state agency. This thing just kept growing. That was a lot of manpower, and Thorpe couldn't see any of the departments using this amount of resources for an extended period of time. TPD barely had enough officers to handle routine calls for service as it was; some calls already held three or four hours before patrol officers were able to respond (even though Tulsa's mayor maintained the department was adequately manned).

Thorpe and Collins would be responding to the nine locations to determine protection deficiencies. He had persuaded Collins not to use the radio so the protection details wouldn't know they were coming. He had persuaded her that it would better show which officers were being lackadaisical. Keeping Phipps in the dark in reference to his whereabouts was Thorpe's true intention.

Collins broke the silence with a loaded question, "What's the relationship between black and white officers on the department?"

Thorpe had anticipated the question but wasn't sure he wanted to discuss the subject. "With the exception of a few who make life miserable on all of us, the relationship is excellent."

"Those few trouble makers, they white or black?" Collins asked.

Thorpe smiled, "That's a hard question to answer without coming off as racist. I suppose it comes down to who you ask."

"Care to be more specific?"

"Not really," Thorpe answered truthfully.

"Please indulge me."

Thorpe didn't know if he wanted to tackle the query; an honest answer might make him appear more appetizing as a suspect. Ultimately he found no reason to lie about it. Ninety-five percent of the department felt the same way he did—though some wouldn't admit it publicly. "Are there white racists on this department? I'm sure there are," Thorpe answered his own question. "But overall, I don't think there *is* friction between individual white and black officers. Almost everyone on this department is college-educated, and they do a pretty good job of judging someone on character rather than race. What friction does exist, in my opinion, was generated by a few malcontents."

Thorpe could probably speak for hours on what he thought were injustices against whites on the department but also knew that blacks could speak for hours about their perceived injustices. Thorpe knew true prejudices were born from an uncompromising belief *you* were the only one who was right. Usually, reality lurked somewhere in between.

"Do you think black officers have any legitimate complaints?" Collins persisted.

"Let's be clear here. Not all black officers are complaining. I'd estimate the percentage to be very small. I can understand some of their viewpoints. I've tried to picture myself on a department comprised of ninety-percent black officers. I can see where I could blame my misfortunes on the color of my skin, and I could also see the perception of special treatment being extended to others. I mean there are some real assholes on this department. I've been treated like shit by some superiors with absolutely no basis whatsoever—in my opinion. If I were a minority, I can see why I might use race as a possible explanation because, in my mind, no others existed. Since I don't have that excuse, I just have to chalk it up to people having a shitty day or them just being an all-American asshole. Also, I've seen some whites on this department get away with some crazy shit. But I don't think it relates to race as much as it does to the good ol' boy system.

"The bottom line is…if you're buddies with a sergeant, captain, major, deputy chief, whatever, it's going to play a part in your disciplinary action on this department—depending on how much stroke your friend has. If you play golf with a deputy chief on a weekly basis, there's going to be some mishaps swept under the carpet. That's not a black-white thing though. It depends on who you are and how much rank you have. But if I were a black officer and I was sitting back watching some of this shit, sure…I'd think, *Those assholes take care of themselves.*" Thorpe wanted to change the subject and chose a statement that'd be effective in doing so. "Maybe these killings have nothing to do with race," Thorpe offered.

"For example?" Agent Collins asked, with an unnaturally neutral tone.

"Maybe someone's pissed for other reasons…some of those guys who were killed were just downright dirty. Maybe one of their own is pissed off about something…Maybe it has nothing at all to do with race at all. Baker was white, explain that."

"Something to consider. But right now our best assumption is a racially motivated white Tulsa police officer or officers," Collins offered.

"With tactical skills," Thorpe added.

Collins looked at Thorpe, "Strong possibility."

THORPE PARKED A HALF BLOCK DOWN from one of the protective details. According to his information, this particular house was being monitored by one of Thorpe's investigators, Jennifer Williams, who was lucky enough to draw an FBI agent as a full-time partner.

"Let's approach on foot," he said, pulling the hoodie back over his head as the two got out of the Ford. They walked down the street toward the house in question. Thorpe recognized Jennifer's car; he figured she would win the argument with the Fed over who drove and which car they took. Thorpe and Collins approached the black Ford Contour from the east. When they were about twenty yards from the rear of Jennifer's car, she scrambled out the driver's side door with her right hand concealed behind her leg. Thorpe knew the hand held a pistol. The passenger door flung open, and a suit stepped out into view, empty handed.

"Don't shoot, it's the PoPo," Thorpe said—using one of the G-rated terms bangers use for the police.

"Fucking Carnac! How 'bout a warning first," Jennifer angrily spat.

"Keeping you on your toes," Thorpe winked.

"If I'd seen the skirt next to you I wouldn't have gotten so excited. Just saw your hooded ass in my side-view mirror." Though Jennifer was a woman, she talked more like a man than most men do.

Thorpe introduced Jennifer and the skirt to one another. Collins asked Jennifer what she thought about the security situation.

Never one to mince words Jennifer gave the run down: "It's a complete cluster-fuck. We're sitting out here like ducks. If someone wanted to get in that house, they could plink us off like steel targets sitting out here in the middle of the street...Or just go in the fucking back door."

Collins defended herself, "As I said in the briefing, your being here is more preventative than actual security. We don't believe the suspect would risk capture by going in the back door with two officers sitting out front. We also don't believe the suspect means harm to anyone other than his intended target."

"You *believe*, but you don't know. You'll know when SIU is scraping my brains off the asphalt," Jennifer argued.

"What do you suggest, Officer Williams?" Collins asked.

"We should be inside the house, sitting in the living room or something," Jennifer suggested.

"Most considered that too intrusive. Would you want two strangers sitting in your living room all day?" Collins explained.

"We're not strangers. We're all fucking cops here. We're not black, we're not white, we're blue. And, no, I wouldn't care. They could sit on my couch and fart in my cushions if they wanted to. If they think we're too intrusive then fuck 'em; let them fend for themselves."

"That is not going to happen," Collins assured her.

Jennifer looked at Thorpe, "This is bullshit."

"I agree, but there's not much we can do about it. If you're worried about getting sniped there are some precautions you can take. First determine where the most likely places are for a sniper to engage you from. Then split up into two different cars so you can both still watch the house and watch each other. Position yourself so it would be difficult to acquire you both as targets in a short amount of time. That should dissuade the shooter enough to wait for a better opportunity—unless of course we have multiple snipers—then you're fucked" Thorpe smiled. He then turned his attention to Collins, "I doubt Agent Collins would have a problem with you being in separate vehicles so long as you can account for one another's whereabouts the entire time."

"Just make sure you can see one another...And no bathroom breaks or trips to the convenience store alone," Collins relented.

The order prompted another retort from Williams. "Does that mean Timothy here wipes my ass for me, or can I actually go inside the restroom all by myself?" The two women gave each other unforgiving looks before Collins turned and began walking back to her car.

Thorpe spoke low. "Cut them some slack, Jennifer. They're just following orders—same as us."

"I don't like being treated like a suspect, John."

"I don't either," Thorpe declared—in spite of the irony. "You want us to watch this house while you go get another car?"

"No. I don't think we're in much trouble of getting whacked. I was just busting her balls...Besides, me and Timmy here are becoming best buddies. Ain't that right, Timmy?" The man in the suit nodded in agreement. "Have fun with the Ice Queen, Carnac."

Thorpe followed Collins back to her vehicle and climbed in behind the steering wheel.

"Cops don't care much for federal agents do they?" Collins asked.

"She's like that with everyone. One of the best undercover officers I've ever seen—but she lacks a bit in the social skills department. Women in particular seem most offended by her."

"I'm not talking about Officer Williams or this assignment in particular. Every officer is being treated like a potential suspect. That's enough to create animosity with anyone. I just mean cops don't like federal agents in general," Collins clarified.

Thorpe considered the question, "Probably narcotics officers more than anyone. We're used to working with DEA and the way they operate. We have a unit, OCDETF, which works in conjunction with the Drug Enforcement Agency, so we're familiar with their procedures. The red tape those guys have to jump through is ridiculous. On TPD, if we have a guy we want to follow, we follow him. If we develop probable cause for a search warrant, we write and serve it. DEA—if they want to follow a guy they have to write it up, send it up, get approval, and wait for it to filter back down to their field agents—and that's just to get permission to conduct surveillance on someone! The hoops they have to jump through—it's a wonder they get anything accomplished. We don't have any problems with the agents themselves—they're generally great guys—just the bureaucracy they have to trudge through to get shit done. I just hope those of you in the FBI don't have the same constraints when it comes to terrorism investigations." Thorpe knew they did; it was a subtle jab. He glanced over at Collins who glumly shook her head.

Thorpe continued, "Every so often we'll have a spike in violent crime or gang activity. In response we'll form a task force which involves our department and several federal agencies. I've been involved in a multitude of these task forces. If the public knew what a sham these media stunts were they'd be outraged. Basically the only thing different is a few more DEA guys will ride shotgun with TPD officers. We still do the same work we always do; we just keep track of the amount of dope, guns, money, and arrests we make during that time period. We get federal prosecutors on board who commit to taking on any eligible cases. The federal government picks up the tab on TPD overtime so Major Duncan actually allows the undercover TPD officers to work. At the end of the assignment the media announces the fruit of the task force. Everyone thinks the DEA descended on the city and took a bunch of guns and criminals off the street. In reality a couple more agents rode around with TPD officers who did what they do every day, week-in, week-out. The feds pick up the overtime bill and get a slap on the back for a job well done."

"So it's a jealousy thing?" Collins said with a broad smile.

Thorpe laughed, "I guess it really is. We do all the work and the feds get all the glory. Your average street cop makes fifty times the arrests any fed ever will."

"Just out of curiosity—what's the opinion of the FBI?"

"I don't know. We don't work as closely with them as the DEA. I guess the general impression the average police officer has is that you guys are mainly accountants and lawyers with a prop pistol on your hip—best suited to white-collar crimes. We have two guys who work with your anti-terrorism unit but they won't say shit about what they do. I know the media says the FBI and local departments are sharing information to fight the war on terror, but the only thing I see is us providing information to you. I don't see it coming back the other direction. However, that's a procedure I happen to agree with. Cops can't keep anything a secret."

"Yeah, we have enough problems keeping secrets within the bureau. I can't imagine eight hundred local cops keeping silent about the local motel owner being the leader of a terrorist cell," Collins agreed.

Thorpe continued, "Hell, about a year ago our police chief got on the news and admitted to having terrorist cells working out of Tulsa. Based on his subsequent statements, he must've had his ass chewed out big time for that blunder."

"Yeah, even *I* heard about it," Collins laughed.

"Quite frankly I don't want to know. I'd probably have to move to North Dakota or something, live on a ranch in the middle of nowhere," Thorpe said, only half kidding.

"It's a scary world," Collins agreed.

"I've talked more in the last thirty minutes than I usually say in a week. How 'bout you give me a break and knock off the questions for a while?"

"Okay. Just one more—you fight professionally or just for fun?"

"What?" *Where did that come from?*

Collins pointed at her own eyebrows as she spoke, "I've noticed you have some scarring in and around your eyebrows—common injuries sustained by boxers. Your knuckles look like you go home and argue with a tree every night, and you also have the beginning of cauliflower ear on the right side—not to mention your nose is slightly askew." Wrestlers often sustain burst blood vessels inside their ears. No external bleeding occurs, but sacs of blood collect inside often causing permanent damage. The condition is commonly referred to as cauliflower ear. Thorpe had noticed he was starting to develop the condition on both ears—just slightly. It could only be noticed under intense scrutiny.

"Gee, thanks. Now you know why I wear a hoodie all the time," Thorpe joked, deflecting the question.

"I'm sorry it doesn't make you unattrac... You're not... It doesn't look bad. It's hardly noticeable," Collins tripped over her words.

"You're such a flatterer. Just had a wild youth is all. Don't look for fights, but sometimes they come my way...You analyze everyone like this?"

"Sorry...bad habit."

Shit. Thorpe felt like this woman was crawling inside his head. Was she here to gather information on the department or on him specifically? There were too many coincidences adding up and Thorpe was beginning to feel the makings of a trap: An extremely attractive FBI agent, who just happens to be a criminal profiler, singles out Thorpe to ride with. She not only is in charge of the protective detail but is also directly involved with the investigation itself. She questions Thorpe about race relations on the department with the result of garnering his opinions as well. Now she's asking questions that were becoming more personal and directed specifically at Thorpe. Based on how the other FBI agents behaved around the woman, Thorpe figured Collins was not a person naturally given to getting personal with her coworkers. Then she subtly implies she may find him attractive—before clumsily trying to word her way out of the statement. Agent Collins, *Doctor* Collins didn't strike Thorpe as a woman who said anything without careful forethought. Thorpe made up his mind—he was definitely being played. "Where to next?"

Collins read off the next address on their checklist. As Thorpe drove, he collected his thoughts and focused on Andrew Phipps. The man had to be somewhere in the city seeking an opportunity to strike. Phipps probably wasn't privy to much information, and if he asked too many questions, he'd draw attention to himself. Still, Phipps would most likely be aware of the locations the protective detail would be guarding. But, since Thorpe was effectively staying off the radio and didn't have an assigned location, Phipps would be limited in his opportunities to isolate him. He would be forced into conducting surveillance on one of the locations and waiting till Thorpe showed his face.

If Phipps were patient enough, sooner or later Thorpe and Collins would roll up to a location and Phipps would have his opportunity. Collins would watch as Thorpe's head was effectively removed from his body. Then she'd have to seriously rethink whatever scenario was playing in her mind. It would all become clearer when crime-scene detectives removed the note from his headless torso. Thorpe decided that if he survived the night he would spend some time explaining recent events in a well-prepared document. Thorpe would place his document and the one from Leatherman's office in a safety deposit box. A box he would make his attorney aware of in case of an untimely death.

Thorpe wasn't sure if Phipps would make a move tonight; if he did it wouldn't be well planned. He decided to play it safe and survey the area before approaching the protection detail from now on. He'd tell Collins he was evaluating the risk potential of each location. She'd probably sense his deceit, but *screw it*, better for her to be suspicious than for him to be dead.

ANDREW PHIPPS WAS HAVING A DIFFICULT TIME. His military training and deployments had been in woodlands and desert. When he had operated in urban areas, it had always been in support of a larger force. Phipps had decided to find a place of cover outside a protected officer's home, where he would wait for Thorpe to show his face then remove it. The difficulty was trying to find a location without being spotted by the protection detail. If he drove his borrowed car down the street to locate the agents, his license plate might be recorded and traced. He'd have to explain why he cruised the area shortly before a TPD sergeant happened to have his head removed with a .308 round. The fact that Phipps was both a current TPD sniper and an ex-Recon marine wouldn't bode well. If he walked by the detail, he might also be subjected to questioning.

His only choice seemed to be moving in by foot and spotting the detail before they spotted him. He would then need to find a nest where he could observe from a distance. If and when Thorpe showed, Phipps would have to be able to take the shot and get to his car before the detail could respond. Even then, the news would be all over the radio, lessening his chances of getting out of the neighborhood undetected. Plus, he'd have to worry about citizens reporting him stalking around with a rifle. Assassinating someone on domestic soil and not getting caught was proving to be more difficult than he'd originally planned.

Phipps considered targeting Thorpe at his home again. But he would have to deal with those *fucking* dogs.

He didn't even know where Thorpe kept the furry bastards. During his last encounter, he hadn't seen the dogs for hours, then all of a sudden they rushed the front fence. And Thorpe had rigged a light curtain on the tree line and opened up on that dumb-ass Shaw with a fucking fully automatic weapon. *Shit.* For all Phipps knew Thorpe had other surprises waiting for him in those woods.

Phipps didn't like any of his options, and he didn't like what he was hearing over the tactical channel. An anonymous caller had reported spotting a man leaving the back door of 1506 West Queen Street—Phipps' residence—and jumping the fence. The protective detail was now reporting that they were at the front door and were unable to make contact with Phipps. Thorpe then came on the radio and told officers on the scene to force entry. *What the hell was going on?* One thing the agents would find for sure: Phipps had slipped out of the house. Now he was going to have to explain his whereabouts and reasons for skulking away. *Shit! And who the hell was sneaking out his back door?*

AGENT COLLINS HAD BEEN ENGAGED in a series of cryptic phone conversations as Thorpe drove to their assorted scouting locations. He wasn't able to gather much information from the mostly one-sided communications; Collins' input consisted mainly of yeses, nos, and uh-huhs. The only thing Thorpe knew for sure was he wasn't a welcome participant in the conversations. She was engaged in one of these exchanges when he heard the call about Phipps' house over the tactical channel. Collins had instantly disengaged from her phone and had instructed Thorpe to tell the officers to force their way in. All relief officers were to start that way.

Thorpe turned his car too, aware he could be driving into a trap. Thorpe advised the dispatcher to notify sub-fleet A and to instruct all available officers to start to the location. Sub-fleet A was the radio channel used by

Gilcrease Division. Thorpe hoped that if this were a trap, the overwhelming number of police officers arriving at the scene would dissuade Phipps.

By the time Thorpe and Collins arrived at Phipps' residence, the protection detail had searched the home and found no signs of an intruder—nor had they found Officer Phipps. Agent Collins was in possession of all the protected officers' contact information. She called Phipps' cell phone number.

PHIPPS WAS ALREADY EN ROUTE BACK TO HIS HOME when his cell phone rang. He didn't recognize the number but figured it would be someone with the department or FBI. He considered not answering the phone but surmised that would create more havoc than picking up. If they were unable to make contact, they'd make a full scale effort to locate him.

"Phipps."

"Officer Phipps, this is Special Agent Collins of the FBI. Are you okay?"

"I'm fine. Thanks for asking." The disclosure was laced with overt sarcasm.

"I'm sorry to say this isn't a social call. We just had a report of a man exiting the back door of your residence. Fearing for your safety, I authorized agents to breech your front door. The agents did, in fact, enter your home, and I was relieved to discover you weren't harmed. What I wasn't happy to learn is that you had purposely slipped away from our protection detail."

Bitch, Phipps thought. *Who was she to order him around?* "I told the FBI, I had no need for a protective detail. Plus, they obviously aren't worth a shit if someone went in and out of my house right under their noses."

"Nevertheless, you do have a detail. In the future, we'd appreciate you keeping us informed of your whereabouts."

"You have no authority over me. I don't have to tell you shit about shit," Phipps barked.

"I have the full cooperation of your chief of police. And I believe he does have authority over you."

"Ma'am, no person has authority over another," Phipps said, trying to put the agent on the defensive.

"We'll have discussions with your command staff in regard to this incident. May I ask where you've been?"

"You can ask."

"Okay, we'll do it your way. You may want to return home and secure your front door."

"I'm en route. I expect the FBI to pay for it," Phipps demanded.

"That would be the least of my worries if I were you," Collins said before she terminated the call.

"PEOPLE CALL *ME* A BITCH?" Collins said out loud—to herself.

Thorpe couldn't help but laugh, "Yeah, I haven't sent him any Christmas cards in quite some time."

"Let's get out of here," Collins said, still a little miffed.

"You don't want to hang around till he gets home and chew on his ass some more?"

"That wouldn't be productive."

"No, but it'd be entertaining." Thorpe was a bit disappointed; he would have liked to see Phipps eye-to-eye for a few minutes. "Where to?"

"Back to SID. We're done for the night; we'll pick up tomorrow where we left off."

The two made their way back to the office. When they parked, Thorpe immediately grabbed his gear bag, told Collins he'd see her tomorrow, and made his way towards an extra car. Collins yelled after him, "You want to go grab a drink somewhere?" *Oh yeah,* he was being played for an easy mark alright; he could almost hear her inner thoughts, let alcohol and hormones cloud his judgment.

"No, thanks, I have some dogs I need to let out before they make a mess all over the place."

"Okay...Tomorrow?"

"Sure," Thorpe relented.

"That's your assigned car?" Collins continued.

Quit with the freaking questions already. "No, I just drive a different one home from time to time...Paranoia, remember?"

"How could I forget?"

Thorpe drove the Mustang out the gate. He made the block and parked. After a couple of minutes, he spotted Agent Collins' gray Crown Victoria pull out of the lot. Thorpe drove back up the ramp and parked next to his truck. It took him less than two minutes to find a GPS tracker attached to the undercarriage of his SID-assigned pickup. Thorpe left the tracking device where he'd found it, then inspected the Mustang. He couldn't readily find one but had no doubt one would be attached to this and the other extra cars before his shift ended tomorrow. *They were on to him. The prevailing racial bullshit was just a convenient ruse.*

Driving home, Thorpe gave his buddy Jeff a call.

"What's up?" Jeff answered.

"You still awake?" Thorpe asked.

"Are you kidding me? I'm not going to get any sleep for the next month."

"We were supposed to go out—where you want to meet?" Thorpe knew Jeff wouldn't be able to go out; he was just giving him hell.

"I can't fucking go out! I'm going to be working twenty-hour days for the rest of my life."

"Relax, man. I was just kidding. Hey, you need anything from the store? I was just about to drop by your house and check on your wife," Thorpe joked.

"Yeah, pick up some skim milk, would you? I don't think I'm going to get off until *ten* or *twelve* tomorrow."

Odd statement, Thorpe thought. "Okay, maybe we can grab lunch during the week or something."

"I doubt it, but I'll give you a call if I can break away," Jeff answered.

Thorpe was troubled by the strange cadence of the conversation. One of his hobbies was studying nonverbal communication. It was a skill his father had imparted. His father had had him read The Silent Language by Edward T. Hall. The first time Thorpe read the book, the information barely registered. But with his father's help, he slowly began to understand the concepts: Less than five percent of a conversation's meaning is conveyed through the actual words spoken. The other ninety-five percent is comprised of time, space, cadence, pitch, body language, facial expressions, eye movement, and so on. Jeff's phone conversation was littered with red flags. Having picked up the distress codes in Jeff's speech patterns, Thorpe focused on the words Jeff had used. Not only had Jeff involuntarily sent warnings, but he had also purposely cautioned Thorpe through the words he chose. First, Jeff had jokingly told Thorpe to pick up some milk. Thorpe happened to know Jeff despised milk. The phrase was no big deal, easily dismissed as part of a sarcastic response, but Jeff also said he wouldn't be home until *ten* or *twelve* tomorrow—putting particular emphasis on the numbers he spoke. Ten-twelve happened to be the department's ten code to inform officers they are not alone. Jeff was warning Thorpe that someone was listening to the conversation. He wondered if someone just happened to be standing next to Jeff or if Thorpe's telephone was tapped. Also, Jeff stated he wouldn't even have time to meet Thorpe for lunch during the week. Everyone has time to eat…something was up. Thorpe felt like the setting sun—everyone was watching him go down.

Twenty-Two

Sunday
February 11th
Early morning

THORPE CLOSED THE DOORS ON DEBORAH'S BARN and extracted his gear bag from the trunk of the Mustang. He climbed a set of stairs to an unused apartment loft and retrieved the AR he'd stashed there before going to work. Thorpe still hadn't destroyed necessary parts of the weapon; he'd better dispose of those tonight. Thorpe stepped out into the dark cold morning. A couple of lights were on inside Deborah's house, but it looked as if he'd make it off her property without encountering the woman. Thorpe crossed the gravel road and began trekking through the woods toward the rear of his property. He'd left Al and Trixie outside and hoped both animals were still alive and well.

Thorpe now had several items on permanent loan from SID, including the pair of night-vision goggles he currently wore. He hadn't officially checked out any of the equipment, and eventually they'd be discovered missing. Thorpe was surprised the high-priced gear hadn't disappeared before this. The procedures for checking out equipment at the office had always been lax. Officers and supervisors alike could borrow gear worth more than of $20,000 a piece without many checks and balances.

Thorpe was using the hand-free goggles to traverse east and slightly north toward the creek that ran behind his house. It was cold outside, hovering around freezing, but the weather was much improved over the night before. The ground foliage was wet from sleet melting throughout the day. As a result, Thorpe could travel more quietly through the woods.

He thought about the night's conversations with Agent Collins. Something didn't track with this lady. She had invited Thorpe for drinks, and while he didn't consider himself unattractive, he was definitely not irresistible. Given the body language of the other agents, it didn't appear she was prone to handing out such invitations. Furthermore, she was a criminal profiler assigned to be Thorpe's personal sidekick. Thorpe wondered if the free time he was being extended wasn't just more rope to hang himself with. He also pondered whether other officers in the unit were being outfitted with GPS tracking devices. Maybe he wasn't the only suspect.

The FBI had been involved in the investigation for less than twenty-four hours. *Was that enough time for him to be developed as a suspect?* The only loose end which could have tied him up that fast was Kaleb Moment. But if the kid had gone straight from his interrogation at the motel to the Feds, Thorpe figured his ass would be in custody by now. Thorpe decided he'd have to do a little investigating of his own. But first he needed to collect the remains of Thadius Shaw and dispose of them somewhere far from his property.

Thorpe was nearing his barn when he heard a low growl and a short bark. A few moments of silence were followed by the thrashings of a large dog with bad intentions. Thorpe had to call off his own dog before it mistakenly took a chunk out of him. Recognizing his voice, the dog slowed but still seemed unsure of him in his goggles. It was Trixie. When she got close enough to recognize Thorpe's scent, her hackles lowered and her ears perked up. Thorpe was greeted by a wagging tail and several licks to the face. Several seconds later, Al showed up for the party. "Good to see you, guys. Guess this means there's no trouble on the homestead." After some belly scratching, Thorpe sent the two dogs out for a search of the property anyway. *No reason to take chances.*

Thorpe connected the electrical cords for the Christmas lights in the tree line. He scanned the trees for movement. He watched his dogs and his surroundings for several minutes but found nothing unusual. He felt secure to walk about his own property but still kept his weapon shouldered as he walked to his front door.

Thorpe had used a drop of candle wax in the crevices of the doors and windows; no intruders could enter undetected. The front door's seal seemed to be intact; Thorpe called for his dogs, unlocked the door, and gave the order to search the home. Immediately Thorpe knew something was wrong. Both dogs lingered in areas too long, taking additional time to gather information through their sense of smell. Whatever information they were gathering put them in a higher state of alert than usual. Thorpe instinctively retreated from the doorway into the shadows. He stayed there—acutely aware of his surroundings—for several minutes trying to gauge where the attack would come from. *Would it come from inside his home, or was his attention being diverted?* Al and Trixie hadn't made a sound. Not wanting to give away his position but fearing for his dogs, Thorpe called for the two animals and immediately changed positions. Both dogs ran out of the house and found their master hunkered down. Maybe no one was in his house now, but he was sure someone had been there sometime during his absence. Thorpe ordered his dogs to remain while he went inside to clear his residence.

Clearing structures of armed men is dangerous. Doing so safely, with one person, is nearly impossible. There are countless angles from which one can be killed inside a multi-roomed building—and every time one moves, those angles change. Thorpe systematically cleared every room in his residence before he was confident the house was secure. When Thorpe finished, he walked back out the front and around the side of his house to the back door. The wax seal was broken; there had definitely been an intruder inside his home.

Thorpe's mind was racing. He doubted Phipps had the knowledge or resources to enter his home without engaging his dogs. They didn't appear to be injured nor lethargic from having been drugged. Besides, if it had been Phipps, the man would have attempted an ambush from inside. *Had the FBI searched his home while he was at work?* Thorpe reentered his home and called his dogs. He followed Al and Trixie through the rooms, taking note of where they lingered. Whoever had been in his house spent considerable time in his closets and dresser drawers—common places for hiding objects.

Thorpe was still amazed at the search warrant services he'd been on. No matter how smart the criminals thought they were, they almost always hid something illegal in the master bedroom closet. Without fail, there would be something illegal somewhere in the master bedroom. Someone had been in Thorpe's house, and that someone was looking for *something—not* someone.

ACROSS THE GRAVEL ROAD, forty yards east of the Christmas-light display, a patch of the forest floor slowly but steadily inched backwards into the darkened recesses of timber. Finally, far from the light, the pile of burlap and jute with intertwined natural foliage rose from the ground and walked away on two legs. The man inside the expertly self-constructed ghillie suit made scarcely a sound as he glided deeper and deeper into the woods.

Twenty-Three

Sunday
February 11th
Morning

IN A LITTLE OVER AN HOUR, THORPE WAS EXPECTED to report to SID, where he'd squander another day shackled to the beguiling Agent Collins. He'd just finished dropping Al and Trixie off at the K-9 center located on the grounds of TPD's Training Academy. Fearing for his dog's safety, Thorpe had talked the sergeant over the K-9 unit to house them in an outside pen for a few days while he "took care of some business."

Before meeting Collins, Thorpe wanted to drop by the detective division and have a chat with Sergeant Hull. The supervisor over homicide hadn't been answering his cell or pager for the last thirty minutes. Thorpe had reached the division's administrative sergeant who informed him all homicide detectives had been in a meeting with the FBI for the last hour and a half. The meeting was due to let out any minute. Thorpe was pulling into the underground parking area of the Main Station when Hull finally returned his call.

"Can you spare a minute for a chat?" Thorpe asked.

"Yeah, bud. Let's do a face to face. Where you at?" Hull asked.

"Just pulled underneath you."

"How 'bout I meet you at the River Parks Café? Ten minutes?"

"See you there," Thorpe confirmed.

Thorpe snapped his phone closed. A lot was conveyed during the short conversation: Hull must have been near people he didn't trust; Thorpe had never heard Hull refer to him—or anyone else—as, "bud." Hull clearly wasn't comfortable speaking over the phone and had suggested they meet at the café— even though both men were already at the main station. The café was an outdoor eatery on the banks of the Arkansas River. In weather like this, it wouldn't even be open for business.

Thorpe hoped Hull had information he'd be willing to share. One thing he knew for sure; Hull wouldn't bullshit him. Thorpe bypassed the café's parking area and stationed himself on the northeast corner of 31st and Riverside Drive. When ten minutes were up, Thorpe called Hull back on his cell. "You ninety-seven yet?" Thorpe asked, using the ten-code officers used when arriving on scene.

"Just pulled in."

Thorpe decided to change the meeting place, "I'm hungry. How 'bout we meet at BBD instead?" BBD was local talk for Brookside by Day, a popular restaurant in the Brookside area. The Brookside neighborhood was home to several trendy restaurants, cafes, and bars. BBD would be bustling with church crowds at this time; the accompanying chatter would provide excellent background noise to muffle any conversation the two men might have.

"What...am I a monkey or something?" Hull asked.

"See you there in five." Thorpe spoke to himself, "A monkey or something?" He let out a short laugh as he got Hull's meaning.

Thorpe waited in the lot and watched as Hull turned from southbound Riverside Drive onto East 31st

Street. Thorpe stayed put for a couple of minutes, trying to ascertain whether or not Hull was in fact a "monkey." If Hull did have a tail, it was up in the air and not dragging on the ground. Thorpe drove to the restaurant another mile to the east. He parked behind it and walked in the back entrance. He found Hull waiting inside.

"Am I a monkey or something," Thorpe laughed.

"Fuck you. I'm not used to this cloak and dagger shit."

"Obviously."

"*You*, on the other hand, seem to be right at home."

"Undercover work…prepares you for it," Thorpe explained.

"Yeah, right."

The two sergeants were shown to a table and both ordered coffee. Hull spoke first, "So what the hell is going on?"

"I was kind of hoping you'd tell me."

The two men sat at the table staring at each other—both trying to force the other's hand.

"Look, John, we can sit here and stare at each other all day long, but the fact is, you need me a hell of a lot more than I need you."

"You're right, Bob. But I don't think you'd want to hear what I have to say—even if I did feel inclined to talk about it."

"Let me ask you this—completely off the record by the way—you have my word…" Hull's word meant something to Thorpe, most men's didn't. "All this shit going on… Does it have anything to do with your wife and daughter's murders?" Hull had just dropped MOAB—the mother of all bombs.

Thorpe sat in stunned silence for a full minute as he made up his mind whether or not to answer the question. Finally Thorpe lifted his head and met Hull's eyes, "It has everything to do with my family's murder."

"I see. And how good is your information? In other words—is there a possibility you may be mistaken?"

"One-hundred-percent positive."

"Shit," Hull mumbled.

"Yeah, shit."

Thorpe looked across the table at his colleague and could tell the man was struggling with a moral dilemma. He didn't want to tell Hull what was going on but the man had somehow already reached certain conclusions. Plus, Bob wasn't going to tell Thorpe a word if he smelled a line of crap. After much mental wrangling, Hull let out a long breath, "What do you need?"

"For some reason, I've captured the attention of the Feds. Why?" Thorpe asked.

"I don't know...I don't. We're being kept in the dark as far as the FBI's role in this thing is concerned. We're doing our own thing, and the FBI's doing theirs. We share our information with them; they don't share shit with us. They were granted access to all personnel files—including yours."

"But you knew I was being looked at specifically. Otherwise we wouldn't be meeting like this," Thorpe pointed out.

"The only reason I knew you were a blip on their radar was because of Agent Collins. She and I had a private meeting during which we discussed the personnel files of several officers—trying to get a feel for potential suspects. Most of those officers we discussed had military or SWAT training. Your file was somewhere near the middle of the stack, and when we discussed it, Agent Collins seemed rather flippant, like she was just going through the motions. I got the impression she was attempting to ascertain as much information about you as possible but not alert me to the intensity of her interest in you. I think the other officer's files were just in there as a cover. Of course I can't really offer you anything to substantiate my impression."

Thorpe smiled, "You don't have to. You're pretty sharp for a tailless monkey."

"She's sharp too—Agent Collins."

"Yeah, I've noticed."

Hull continued, "Some information about you I had to pass on. They'd find it sooner or later. Some information I kept to myself—information about your father and your extracurricular activities inside the ring. But if I found it, they'll find it."

"I appreciate that, Bob. If you don't mind me asking—what did you find out about my father?"

"Not much. He was probably Army Special Forces before he went to work for a private security *company*. I figure the work he did for this company was probably related to his Army skills. I also figured he passed some of those skills on to his son."

"You did a lot of figuring, Bob. To tell you the truth I don't know what the hell my father did for a living. All I know is he wanted to keep me isolated from whatever it was—but it did make for an interesting childhood."

"I bet."

"I'm thinking you started figuring I may have been involved in this mess before the Feds even showed up. You want to tell me how?"

Hull shook his head, "I got a lot of stuff that doesn't add up to shit. Just had a feeling...like you had a feeling some meth-head was going to blow your head off with a shotgun."

Thorpe considered the statement, "People ought to trust their instincts more. I'd best get going; I'm supposed to hook up with *Doctor* Collins in twenty minutes. Don't want her to think I'm up to no good." Thorpe took out a piece of paper, wrote down three names, and passed the note to Hull. "Those three are also involved. I have a document and corroborating evidence in a safety deposit box at the Mid-First Bank at 91st Street and Yale. If something happens to me before they answer for what they did, make sure you retrieve and use it. By the way, I didn't have anything to do with Cole Daniels; I think it was them tying up some loose ends." Thorpe rose from the table, plopped down a couple of bucks for his untouched coffee, and made his way towards the back door.

"Hey, John..."

Thorpe turned to look at Hull who still sat glumly at the table, "Yeah?"

Hull met Thorpe's eyes. "I'd have done the same thing," he offered.

Thorpe slowly nodded, turned, and walked out into the bright February afternoon. He had a Marine Force-Recon/TPD sniper trying to kill him and an FBI criminal-profiler trying to arrest him. The chances of Thorpe avoiding death or prison were almost zero.

Twenty-Four

Sunday
February 11th
Morning

FIFTEEN MINUTES LATER, THORPE ENTERED HIS OFFICE to find Agent Collins waiting on his couch. She was dressed much more casually in a pair of blue jeans and a dark, snug sweater.

"You feel bad about outclassing me in the sushi joint?" Thorpe asked.

"Don't need a suit to accomplish that," Collins said with a wry smile.

"Ouch. FBI one...PD zero," Thorpe said. "What's on the agenda tonight—more of the same?"

"Pretty much."

"Ready to get going?"

Collins remained on the couch. "Let's discuss some of your troops first. Give me your impression of them."

"I can do that in the car," Thorpe suggested.

"Please," Collins gestured for Thorpe to have a seat behind his desk. She was stalling, probably giving one of her colleagues time to hardwire a tracking device to the

Mustang. Thorpe sat behind his desk and defended each and every one of his troops for the next twenty minutes. After the charade was over, Agent Collins announced she was ready to leave. To Thorpe's surprise, he successfully talked Agent Collins into taking one of SID's extra cars. She must have anticipated this request, ensuring every extra unit assigned to SID was now outfitted with GPS.

Thorpe retrieved a couple of bags from the Mustang and tossed them into the small back seat of the green Jeep Wrangler. Adding to his suspicion, he noticed Collins had a bag packed as well. They both climbed into the small four-wheel-drive vehicle and discussed which addresses they'd survey during the next twelve hours.

Every officer with protective details had been granted time-off with pay. That meant Phipps had the freedom of choosing a place and time to target Thorpe. Meanwhile, Thorpe was tethered to a federal agent. In addition to avoiding death, Thorpe was going to have to deal with the mental probings of the good doctor. He was beginning to develop a headache, a condition he generally never experienced unless it was preceded by someone's fist colliding with the side of his head. The stress of the last few days was beginning to take a toll on his body and mind. He'd spent half of last night wrestling with the rigid corpse of the late Mr. Shaw while wondering if the FBI were going to pounce on him at any minute.

Thorpe thought he might have to use his first-ever sick day tomorrow, which would really put the FBI on high alert. They'd surely figure Thorpe to be on the prowl. For now he'd just concentrate on two things: not getting arrested or killed in the next twelve hours.

The Jeep was equipped with a hard-top and limo tint. Because of the added privacy, Thorpe didn't worry about covering his face with his hoodie as he and his jean-clad, federal agent pulled away from the office.

"We going to be together all night, or you going to give me a reprieve for a few hours?" Thorpe asked.

"Why, you don't like my company?"

"It's not that. I just have some people to kill, and you're putting a cramp in my style." Thorpe was joking—well not really—he was pretending to be joking. *How would the good doctor take the comment?*

After several moments of silence, Collins finally responded, "Is that one of your attempts at humor again?"

"Was it funny?" Thorpe asked.

"No."

"Then it wasn't. I'm always humorous when I make the attempt."

"You realize I am a federal agent assigned to this investigation. It's not in your best interest to make those kind of statements in case one or both of us end up in federal court?"

"Shit, you've lost your entire sense of humor overnight." Thorpe had a feeling their conversation was being monitored and recorded. She was trying to avoid an ambiguous conversation.

Thorpe decided to have a little fun, "Agent Collins, what are you doing?"

"What are you talking about?"

Thorpe began speaking with agitation, "Agent Collins, please do not grab my crotch again. I have a girlfriend, and while I find you mildly attractive, I'm not interested."

"What the hell are you talking about? Have you lost your mind? I haven't touched you."

"Agent Collins, please pull your sweater back down…I don't want to see those. Oh, my god, they're hideous!"

"Sergeant Thorpe! I don't know what you're trying to pull but…"

Thorpe cut her off, "Oh my God, don't pull your pants down. Holy shit…when was the last time that thing saw a pair of scissors?"

"Sergeant Thorpe!"

"Screaming my name doesn't do it for me. Damn, it looks like you have Don King in a leg lock down there."

Agent Collins' face was flushed red. Thorpe couldn't tell if it was from anger or embarrassment. She began to raise her voice again but a look of recognition washed over her face. "You think I'm wearing a wire?" She still looked pissed.

"Aren't you?" Thorpe asked.

"No."

"Is someone listening to us?"

"No."

"If there is—they're laughing their asses off."

"Damn, you're a prick. I thought you'd lost your mind." Agent Collins face began to regain some of its natural color, and Thorpe heard her giggle as she repeated, "Don King in a leg lock. Ugh, you're an asshole."

"Admitted. What would you do if one of your FBI buddies treated you like this?"

"I'd chew his ass up one side and down the other. I'd let him know if he ever did it a second time, it'd be his last time."

"That's what I figured."

"Based on what information?" Collins asked.

"Based on how your coworkers act around you. They treat you like you're a real..."

"Bitch? They might be right."

"How 'bout me... Going to write me up?"

"You? No. I have to work with those guys..." Agent Collins had a slight smile as she completed her thought, "You, on the other hand, I'll never have to see your sorry ass again."

Thorpe doubted Agent Collins was telling the truth; he figured the conversation was being monitored. Plus, she'd forgiven his outburst way too easily. Thorpe pictured a room full of suits all nodding their heads when the word "bitch" was mentioned.

A dispatcher making an announcement over the protective detail's sub-fleet interrupted their verbal Judo. "All units be advised a large group of demonstrators are gathering outside the Main Station. Officers at the location are requesting additional units. Officers report the crowd is growing in size and in animosity towards police."

A famous national figure in the black community had scheduled a 9 a.m. press conference downtown at the main station to address the recent killings. Several uniformed officers and the mounted patrol had been assigned as security for the speaker. Because of the early hour, the event was expected to be relatively peaceful. Agent Collins grabbed the radio and advised all units on protective detail to remain in their current positions.

Thorpe took exception with the order, "If some cop gets hurt down there because they didn't have enough bodies, there's going to be hell to pay."

"And if someone gets killed because we abandon our posts there's going to be hell to pay."

"At least let the relief units head that way."

"Fine," Collins said, relenting.

Thorpe picked up the microphone and instructed the relief units to head to the area to assist on-scene officers. Thorpe than redirected the Jeep towards downtown.

"Where are you going?" Collins asked.

"We're headed to the officers in need."

"No, we're not. We will continue with our assignment."

"I'm going to help those officers. Do you want me to let you out?"

"Sergeant Thorpe, who is in charge here?"

"You are," Thorpe said.

"Then you *will* turn this car around and continue with our current assignment."

"No, I will not. Now unless you plan on physically restraining me, this argument is over." Thorpe risked a glance over at Agent Collins who stared straight ahead at the road with a clenched jaw. *At least, for the moment, the jaw was shut.*

Thorpe traveled down the Broken Arrow Expressway taking the Inner Dispersal Loop around the south side of the city. He exited the highway on Denver Avenue and turned north. When Thorpe reached 6th Street, he found the intersection was blockaded so that vehicles couldn't travel in front of the Main Station. Thorpe jumped the curb and illegally parked on the east side of Denver, a half-block from the agitated crowd.

This was exactly what Thorpe feared would happen, and he felt personally responsible for having set events in motion. This was not about race, it was personal. This was about some crooked-assed cops, a few of whom were black, who'd made a fatal error. Unfortunately, Thorpe couldn't just get on the news and announce the reason behind the killings. But if some innocent person were hurt—and God forbid it be a fellow officer—he'd never forgive himself. He had enough blood on his hands already.

Investigators with the intelligence unit usually integrated themselves into volatile crowds. Whether it was the KKK, or that dumb-ass church group that picketed military funerals, the Intel guys were usually in the mix looking for trouble makers before they could instigate civil disobedience—today's politically correct name for a riot. Besides infiltrating the crowds, one or more were usually discretely filming. It was always good to have video contradicting a demonstrator's edited version of events. Because SID was stretched thin by the protective details, no such provisions had been made for this speech.

Thorpe grabbed a radio, ensured he was on the proper sub-fleet, and concealed the radio inside his jacket with the ear-bud securely attached. He left the Jeep, walking briskly towards 6th Street. Agent Collins was in hot pursuit. Thorpe rounded the corner on the south side of 6th and noticed additional units responding. They included a couple of unmarked cars. He recognized two day-shift narcotics investigators piling out of their cars. He flagged them over.

They hurried over to Thorpe, "What's up, sarge?"

"Stay next to me. Look for troublemakers. And let's try not to get our asses kicked." Thorpe headed off toward the crowd.

Thorpe observed the famed civil rights leader on the north side of 6th Street, behind a podium. The podium was at the top of a flight of concrete steps. Above the podium was another set of steps. The speaker was surrounded by his own personal protective detail, four large black males in expensive suits. Uniformed officers covered the stairs in front of and behind the speaker. The mounted patrol unit—six officers on horseback—completed the detail. The size of the police force was growing by the minute.

Thorpe and company approached the back of the crowd. The throng of people was diverse, comprised of various minorities and a sprinkling of whites. Most of those assembled were peaceful, but there was a small core with trouble on their minds.

"Agent Collins, get your identification out, and join the officers across the street," Thorpe ordered.

"Bullshit, I'm coming with you."

"I need you on the other side of the street. I've seen this before. There are some in this group looking for any opportunity to cause trouble. And believe me...you're an opportunity."

"I can take care of myself," Collins shouted.

Thorpe swung around and pointed his index finger at Collins. "I'm sure you can. But if someone decides to cop-a-feel, and we have to take them down, the fight's going to be on. Then all those officers across the street are going to have to come over here to save our asses. And if one of them gets hurt, it'll be your fault."

Agent Collins gave a simple nod and crossed the street towards the uniformed police officers. When she reached the line of blue, she produced identification and was allowed inside the perimeter. Thorpe watched as Collins ascended the steps and took an elevated position where she could observe the crowd and Thorpe.

The minister's words called for peace, but his speech and mannerisms hinted at insurrection. Thorpe felt pride as he looked at the stoic faces of the police officers gathered around protecting the man who was unjustly insulting them. Thorpe's pride in his fellow officers was tainted with personal shame because his actions had tarnished one of the finest police departments in the country.

Thorpe estimated the crowd to be near three hundred, with fifty of those having the potential to make trouble. They were the young and angry, those who were convinced they'd been the victims of white injustice—and the police were the greatest symbol of the white justice system.

The angry vocal group had worked its way toward the front of the crowd. Within this assemblage, Thorpe identified an even smaller click of five. Each one wore long white t-shirts which were visible below their coats. All but one were hurling racial insults at the officers across the street. It was the quiet one who most troubled Thorpe. He was younger than the rest, maybe sixteen or seventeen, and was pacing up and down like a caged predator. It looked as though he was working up the courage to do something he shouldn't. Whatever he was planning, it was bothering the kid enough he wasn't engaging in verbal confrontation with the police. The kid seemed to be *somewhere else* entirely.

Thorpe risked moving through the crowd to get a closer look. His group of three was able to maneuver within several feet of the kids, who were focused on the uniformed officers. The quiet one continued to pace behind his buddies and kept looking down at his waist, sweating despite the cool weather. *Shit*. Thorpe had little doubt the kid had a pistol in his waistband.

People carrying weapons often continuously touched them or glanced down to where they had them concealed. They feared the handle might be protruding through their clothing or that the weapon was visible in some other way. Instead of a bulge in a jacket giving away the gun, it was usually their behavior.

Thorpe glanced at the two narcotics officers. A nod of their heads indicated they'd also recognized the potential threat. The tricky part was what to do about it. Taking down an armed man in a hostile crowd was never easy work, but Thorpe had to do something before the kid worked up the nerve to do what he was contemplating.

The three undercover officers formed a small huddle and discussed their play. "Snatch and grab," Thorpe began. "I'm going to wrap him up around the waist and pin his arms. Tanner, as soon as I wrap him up, you're going to grab his legs. Frank, you're going to make a hole for us right toward our skirmish line. Understand?"

Both men nodded. Thorpe looked up at Collins who was staring back intently. He made a circle above his head with his finger pointed down indicating the three of them. Then—continuing with the football analogy—made a motion similar to the tomahawk chop popular at so many sports arenas. Thorpe didn't want the skirmish line to think they were demonstrators breaking ranks. Collins seemed to understand, as she descended the stairs and spoke to the sergeant in charge of the front line officers.

"Hard and fast. Let's go," Thorpe commanded.

Thorpe hoped to hell the kid had a gun. Their makeshift fullback, Frank, had just knocked two guys out of the way and kicked over the wooden barricade while Thorpe and Tanner followed carrying their "football" through the defensive line. If Thorpe had guessed wrong, and the kid was unarmed, they were all going to get their asses sued off. Never mind they were trying to save someone's life.

Having safely crossed the plane of the end-zone, or in this case the skirmish-line, Tanner unloaded his share of the burden. Thorpe went crashing to the pavement on top of the pigskin. It was then that Thorpe heard one of the sweetest sounds ever—the sound of a metal object striking the concrete sidewalk. Fumble. Thorpe rolled the kid over and was rewarded with the sight of a chrome handgun. Thank God. If the kid had been unarmed, there would have been ten different camera angles of Thorpe's actions posted on YouTube before dinner was served at Furr's cafeteria. He and the department would've been crucified.

Thorpe's relief was short-lived. The football's friends had stood in shock for a few seconds but now realized one of their own had just lost a brutal game. They stepped over the fallen barricade in an ill-conceived plan to retrieve their comrade. Others in the crowd, believing they'd just witnessed Thorpe face plant a black man for no good reason, decided to join in the festivities.

Then chaos broke out. The crowd, which had been headed straight toward Thorpe and his prisoner, were now headed every direction but—thanks to six mounted police officers and seven thousand pounds of horse meat. Most people were just trying to get the hell out of the way; but the fifty or so who'd been looking for an opportunity had found it. Several youths had entered the parking lot to the southeast and were now in the process of expressing their freedom of speech by smashing car windows.

His fellow officers were going to be busy for a while, but Thorpe had had enough. He passed his prisoner off to a uniformed patrolman, dropped the magazine out of the suspect's handgun, and jacked a round out of the chamber.

"Hey, Tanner, Frank, good job. You two ever want to come over to Gangs just say the word."

"No offense, John, but fuck you," Tanner smiled.

"Oh, come on. It's the land of milk and honey. Hey, could you do me a favor and turn in this gun? There's nothing left for you guys to do here anyway. I think your cover has officially been blown."

"Yeah, no problem."

Thorpe looked at Collins who'd joined his side, "Let's get inside." He nodded toward the rivers of fleeing people between them and the Jeep, "I don't think we'll be able to get to our ride for a few minutes."

The two ascended the stairs and headed toward the entrance to the main station. "You did a good job back there, you know?" Collins offered. "Probably saved someone's life, the kid's for sure."

"Yeah, now he'll have a chance to grow up and learn how to kill a cop without getting caught," Thorpe answered.

Collins shook her head, "Don't make this something ugly. You know you can't have control over everyone and everything. Some things are just going to...be."

"And some things can be prevented," Thorpe argued.

"Look, tragedies happen every minute of every day. Someone's mother dies in a car wreck because her daughter took ten seconds to give her a hug in the morning. Someone's son dies because he was on his way home for Mother's Day when a truck driver sneezes at an intersection. Someone's father dies because he made an oath to protect others with his life if need be. None of it can be predicted, and yet we all wallow in guilt."

Thorpe was already thinking Collins sounded a bit rehearsed when she stopped and put a hand on his shoulder.

"You're hurt," she said.

"Look, you've obviously done your homework on me, and you know what happened to my family. If I want your psychobabble I'll lie down on your couch and pay you a couple hundred bucks."

"No," Collins nodded down at Thorpe's hand, "I mean you're physically hurt."

Thorpe was dripping blood on the sun-bleached concrete. He looked back noticing a blood trail up the stairs.

He felt embarrassed for misunderstanding Collins and for reprimanding her. "Look, I'm sorry, I…"

"Forget about it," Collins said, cutting him off. "Is it painful?"

"Not till you pointed it out. Guess I still have a bit of an adrenaline dump."

"Let's get it cleaned up."

Twenty-Five

Sunday
February 11th
Afternoon

Ambretta followed Thorpe along the mostly empty hallways of the main station. Because it was Sunday the station was closed to the public and few detectives were on duty. Thorpe led her to the offices of the Domestic Violence Unit, where he remembered seeing a first aid kit bolted to the wall. While she sifted through the metal box, she noticed him step into a separate office, turn his back, and make a phone call. He either wasn't able to reach who he'd dialed or didn't have much to say, because thirty seconds later he sat down in a padded chair just behind her.

When Ambretta had arrived in Tulsa, she'd been given four tasks, two of which were secondary to the others. One task was to coordinate protective details using local officers and federal agents. Another was to monitor the progress of the investigative unit. Her main objectives were monitoring the movements of Sergeant Jonathan Thorpe and learning as much as possible about the man. Normally this would be a simple task; she generally had no problem getting men to do just about anything she wanted.

It was a skill that had served her well over the last two years.

Thorpe, however, was proving to be a difficult case. If he admired her looks, he hid it well. And he'd turned her down for drinks once already—something that had never happened to her before—even with married men. He claimed to have a girlfriend which she knew to be a lie. Not unless he kept her locked away in a subterranean mew. Of course, if the man really were running around killing people at night, then he *was* a tad busy.

Ambretta felt she excelled at appraising the quality of a man, and Thorpe didn't strike her as a serial murderer. At least not one motivated by racial issues. He was obviously capable of violence when necessary. And what had happened to his family would cause anyone to lose moral footing; Ambretta knew that first hand. Still, there was something *different* about Thorpe. He had an abundance of scar tissue in the eyebrow area. He had battered ears and calloused knuckles. Still...he was good looking. And those green eyes...wow. Attraction wasn't something she'd felt in a long time, but she recognized the familiar pang. She realized part of it was because of their shared experiences; they'd each lost loved ones to unspeakable acts of cowardice. Regardless, she had a job to do and she was not accustomed to failing.

Having gathered what she needed from the kit, Ambretta turned around and caught Thorpe looking at her ass. *So he's a man after all.*

"Please take off your jacket and sweatshirt."

"I usually demand my date buy me dinner first."

"I saw you looking, Big Boy. You may as well give up on that dream right now."

Thorpe laughed. As he dragged the sweatshirt over his head, it pulled up the t-shirt, exposing his washboard stomach and yet another laceration. She didn't know when she'd seen a man in such phenomenal shape. Except on the cover of magazines. But those guys trained for months and then dehydrated themselves for the photo shoot. This guy resembled a middleweight boxer at a pre-fight weigh-in. There was no fat at all on him. And, for some reason, the scars didn't detract from his looks.

"Where'd you get the cut?"

"Police work is dangerous."

Does this guy ever give a straight answer? "Right," she said with arched eyebrows. Ambretta sat on a rolling chair and slid in front of Thorpe. She opened a bottle of hydrogen peroxide. One of his knees was between hers.

"You know what I say here, right?" Collins asked.

"This is going to hurt a little?" Thorpe said.

"Close enough."

She tipped the bottle, and liquid foamed on the abrasion. She repeated the process two more times until satisfied she'd flushed the wound. Then she grabbed a roll of gauze and began wrapping the damaged hand and wrist. *Those damned eyes of his.*

Thorpe looked directly into hers, "Isn't this where we gaze at each other and fall into a long kiss?"

Ambretta was used to men looking at her the way Thorpe was now. The only difference was she'd been attracted to few, if any. There were so many freaks out there. If they weren't self absorbed braggarts, they usually had good reason. The so-called sensitive ones, the ones who actually gave a damn what you had to say, were usually a teaspoon of estrogen away from being women. Yeah, they knew how to hold open a door for you, but just try to find one with the steel to stand up and do what's right when things went to hell. And if they were a man's man, they might offer a pair of broad shoulders, but there's no way in hell they'd give you their time, heart, or, God forbid, their loyalty.

Ambretta knew she was comparing every man to her father—an unfair comparison for anyone. He might not have been the perfect man, but he was the perfect father. He would've given his life, his heart, his loyalty, his everything for his little girl. The only problem was that her father would also have given his life for complete strangers—which, ultimately, he did.

Ambretta gazed back into Thorpe's eyes: *If only circumstances were different.* She said, "Even if I didn't know what an ass you were, you still wouldn't have a chance."

"Ouch. That hurt worse than my hand."

"Somehow I think you'll survive both injuries. All finished."

Thorpe made a fist a couple of times. "Nice work. Well, on my hand at least. As for my ego..."

"Your hand is far more manageable than your ego," Ambretta said as she leaned back and crossed her arms. His knee was still between hers, his eyes still on hers.

Ambretta heard the office door open.

She looked up to see Jeff Gobin, Thorpe's best friend, standing at the door. "Hey, John. You ready?"

"I'm ready," Thorpe responded.

Ambretta reestablished eye contact, "Ready for what?"

"Jeff here is taking me home, seeing that I'm injured and all."

Their eyes remained locked on each other. *The asshole.*

"The phone call you made?" she said.

"The phone call I made," he confirmed.

Ambretta found herself in the backseat of Jeff's car spitting mad and trying desperately not to show it. Thorpe had graciously offered for Jeff to drop her off at the Jeep on the way out. *How did he put it?* "I wouldn't want someone else to take a crack at my dream." Ugh. She didn't bother arguing. She already knew it'd be useless to try and keep him at work. If he wanted to use sick time or injury leave or whatever the hell, she couldn't stop him.

Jeff stopped next to the Jeep, and Thorpe stepped out followed by Ambretta. He unlocked the door, retrieved his gear, and tossed her the keys.

"I hope you don't mind," he said.

Thorpe had left the passenger door on Jeff's car open so he could make a quick escape. Ambretta slammed it shut. "What are you doing?"

"Are you a man who keeps his promises?"

OH SHIT, WHERE WAS THIS GOING? Thorpe was a man who kept his promises. His father would roll over in his grave. "I am."

"Yesterday, you promised to have drinks with me tonight," Ambretta reminded him.

"I didn't exactly promise," Thorpe argued.

"Are you going to argue over semantics now?" Then, "John...what if I buy all the drinks and promise not to talk shop?"

She referred to him by his first name—*pulling out the big guns*. He could use a couple of drinks, and he could absolutely use the company of an attractive woman—beautiful, really—but not one who was trying to put him in federal prison.

"I'll tell you what. You buy the drinks, you don't talk shop, you don't ask any questions about me, and you let me call you Ambretta. Then you have a deal."

"Deal. In private you may refer to me by Ambretta."

"Okay, Ambretta. Jeff is taking me home first; I have some things I need to take care of."

"I can drive you home."

"I appreciate it. But Jeff and I have some catching up to do."

"What time shall we meet?" Collins asked.

Thorpe was quietly cussing himself, *Shit, how'd I let this happen?* He'd finally gotten a free pass away from this woman only to make what sounded a lot like a date with her. "How 'bout seven?" Thorpe answered.

"Done. If you don't show, I'm going to come looking for you."

"Of that, I have no doubt," Thorpe replied as he climbed into Jeff's city-issued Ford Taurus.

Thorpe looked at Jeff and put his index finger up to his own mouth as an indication to Jeff he didn't feel comfortable speaking confidentially in the car. Jeff left, turning south onto Denver.

"Let's grab a couple beers before you take me home."

"Okay. Where to?"

"Let's go to Los Cabos at the Riverwalk; it'll have a good crowd on a Sunday afternoon."

Twenty-Six

Sunday
February 11th
Afternoon

LOS CABOS WAS A MEXICAN RESTAURANT. It was part of Riverwalk Crossing, a collection of shops, bars, restaurants, and theaters that sat on the west side of the Arkansas River in the town of Jenks on Tulsa's southwest border. The restaurant wouldn't be too out of the way for the drive to Thorpe's *compound*, as Jeff liked to refer to it. When they arrived at the eatery, Thorpe removed his cell phone and left it in the car, motioning for Jeff to do the same. Once the two were seated at a booth inside the noisy restaurant, Thorpe felt free to speak, but it was Jeff who initiated the conversation, "John, what the hell is going on?"

"It's obvious the FBI considers me a suspect in these murders."

"I know *that*, but why? Why the *hell* would you kill those guys? I mean I know they weren't your favorite people—mine either, for that matter. But them being assholes is no reason to kill a man."

"Maybe I'm a closet racist, Jeff. Maybe I befriended you, just to get near you. Make you feel all comfortable around me then..." Thorpe snapped his fingers and smiled.

"The only thing you're killing me with are your lame jokes, John. And it's a slow-ass death, let me tell ya."

"I've been getting that a lot lately. I think my timing's off."

"Could you be serious for one fucking minute? You have an airtight alibi for Daniels' murder. You were in the middle of a search warrant with your entire squad when he was killed. So why do they suspect you?"

"Why don't you tell me, Jeff? You know something, you've avoided me like an infectious disease since the Feds blew into town."

"Do you have anything to do with this?" Jeff pointedly asked.

Thorpe didn't want to lie to his friend, but telling the truth wouldn't benefit either man and would only put Jeff in a predicament. Jeff would have to turn Thorpe in—or keep the secret and become an accessory. Hull had figured out matters on his own. Jeff was still struggling for answers—but he knew something. "Jeff, you know me better than anyone on the department, maybe better than anyone living on this planet with the exception of my sister. Do you think I'd commit cold-blooded murder just because of someone's fucked-up views?"

"No."

Thorpe hadn't lied, but he hadn't exactly answered Jeff's question either. "You know I wouldn't. Jeff, please tell me what you know—so I can figure out what the hell is going on myself."

"You repeat it, I'll be fired and tossed in prison."

"Again, you know me better than that. Whatever you say here will never be repeated."

"Fuck." Jeff shook his head. "First of all, what I know I'm not supposed to know. I'm not going to tell you who I got my information from, so don't ask. All I can tell you is that they're a reliable source." Jeff looked nervously around the restaurant. "From what I understand, the FBI received a phone call from some kid named Kaleb Moment. You know him?"

Thorpe nodded his head. *Should've killed that little snitch bastard.* Thorpe could justify the other killings to himself—as some kind of justice. Killing Kaleb would've been purely out of self-preservation. Thorpe had tried to salvage part of his soul by releasing the kid from that motel room. *No good deed goes unpunished.*

Jeff continued, "Anyway, I guess this Kaleb kid calls up a Texas FBI office and tells them some Tulsa police sergeant is fixing to go off the reservation. Tells them there's some Tulsa police officers about to get killed. Tells them this sergeant will be the one responsible for their murders. Tells them you, Sergeant John Thorpe, is the one who'll be responsible. Tells them that other TPD officers are involved, so he can't go to the police.

"Kaleb demands to be placed in the witness protection program and wants a document promising this placement. He called the Texas FBI because he's so freaked out. He's afraid you have friends in high places. I guess the agent who took the call is thinking, 'Yeah, right, another caller with conspiracy theories.' But he tells the kid to drive on in, and he'll take the statement. If the information turns out to be good, and TPD officers start getting whacked, he'll make sure he gets in the program."

Jeff nervously looked around the restaurant before he continued, "Well, guess what happens? Stephen Price gets killed with a bow and arrow, and Cole Daniels gets sniped in his living room, and this kid never shows up for his meeting with the Texas FBI agent. Meanwhile, the agent catches the national news and thinks, 'Oh shit! The kid was legit.' He contacts Tulsa's FBI office and relates the discussion he had with Kaleb on the phone.

"The FBI, having been given your name and a tip that other TPD officers are involved, calls a private meeting with several members of TPD management. No one from Homicide or Internal Affairs is invited to this meeting. I guess they discuss their options and decide to go out to your house and pick you up for questioning. At least that was the plan—until Agent Collins entered the meeting…"

Thorpe listened to Jeff and thought he had a lot of information for someone who wasn't supposed to be in the know. Most likely, Jeff's source was a certain deputy chief he'd befriended. Thorpe listened as Jeff continued.

"…I guess the special agent in charge of the Tulsa office doesn't know Agent Collins from squat. She walks in, produces her credentials, and tells them in no uncertain terms that she is now in charge. The SAC protests but Collins tells him to take it up with his boss and spits out the man's cell phone number from memory. According to my source, the SAC phones his boss and—based on the subsequent expression on his face—was told he was subordinate to Agent Collins.

"Agent Collins addressed the group and informed them *you* have an airtight alibi for the murder of Cole Daniels. So if you *are* a suspect, there are others involved as well. She also tells them the only reason you were named as a suspect was because of the phone call from the now missing Kaleb Moment. If you were indeed involved, they had no corroborating evidence and would only be 'showing their hand' if they brought you in for an interview so early in the investigation. Agent Collins went on to say that the best course of action would be to monitor your activities. She then excused the few TPD personnel from the room and had a private meeting with the local FBI officials. According to my source, when the local Feds walked out, they looked like they'd all been kicked in the balls. The same night they had this meeting, Brandon Baker was killed and set on fire, and Thadius Shaw went missing.

"Other than that, I don't know much. After the initial meeting, the FBI has disclosed little to TPD. I was threatened with having my balls cut off and shoved up my ass if I relayed any of this information. Anyway, Agent Collins is in charge of this whole investigation, and she's been riding around with you for seven or eight hours a day. I wouldn't trust her for shit if I were you."

"Yeah. I should definitely stay away from her," Thorpe agreed.

"By the way, what'd she say to you outside my car?"

"Oh, nothing. We were just planning our date for this evening."

"What? That your sorry-ass sense of humor again?"

"No. That's just my sorry-ass decision making," Thorpe shrugged.

Jeff was laughing. "You dumb-ass. You never were very smart with women."

"Shit, I don't even know how it happened, Jeff."

"I do. If she were five-foot-three and four-hundred pounds you wouldn't be in this position. The Feds probably sent her on purpose. Well, at least you have nothing to worry about since you're not involved in this shit. She's just wasting her time. Damn good looking, though—doesn't even wear much make-up. Female feds never look like her—'cept in the movies."

After a couple more beers, the two men loaded up in the car and continued to Thorpe's residence. As Jeff entered the neighborhood, he didn't pay much attention when Thorpe asked to pull over to the side of the road—not until Thorpe grabbed his gear bag and climbed out of the Ford.

"You're walking?"

"Yeah, the Feds are keeping tabs on me, and I don't like to make things easy for anyone." In reality Thorpe was cognizant he had a Special Forces Marine still stalking his ass. "Jeff, thanks."

"No problem, and be careful around Agent Collins. Don't let her use her feminine wares against you."

"You know me. I'm like a rock."

"Yeah. 'Bout as smart as one," Jeff replied.

"If you don't mind, don't drive by my house. Just back up and head out the way we came."

Jeff's nod turned into a disappointed shake as he watched his best friend disappear into the woods. He'd expected Thorpe to have more faith in him.

Twenty-Seven

Sunday
February 11th
Evening

THORPE SPED ALONG TOWARD TULSA under a clear, starlit night. Earlier he'd arrived home and, after a close inspection of his wax seals, was confident no one had entered the house in his absence. He'd taken a nervous shower, half expecting the bathroom door to burst open while he stood naked, armed only with shampoo and the wrong kind of gun.

Following the shower, Thorpe had settled into a chair to think. Instead, he had instantly fallen asleep and hadn't woken until nearly two hours later—the toll of the last few days demanding payment. Later, he had donned a pair of coveralls to protect his date garb and packed dress shoes in his ever-present gear bag. Then he plodded through the woods to retrieve his personal truck from Deborah's barn.

Now, as Thorpe neared the Creek Turnpike, he retrieved his phone and called Ambretta.

"I was beginning to think you were going to stand me up," she answered.

"I'm a man of my word. I'm almost to Tulsa now. Where do you want to meet?"

"I'm staying at the Renaissance Hotel on 71st Street. You mind picking me up here?"

"I'll be there in fifteen or less."

Thorpe cursed himself for agreeing to this meeting. He still had three hostiles at large: Phipps, Corn, and McDonald, all of whom wanted him dead. But instead of dealing with these somewhat pressing issues, he was driving straight into the lion's den for a *date* with the FBI agent in charge of his investigation. Thorpe shook his head. Though logic told him to avoid this encounter, his intuition directed him otherwise. Or maybe it was testosterone rather than intuition providing direction—he was definitely attracted to the woman. Hopefully, his judgment wasn't fatally clouded.

The Renaissance Hotel was located just north of 71st Street and just west of Highway 169. It was one of Tulsa's nicest and newest hotels. The 71st Street corridor was a Mecca of shops, malls, restaurants, and bars. He redialed Ambretta's number to tell her he'd arrived.

Ambretta answered, "I just ordered a drink inside the hotel bar, Merlots I believe it's called. Care to join me?"

Thorpe walked inside the large hotel. He was dressed in black slacks and a tailored, long-sleeve dress shirt. He found Ambretta sitting at the bar facing the entrance—as all good cops do. She was dressed in a simple form-fitting black dress that, as she sat, came to about mid-thigh. It was the first time he'd seen her with her hair down—literally. Her wavy black tresses were draped in front of her left shoulder, exposing her long slender neck. She was posing rather nicely. On the other side of the horseshoe-shaped bar were two middle-aged men in business suits who appeared as if they were trying to work up the courage to approach the beauty across from them. Thorpe muttered to himself as he crossed the room, "I might as well turn myself in and get it over with." As Thorpe stepped up to the bar, Ambretta gave a warm smile—her full red lips framing her perfectly white teeth. *Shit.*

"John."

It sounded odd to hear her refer to him by his first name. "Ambretta."

"Were you talking to yourself?"

"Yes. And it wasn't a pleasant conversation," Thorpe admitted.

Ambretta laughed. "You clean up pretty well," she said touching his arm.

"Didn't want you to outclass me. But I see I've failed in that endeavor yet again."

"I'll consider that a compliment. I promised to buy the drinks...What'll you have?"

Ambretta was offering him a drink. And he noticed that despite the outside temperature she hadn't brought a jacket down from her room; she wasn't planning on going anywhere. That was either very good for Thorpe—or very bad. Was he going to be heading up to her room, or was he going to be leaving here in handcuffs? "What are you having?" Thorpe asked, nodding to the drink sitting in front of Ambretta.

"It's called a Red Rider."

"May I?" Thorpe asked.

"Be my guest."

Thorpe didn't have any intention of ordering the drink for himself, he was just curious if she were actually drinking alcohol. He raised the heavy glass to his lips smelling the bourbon before tasting it. "Not bad, but I think I'll just stick to beer." Thorpe glanced across the bar at the two suits; based on their sour expressions, you'd think someone had pissed in their drinks. Other than the suits—who as far as Thorpe knew were Ambretta's back-up—and the bartender, he and Ambretta were the only ones in the bar on this Sunday evening. Since Oklahoma still operated under antiquated liquor laws, Thorpe ordered an imported beer, avoiding the low-point domestic product typically served in the state.

When the bartender set down his beer, Ambretta suggested they sit in the lounge area. Thorpe watched as she slid off the stool, grabbed a small handbag, and sauntered towards a couch in her black pumps. Thorpe couldn't help but look back at the two suits seated at the bar. He winked. One tipped his drink towards Thorpe in a "good luck" gesture. He couldn't be positive, but the men didn't strike him as FBI material. Ambretta selected a couch near an end table, gracefully sat, and crossed her legs. Rather than accompany her on the couch, Thorpe opted for a chair sitting at a ninety-degree angle to the sofa. *Like a rock.*

"So, as per your terms, I have opened a bar tab under my name. Well, actually under my room, which the FBI will graciously pay. I will not ask you any questions, and I can't talk about work. Which means you're going to have to carry the bulk of the conversation tonight."

"Not so...I can ask you questions."

"You forget who I work for. I'm much better at asking questions rather than answering them," Ambretta responded, smiling.

"Maybe we'll just order drinks and stare at each other uncomfortably."

"I don't find looking at you uncomfortable, John."

"Ambretta, you're laying it on a little thick, aren't you?"

"You like subtleties?"

I don't like being played the fool. "I like honesty."

"Have you been completely honest with me, John?"

Good point. "Ambretta, I do believe your statement was in the form of a question *which* is a direct violation of our agreement. Just consider tonight to be the antithesis of Jeopardy," Thorpe replied with a smile of his own.

"All right, John, consider the last question rhetorical. So what would you like to discuss?"

Thorpe laughed, "You can't speak without asking a question."

Ambretta gave Thorpe a fake go-to-hell smile. *Damn, she looked good.*

"Ambretta, how does a lady like *you* find herself employed by the FBI?"

"It's my turn under the microscope, is it?"

"Now you're answering questions with questions," Thorpe pointed out.

Ambretta laughed, "Shit! I *can* only communicate in the form of a question."

AMBRETTA HAD REHEARSED FOR THIS EVENING using one of many cover stories filed away in her nearly photographic memory. There were several "truths" she was permitted and willing to impart to Thorpe. Normally it's best to let these truths slip out slowly over time so your mark thinks he or she is making progress—thereby keeping yourself valuable. In Ambretta's world, once one loses value, her existence is no longer crucial. Certainly, this assignment was different than most. Ambretta wasn't even sure what the ultimate goal of her assignment was, though that was not uncommon. What she did know, and had only recently learned, was John had killed one or more of the recent "victims." She had also learned it was not racially motivated; his fellow police officers been responsible for the murder of his wife and daughter—circumstances with which she was all too familiar.

Ambretta's mother had died of a prolonged illness when she was only eleven-years-old. Her father, a NYPD officer, had raised her as a single parent. He had done the best he could. Ambretta—always academically advanced—had been offered full scholarships at prominent universities around the nation. Not wanting to venture far from her father, she attended Cornell University in Ithaca, where she studied linguistics and dabbled in psychology. She was in her second year of graduate studies when she watched the horrific events of September 11 unfold on her dorm-room television. Shortly after, Ambretta learned her father was among the heroes who had perished trying to save others in the World Trade Center. There she was—24-years-old, her academic achievements seemingly inconsequential, contemplating joining the United States Army. With all her talents and potential, the only thing she wanted to do was pick up a rifle and send a chunk of lead three-thousand feet per second into the brain of a radical Islamic. She came to realize that, being female, her chances of seeing combat and exacting the revenge she so desperately sought were minuscule.

She came to recognize her particular talents lent themselves to more specialized work—with the goal of stopping subsequent attacks on U.S. soil. Her education was redirected and honed at alternative institutions of higher learning. Despite what she'd told John, she did not hold a doctorate in clinical psychology and had never attended Boston University. In her experience, she'd found if people think they've discovered a truth on their own, they're more apt to believe it; so she simply played up the scenario John had invented.

So why was she tied up on a domestic issue in Tulsa, Oklahoma? All she knew was the assignment shouldn't last more than a couple of weeks and then it would be back to stanching the cancerous seepage that oozed across the U.S. border on a daily basis.

To use one of these cover stories on John seemed to be an affront to the man. She and John both lost their families to acts of violence prompting similar responses. She'd taken up arms against the evil that had taken her father's life just as John had sought his own justice against another evil. Though his outward appearance seemed confident and calm, she could see the ruin deep within his eyes—even as he masked himself with humor. She truly didn't know what this investigation would yield, but she knew she was feeling a deep attraction for this man. He was smart, funny, good-looking, and reminiscent of her father.

Ultimately, Ambretta attempted to answer John's question without lying: "That's a complicated question. Simply put, I want to put bad people in a place where they can't hurt others any longer."

THORPE THOUGHT THROUGH THE ANSWER. Most cops will say "to put bad guys in jail." That is, unless they are in an interview or speaking to a group of civvies, then they'll say "because I want to help people." But Ambretta had said, "To put bad people in a *place* where they can't hurt others any longer."

"I was hoping you'd be a little more specific. You obviously have the intelligence to make a fair amount of money in the private sector," Thorpe replied.

"Money isn't everything. In fact your personnel file indicates you graduated from college at the top of your class. The same could be said for you."

"Maybe. You just don't strike me as the FBI type... And remember, you can't ask me what I consider an FBI type to be," Thorpe smiled.

"I'm at a severe disadvantage in this conversation. Okay, more specifically, I lost my father to an act of violence, and I entered law enforcement to get revenge on the bastards responsible."

AMBRETTA WATCHED AS THE DISTRUST FLOODED into John's eyes, facial muscles, and posture. "John, I promise you that's the truth." Ambretta instantly regretted giving him the truth—the similarities would be hard for him to digest. In this case, her truth and John's truth were eerily similar. John was not a trusting man, and he'd see it as a tactic being used against him.

THORPE WAS HAVING A DIFFICULT TIME reading this woman. He'd spent considerable time with her and couldn't nail down her characteristics. Usually when someone is recalling a fact they will look up and to one side—the same side—each time. When someone is using the creative side of their mind, a.k.a. the lying side, they will often look to the opposite direction. A myriad of other behaviors combine with these cues, including breathing rate, the relaxation and tensing of facial muscles, sometimes even ticks. Often people will touch their face when lying, particularly their nose or mouth. They will assume a defensive posture—crossing their arms or legs or leaning away from their interviewer. These subconscious cues were available for scrutiny by the trained observer. Ambretta was inconsistent; if anything she seemed even calmer when the validity of her statements was in question.

Her last statement was too much. She'd been in full flirt mode since he walked in the hotel, and now this. *Look how much we have in common. People killed my family, and I'm out for revenge just like you. Bullshit!* "Agent Collins, you'd better get on the phone with your boss and find out just how much you're willing to tell me because I've had about enough of this shit. Either put me in handcuffs right now, or let me walk out of here—but let's end this charade."

"I don't have to call my boss. I know what I can tell you. I haven't told you one lie…not tonight anyway. You, more than anyone else, should know things aren't always what they seem."

Thorpe stood, walked to the bar and ordered another beer. He looked over at the two suits who seemed anxious to hear the news. He told them: "Turns out she's a high-priced prostitute. Wanted four-hundred for the night. Can you believe that shit?" Thorpe took his beer and walked out of the bar.

Ambretta pulled out her phone. "He's pissed and he's moving."

Twenty-Eight

Sunday
February 11th
Evening

THORPE STORMED OUT TO HIS TRUCK, opened the cab, and retrieved a flashlight. Despite his attire, he dropped to the pavement and shimmied beneath the undercarriage. He found a tracking device that had been attached while he'd been inside the hotel. He ripped it loose from the truck. Thorpe stood, threw the device toward the lobby, and felt the loss of control. The bottled emotion of the last year, compounded by the stress of the last week, was dealing a devastating blow. He recognized the loss of restraint but still couldn't stop the downward spiral.

Thorpe slammed his foot down on the accelerator. A lone car on the access road forced him to slam on his breaks to avoid a collision. He felt the antilock brakes vibrate through the pedal and up into his leg. He also felt something slide into his heel. He bent over and retrieved the object. It was his daughter's old Game Boy. She'd lost it shortly before her murder and Thorpe had scolded her for being careless with the expensive toy. The memory sent a towering wave of guilt crashing over his body. His chest suddenly felt constricted. His eyesight went in and out of focus. Yet he drove.

Visions of his daughter replaced traffic-filled streets. They burst in his mind like fireworks. They were images he'd managed to suppress over the last few months: Ella singing on her karaoke machine, laughing across from her daddy as they spun on the teacup ride, giggling as her mother bathed her fragile body in the kitchen sink. Her shame as Thorpe reprimanded her for being irresponsible. Images of him holding her lifeless body. Of sitting in the patrol car outside his home awash in red and blue lights. Of the pity on his fellow officer's faces. Still other phantasms tore at Thorpe: Images of himself ripping flesh from Marcel Newman, of dislocating Leon's shoulders, of fear-filled eyes as he slit Shaw's throat. Who had he become—surely not the man his father had hoped he would be? *My father.* Thorpe remembered a quote his father had sometimes recited, "Action is the antidote to despair."

NEARLY THIRTY MILES SOUTHWEST, Andrew Phipps lay secreted inside Thorpe's house with much on his mind—not the least of which was Cornelius Johnson and his labored breathing from the next room. Another was the mystery location of Thorpe's guard dogs. He had no idea where Thorpe kept the beasts; he and Corn had searched the property without success. One thing was for certain: If the two shepherds led their master into the home, things were going to get *real ugly, real fast.*

Both men had been hiding here since slightly after 9 p.m., and the tension was about to boil over—especially for Corn who wasn't used to combat situations. Being still for hours—while anticipating a gun battle that will occur on an unknown schedule—is enough to test any man's iron. The men had taken up positions where they could cover the front and back doors. When Thorpe stepped into the home, his body would be transformed into a sieve.

Watching the front door, Phipps was armed with a Remington 1911 .45 caliber pistol—a very reliable weapon. Corn was armed with a 12-gauge shotgun loaded with double-ought buckshot. He was covering the back door between bathroom breaks. Because of nerves, he'd been relieving himself far too frequently, which was yet another concern for Phipps; he hoped to hell Thorpe wouldn't slip in the back door during an ill-timed bladder movement.

Phipps was going to kill Corn when this was over. The man was a nervous wreck, and he'd probably sprayed DNA evidence all over Thorpe's bathroom every time he pissed in the dark. Corn would eventually get caught and undoubtedly give up Phipps in the aftermath. Corn would have to die. So would Sergeant McDonald.

First things first. He had to kill Thorpe. *Where was that motherfucker?*

THORPE WIPED HIS SALTY FACE with his shirt sleeve and—uncertain how he'd arrived or for how long he'd been there—found himself in the parking lot of Jasmine's Lounge on the northeast side of town. The establishment was a cheesy strip-bar and the location of several shootings and stabbings. Thorpe was shaking as he stuffed a small pistol down the front of his pants and approached the bar. He wouldn't admit to himself why he was here but knew it wasn't to ogle the less-than-attractive dancers.

Entering the bar, he received a pat-down by the unarmed, long-haired security guard at the front door. The guy was making a feeble attempt at keeping weapons out of the business but neglected to pat down Thorpe's genitals—a mistake heterosexual security guards often make.

Walking through the strip-bar, Thorpe noticed several seedy patrons inside. Wearing slacks and a button down, he didn't exactly fit in with the regulars. Thorpe went directly to the men's bathroom and entered a stall. Before urinating, he removed the small Glock 27 from his crotch and placed the weapon in the waistband of his pants. Reconsidering, Thorpe removed the pistol, stood on the stool, and hid the weapon in the drop-down ceiling of the bathroom. He hadn't come here to kill someone.

Thorpe left the men's room, selected a stool at the bar, and ordered a bottle of beer. He wasn't about to drink from a glass at this shit-hole; plus bottles make great impromptu weapons. Thorpe scanned the room until his eyes found a table consisting of three white males with an assortment of prison tattoos. He kept his eyes focused on the group, knowing full well what the gaze would reap. It didn't take long for one of the men in the group to notice the unwanted attention. Thorpe read the man's lips—"what the fuck," followed by the other two men turning their attention his way. None of the three men was huge, but they all had prison muscle. Thorpe felt his adrenaline spike, a welcome alternative to crushing despair.

"We don't want any trouble in here, mister." It was the bartender.

"You won't have any from me," Thorpe said, never taking his eyes off the three men.

"Then quit fuckin' with folks."

"I'm just sitting here enjoying my adult beverage."

"Bullshit! Those three are about to shove your head up your Polo-wearing ass."

"Claiborne," Thorpe corrected.

"What?"

"Those three are about to shove my head up my 'Claiborne' wearing ass."

"You think you're fucking funny or something?"

"That's been a matter of contention lately," Thorpe admitted.

"I hope they kill your funny ass."

"I hope they do too."

The one seated in the middle of the group was the first to rise, probably the alpha male of the pack. The other two were happy to be at his side. The alpha male strode smoothly toward Thorpe, seemingly relaxed and unconcerned. Thorpe noticed he had a tattoo on his neck that read "Momma Tried." *Clever.* The other two backed up their buddy. One clumsily knocked into a chair on his way over;

his muscles were tight, and he moved in a jerky manner. He was nervous and would be the weakest of the three threats. Thorpe slid off the back of his stool, keeping the piece of wood between himself and his new inked-up friends.

"What the fuck you looking at?" asked the man with the neck tattoo.

"I couldn't help but notice…"

"You couldn't help but notice what, asshole?"

"Momma didn't try hard enough," Thorpe said with a grin.

Like a good fighter, Momma Tried didn't run his mouth. Instead he threw a right cross meant to deliver a fight-ending blow. Because of the wooden stool obstacle, Momma Tried couldn't fully step into the punch and Thorpe easily rocked back, avoiding the strike while simultaneously kicking the stool into Momma Tried's legs. Momma Tried picked up the stool, wielding it as a weapon. He cocked it like a baseball bat. As he did, Thorpe stepped in and drove his left elbow into the Momma Tried's face. He fell back on the dirty carpet as Ink man number two began circling around to Thorpe's right. Thorpe could tell Ink man number three wanted to haul ass out of there but was probably afraid of the retribution he'd receive from Momma Tried.

Ink Man number three—chickenshit that he was—produced a knife, promoting himself from weakest to greatest threat. Momma Tried had successfully sprouted from the floor and was once again in the fray. Thorpe now had Knife Man on his left, Momma Tried dead ahead, and no nickname man on his right. Thorpe picked up his beer bottle, realizing he might have taken on more than he could handle.

Just then the wooden stool came crashing down on Knife Man's head. Unlike the movies, the stool didn't shatter into a hundred pieces, but based on the sound, the same couldn't be said about the man's skull.

Totally surprised by the unexpected attack, Momma Tried momentarily shifted his focus to the new development—*mistake*. Thorpe shoved the beer bottle, neck first, into his teeth. The blow sent Momma Tried reeling backward onto the floor in a bloodied heap; he was done. No Nickname Man simply held his hands up, palms facing Thorpe in a gesture of surrender. He backed into the bathroom.

"John, we need to get the hell out of here! The police are en route," said the wielder of wooden stool—Ambretta. She had changed out of her dress and pumps into jeans and tennis shoes. Her make-up was still perfect. Her hair was a bit tousled, making it look sexier than ever. Thorpe ignored Ambretta and followed the man into the bathroom.

"John, let's go! It's over!" Ambretta yelled as she followed both men into the restroom.

When Thorpe entered the bathroom, his former assailant looked like he was going to shit himself. *Appropriate place to do it.* "Get the fuck out of here, I gotta piss," Thorpe hissed at the man. The man looked relieved as he slid past Ambretta.

"Damn, John, I thought you were going to kill him," Ambretta said.

"I just have to retrieve something before we leave," Thorpe replied, as he stepped on the stool to retrieve his weapon from the ceiling. When he stepped down and out of the stall, Ambretta grabbed him by the back of the neck, rose up, and kissed him longingly. Despite the location, it was the best first kiss Thorpe had ever experienced.

"We have to go," she said.

The two hurried out of the restroom and crossed the murky expanse of barroom floor toward the unarmed security guard. The guard, probably unarmed because he was an ex-con, made no attempt to stop them as they left the establishment.

"Give me your keys," Ambretta barked as the two headed for Thorpe's truck.

Thorpe was too embarrassed with his recent behavior to try and argue. He tossed her the keys. He was thrust back into his seat as Ambretta tore out of the lot.

"I found your tracking device. How'd you follow me?" Thorpe asked.

"You found the one we wanted you to find."

"Why...?"

Ambretta cut him off. "Just shut the fuck up, John. Give me a minute."

After a few minutes of silence, Thorpe asked "What should we do on our second date?"

"Not this."

"By the way, I had them just where I wanted 'em."

"Bullshit. I saved your ass, and you know it."

Thorpe did know it; at the very least he was about to earn a few more lacerations. "I guess I owe you one. I'll pay you back after I'm finished serving the sentence you hang on me."

Ambretta reached over and touched Thorpe lightly on the cheek with the back of her fingers. A look of genuine concern enveloped her face. "Just give me a chance to earn your trust."

They rode in silence the rest of the way to Ambretta's hotel. There, she took his hand and led him up to her room. Once inside, Ambretta began unbuttoning Thorpe's shirt as the two shared their second kiss. Once his shirt was off, Ambretta pulled his t-shirt over his head, exposing his muscular but scarred form. Ambretta whispered, "What have you been into?" not expecting an answer as she traced the scars with her index finger. She pulled Thorpe over to the bed and down on top of her. They made love. It wasn't as rabid as being with Deborah, but it was equally intense—and much more meaningful. When they'd finished, they showered together and fell into another lovemaking session. No words were spoken as they fell asleep in one another's arms.

Twenty-Nine

Monday
February 12th
Morning

Corn's whining was intensifying hourly. They'd been in the house all night. Both were reaching their breaking points. Corn wanted to leave, and only one argument had been able to keep the man inside the house. "What if you run into that Rambo motherfucker when you're trekking through the woods? Best we wait in here and finish this thing—'less you wanna be looking over your shoulder for the rest of your life." Phipps knew Corn wasn't about to walk out the door and head though the woods on his own. But, at times Corn was breathing so loudly Phipps was afraid he could be heard outside Thorpe's home.

Phipps himself was both thirsty and hungry; he'd been avoiding fluids so as not to have to use the bathroom. *And sure as the sun rises every morning, as soon as I make a move for the refrigerator, that asshole will walk in the front door.* Speaking of the sun—it was rising. It was still dim in the interior but soon the room would be well lit. Phipps was considering his options when he heard someone working the rear door knob. *Shit.*

He didn't trust Corn to cover his area of responsibility but hesitated to leave his own post. Thorpe could be causing a diversion at the back door with the intent of bursting through the front. As the back door creaked open, he heard Corn nervously breathe the word, "Fuck!" *Jesus Christ, he had to do everything.* As Phipps rounded the corner with his weapon at the ready, he heard something metallic skidding across the kitchen floor.

THORPE WOKE AT SLIGHTLY AFTER SIX IN THE MORNING not quite sure where he was. The warm, smooth skin of Ambretta pressed against his abdomen cleared his mind. He caressed her side, pausing at the waist before gliding his hand up the steep incline of her hips. She responded by pushing her buttocks deeper into Thorpe's groin. They made love again. When they finished, he wanted answers; or maybe he didn't. He didn't ask for any. He showered, dressed, kissed Ambretta, and walked out the hotel door without either of them saying a word.

He didn't know what do anymore. Maybe he should just go to investigators with what little corroborating evidence he had. Maybe he thought he had something to live for again—Ambretta. On the other hand, what future could they have with him spending the rest of his life in prison? He was tired, tired of the killing and tired of the lying. But mostly he was tired of the visceral tug of war with his rope of a soul.

As Thorpe walked out of the hotel, he fell in behind a young family of three. A man was walking with a woman on his right arm, and a girl of about seven clinging to his left hand. Thorpe felt the familiar gnawing in his chest as he witnessed a vision of what he'd been denied. It was time to finish this thing, even if he had to march right into Phipps' house under the watchful eye of the FBI. As Thorpe drove back towards his home, he considered the night he'd spent with Agent Collins—Ambretta.

If he were the prime suspect in these murders, would she sacrifice the FBI's case and her career by sleeping with him? *Unlikely.* He'd never use the relationship to avoid prison, but there was no way she could trust him to do that—*was there?* Thorpe had too many questions and not enough answers. The only thing he knew for sure was he'd better extract his head from his anal cavity before Phipps put a bullet in it.

Thorpe pulled into Deborah's barn not remembering much of the twenty-five minute drive home. *Shit!* He'd better get his head in the game. Thorpe slipped coveralls over his dress clothes and exchanged his shoes for a pair of boots. He was armed with his Sig Sauer and department-issued, bullet-resistant vest. Other than that, he wasn't much prepared for combat. As Thorpe started walking towards the road, he noticed Mr. Jennings's Mercedes was parked in front of their home. Thorpe didn't know what to make of it, and he didn't really care. He just hoped Deborah would find some happiness somehow. As Thorpe trudged through the woods, he was overcome with a sense of finality, as if everything was about to come to an end. He also had the uncanny feeling of being watched, though he didn't feel threatened. *Al and Trixie, I wish I'd kept you here; my senses are all fucked up.*

Thorpe scrambled up the creek bank and poked his head over the berm. Everything seemed normal though a bit unkempt. The sun was bright in the sky, and it seemed an unlikely time to be attacked. Of course, that's generally when it happens. Thorpe retreated back down into the creek with the feeling he'd lost his edge somehow. He sat down with his back to a tree and retrieved a picture of his daughter from his wallet. "I'm sorry, baby. Daddy should have been there."

After a solid minute of staring at the image, Thorpe returned the photograph to his wallet and placed it on the ground. He removed his constrictive coveralls, dress shirt, and t-shirt. Dressed only in black boots and black slacks, he pulled the dark, bullet-resistant vest over his bare torso. He removed a hunting knife from his gear bag and strapped it to his leg. With the .357 in his right hand, Thorpe tore out of the creek and sprinted to the rear of his home. He cleared the open expanse without incident but felt exposed against the side of the house. Staying below the windows, Thorpe crept towards the rear door, discovering a broken wax seal—someone had been, or was *still*, inside his home.

The smart thing to do would be to back away and watch his house from a distance. If Phipps or someone was inside, they'd eventually tire and leave—giving Thorpe the advantage. Of course inside they had access to food and drink, and Thorpe didn't have either, nor was he dressed to spend a potential overnighter in the elements. He considered that it was just as likely the FBI had served a search warrant on his home while the capable Agent Collins had kept him occupied. If that were the case, he would be sitting in the woods for hours for nothing. Thorpe was tired of waiting. It was time to end this thing.

He tried the back door and found the deadbolt already disengaged. He cracked the barrier open, paused, and burst in, weapon up. He saw a figure on the floor. Thorpe put a bullet in the man's forehead before registering that he was shooting at a corpse.

The smell of magnesium and blood hung thickly in the air. *What the hell?* Thorpe didn't linger on the dead body, just registered it was Corn Johnson. He kept moving though the house. The next five minutes were as tense as any in the last year as he cleared the rest of the home. He found nothing. Thorpe checked the front door. Locked. He returned to the back door, locked it, and examined Corn's body lying on the floor. Corn had been shot in the head—almost exactly where Thorpe had placed his own bullet.

Because of the damage to Corn's face, it was impossible to tell how many times he'd been shot before Thorpe's own contribution. Whoever did it was a professional. Thorpe noticed scorch marks and remnants of a Flash-bang not far from Corn's body—law-enforcement and military use the devices to incapacitate suspects. The grenades are designed to stun, not injure or kill, and are often used in hostage situations. Attached to Corn's jacket was a piece of paper with one handwritten word in ink; it simply read, "BARN."

Once more Thorpe was struggling to understand the situation. *Had Phipps or McDonald killed Corn and left him in his home? Am I being set up?* Too many things weren't adding up. Thorpe gripped his pistol, cracked open the back door, and scanned the area. Having cautiously crossed the fifty yards separating his house and barn, Thorpe arrived at the rear entrance and tried the door. It was unlocked. He turned the doorknob, and once again cracked open the door before entering. Tactical teams refer to this process as "letting the room cook." An impatient shooter would start firing when the door first opened or shortly after.

Staying off to the side, Thorpe heard nothing. He noticed the barn's interior lights were on but couldn't sense any movement. Thorpe entered the barn low and fast—damn near shooting Andrew Phipps as he sat in the southwest corner of the barn. The only thing preventing Thorpe's finger from depressing the trigger was the sight of a gag in the man's mouth and the fact he was bound to a metal support pole. Phipps was positioned much like how Thorpe had last seen Marcel Norman—except Phipps was still alive and staring at Thorpe with malevolent eyes.

Thorpe cleared the rest of the barn, passing behind Phipps and confirming he was secured to the pole with a pair of flex-cuffs. He ascended a set of stairs and cleared a loft area which sat above the south third of the barn. Confident the rest of the structure was secure, Thorpe descended the stairs and locked the metal rear door from the inside.

What in the fuck is going on! Thorpe extracted the long blade from the sheath attached to his thigh and approached Phipps. Few weapons have quite the same psychological impact as a large, sharp knife. Thorpe walked around Phipps twice, noticing the bound man had a large contusion just above his right jawline, near the ear. On a third pass, Thorpe searched Phipps for weapons, then knelt down and slid the flat side of the blade down Phipps cheek and underneath the gag. Thorpe twisted the blade so the sharp edge faced the cloth. He cut it loose from Phipps' mouth. The point of the knife incidentally took out a sizable chunk of Phipps fleshy cheek—*whoops*. Thorpe walked about ten feet in front of Phipps and sat down on the concrete floor.

Thorpe stared at Phipps without saying a word; sometimes the best interview technique is to say nothing at all, particularly when your subject is nervous. In this case Phipps had a lot more to be nervous about than Thorpe. After about a minute of silence, Phipps began talking. "You ought to get on with killing me. If I get a chance I'm going to gut you like a pig."

Thorpe remained quiet.

"Why'd you fucking tie me up, motherfucker? I don't know shit. The longer you let me live the more chances I get to kill your white ass."

Thorpe realized Phipps wasn't going to be able to provide any answers; he thought Thorpe had tied him up to torture him for information. Whoever had put Phipps in this predicament must have done it while the man was unconscious—*probably cold-cocked him after he was disoriented with the stun grenade*. Thorpe stood, walked over to a weight bench where he removed the Sig Sauer, dropped the magazine, broke the weapon down, and carefully placed the parts on the bench. With his back to Phipps, Thorpe pulled off his bullet resistant vest, putting his scarred and developed body on full display. Thorpe once again extracted the knife, passed behind Phipps, and cut the flex-cuffs—releasing his captive. Then Thorpe walked back to the metal door—his back facing Phipps as though he weren't a concern. He unlocked the door and threw the knife outside. Thorpe relocked the back door and returned his attention to Phipps who had risen off the floor. He stood motionless next to the pole.

Thorpe returned to a position ten feet in front of Phipps and assumed a fighting stance.

Phipps smiled, "Oh, you *fucked-up* boy. Gone up a lot tougher than your skinny white ass," Phipps replied with false bravado. Thorpe could hear the shimmer in his voice.

Phipps wasn't nearly as lean as Thorpe; he was thirty pounds heavier and probably stronger. Thorpe had at least one thing in his favor, though; he hadn't recently been knocked unconscious as Phipps had. *Too bad for him.*

Phipps removed his own shirt, revealing a myriad of tattoos and a fraternity brand on his left tricep. He assumed a boxer's stance and approached Thorpe with his healed, third-degree-burned shoulder turned away. *That was odd.* Thorpe had noticed Phipps' holster was on his right hip—indicating he was right handed. But Phipps was in a southpaw stance. He was either ambidextrous or was going to attempt a kick or a takedown.

And a kick it was, a poorly executed one that Thorpe easily avoided. When Phipps' foot landed, he took the stance of a traditional right-handed boxer. Thorpe moved in and caught a left jab on the forehead that rocked him back a few inches. It was a hard punch for a jab.

"That's right, bitch! Come get you some more!" Phipps encouraged.

Phipps had fast hands and was probably well versed in hand-to-hand combat given his history in the Marine Corps. Thorpe got within striking distance again and fired a kick at the outside of Phipps' lead leg. He was hoping to impact the sciatic nerve—the largest and longest single nerve in the entire body. When traumatized, the sciatic nerve greatly affects the workings of the legs. The kick landed, but Thorpe received an overhand right to the left side of his head. Though the impact to his head was solid, it wasn't a stunning blow. Thorpe feigned a wobble of the legs and a buckle of the knees. Phipps saw a wounded animal in front of him and took the bait; he rushed in. Another overhand right was hurtling towards Thorpe's face as he ducked the punch and drove into Phipps' hips. Thorpe wrapped his arms around his assailant, lifted him off the ground, and arched his own back. Then, using all the strength in his back, abs, and legs, Thorpe torqued his body forward, driving his right shoulder into Phipps' abdomen. The move was so violent that Thorpe's own feet left the ground as he slammed the back of Phipps' head onto the gray concrete floor. Thorpe couldn't see the impact, but the wet watermelon-like sound left little doubt Phipps had sustained a catastrophic head injury. Even as Thorpe rose to deliver more punishment, he noticed the slack in Phipps' facial muscles. He was dead.

Thorpe stood and rubbed the side of his own head. His adrenaline was fading. The pain from Phipps' punch was beginning to register. He felt a good-sized knot behind and above his temple. Good thing the punch hadn't land two or three inches forward or Thorpe might have been the slab of meat lying on the floor right now. Three inches stood between victim and victor.

Thorpe left the body and walked into the daylight leaving his unassembled pistol behind in the barn. It was the first time in days that he felt he could walk on his own property without the prospect of a bullet stopping him dead. Before heading back to his house, he retrieved his discarded coveralls and used them to protect himself from the brisk February weather. Back inside the house, he walked past the remains of Corn Johnson and retrieved a six pack of beer from his refrigerator. Thorpe popped open one of the beers in the kitchen and tipped it towards Corn in mock salute as he walked back out the door.

Thorpe took the beer into his backyard, lifted it above his head, and turned around in a complete circle. He then tore off three beers and trekked fifty yards into the woods. He left the beers on a fallen tree—an offering to his unseen, unknown accomplice. He returned to his backyard and built a fire in his pit then sat down with his back to the tree line.

As Thorpe took a long pull off his cold beer, he wondered if he'd ever know who his accomplices were or what their motivation was. Someone had gone to a lot of trouble to remain anonymous. As he reviewed the events of the last few days, he remembered the man who had been reported leaving the back door of Phipps' home. Later it was discovered Phipps hadn't been present. *Was that man the same one who'd sprung a trap on Phipps and Corn today?*

There were too many loose ends, and every time he tried to grab one he only reeled in more questions. One possibility nagged at him: What if Ambretta Collins' assignment had been to protect Thorpe not to prosecute him? She seemed too smart to become romantically involved with a serial murderer no matter how dashing Thorpe hoped he was. If she *had* been there to help Thorpe, she'd gone to great lengths to hide her true objective.

One thing was certain, he was due some answers and she was going to provide them. But he had one more visit to make first. There was still one collaborator left, Sergeant McDonald.

Thorpe stood and walked into his home—not bothering to turn and see if his beer offering had been accepted.

Thirty

Tuesday
February 13th
Morning

THORPE ROSE AT 7 A.M. prepared to begin his quest for Sergeant McDonald but unsure how to go about accomplishing the task without drawing attention. He'd spent the previous day dealing with the bodies of Phipps and Corn Johnson. Because of potential tracking devices attached to his personal truck and without access to SID units, Thorpe was limited in his disposal options. Ultimately, he waited for Deborah to leave her home then loaded the tarp-wrapped bodies into the back of his pickup and pulled into Deborah's barn. Afterwards he trekked back to his home and fetched the Polaris ATV he used to work on his property. He loaded both bodies onto an attached four-wheel metal wagon and drove them several miles west of Deborah's property. After digging one large grave with a pick and shovel, Thorpe tossed the bodies in. He'd move them some day when surveillance was less of a worry.

Having no bodies to worry about now, Thorpe was showered, dressed, and ready to leave the house by 8 a.m.

Thorpe picked up his phone and called Ambretta's cell. He got a recorded voice telling him the number he'd dialed was "no longer in service." A follow-up phone call to the Renaissance Hotel informed him Miss Ambretta Collins had checked out of the hotel yesterday morning. He was trying to process her disappearance when the phone rang. Thorpe excitedly snatched the phone off the counter, "Hello?"

"It's Hull."

"Oh," Thorpe replied, disappointed.

"That was a warm welcome."

"Sorry, I was expecting a call."

"Don't be too sorry. I've got some good news. You home?"

"Yeah."

"I'm five minutes out. Don't go anywhere."

Good news? He could use some. Thorpe walked out to his gate, opened it, and returned to his front porch. As promised, five minutes after the call, Hull rolled onto the gravel driveway, and climbed from his car.

"What's so important to get you out in the boonies this time of the morning?" Thorpe asked.

"You're not going to believe what's happened. I tricked myself into thinking I knew what the fuck was going on, but I guess I didn't. Jesus H. Christ," Hull said with obvious excitement.

"Spit it out, Bob, you're killing me."

"I was called into a meeting with the FBI this morning—freaking *six* in the morning. Thought for sure it'd be bad news. Thought they were probably getting ready to come out here and hem your ass up."

"Was Ambretta there?" Thorpe asked, surprised this was his first concern.

Hull got a sour look on his face, "What? Uh...Not exactly...I thought you were in a hurry to hear what happened?"

"Sorry, Bob, go on."

"Last night, Sergeant McDonald killed himself in a Wichita hotel room. Fucking hung himself from a doorknob," Hull explained.

"No shit?" Thorpe uttered the words not believing for a moment McDonald died by his own hand. The man was too narcissistic to commit suicide.

"No shit. But that's not the best part. In his jacket pocket was a digital recorder, and you won't believe what was on it…"

"Let me guess…McDonald recorded a statement implicating himself in all these recent murders."

Hull stepped back and looked hard at Thorpe, "What?! I guess that's why they call you Carnac. I haven't heard the tape, but apparently he admits to engineering a plan to kill black officers who've been vocal in racial allegations against the department. He stated he'd paid Kaleb Moment to phone the FBI implicating you in some forthcoming murders. Knowing Kaleb is a snitch and can't be trusted, he admitted to killing the kid after he made the phone call. Then he killed Stephen Price."

Hull shook his head as though he couldn't believe his own words as he continued, "McDonald goes on to say he and Brandon Baker were responsible for killing Daniels and Shaw. He says Baker started acting strange after those two murders. He was afraid Baker was going to go to the police so he killed him and set the Durango on fire because his own fingerprints were all over the interior.

"Now get this. He also says he killed Andrew Phipps and Corn Johnson last night before fleeing to Wichita. We haven't been able to reach Phipps or Corn on the phone. They haven't been home since yesterday afternoon, and they're completely off the grid. We haven't found their bodies yet, but we suspect McDonald's telling the truth. About them being dead anyway.

"Toward the end of the recording, McDonald breaks down. Starts babbling about not being the man he once was. The last words on the tape were apologies to his family. Then he dialed 911, left the phone off the hook, and hung himself from a door knob with a neck tie." Hull's head was still unconsciously wagging back-and-forth as though his body was calling his mouth a liar.

"And the FBI doesn't suspect it was a murder staged to look like a suicide?" Thorpe asked.

"They said there wasn't a mark on the man. Nothing to indicate the recording had been coerced. Plus, who the hell could make a guy kill himself with a tie and a door-knob."

Yeah...Who could? "Still, they've gotta be considering me?"

"Nope. McDonald was checked into an out-of-state hotel he paid for with cash under an assumed name. The FBI didn't even know where he was staying. How the hell could you have found him while you were under their surveillance? They apparently have a GPS unit on your truck and confirmed it'd never left the Mounds area all day yesterday. Plus Agent Collins stated she'd conducted direct surveillance on you all Sunday—and Sunday night."

"Collins is my alibi?" Thorpe tilted his head, perplexed. "I thought she wasn't at this meeting?"

"She wasn't. I guess she's been reassigned...whatever. We had her on a conference call." Hull held his hands up, palms facing Thorpe. "John, I don't know what the hell is going on—and to tell you the truth—I don't want to know. The fact is...you're off the hook. They have a taped confession that, so far, pans out. And you have a federal agent who can attest to your whereabouts."

Thorpe and Hull continued talking for several minutes but not many more pertinent details were available. It seemed the case had been neatly wrapped up with a pretty silk bow—or in this case—a silk tie. The Feds were preparing to descend on McDonald's house with a search warrant. Thorpe had little doubt they'd find evidence inside the home tying him to one or more of the murders. Evidence likely planted by the man who'd been seen slipping out of the back of Phipps' home. Whoever Thorpe's mysterious new friends were, they were quite capable. Eventually Hull slapped Thorpe on the back and assured him he'd demand answers during his retirement party. The homicide detective strode back to his car and pulled away, head still shaking.

Who was Ambretta Collins and why had she saved his ass? It was a question he might never know the answer to. Strangely, it wasn't the most paramount question Thorpe was asking himself. Instead, he was more concerned whether the woman's feelings for him had been genuine or just a ruse to keep him away from his property. Of all his experiences over the last week, he was amazed his most pressing question didn't concern her true identity but rather whether her affections for him were true.

Thorpe pulled himself off his porch and retrieved his private vehicle. He had a visit to make, one he'd been avoiding far too long.

Thirty-One

Tuesday
February 13th
Afternoon

AMBRETTA COLLINS SAT IN THE DARKENED CONFINES of a parked 2006 Toyota Sequoia. Most government agents drove American-made, non-descript vehicles, a fact not unnoticed by enemies of the United States. And that was precisely why she didn't drive one. Ambretta was not an FBI agent. Ambretta wasn't even Ambretta.

She *was* a government agent. She *assumed* she worked for the CIA, at least indirectly, though she'd never receive a paycheck stamped Central Intelligence Agency. And the memo line would never read, "For snatching Mohammad from bed in the middle of the night."

Her job...her mission, was to identify, infiltrate, and decimate terrorist cells operating inside the US border. If only the average American citizen were aware of the target-rich-environment in which she worked. If they realized the threat America faced everyday, Ambretta might not need to be a spy in her own damn country. The US border was a sieve. Thousands of illegals crossed the Mexican border every single day. Did people really believe Muslim extremists weren't among them?

America was a nation of laws—and, to a much larger degree, lawyers. The constitution was often perverted to such a degree that law enforcement was unable to do its job. Ambretta doubted the founding fathers meant for constitutional protections to apply to foreign terrorists who entered this country with the sole intent of bringing about its destruction. Many Americans felt these animals should be provided the same liberties enjoyed by United States' own law-abiding citizens. Others believed terrorists should at least be handled under rules of the Geneva Convention, though these non-uniformed "combatants" clearly didn't meet the criteria. All of these rules were applied to men who recruited mentally and physically handicapped women and children to blow themselves up in the name of Allah—while the men themselves sat on the sidelines masturbating to pornography.

Ambretta knew there had always been patriots doing the dirty work of protecting the very freedoms that others wished to extend to enemies of this country. Many of those patriots had to toil in the shadows. Ambretta was such a person.

She made people disappear to someplace discreet, dank, and dark. There, they were most likely milked of information until the tit ran dry. She couldn't say for certain. She wasn't privy to everything. She was only a cog in the machine, undoubtedly a small, but efficient, machine. Her service to her country would never be printed in any newspaper, not unless she was someday uncovered. But even then, even if she talked, what information could she provide?

In many ways she operated much like the terrorist cells she observed and dismantled. These cells generally had a single objective, remaining unaware of how their plans impacted the overall mission. They didn't know what other cells were doing, where they were operating, or what their names were. If one cell was compromised, the collective goal remained intact.

In fact, some terrorist cells' only objective was to appear suspicious, thereby diverting limited investigative resources from more integral members. These "dummy" cells were unwitting bait; they thought they were playing a larger role than that of a clay pigeon.

If Ambretta were to be uncovered by the terrorists she investigated, torture, rape, and death, were sure to follow. And then maybe rape again.

If she were uncovered by American watchdogs and picked-up for questioning at least she'd be in the soft, manicured hands of the FBI. The FBI didn't resort to such "distasteful" interrogation techniques. Somehow she found its hands-off approach both disturbing and reassuring: Disturbing because the enemy was afforded the same protections. Reassuring because they wouldn't break her either. The only threat they could muster would be the loss of her freedom. Her freedom she'd willingly give. So many others had given so much more.

If she *were* imprisoned and *did* feel compelled to "talk" for consideration of a lesser sentence, she knew the next disappearing act would be her own. No one could protect her. No facility would be safe.

It didn't matter. For now, Ambretta wasn't yet permitted to have a broader view of the game in which she played. Sometimes the only information she was provided was just enough to keep her operating safely. More often than not, she sent information up through her handler with little information filtering back down. Though accustomed to operating in the dark, recent events had been highly unusual. Why had she been sent to Tulsa? What exactly had been her mission? And what in the hell were they doing in this graveyard?

Ambretta looked out the window at her handler. The old man had directed her to a location in the sprawling cemetery, then told her to wait in the car. He had solemnly walked to a gravesite about fifty yards off one of the private drives.

Just six days ago, Ambretta had been on assignment in Atlanta, Georgia. She'd been working a case there for nearly a month when she'd received a phone call from her handler telling her to pack up everything and head to Tulsa. She detected a bit of urgency in the old man's usually cool and indifferent manner.

Her handler was nearly as much a mystery today as the morning he'd first made contact. He'd promised a rewarding career, but most importantly he had appealed to Ambretta's fervor to strike back at those who'd cut down her father. It was her handler who'd chosen the name she currently used. She'd always thought Ambretta an odd choice, given most in the business had common, more forgettable names.

She did know the old man was a former commando, and he'd been doing this for a *very* long time. She also knew he'd spent considerable time in a foreign prison and had suffered from brutal torture sessions that had left him physically and mentally scarred. He didn't complain about the abuse, and only mentioned it to stress that Ambretta always be cautious.

When she and her handler arrived in Tulsa, she found the pipeline of information clogged more than ever. She knew he'd arranged for her to have FBI credentials and had given her considerable oversight over her "fellow" FBI agents. Her handler told her the NSA had intercepted a phone call indicating multiple threats against a company asset, one Jonathan Thorpe. Her handler had subsequently interrogated the caller (a man named Kaleb Moment), and had obtained from him a list of potential assassins. Her handler had also provided her with the same information the FBI was acting upon—so she could carry out her assignment intelligently. Her assignment had been to "saddle up" next to Sergeant Thorpe while her handler dealt with potential threats. For the next six days, her only communication with her handler had been conducted via telephone.

Even though Thorpe was supposedly a "company asset," she was not to break from the cover she'd been given, and as the assignment continued, she began to feel like one of those "dummy" cells. Through her investigation into Thorpe's background, reading his file, and personal experiences with the man, she began to seriously doubt he was connected to the company in any way. Still, she trusted her handler and dutifully carried on with her assignment.

What she hadn't expected was the emotional and physical attraction she'd developed for Sergeant Thorpe. John. Upon meeting him, she had recognized he was a strong man, but she also perceived suffering—deep within the recesses of those bright green eyes. He'd tragically lost his family only thirteen months earlier, and she had empathized with the empty shell before her. It was the same emptiness she had felt for several years—and if she were completely honest with herself—an emptiness she still carried. She knew their shared experiences were part of the foundation of their budding relationship. She also recognized John was smart, funny, and considerate. She had had no intentions of developing feelings for the man, knowing full well the assignment would be temporary. But some things can't be overridden with reason.

On their last night together, her handler had informed her multiple tangos were preparing an ambush in Thorpe's home. She was to keep John from returning at any cost. When he'd become upset with her and left the hotel, she was greatly concerned—not because she had failed in her assignment—but for the well being of the man with whom she'd fallen in love. When she'd fetched John from the bar, she was armed with rohypnol and could have easily slipped him the drug, rendering him unconscious. Despite reason, despite logic, she'd led him up to her room where they had made love. The night was not only a physical release, but an emotional one as well. She hoped

Thorpe realized the lovemaking had been genuine; she hadn't seduced him as part of a job assignment. *Her job assignment*—she still didn't know what it'd been all about. *And why was her handler visiting a grave when they should be making their way out of Tulsa?*

Because an unexpected meeting with Thorpe would be "messy," as her handler had put it, Thorpe's personal truck was still outfitted with a GPS tracker, which they were still monitoring. Someone else would remove the device later. (As on many of Ambretta's assignments, this someone would have no clue why the device had been installed in the first place; they'd have a simple task to perform, no questions asked.)

As Ambretta sat pondering the past six days she observed a blip on her GPS monitor headed straight for their location. Ambretta stepped out of the car, the movement attracting the attention of her handler who'd been standing over a grave. She didn't shout but simply made a hand gesture to the old man conveying they had to leave immediately.

The old man. The same mumbling old man who'd tried to purchase crack from Phipps in the motel room. The same figure who'd glided out of Thorpe's woods in a ghillie suit. The same man who had exited Phipps' back door and nimbly jumped a fence.

This old man now walked briskly towards the waiting Toyota, dark sunglasses shielding his eyes from the bright February sun. Parked on the north end of a long loop, the old man entered the Toyota as Ambretta realized they wouldn't make the exit before Thorpe pulled onto the property. She couldn't allow the cars to meet head-on, so she drove halfway around the one-way circle drive. Thirty seconds later, she observed Thorpe's pickup enter the property and park at the same location they'd just left. "Ben, what the hell is going on?" Ambretta uncharacteristically demanded of her handler.

The old man removed his sunglasses and watched as John walked towards the same gravesite he himself had just departed. She'd never seen much in the way of emotion from Ben before, but now she watched as a single tear rolled down the old man's wrinkled and scarred left cheek. When he turned to her and told her to drive, she saw the pain in his old green eyes—those familiar green eyes—and she knew.

THORPE WALKED THROUGH THE GRAVEYARD a free man, though one couldn't tell based on the apprehension in his gait. He'd recently walked into gun fights with calmer dispositions. As his legs resisted moving toward his wife's and daughter's final resting place, his mind resisted by drifting back to the events of the last six days.

Someone had gone through great lengths to protect him, physically and legally. Several people—he noted the plural—had kept him out of harm's way and had constructed irrefutable alibis. No single person would have the resources to accomplish what'd been done for him over the last week. Who and why?

Who was Ambretta Collins, and why had she and others risked their necks for him? The question gnawed at Thorpe. Like smoke, the answer was there, but hell if he could grasp it. Was Ambretta even her real name? Had she seduced him into her bed only to keep him isolated, while a person or persons flushed rats out of his house? Were GPS units attached to his vehicle only to keep him safe and provide extra "proof" he was not responsible for Sergeant McDonald's "suicide?" Did Ambretta have genuine feelings for him? Did she love him?

Of all the questions the last two consumed him like a towering wave. He'd never experienced what he now felt. It tore him inside-out, leaving him exposed. He loved someone and was desperate to know if she loved him in return. He hated the feeling, despised it; It was a loss of control. Someone had power over him, and it made him feel weak.

Lost in these thoughts, Thorpe found himself at the foot of his wife's grave staring down at her marker.

Erica Hessler Thorpe
Mother and daughter, together forever
Love has no end

Thorpe dropped to his knees at the foot of her grave with a sudden realization—but something he'd probably always known, something he'd subconsciously blocked over the last year. Thorpe had forced his wife to live for years the way he felt now. Erica had loved him, he knew that now. Had he denied her love in return? Had the unexpected pregnancy festered resentment?

It sure as hell hadn't been Erica's fault. She hadn't trapped him, hadn't pressured him to marry her, hadn't needed him financially. It took two to have a child. Had he married out of an overwhelming sense of responsibility? She was owed more than that. Their daughter was owed more than that. Thorpe had his character flaws for sure; he'd never pretended otherwise. But Erica and Ella had deserved more from him during their short time on this earth.

Thorpe crawled across the ground and sat between his wife's and daughter's markers. They'd been buried more than a year, and he hadn't visited once since the funeral. A tremendous amount of guilt had kept him away—guilt that stemmed from more than his failure to protect his family. Thorpe sat and told his wife he was sorry. Sorry for not saying he loved her. Sorry for not showing it. Sorry for being absent the night death came calling. Sorry, sorry, sorry.

The other headstone sat just right of Erica's.

Ella Ambretta Thorpe
My World

Thorpe had chosen the epitaph. It was simple but said everything. The middle name clawed at him as he read it now. *Coincidence? Had to be. But what were the chances? So many questions.*

Erica had fought with him over the middle name because of the word the initials spelled. She was afraid it would lead to childhood teasing. But he loved the name, wanted it to be her first. Ultimately Erica had won the argument, as mothers generally do. The middle name was granted Thorpe as a compromise.

Thorpe's love for his daughter had never been in doubt. Shortly after coming home, she became his everything. The pain of losing her had been crushing; an all-encompassing despair he hoped never to feel again. He'd prefer to never feel *anything* else. Like many before him, his way of dealing with the pain had been to not deal with it at all. Over the past months, he'd filled the empty hole inside himself with hatred and promises of revenge.

Thorpe knew he couldn't bring back his wife and daughter but he could bring those responsible for their murders to justice. His kind of justice. While he had failed in protecting his wife and daughter, he would not fail in avenging them. In the process he knew he'd lost a bit of himself, turning a corner there would be no coming back from.

Those responsible for the deaths had answered for their sins. Yet he still had a hole in his heart, a hole he doubted would ever be filled. Thorpe placed a single red rose on each grave, realizing as he did that there were others who needed to be brought to justice—many others. And he was good at it.

Acknowledgments

Thanks to:

God, for giving me the ability to write (my bad on the subject matter).

Each and every member of the U.S. military: past, present, and future for giving me the freedom to write.

My fellow LE brothers and sisters for providing the protection to write. Thank you for doing your thankless jobs.

Andrew, Kevin, and all my proofreaders and supporters. Thank you.

A special thanks to Kelli for giving me a chance, a voice, and a guiding hand.

Sonya, Julia, Ally, for the inspiration. Without my immeasurable love for you, I wouldn't have been able to realize the depth of Jonathan Thorpe's loss.

About the author

Gary Neece is a sergeant and 18-year veteran of the Tulsa Police Department in Tulsa, Oklahoma. He has vast experience in specialty units for violent-crime reduction and drug enforcement. Much of the inspiration for his writing springs from his time in the Special Investigations Division, where he supervised the department's undercover Vice/Narcotics Unit. He lives near Tulsa with his wife and two daughters.

CPSIA information can be obtained at www.ICGtesting.com
260671BV00002B/2/P